'The single most beautiful, solid, unearthly and unjustifiably forgotten novel of the twentieth century . . . a little golden miracle of a book'
NEIL GAIMAN

'A Shakespearian tragi-comedy, a murder mystery and a multi-faceted allegory all in one: and a damn good story too'
MARY GENTLE

'[Hope Mirrlees was] a very self-conscious, wilful, prickly and perverse young woman, rather conspicuously well dressed and pretty, with a view of her own about books and style, an aristocratic and conservative tendency in opinion and a corresponding taste for the beautiful and elaborate in literature'
VIRGINIA WOOLF

'What we have here is that rarest of creatures, the fantasy novel of ideas'
MICHAEL SWANWICK

'The tone is assured and urbane, with aphorisms dripping from every other sentence and a real sense of the menacing and the bizarre. It has been a major influence on genre fantasy since its republication in the late 1960s'
ROZ KAVENEY, *Cambridge Guide to Women Writers*

HOPE MIRRLEES was born in 1887 in England. A scholar and translator, she published three novels during the nineteen twenties, of which *Lud-in-the-Mist* (1926) is the most well-known. A contemporary and associate of Virginia Woolf, Bertrand Russell, Walter de la Mare, T.S. Eliot and W.B. Yeats, she appears fleetingly in a number of their diaries and biographies. Woolf described her as 'a very self-conscious, wilful, prickly and perverse young woman, rather conspicuously well dressed and pretty, with a view of her own about books & style, an aristocratic and conservative tendency in opinion, and a corresponding taste for the beautiful and elaborate in literature' and concluded she was 'rather an exquisite apparition'. Another contemporary described Hope Mirrlees as 'a cross between a pixy and a genius'. She lived and worked with Jane Ellen Harrison, the classical scholar, from about 1921 onwards. After Harrison's death in 1928 her only published work was the first part of a biography of Cotton the Antiquarian (*A Fly in Amber*). Hope Mirrlees died in 1978. Following its republication in the 1960s, *Lud-in-the-Mist* became highly influential on fantasy, and was championed by authors including Neil Gaiman and Michael Swanwick.

*Also by Hope Mirrlees*

FICTION

Madeleine: One of Love's Jansenists (1919)

The Counterplot (1924)

POETRY

Paris: A Poem (1919)

Poems (1963)

Mood and Tensions (1976)

NON-FICTION

Listening to the Past (1926)

The Religion of Women (1926)

Gothic Dreams (1928)

Bedside Books (1928)

A Fly in Amber (1962)

HOPE MIRRLEES

GOLLANCZ
LONDON

This edition first published in Great Britain in 2018 by Gollancz

First published in Great Britain in 2008 by Gollancz
an imprint of the Orion Publishing Group Ltd
Carmelite House, 50 Victoria Embankment
London EC4Y 0DZ

An Hachette UK Company

7 9 10 8

Copyright © Hope Mirrlees, 1926
Introduction copyright ©Neil Gaiman, 2000

The moral right of Hope Mirrlees to be identified as the author of this work has been asserted in accordance with the Copyright, Designs and Patents Act of 1988.

All rights reserved. No part of this publication may be reproduced, stored in a retrieval system, or transmitted in any form or by any means, electronic, mechanical, photocopying, recording, or otherwise, without the prior permission of both the copyright owner and the above publisher of this book.

All the characters in this book are fictitious, and any resemblance to actual persons, living or dead, is purely coincidental.

A CIP catalogue record for this book is available from the British Library.

ISBN 978 1 473 22556 5

Printed and bound in Great Britain by Clays Ltd, Elcograf S.p.A.

www.orionbooks.co.uk
www.gollancz.co.uk

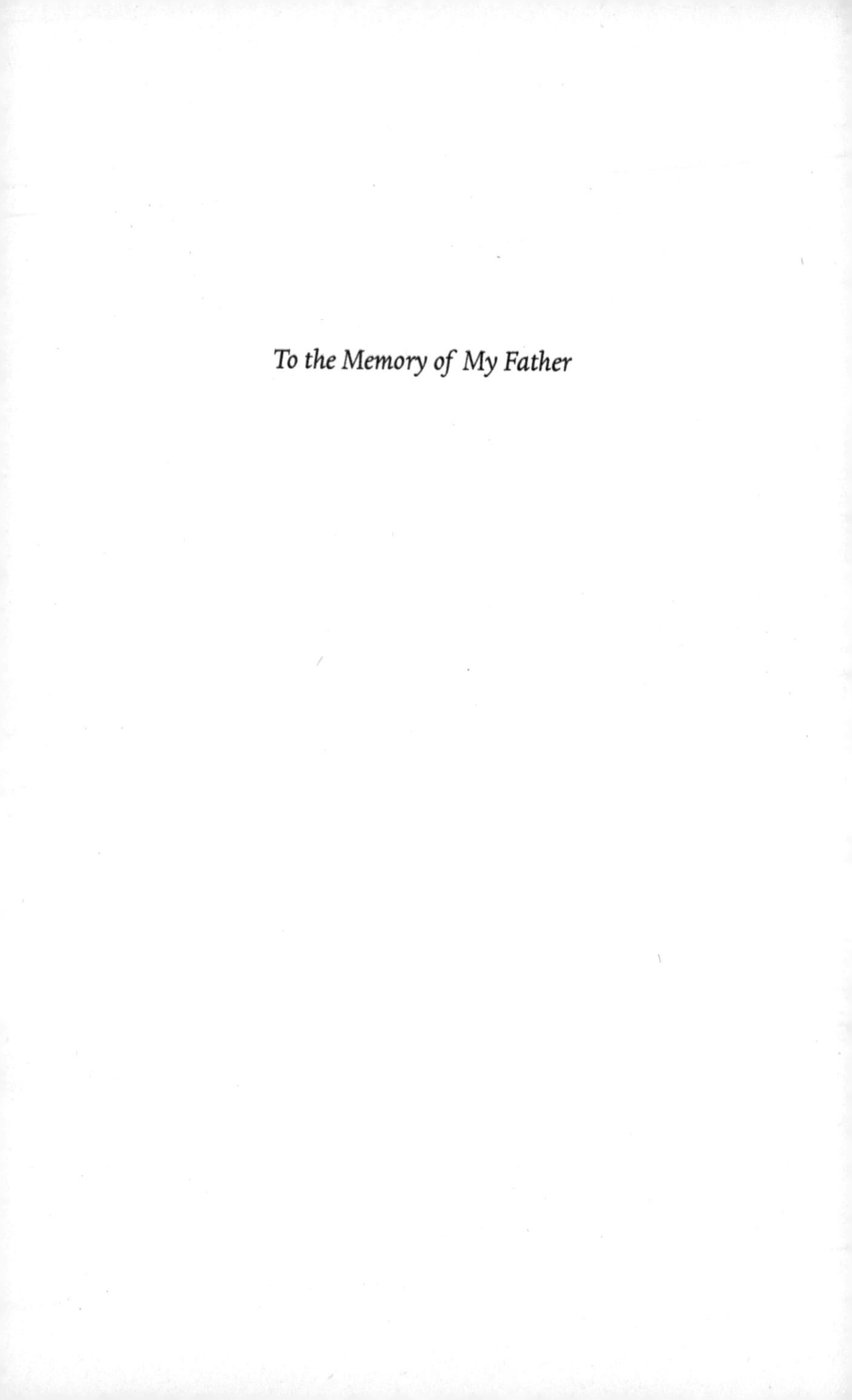

*To the Memory of My Father*

# INTRODUCTION

Hope Mirrlees only wrote one fantasy novel, but it is one of the finest in the English language.

The country of Dorimare (fundamentally English, although with Flemish and Dutch threads in the weave) expelled magic and fancy when it banished hunchbacked libertine Duke Aubrey and his court, two hundred years before our tale starts. The prosperous and illusion-free burghers of the town swear by 'toasted cheescrumbs' as easily as by the 'Sun, Moon, Stars and Golden Apples of the West'. Faerie has become, explicitly, obscenity.

But fairy fruit is still being smuggled over the border from Fairyland. Eating it gives strange visions and can drive people to madness and beyond. The fruit is so illegal that it cannot even be named: smugglers of fruit are punished for smuggling silk, as if the changing of the name will change the thing itself.

The Mayor of Lud-in-the-Mist, Nat Chanticleer, is less prosaic than he would have others believe. His life is a fiction he subscribes to, or would like to, of a sensible life like everyone else's – and particularly like the dead that he admires. His world is a shallow thing, though, as he will soon learn: without his knowledge, his young son, Ranulph, has been fed fairy fruit.

Now the fairy world – which is also, as in all the oldest folk tales, the world of the dead – begins to claim the town: a puck named Willy Wisp spirits away the lovely young ladies of Miss Crabapple's Academy for Young Ladies, over the hills and far away; Chanticleer stumbles upon the fruit smugglers, and his life takes a turn for the worse; Duke Aubrey is sighted; old murders will out; and, in the end, Chanticleer must cross the Elfin Marches to rescue his son.

The book begins as a travelogue or a history, becomes a pastorale, a low comedy, a high comedy, a ghost story and a detective story. The writing is elegant, supple, effective and haunting: the author demands a great deal from her readers, which she repays many times over.

The magic of *Lud-in-the-Mist* is built from English folklore – it is not such a great step from Aubrey to Oberon, after all; Willy Wisp's Ho-ho-*hoh* is Robin Goodfellow's, from a song they say Ben Jonson wrote; and it will not come as a surprise to the folklorist that old Portunus says nothing and eats live frogs. The 'lily, germander and sops in wine' song is first recorded in the seventeenth century, under the name of 'Robin Good-Fellow or, the Hob-Goblin'.

I have seen editions of *Lud-in-the-Mist* which proclaim it to be a thinly disguised parable for the class struggle. Had it been written in the 1960s it would, I have no doubt, have been seen as a tale about mind-expansion. But it seems to me that this is, most of all, a book about reconciliation – the balancing and twining of the mundane and the miraculous. We need both, after all.

It is a little golden miracle of a book, adult, in the best sense, and, as the best fantasy should be, far from reassuring.

Neil Gaiman
August 2000

The Sirens stand, as it would seem, to the ancient and the modern, for the impulses in life as yet immortalised, imperious longings, ecstasies, whether of love or art, or philosophy, magical voices called to a man from his 'Land of Hearts Desire', and to which if he hearken it may be that he will return no more – voices, too, which, whether a man sail by or stay to hearken, still sing on.

JANE HARRISON

# 1
## MASTER NATHANIEL CHANTICLEER

The free state of Dorimare was a very small country, but, seeing that it was bounded on the south by the sea and on the north and east by mountains, while its centre consisted of a rich plain, watered by two rivers, a considerable variety of scenery and vegetation was to be found within its borders. Indeed, towards the west, in striking contrast with the pastoral sobriety of the central plain, the aspect of the country became, if not tropical, at any rate distinctly exotic. Nor was this to be wondered at, perhaps; for beyond the Debatable Hills (the boundary of Dorimare in the west) lay Fairyland. There had, however, been no intercourse between the two countries for many centuries.

The social and commercial centre of Dorimare was its capital, Lud-in-the-Mist, which was situated at the confluence of two rivers about ten miles from the sea and fifty from the Elfin Hills.

Lud-in-the-Mist had all the things that make an old town pleasant. It had an ancient Guildhall, built of mellow golden bricks and covered with ivy and, when the sun shone on it, it looked like a rotten apricot; it had a harbour in which rode vessels with white and red and tawny sails; it had flat brick houses – not the mere carapace of human beings, but ancient living creatures, renewing and modifying themselves with each generation under their changeless antique roofs. It had old arches, framing delicate landscapes that one could walk into, and a picturesque old graveyard on the top of a hill, and little open squares where comic baroque statues of dead citizens held levees attended by birds and lovers and insects and children.

It had, indeed, more than its share of pleasant things; for, as we have seen, it had two rivers.

Also, it was plentifully planted with trees.

One of the handsomest houses of Lud-in-the-Mist had belonged for generations to the family of Chanticleer. It was of red brick, and the front, which looked on to a quiet lane leading into the High Street, was covered with stucco, on which flowers and fruit and shells were delicately modelled, while over the door was emblazoned a fine, stylized cock – the badge of the family. Behind, it had a spacious garden, which stretched down to the river Dapple. Though it had no lack of flowers, they did not immediately meet the eye, but were imprisoned in a walled kitchen-garden, where they were planted in neat ribands, edging the plots of vegetables. Here, too, in spring was to be found the pleasantest of all garden conjunctions – thick yew hedges and fruit trees in blossom. Outside this kitchen-garden there was no need of flowers, for they had many substitutes. Let a thing be but a sort of punctual surprise, like the first *cache* of violets in March, let it be delicate, painted and gratuitous, hinting that the Creator is solely preoccupied with *æsthetic* considerations, and combines disparate objects simply because they *look* so well together, and that thing will admirably fill the role of a flower.

In early summer it was the doves, with the bloom of plums on their breasts, waddling on their coral legs over the wide expanse of lawn, to which their propinquity gave an almost startling greenness, that were the flowers in the Chanticleers' garden. And the trunks of birches are as good, any day, as white blossom, even if there had not been the acacias in flower. And there was a white peacock which, in spite of its restlessness and harsh shrieks, had something about it, too, of a flower. And the Dapple itself, stained like a palette, with great daubs of colour reflected from sky and earth, and carrying on its surface, in autumn, red and yellow leaves which may have fallen on it from the trees of Fairyland, where it had its source – even the Dapple might be considered as a flower growing in the garden of the Chanticleers.

There was also a pleached alley of hornbeams.

To the imaginative, it is always something of an adventure to walk down a pleached alley. You enter boldly enough, but very soon you find yourself wishing you had stayed outside – it is not air that you are breathing, but silence, the almost palpable silence of trees. And is the only exit that small round hole in the distance? Why, you will never be able to squeeze through *that!* You must turn back . . . too late! The spacious portal by which you entered has in its turn shrunk to a small round hole.

Master Nathaniel Chanticleer, the actual head of the family, was a typical Dorimarite in appearance; rotund, rubicund, red-haired, with hazel eyes in which the jokes, before he uttered them, twinkled like trout in a burn.

Spiritually, too, he passed for a typical Dorimarite; though, indeed, it is never safe to classify the souls of one's neighbours; one is apt, in the long run, to be proved a fool. You should regard each meeting with a friend as a sitting he is unwillingly giving you for a portrait – a portrait that, probably, when you or he die, will still be unfinished. And, though this is an absorbing pursuit, nevertheless, the painters are apt to end pessimists. For however handsome and merry may be the face, however rich may be the background, in the first rough sketch of each portrait, yet with every added stroke of the brush, with every tiny readjustment of the 'values,' with every modification of the chiaroscuro, the eyes looking out at you grow more disquieting. And, finally, it is your *own* face that you are staring at in terror, as in a mirror by candle-light, when all the house is still.

All who knew Master Nathaniel would have been not only surprised, but incredulous, had they been told he was not a happy man. Yet such was the case. His life was poisoned at its springs by a small, nameless fear; a fear not always active, for during considerable periods it would lie almost dormant – *almost*, but never entirely.

He knew the exact date of its genesis. One evening, many years ago, when he was still but a lad, he and some friends decided as a frolic to dress up as the ghosts of their ancestors and frighten the servants. There was no lack of properties; for the attics of the Chanticleers were filled with the lumber of the past: grotesque wooden masks, old weapons and musical instruments, and old costumes – tragic, hierophantic robes that looked little suited to the uses of daily life. There were whole chests, too, filled with pieces of silk, embroidered or painted with curious scenes. Who has not wondered in what mysterious forests our ancestors discovered the models for the beasts and birds upon their tapestries; and on what planet were enacted the scenes they have portrayed? It is in vain that the dead fingers have stitched beneath them – and we can picture the mocking smile with which these crafty cozeners of posterity accompanied the action – the words *February*, or *Hawking*, or *Harvest*, having us believe that they are but illustrations of the activities proper to the different months. We know better. These are not the normal activities of mortal men. What kind of beings peopled the earth four or five centuries ago, what strange lore they had acquired, and what were their sinister doings, we shall never know. Our ancestors keep their secret well.

Among the Chanticleers' lumber there was also no lack of those delicate, sophisticated toys – fans, porcelain cups, engraved seals – that, when the civilisation that played with them is dead, become pathetic and appealing, just as tunes once gay inevitably become plaintive when the generation that first sang them has turned to dust. But those particular toys, one felt, could never have been really frivolous – there was a curious gravity about their colouring and lines. Besides, the moral of the ephemeral things with which they were decorated was often pointed in an aphorism or riddle. For instance, on a fan painted with wind-flowers and violets were illuminated these words: *Why is Melancholy like Honey? Because it is very sweet, and it is culled from Flowers.*

These trifles clearly belonged to a later period than the masks and costumes. Nevertheless, they, too, seemed very remote from the daily life of the modern Dorimarites.

Well, when they had whitened their faces with flour and decked themselves out to look as fantastic as possible, Master Nathaniel seized one of the old instruments, a sort of lute ending in the carving of a cock's head, its strings rotted by damp and antiquity, and, crying out, 'Let's see if this old fellow has a croak left in him!' plucked roughly at its strings.

They gave out one note, so plangent, blood-freezing and alluring, that for a few seconds the company stood as if petrified.

Then one of the girls saved the situation with a humorous squawk, and, putting her hands to her ears, cried, 'Thank you, Nat, for your cat's concert! It was worse than a squeaking slate.' And one of the young men cried laughingly, 'It must be the ghost of one of your ancestors, who wants to be let out and given a glass of his own claret.' And the incident faded from their memories – but not from the memory of Master Nathaniel.

He was never again the same man. For years that note was the apex of his nightly dreams; the point towards which, by their circuitous and seemingly senseless windings, they had all the time been converging. It was as if the note were a living substance, and subject to the law of chemical changes – that is to say, as that law works in dreams. For instance, he might dream that his old nurse was baking an apple on the fire in her own cosy room, and as he watched it simmer and sizzle she would look at him with a strange smile, a smile such as he had never seen on her face in his waking hours, and say, 'But, of course, you know it isn't really the apple. *It's the Note.*'

The influence that this experience had had upon his attitude to daily life was a curious one. Before he had heard the note he had caused his father some uneasiness by his impatience of routine and his hankering after travel and adventure. He had, indeed, been heard to vow that he would rather be the captain of one of his father's ships than the sedentary owner of the whole fleet.

But after he had heard the Note a more stay-at-home and steady young man could not have been found in Lud-in-the-Mist. For it had generated in him what one can only call a wistful yearning after the prosaic things he already possessed. It was as if he thought he had already lost what he was actually holding in his hands.

From this there sprang an ever-present sense of insecurity together with a distrust of the homely things he cherished. With which familiar object – quill, pipe, pack of cards – would he be occupied, in which regularly recurrent action – the pulling on or off of his nightcap, the weekly auditing of his accounts – would he be engaged when IT, the hidden menace, sprang out at him? And he would gaze in terror at his furniture, his walls, his pictures – what strange scene might they one day witness, what awful experience might he one day have in their presence?

Hence, at times, he would gaze on the present with the agonizing tenderness of one who gazes on the past: his wife, sitting under the lamp embroidering, and retailing to him the gossip she had culled during the day; or his little son, playing with the great mastiff on the floor.

This nostalgia for what was still there seemed to find a voice in the cry of the cock, which tells of the plough going through the land, the smell of the country, the placid bustle of the farm, as happening *now*, all round one; and which, simultaneously, mourns them as things vanished centuries ago.

From his secret poison there was, however, some sweetness to be distilled. For the unknown thing that he dreaded could at times be envisaged as a dangerous cape that he had already doubled. And to lie awake at night in his warm feather bed, listening to the breathing of his wife and the soughing of the trees, would become, from this attitude, an exquisite pleasure.

He would say to himself, 'How pleasant this is! How safe! How warm! What a difference from that lonely heath when I had no cloak and the wind found the fissures in my doublet, and my feet were aching, and there was not moon enough to prevent my stumbling, and IT was lurking in the darkness!' enhancing thus his present well-being by imagining some unpleasant adventure now safe behind him.

This also was the cause of his taking a pride in knowing his way about his native town. For instance, when returning from the Guildhall to his own house he would say to himself, 'Straight across the market-place, down Appleimp Lane, and round by the

Duke Aubrey Arms into the High Street . . . I know every step of the way, every step of the way!'

And he would get a sense of security, a thrill of pride, from every acquaintance who passed the time of day with him, from every dog to whom he could put a name. 'That's Wagtail, Goceline Flack's dog. That's Mab, the bitch of Rackabite the butcher, *I* know them!'

Though he did not realise it, he was masquerading to himself as a stranger in Lud-in-the-Mist – a stranger whom nobody knew, and who was thus almost as safe as if he were invisible. And one always takes a pride in knowing one's way about a strange town. But it was only this pride that emerged completely into his consciousness.

The only outward expression of this secret fear was a sudden, unaccountable irascibility, when some harmless word or remark happened to sting the fear into activity. He could not stand people saying, 'Who knows what we shall be doing this time next year?' and he loathed such expressions as 'for the last time', 'never again', however trivial the context in which they appeared. For instance, he would snap his wife's head off – why, she could not think – if she said, '*Never again* shall I go to that butcher', or 'That starch is a disgrace. *It's the last time* I shall use it for my ruffs'.

The fear, too, had awakened in him a wistful craving for other men's shoes that caused him to take a passionate interest in the lives of his neighbours; that is to say if these lives moved in a different sphere from his own. From this he had gained the reputation – not quite deserved – of being a very warmhearted, sympathetic man, and he had won the heart of many a sea-captain, of many a farmer, of many an old working woman by the unfeigned interest he showed in their conversation. Their long, meandering tales of humble normal lives were like the proverbial glimpse of a snug, lamp-lit parlour to a traveller belated after nightfall.

He even coveted *dead* men's shoes, and he would loiter by the hour in the ancient burying ground of Lud-in-the-Mist, known from time immemorial as the Fields of Grammary. He could justify this habit by pointing to the charming view that one got thence of both Lud and the surrounding country. But though he sincerely loved the view, what really brought him there were such epitaphs as this:

HERE LIES
EBENEEZOR SPIKE
BAKER
WHO HAVING PROVIDED THE CITIZENS OF
LUD-IN-THE-MIST
FOR SIXTY YEARS WITH FRESH SWEET LOAVES
DIED AT THE AGE OF
EIGHTY-EIGHT
SURROUNDED BY HIS SONS AND GRANDSONS

How willingly would he have changed places with that old baker! And then the disquieting thought would come to him that perhaps after all epitaphs are not altogether to be trusted.

# 2

# THE DUKE WHO LAUGHED HIMSELF OFF A THRONE AND OTHER TRADITIONS OF DORIMARE

Before we start on our story it will be necessary, for its proper understanding, to give a short sketch of the history of Dorimare and the beliefs and customs of its inhabitants.

Lud-in-the-Mist was scattered about the banks of two rivers, the Dapple and the Dawl, which met on its outskirts at an acute angle, the apex of which was the harbour. Then there were more houses up the side of a hill, on the top of which stood the Fields of Grammary.

The Dawl was the biggest river of Dorimare, and it became so broad at Lud-in-the-Mist as to give that town, twenty miles inland though it was, all the advantages of a port; while the actual seaport town itself was little more than a fishing village. The Dapple, however, which had its source in Fairyland (from a salt inland sea, the geographers held) and flowed subterraneously under the Debatable Hills, was a humble little stream, and played no part in the commercial life of the town. But an old maxim of Dorimare bade one never forget that *The Dapple flows into the Dawl.* It had come to be employed when one wanted to show the inadvisability of despising the services of humble agents; but, possibly, it had had originally another application.

The wealth and importance of the country was mainly due to the Dawl. It was thanks to the Dawl that girls in remote villages of Dorimare wore brooches made out of walrus tusks, and applied bits of unicorns' horns to their toothache, that the chimney-piece in the parlour of almost every farm-house was adorned with an ostrich egg, and that when the ladies of Lud-in-the-Mist went out shopping or to play cards with their friends, their market-basket or ivory markers were carried by little indigo pages in crimson turbans from the Cinnamon Isles, and that pigmy pedlars from the far North hawked amber through the streets. For the Dawl had turned Lud-in-the-Mist into a town of merchants, and all the power and nearly all the wealth of the country was in their hands.

But this had not always been the case. In the old days Dorimare had been a duchy, and the population had consisted of nobles and peasants. But gradually there had arisen a middle-class. And this class had discovered – as it always does – that trade was seriously hampered by a ruler unchecked by a constitution, and by a ruthless, privileged class. Figuratively, these things were damming the Dawl.

Indeed, with each generation the Dukes had been growing more capricious and more selfish, till finally these failings had culminated in Duke Aubrey, a hunchback with a face of angelic beauty, who seemed to be possessed by a laughing demon of destructiveness. He had been known, out of sheer wantonness, to gallop with his hunt straight through a field of standing corn, and to set fire to a fine ship for the mere pleasure of watching it burn. And he dealt with the virtue of his subjects' wives and daughters in the same high-handed way.

As a rule, his pranks were seasoned by a slightly sinister humour. For instance, when on the eve of marriage a maid, ac-cording to immemorial custom, was ritually offering her virginity to the spirit of the farm, symbolised by the most ancient tree on the freehold, Duke Aubrey would leap out from behind it, and, pretending to be the spirit, take her at her word. And tradition said that he and one of his boon-companions wagered that they would succeed in making the court jester commit suicide of his own free will. So they began to work on his imagination with plaintive songs, the burden of which was the frailty of all lovely things, and with grim fables comparing man to a shepherd, doomed to stand by impotent while his sheep are torn, one by one, by a ravenous wolf.

They won their wager; for coming into the jester's room one morning they found him hanging from the ceiling, dead. And it was believed that echoes of the laughter with which Duke Aubrey greeted this spectacle were, from time to time, still to be heard proceeding from that room.

But there had been pleasanter aspects to him. For one thing, he had been an exquisite poet, and such of his songs as had come down were as fresh as flowers and as lonely as the cuckoo's cry. While in the country stories were still told of his geniality and tenderness – how he would appear at a village wedding with a cart-load of wine and cakes and fruit, or of how he would stand by the bedside of the dying, grave and compassionate as a priest.

Nevertheless, the grim merchants, obsessed by the will to wealth, raised up the people against him. For three days a bloody battle raged in the streets of Lud-in-the-Mist, in which fell all the nobles of Dorimare. As for Duke Aubrey, he vanished – some said to Fairyland, where he was living to this day.

During those three days of bloodshed all the priests had vanished also. So Dorimare lost simultaneously its Duke and its cult.

In the days of the Dukes, fairy things had been looked on with reverence, and the most solemn event of the religious year had been the annual arrival from Fairyland of mysterious, hooded strangers with milk-white mares, laden with offerings of fairy fruit for the Duke and the high-priest.

But after the revolution, when the merchants had seized all the legislative and administrative power, a taboo was placed upon all things fairy.

This was not to be wondered at. For one thing, the new rulers considered that the eating of fairy fruit had been the chief cause of the degeneracy of the Dukes. It had, indeed, always been connected with poetry and visions, which, springing as they do from an ever-present sense of mortality, might easily appear morbid to the sturdy common sense of a burgher-class in the making. There was certainly nothing morbid about the men of the revolution, and under their *régime* what one can only call the tragic sense of life vanished from poetry and art.

Besides, to the minds of the Dorimarites, fairy things had always spelled delusion. The songs and legends described Fairyland as a country where the villages appeared to be made of gold and cinnamon wood, and where priests, who lived on opobalsum and frankincense, hourly offered holocausts of peacocks and golden bulls to the sun and the moon. But if an honest, clear-eyed mortal gazed on these things long enough, the glittering castles would turn into old, gnarled trees, the lamps into glow-worms, the precious stones into potsherds, and the magnificently-robed priests and their gorgeous sacrifices into aged crones muttering over a fire of twigs.

The fairies themselves, tradition taught, were eternally jealous of the solid blessings of mortals, and, clothed in invisibility, would crowd to weddings and wakes and fairs – wherever good victuals, in fact, were to be found – and suck the juices from fruits and meats – in vain, for nothing could make them substantial.

Nor was it only food that they stole. In out-of-the-way country places it was still believed that corpses were but fairy cheats, made to resemble flesh and bone, but without any real substance – otherwise, why should they turn so quickly to dust? But the real person, for which the corpse was but a flimsy substitute, had been carried away by the Fairies, to tend their blue kine and reap their fields of gillyflowers. The country people, indeed, did not always clearly distinguish between the Fairies and the dead. They called them both the 'Silent People'; and the Milky Way they thought was the path along which the dead were carried to Fairyland.

Another tradition said that their only means of communication was poetry and music; and in the country poetry and music were still called 'the language of the Silent People'.

Naturally enough, men who were teaching the Dawl to run gold, who were digging canals and building bridges, and seeing that the tradesmen gave good measure and used standard weights, and who liked both virtues and commodities to be solid, had little patience for flimsy cheats. Nevertheless, the new rulers were creating their own form of delusion, for it was they who founded in Dorimare the science of jurisprudence, taking as their basis the primitive code used under the Dukes and adapting it to modern conditions by the use of legal fictions.

Master Josiah Chanticleer (the father of Master Nathaniel), who had been a very ingenious and learned jurist, had drawn in one of his treatises a curious parallel between fairy things and the law. The men of the revolution, he said, had substituted law for fairy fruit. But whereas only the reigning Duke and his priests had been allowed to partake of the fruit, the law was given freely to rich and poor alike. Again, fairy was delusion, so was the law. At any rate, it was a sort of magic, moulding reality into any shape it chose. But, whereas fairy magic and delusion were for the cozening and robbing of man, the magic of the law was to his intention and for his welfare.

In the eye of the law, neither Fairyland nor fairy things existed. But then, as Master Josiah had pointed out, the law plays fast and loose with reality – and no one really believes it.

Gradually, an almost physical horror came to be felt for anything connected with the Fairies and Fairyland, and society followed the law in completely ignoring their existence. Indeed, the very word 'fairy' became taboo, and was never heard on polite lips, while the greatest insult one Dorimarite could hurl at another was to call him 'Son of a Fairy'.

But, on the painted ceilings of ancient houses, in the peeling frescoes of old barns, in the fragments of bas-reliefs built into modern structures, and, above all, in the tragic funereal statues of the Fields of Grammary, a Winckelmann, had he visited Dorimare, would have found, as he did in the rococo Rome of the eighteenth century, traces of an old and solemn art, the designs of which served as *poncifs* to the modern artists. For instance, a well-known advertisement of a certain cheese, which depicted a comic, fat little man menacing with knife and fork an enormous cheese hanging in the sky like the moon, was really a sort of unconscious comic reprisal made against the action depicted in a very ancient Dorimarite design, wherein the moon itself pursued a frieze of tragic fugitives.

Well, a few years before the opening of this story, a Winckelmann, though an anonymous one, actually did appear in Lud-in-the-Mist; although the field of his enquiries was not limited to the plastic arts. He published a book, entitled *Traces of Fairy in the Inhabitants, Customs, Art, Vegetation and Language of Dorimare.*

His thesis was this: that there was an unmistakable fairy strain running through the race of Dorimarites, which could only be explained by the hypothesis that, in the olden days, there had been frequent intermarriage between them and the Fairies. For instance, the red hair, so frequent in Dorimare, pointed, he maintained, to such a strain. It was also to be found, he asserted, in the cattle of Dorimare. For this assertion he had some foundation, for it was undeniable that from time to time a dun or dapple cow would bring forth a calf of a bluish tinge, whose dung was of a ruddy gold. And tradition taught that all the cattle of Fairyland were blue, and that fairy gold turned into dung when it had crossed the border. Tradition also taught that all the flowers of Fairyland were red, and it was indisputable that the cornflowers of Dorimare sprang up from time to time as red as poppies, the lilies as red as damask roses. Moreover, he discovered traces of the Fairies' language in the oaths of the Dorimarites and in some of their names. And, to a stranger, it certainly produced an odd impression to hear such high-flown oaths as; by the Sun, Moon and Stars; by the Golden Apples of the West; by the Harvest of Souls; by the White Ladies of the Fields; by the Milky Way, come tumbling out in the same breath with such homely expletives as Busty Bridget; Toasted Cheese; Suffering Cats; by my Great-Aunt's Rump; or to find names like Dreamsweet, Ambrose, Moonlove, wedded to such grotesque surnames as Baldbreech, Fliperarde, or Pyepowders.

With regard to the designs of old tapestries and old bas-reliefs, he maintained that they were illustrations of the *flora, fauna* and history of Fairyland, and scouted the orthodox theory which explained the strange birds and flowers as being due either to the old artists' unbridled fancy or to their imperfect control of their medium, and considered that the fantastic scenes were taken from the ritual of the old religion. For, he insisted, all artistic types, all ritual acts, must be modelled on realities; and Fairyland is the place where what *we* look upon as symbols and figures actually exist and occur.

If the antiquary, then, was correct, the Dorimarite, like a Dutchman of the seventeenth century, smoking his churchwarden among his tulips, and eating his dinner off Delft plates, had trivialised to his own taste the solemn spiritual art of a remote, forbidden land, which he believed to be inhabited by grotesque and evil creatures given over to strange vices and to dark cults . . . nevertheless in the veins of the Dutchman of Dorimare there flowed without his knowing it the blood of these same evil creatures.

It is easy to imagine the fury caused in Lud-in-the-Mist by the appearance of this book. The printer was, of course, heavily fined, but he was unable to throw any light on its authorship. The manuscript, he said, had been brought him by a rough, red-haired lad, whom he had never seen before. All the copies were burned by the common hangman, and there the matter had to rest.

In spite of the law's maintaining that Fairyland and everything to do with it was non-existent, it was an open secret that, though fairy fruit was no longer brought into the country with all the pomp of established ritual, anyone who wanted it could always procure it in Lud-in-the-Mist. No great effort had ever been made to discover the means and agents by which it was smuggled into the town; for to eat fairy fruit was regarded as a loathsome and filthy vice, practised in low taverns by disreputable and insignificant people, such as indigo sailors and pigmy Norsemen. True, there had been cases known from time to time, during the couple of centuries that had elapsed since the expulsion of Duke Aubrey, of youths of good family taking to this vice. But to be suspected of such a thing spelled complete social ostracism, and this, combined with the innate horror felt for the stuff by every Dorimarite, caused such cases to be very rare.

But some twenty years before the opening of this story, Dorimare had been inflicted with a terrible drought. People were reduced to making bread out of vetches and beans and fern-roots; and marsh and tarn were rifled of their reeds to provide the cattle with food, while the Dawl was diminished to the size of an ordinary rill, as were the other rivers of Dorimare – with the exception of the Dapple. All through the drought the waters of the Dapple remained unimpaired; but this was not to be wondered at, as a river whose springs are in Fairyland has probably mysterious sources of moisture. But, as the drought burned relentlessly on, in the country districts an ever-increasing number of people succumbed to the vice of fairy fruit-eating . . . with tragic results to themselves, for though the fruit was very grateful to their parched throats, its spiritual effects were most alarming, and every day fresh rumours reached Lud-in-the-Mist (it was in the country districts that this epidemic, for so we must call it, raged) of madness, suicide, orgiastic dances, and wild doings under the moon. But the more they ate the more they wanted, and though they admitted that the fruit produced an agony of mind, they maintained that for one who had experienced this agony life would cease to be life without it.

How the fruit got across the border remained a mystery, and all the efforts of the magistrates to stop it were useless. In vain they invented a legal fiction (as we have seen, the law took no cognisance of fairy things) that turned fairy fruit into a form of woven silk and, hence, contraband in Dorimare; in vain they fulminated in the Senate against all smugglers and all men of depraved minds and filthy habits – silently, surely, the supply of fairy fruit continued to meet the demand. Then, with the first rain, both began to decrease. But the inefficiency of the magistrates in this national crisis was never forgotten, and 'feckless as a magistrate in the great drought' became a proverb in Dorimare.

As a matter of fact, the ruling class of Dorimare had become incapable of handling any serious business. The wealthy merchants of Lud-in-the-Mist, the descendants of the men of the revolution and the hereditary rulers of Dorimare had, by this time, turned into a set of indolent, self-indulgent, humorous gentlemen, with hearts as little touched to tragic issues as those of their forefathers, but with none of their forefathers' sterling qualities.

A class struggling to assert itself, to discover its true shape, which lies hidden, as does the statue in the marble, in the hard, resisting material of life itself, must, in the nature of things, be different from that same class when chisel and mallet have been laid aside, and it has actually become what it had so long been struggling to be. For one thing, wealth had ceased to be a delicate, exotic blossom. It had become naturalised in Dorimare, and was now a hardy perennial, docilely renewing itself year after year, and needing no tending from the gardeners.

Hence sprang leisure, that fissure in the solid masonry of works and days in which take seed a myriad curious little flowers – good cookery, and shining mahogany, and a fashion in dress that, like a baroque bust, is fantastic through sheer wittiness, and porcelain shepherdesses, and the humours, and endless jokes – in fact, the toys, material and spiritual, of civilisation. But they were as different as possible from the toys of that older civilisation that littered the attics of the Chanticleers. About these there had been something tragic and a little sinister; while all the manifestations of the modern civilisation were like fire-light – fantastic, but homely.

Such, then, were the men in whose hands lay the welfare of the country. And, it must be confessed, they knew but little and cared still less about the common people for whom they legislated.

For instance, they were unaware that in the country Duke Aubrey's memory was still green. It was not only that natural children still went by the name of 'Duke Aubrey's brats'; that when they saw a falling star old women would say, 'Duke Aubrey has shot a roe'; and that on the anniversary of his expulsion, maids would fling into the Dapple, for luck, garlands woven out of the two plants that had formed the badge of the Dukes – ivy and spills. He was a living reality to the country people; so much so that, when leakages were found in the vats, or when a horse was discovered in the morning with his coat stained and furrowed with sweat, some rogue of a farm-hand could often escape punishment by swearing that Duke Aubrey had been the culprit. And there was not a farm or village that had not at least one inhabitant who swore that he had seen him, on some midsummer's eve, or some night of the winter solstice, galloping past at the head of his fairy hunt, with harlequin ribbands streaming in the wind, to the sound of innumerable bells.

But of Fairyland and its inhabitants the country people knew no more than did the merchants of Lud-in-the-Mist. Between the two countries stood the barrier of the Debatable Hills, the foothills of which were called the Elfin Marches, and were fraught, tradition said, with every kind of danger, both physical and moral. No one in the memory of man had crossed these hills, and to do so was considered tantamount to death.

# 3

# THE BEGINNING OF TROUBLE

The social life of Lud-in-the-Mist began in spring and ended in autumn. In winter the citizens preferred their own firesides; they had an unreasoning dislike of being out after nightfall, a dislike due not so much to fear as to habit. Though the habit may have sprung from some forgotten danger that, long ago, had made their ancestors shun the dark.

So it was always with relief as well as with joy that they welcomed the first appearance of spring – scarcely crediting at first that it was a reality shared by all the world, and not merely an optical delusion confined to their own eyes in their own garden. There, the lawn was certainly green, the larches and thorns even startlingly so, and the almonds had rose-coloured blossoms; but the fields and trees in the hazy distance beyond their own walls were still grey and black. Yes, the colours in their own garden must be due merely to some gracious accident of light, and when that light shifted the colours would vanish.

But everywhere, steadily, invisibly, the trees' winter foliage of white sky or amethyst grey dusk was turning to green and gold.

All the world over we are very conscious of the trees in spring, and watch with delight how the network of twigs on the wych-elms is becoming spangled with tiny puce flowers, like little beetles caught in a spider's web, and how little lemon-coloured buds are studding the thorn. While as to the long red-gold buds of the horse-chestnuts – they come bursting out with a sort of a visual bang. And now the beech is hatching its tiny perfectly-formed leaves – and all the other trees in turn.

And at first we delight in the diversity of the colours and shapes of the various young leaves – noting how those of the birch are like a swarm of green bees, and those of the lime so transparent that they are stained black with the shadow of those above and beneath them, and how those of the elm diaper the sky with the prettiest pattern, and are the ones that grow most slowly.

Then we cease to note their idiosyncrasies, and they merge, till autumn, into one solid, unobtrusive green curtain for throwing into relief brighter and sharper things. There is nothing so dumb as a tree in full leaf.

It was in the spring of his fiftieth year that Master Nathaniel Chanticleer had his first real anxiety. It concerned his only son Ranulph, a little boy of twelve years old.

Master Nathaniel had been elected that year to the highest office in the state – that of Mayor of Lud-in-the-Mist and High Seneschal of Dorimare.

*Ex officio*, he was president of the Senate and chief justice on the Bench. According to the constitution, as drawn up by the men of the revolution, he was responsible for the safety and defence of the country in case of attack by sea or land; it was for him to see that both justice and the country's revenues were properly administered; and his time was held to be at the disposal of the most obscure citizen with a grievance.

Actually – apart from presiding on the Bench – his duties had come to consist of nothing more onerous than being a genial and dignified chairman of a comfortable and select club, for that was what in reality the Senate had now become. Nevertheless, though it was open to question whether his official duties were of the slightest use to anyone, they were numerous enough to occupy most of his time and to cause him to be unconscious of the undercurrents in his home.

Ranulph had always been a dreamy, rather delicate child, and backward for his years. Up to the age of seven, or thereabouts, he had caused his mother much annoyance by his habit, when playing in the garden, of shouting out remarks to an imaginary companion. And he was fond of talking nonsense (according to the ideas of Lud-in-the-Mist, slightly obscene nonsense) about golden cups, and snow-white ladies milking azure cows, and the sound of tinkling bridles at midnight. But children are apt, all the world over, to have nasty little minds; and this type of talk was not uncommon among the children of Lud-in-the-Mist, and, as they nearly always grew out of it, little attention was paid to it.

Then, when he was a few years older, the sudden death of a young scullerymaid affected him so strongly that for two days he would not touch food, but lay with frightened eyes tossing and trembling in his bed, like a newly-caught bird in a cage. When his shocked and alarmed mother (his father was at the seaport town on business at the time) tried to comfort him by reminding him that he had not been particularly fond of the scullerymaid while she was alive, he had cried out irritably, 'No, no, it isn't *her* . . . it's the thing that has happened to her!'

But all that was when he was still quite a little boy, and, as he grew older, he had seemed to become much more normal.

But that spring his tutor had come to Dame Marigold to complain of his inattention at his studies, and sudden unreasonable outbreaks of passion. 'To tell you the truth, ma'am, I think the little fellow can't be well,' the tutor had said.

So Dame Marigold sent for the good old family doctor, who said there was nothing the matter with him but a little overheating of the blood, a thing very common in the spring; and prescribed sprigs of borage in wine: 'the best cordial for lazy scholars,' and he winked and pinched Ranulph's ear, adding that in June he might be given a fusion of damask roses to complete the cure.

But the sprigs of borage did not make Ranulph any more attentive to his lessons; while Dame Marigold had no longer need of the tutor's hints to realise that the little boy was not himself. What alarmed her most in his condition was the violent effort that he had evidently to make in order to react in the least to his surroundings. For instance, if she offered him a second helping at dinner, he would clench his fists, and beads of perspiration would break out on his forehead, so great an effort did it require to answer Yes or No.

There never had been any real sympathy between Ranulph and his mother (she had always preferred her daughter, Prunella), and she knew that if she were to ask him what ailed him he would not tell her; so, instead, she asked Ranulph's great ally and confidant, Master Nathaniel's old nurse, Mistress Hempen.

Hempie, as they called her, had served the family of Chanticleer for nearly fifty years, in fact ever since the birth of Master Nathaniel. And now she was called the housekeeper, though her duties were of the lightest, and consisted mainly of keeping the store-room keys and mending the linen.

She was a fine, hale, old country-woman, with a wonderful gift for amusing children. Not only did she know all the comic nursery stories of Dorimare (Ranulph's favourite was about a pair of spectacles whose ambition was to ride on the nose of the Man-in-the-Moon, and who, in vain attempts to reach their goal, were always leaping off the nose of their unfortunate possessor), but she was, as well, an incomparable though sedentary playfellow, and from her arm-chair would direct, with seemingly unflagging interest, the manœuvres of lead soldiers or the movements of marionettes. Indeed, her cosy room at the top of the house seemed to Ranulph to have the power of turning every object that crossed its threshold into a toy: the ostrich egg hanging from the ceiling by a crimson cord, the little painted wax effigies of his grandparents on the chimney-piece, the old spinning-wheel, even the empty bobbins, which made excellent wooden soldiers, and the pots of jam standing in rows to be labelled – they all presented infinite possibilities of being played with; while her fire seemed to purr more contentedly than other fires and to carry prettier pictures in its red, glowing heart.

Well, rather timidly (for Hempie had a rough edge to her tongue, and had never ceased to look upon her mistress as a young and foolish interloper), Dame Marigold told her that she was beginning to be a little anxious about Ranulph. Hempie shot her a sharp look over her spectacles, and, pursing her lips, drily remarked, 'Well, ma'am, it's taken you a long time to see it.'

But when Dame Marigold tried to find out what she thought was the matter with him, she would only shake her head mysteriously, and mutter that it was no use crying over spilt milk, and least said soonest mended.

When finally the baffled Dame Marigold got up to go, the old woman cried shrilly: 'Now, ma'am, remember, not a word of this to the master! He was never one that could stand being worried. He's like his father in that. My old mistress used often to say to me, "Now, Polly, we won't tell the master. *He can't stand worry.*" Aye, all the Chanticleers are wonderful sensitive.' And the unexpressed converse of this last statement was, 'All the Vigils, on the other hand, have the hides of buffaloes.'

Dame Marigold, however, had no intention of mentioning the matter as yet to Master Nathaniel. Whether or not it was due to the Chanticleers' superior sensitiveness of soul, the slightest worry, as she knew to her cost, made him unbearably irritable.

He had evidently, as yet, noticed nothing himself. Most of his day was spent in the Senate and his counting-house; besides, his interest in other people's lives was not extended to those of his own household.

As to his feelings for Ranulph, it must be confessed that he looked upon him more as an heirloom than as a son. In fact, unconsciously, he placed him in the same category as the crystal goblet with which Duke Aubrey's father had baptized the first ship owned by a Chanticleer, or the sword with which his ancestor had helped to turn Duke Aubrey off the throne – objects that he very rarely either looked at or thought about, though the loss of them would have caused him to go half mad with rage and chagrin.

However, one evening, early in April, the matter was forced upon his attention in a very painful manner.

By this time spring had come to all the world, and the citizens of Lud-in-the-Mist were beginning to organise their life for summer – copper vessels were being cleaned and polished for the coming labours of the still-room, arbours in the gardens swept out and cleaned, and fishing-tackle overhauled; and people began to profit by the longer days by giving supper-parties to their friends.

Nobody in Lud-in-the-Mist loved parties more than Master Nathaniel. They were a temporary release. It was as if the tune of his life were suddenly set to a different and gayer key; so that, while nothing was substantially changed, and the same chairs stood in the same places, with people sitting in them that he met every day, and there was even the same small, dull ache in one of his teeth, nevertheless the sting, or rather the staleness, was taken out of it all. So it was very gleefully that he sent invitations to all his cronies to come 'and meet a Moongrass cheese' – as he had done every April for the last twenty-five years.

Moongrass was a village of Dorimare famous for its cheeses – and rightly so, for to look at they were as beautiful as Parian marble veined with jade, and they had to perfection the flavour of all good cheeses – that blending of the perfume of meadows with the cleanly stench of the byre. It was the Moongrass cheeses that were the subject of the comic advertisement described in a previous chapter.

By seven o'clock the Chanticleers' parlour was filled with a crowd of stout, rosy, gaily-dressed guests, chattering and laughing like a flock of paroquets. Only Ranulph was silent; but that was to be expected from a little boy of twelve years old in the presence of his elders. However, he need not have skulked in a corner, nor responded quite so surlily to the jocular remarks addressed him by his father's guests.

Master Nathaniel, of course, had a well-stored cellar, and the evening began with glasses of delicious wild-thyme gin, a cordial for which that cellar was famous. But, as well, he had a share in a common cellar, owned jointly by all the families of the ruling class – a cellar of old, mellow jokes that, unlike bottles of wine, never ran dry. Whatever there was of ridiculous or lovable in each member of the group was distilled into one of these jokes, so that at will one could intoxicate oneself with one's friends' personalities – swallow, as it were, the whole comic draught of them. And, seeing that in these old jokes the accumulated irritation that inevitably results from intimacy evaporated and turned to sweetness, like the juice of the grape they promoted friendship and cordiality – between the members of the group, that is to say. For each variety of humour is a sort of totem, making at once for unity and separation. Its votaries it unites into a closely-knit brotherhood, but it separates them sharply off from all the rest of the world. Perhaps the chief reason for the lack of sympathy between the rulers and the ruled in Dorimare was that, in humour, they belonged to different totems.

Anyhow, everyone there tonight shared the same totem, and each one of them was the hero of one of the old jokes. Master Nathaniel was asked if his crimson velvet breeches were a *blackish* crimson; because, many years ago, he had forgotten to go into mourning for his father-in-law; and when Dame Marigold had, finally, tentatively pointed out to him his omission, he had replied angrily, 'I *am* in mourning!' Then, when with upraised eyebrows she had looked at the canary-coloured stockings that he had just purchased, he had said sheepishly, 'Anyhow, it's a *blackish* canary'.

Few wines have as strong a flavour of the grape as this old joke had of Master Nathaniel. His absent-mindedness was in it, his power of seeing things as he wanted them to be (he had genuinely believed himself to be in mourning) and, finally, in the '*blackish* canary' there was the tendency, which he had inherited, perhaps, from his legal ancestors, to believe that one could play with reality and give it what shape one chose.

Then, Master Ambrose Honeysuckle was asked whether the Honeysuckles considered a Moongrass cheese to be a cheese; the point being that Master Ambrose had an exaggerated sense of the importance of his own family, and once in the law-courts, when the question arose as to whether a dragon (there were still a few harmless, effete dragons lurking in caves in out-of-the-way parts of Dorimare) were a bird or a reptile, he had said, with an air of finality, 'The Honeysuckles have always considered them to be *reptiles*'. And his wife, Dame Jessamine, was asked if she wanted her supper 'on paper', owing to her habit of pinning her husband down to any rash promise, such as that of a new barouche, by saying, 'I'd like that on paper, Ambrose'.

And there was Dame Marigold's brother, Master Polydore Vigil, and his wife, Dame Dreamsweet, and old Mat Pyepowders and his preposterous, chattering dame, and the Peregrine Laquers and the

Goceline Flacks and the Hyacinth Baldbreeches – in fact, all the cream of the society of Lud-in-the-Mist, and each of them labelled with his or her appropriate joke. And the old jokes went round and round, like bottles of port, and with each round the company grew more hilarious.

The anonymous antiquary could have found in the culinary language of Dorimare another example to support his thesis; for the menu of the supper provided by Dame Marigold for her guests sounded like a series of tragic sonnets. The first dish was called *The Bitter-Sweet Mystery* – it was a soup of herbs on the successful blending of which the cooks of Lud-in-the-Mist based their reputation. This was followed by *The Lottery of Dreams*, which consisted of such delicacies as quail, snails, chicken's liver, plovers' eggs, peacocks' hearts, concealed under a mountain of boiled rice. Then came *True-Love-in-Ashes*, a special way of preparing pigeons; and last, *Death's Violets*, an extremely indigestible pudding decorated with sugared violets.

'And now!' cried Master Nathaniel gleefully, 'here comes the turn of our old friend! Fill your glasses, and drink to the King of Moongrass cheeses!'

'To the King of Moongrass cheeses!' echoed the guests, stamping with their feet and banging on the table. Whereupon Master Nathaniel seized a knife, and was about to plunge it into the magnificent cheese, when suddenly Ranulph rushed round to his side and, with tears in his eyes, implored him, in a shrill terrified voice, not to cut the cheese. The guests, thinking it must be some obscure joke, tittered encouragingly, and Master Nathaniel, after staring at him in amazement for a few seconds, said testily, 'What's taken the boy? Hands off, Ranulph, I say! Have you gone mad?' But Ranulph's eyes were now starting out of his head in fury, and, hanging on to his father's arm, he screamed in his shrill, childish voice, 'No, you won't! You won't, you won't! I *won't* let you!'

'That's right, Ranulph!' laughed one of the guests. 'You stand up to your father!'

'By the Milky Way! Marigold,' roared Master Nathaniel, beginning to lose his temper, 'what's *taken* the boy, I ask?'

Dame Marigold was looking nervous. 'Ranulph! Ranulph!' she cried reproachfully, 'go back to your place, and don't tease your father.'

'No! No! No!' shrieked Ranulph still more shrilly, 'he shall not kill the moon . . . he shall *not*, I say. If he does, all the flowers will wither in Fairyland.'

How am I to convey to you the effect that these words produced on the company? It would not be adequate to ask you to imagine your own feelings were your host's small son suddenly, in a mixed company, to pour forth a stream of obscene language; for Ranulph's words were not merely a shock to good taste – they aroused, as well, some of the superstitious terror caused by the violation of a taboo.

The ladies all blushed crimson, the gentlemen looked stern, while Master Nathaniel, his face purple, yelled in a voice of thunder, 'Go to bed *this instant*, Ranulph . . . and I'll come and deal with you later on'; and Ranulph, who suddenly seemed to have lost all interest in the fate of the cheese, meekly left the room.

There were no more jokes that evening, and on most of the plates the cheese lay neglected; and in spite of the efforts of some of the guests, conversation flagged sadly, so that it was scarcely nine o'clock when the party broke up.

When Master Nathaniel was left alone with Dame Marigold he fiercely demanded an explanation of Ranulph's behaviour. But she merely shrugged her shoulders wearily, and said she thought the boy must have gone mad, and told him how for some weeks he had seemed to her unlike himself.

'Then why wasn't I told? Why wasn't I told?' stormed Master Nathaniel. Again Dame Marigold shrugged her shoulders, and, as she looked at him, there was a gleam of delicate, humorous contempt in her heavily-lidded eyes. Dame Marigold's eyes, by the way, had a characteristic, which was to be found often enough among the Ludites – you would have called them dreamy and languorous, had it not been for the expression of the mouth, which with its long satirical upper lip, like that of an old judge, and the whimsical twist to its corners, reacted on the eyes, and made them mocking and almost too humorous – never more so than when she looked at Master Nathaniel. In her own way she was fond of him. But her attitude was not unlike that of an indulgent mistress to a shaggy, uncertain-tempered, performing dog.

Master Nathaniel began to pace up and down the room, his fists clenched, muttering imprecations against inefficient women and the overwhelming worries of a family man – in his need for a victim on whom to vent his rage, actually feeling angry with Dame Marigold for having married him and let him in for all this fuss and to-do. And his shadowy fears were more than usually clamorous.

Dame Marigold, as she sat watching him, felt that he was rather like a cockchafer that had just flounced in through the open window, and, with a small, smacking sound, was bouncing itself backwards and forwards against its own shadow on the ceiling – a shadow that looked like a big, black, velvety moth. But it was its clumsiness, and blundering buzzing ineffectualness that reminded her of Master Nathaniel; not the fact that it was banging itself against its shadow.

Up and down marched Master Nathaniel, backwards and forwards bounced the cockchafer, hither and thither flitted its soft, dainty shadow. Then, suddenly, straight as a die, the cockchafer came tumbling down from the ceiling and, at the same time, Master Nathaniel – calling over his shoulder, 'I must go up and see that boy,' – dashed from the room.

He found Ranulph in bed, sobbing his heart out, and as he looked at the piteous little figure he felt his anger evaporating. He laid his hand on the boy's shoulder and said not unkindly: 'Come, my son; crying won't mend matters. You'll write an apology to Cousin Ambrose, and Uncle Polydore, and all the rest of them, to-morrow; and then – well, we'll try to forget about it. We're none of us quite responsible for what we say when we're out of sorts . . . and I gather from your mother you've not been feeling quite the thing these past weeks.'

'It was something *made* me say it!' sobbed Ranulph.

'Well, that's a nice, easy way of getting out of it,' said Master Nathaniel more sternly. 'No, no, Ranulph, there's no excuse for behaviour like that, none whatever. By the Harvest of Souls!' and his voice became indignant, 'Where did you pick up such ideas and such expressions?'

'But they're true! They're true!' screamed Ranulph.

'I'm not going into the question of whether they're *true* or not. All I know is that they're not the things talked about by ladies and gentlemen. Such language has never before been heard under my roof, and I trust it never will be again . . . you understand?'

Ranulph groaned, and Master Nathaniel added in a kinder voice, 'Well, well say no more about it. And now what's all this I hear from your mother about your being out of sorts, eh?'

But Ranulph's sobs redoubled. 'I want to get *away!* To get *away!*' he moaned.

'Away? Away from where?' and there was a touch of impatience in Master Nathaniel's voice.

'From . . . from things *happening*,' sobbed Ranulph.

Master Nathaniel's heart suddenly contracted; but he tried not to understand. 'Things happening?' he said in a voice that he endeavoured to make jocular. 'I don't think anything very much happens in Lud, does it?'

'*All* the things,' moaned Ranulph, 'summer and winter, and days and nights. *All* the things!'

Master Nathaniel had a sudden vision of Lud and the surrounding country, motionless and soundless, as it appeared from the Fields of Grammary.

Was it possible that Ranulph, too, was a *real* person, a person inside whose mind things happened? He had thought that he himself was the only real person in a world of human flowers. For Master Nathaniel that was a moment of surprise, triumph, tenderness, alarm.

Ranulph had now stopped sobbing, and was lying there quite

still. 'The whole of me seems to have got inside my head, and to hurt . . . just like it all gets inside a tooth when one has toothache,' he said wearily.

Master Nathaniel looked at him. The fixed stare, the slightly-open mouth, the rigid motionless body, fettered by a misery too profound for restlessness – how well he knew the state of mind these things expressed! But there must surely be relief in thus allowing the mood to mould the body's attitude to its own shape.

He had no need now to ask his son for explanations. He knew so well both that sense of emptiness, that drawing in of the senses (like the antennæ of some creature when danger is no longer imminent, but *there*), so that the physical world vanishes, while you yourself at once swell out to fill its place, and at the same time shrink to a millionth part of your former bulk, turning into a mere organ of suffering without thought and without emotions; he knew also that other phase, when one seems to be flying from days and months, like a stag from its hunters – like the fugitives, on the old tapestry, from the moon.

But when it is another person who is suffering in this way, in spite of one's pity, how trivial it all seems! How certain one is of being able to expel the agony with reasoning and persuasion!

It was in a slightly husky voice that, laying his hand on Ranulph's, he said, 'Come, my son, this won't do.' And then, with a twinkle, he added, 'Chivvy the black rooks away from the corn.'

Ranulph gave a little shrill laugh. 'There are no black rooks – all the birds are golden,' he cried.

Master Nathaniel frowned – with *that* sort of thing he had no patience. But he determined to ignore it, and to keep to the aspect of the case for which he had real sympathy. 'Come, my son!' he said, in a tenderly rallying voice. 'Tell yourself that tomorrow it will all be gone. Why, you don't think you're the only one, do you? We all feel like that at times, but we don't let ourselves be beaten by it, and mope and pine and hang our heads. We stick a smile on our faces and go about our business.'

Master Nathaniel, as he spoke, swelled with complacency. He

had never realised it before, but really it was rather fine the way he had suffered in silence, all these years!

But Ranulph had sat up in bed, and was looking at him with a strange little smile.

'I'm not the same as you, father,' he said quitely. And then once more he was shaken by great sobs, and screamed out in a voice of anguish, 'I have eaten fairy fruit!'

At these terrible words Master Nathaniel stood for a moment dizzy with horror; then he lost his head. He rushed out on to the landing, calling for Dame Marigold at the top of his voice.

'Marigold! Marigold! *Marigold!*'

Dame Marigold came hurrying up the stairs, calling out in a frightened voice, 'What is it, Nat? Oh, dear! What *is* it?'

'By the Harvest of Souls, hurry! *Hurry!* Here's the boy saying he's been eating . . . the stuff we don't mention. Suffering cats! I'll go mad!'

Dame Marigold fluttered down on Ranulph like a plump dove.

But her voice had none of the husky tenderness of a dove as she cried, 'Oh, Ranulph! You naughty boy! Oh, dear, this is *frightful!* Nat! Nat! What *are* we to do?'

Ranulph shrank away from her, and cast an imploring look towards his father. Whereupon Master Nathaniel took her roughly by the shoulders and pushed her out of the room, saying, 'If *that* is all you can say, you'd better leave the boy to me.'

And Dame Marigold, as she went down the stairs, terrified, contemptuous, sick at heart, was feeling every inch a Vigil, and muttering angrily to herself, 'Oh, these *Chanticleers!*'

We are not yet civilised enough for exogamy; and, when anything seriously goes wrong, married couples are apt to lay all the blame at its door.

Well, it would seem that the worst disgrace that could befall a family of Dorimare had come to the Chanticleers. But Master Nathaniel was no longer angry with Ranulph. What would it serve to be angry? Besides, there was this new tenderness flooding his heart, and he could not but yield to it.

Bit by bit he got the whole story from the boy. It would seem that some months ago a wild, mischievous lad called Willy Wisp who, for a short time, had worked in Master Nathaniel's stables, had given Ranulph one sherd of a fruit he had never seen before. When Ranulph had eaten it, Willy Wisp had gone off into peal upon peal of mocking laughter, crying out, 'Ah, little master, what you've just eaten is FAIRY FRUIT, and you'll never be the same again . . . ho, ho, *hoh!*'

At these words Ranulph had been overwhelmed with horror and shame: 'But now I nearly always forget to be ashamed,' he said. 'All that seems to matter now is to get away . . . where there are shadows and quiet . . . and where I can get . . . more *fruit*.'

Master Nathaniel sighed heavily. But he said nothing; he only stroked the small, hot hand he was holding in his own.

'And once,' went on Ranulph, sitting up in bed, his cheeks flushed, his eyes bright and feverish, 'in the garden in full daylight I saw them dancing – the Silent People, I mean – and their leader was a man in green, and he called out to me, "Hail, young Chanticleer! Some day I'll send my piper for you, and you will up and follow him!" And I often see his shadow in our garden, but it's not like our shadows, it's a bright light that flickers over the lawn. And I'll go, I'll go, I'll *go*, I'll *go*, some day, I know I shall!' and his voice was frightened and, at the same time, triumphant.

'Hush, hush, my son!' said Master Nathaniel soothingly, 'I don't think we'll let you go.' But his heart felt like lead.

'And ever since . . . since I ate . . . the *fruit*,' went on Ranulph, 'everything has frightened me . . . at least, not only since then, because it did before too, but it's much worse now. Like that cheese tonight . . . anything can suddenly seem queer and terrible. But since . . . since I ate that fruit I sometimes seem to see the reason why they're terrible. Just as I did tonight over the cheese, and I was so frightened that I simply couldn't keep quiet another minute.'

Master Nathaniel groaned. He too had felt frightened of homely things.

'Father,' said Ranulph suddenly, 'What does the cock say to *you?*'

Master Nathaniel gave a start. It was as if his own soul were speaking to him.

'What does he say to me?'

He hesitated. Never before had he spoken to anyone about his inner life. In a voice that trembled a little, for it was a great effort to him to speak, he went on, 'He says to me, Ranulph, he says . . . that the past will never come again, but that we must remember that the past is made of the present, and that the present is always here. And he says that the dead long to be back again on the earth, and that . . .'

'No! No!' cried Ranulph fretfully, 'he doesn't say that to *me*. He tells me to come away . . . away from real things . . . that bite one. That's what he says to *me*.'

'No, my son. *No*,' said Master Nathaniel firmly. 'He *doesn't* say that. You have misunderstood.'

Then Ranulph again began to sob. 'Oh, father! father!' he moaned, 'they hunt me so – the days and nights. Hold me! Hold me!'

Master Nathaniel, with a passion of tenderness such as he had never thought himself capable of, lay down beside him, and took the little, trembling body into his arms, and murmured loving, reassuring words.

Gradually Ranulph stopped sobbing, and before long he fell into a peaceful sleep.

# 4

# ENDYMION LEER PRESCRIBES FOR RANULPH

Master Nathaniel awoke the following morning with a less leaden heart than the circumstances would seem to warrant. In the person of Ranulph an appalling disgrace had come on him, and there could be no doubt but that Ranulph's life and reason were both in danger. But mingling with his anxiety was the pleasant sense of a new possession – this love for his son that he had suddenly discovered in his heart, and it aroused in him all the pride and the pleasure that a new pony would have done when he was a boy.

Besides, there was that foolish feeling of his that reality was not solid, and that facts were only plastic toys; or, rather, that they were poisonous plants, which you need not pluck unless you choose. And, even if you do pluck them, you can always fling them from you and leave them to wither on the ground.

He would have liked to vent his rage on Willy Wisp. But during the previous winter Wily had mysteriously disappeared. And though a whole month's wages had been owing to him, he had never been seen or heard of since.

However, in spite of his attitude to facts, the sense of responsibility that had been born with this new love for Ranulph forced him to take some action in the matter, and he decided to call in Endymion Leer.

Endymion Leer had arrived in Lud-in-the-Mist some thirty years ago, no one knew from where.

He was a physician, and his practice soon became the biggest in the town, but was mainly confined to the tradespeople and the poorer part of the population, for the leading families were conservative, and always a little suspicious of strangers. Besides, they considered him apt to be disrespectful, and his humour had a quality that made them vaguely uncomfortable. For instance, he would sometimes startle a polite company by exclaiming half to himself, 'Life and death! Life and death! They are the dyes in which I work. Are my hands stained?' And, with his curious dry chuckle, he would hold them out for inspection.

However, so great was his skill and learning that even the people who disliked him most were forced to consult him in really serious cases.

Among the humbler classes his was a name to conjure with, for he was always ready to adapt his fees to the purses of his patients, and where the purses were empty he gave his services free. For he took a genuine pleasure in the exercise of his craft for its own sake. One of the stories told about him was that one night he had been summoned from his bed to a farm-house that lay several miles beyond the walls of the town, to find when he got there that his patient was only a little black pig, the sole survivor of a valuable litter. But he took the discovery in good part, and settled down for the night to tend the little animal; and by morning he was able to declare it out of danger. When, on his return to Lud-in-the-Mist, he had been twitted for having wasted so much time on such an unworthy object, he had answered that a pig was thrall to the same master as a Mayor, and that it needed as much skill to cure the one as the other; adding that a good fiddler enjoys fiddling for its own sake, and that it is all the same to him whether he plays at a yokel's wedding or a merchant's funeral.

He did not confine his interests to medicine. Though not himself by birth a Dorimarite, there was little concerning the ancient customs of his adopted country that he did not know; and some years ago he had been asked by the Senate to write the official history of the Guildhall, which, before the revolution, had been the palace of the Dukes, and was the finest monument in Lud-in-the-Mist. To this task he had for some time devoted his scanty leisure.

The Senators had no severer critic than Endymion Leer, and he was the originator of most of the jokes at their expense that circulated in Lud-in-the-Mist. But to Master Nathaniel Chanticleer he seemed to have a personal antipathy; and on the rare occasions when they met his manner was almost insolent.

It was possible that this dislike was due to the fact that Ranulph when he was a tiny boy had seriously offended him; for pointing his fat little finger at him he had shouted in his shrill baby voice:

*'Before the cry of Chanticleer*
*Gibbers away Endymion Leer.'*

When his mother had scolded him for his rudeness, he said that he had been taught the rhyme by a funny old man he had seen in his dreams. Endymion Leer had gone deadly white – with rage, Dame Marigold supposed; and during several years he never referred to Ranulph except in a voice of suppressed spite.

But that was years ago, and it was to be presumed that he had at last forgotten what had, after all, been nothing but a piece of childish impudence.

The idea of confiding to this upstart the disgraceful thing that had happened to a Chanticleer was very painful to Master Nathaniel. But if anyone could cure Ranulph it was Endymion Leer, so Master Nathaniel pocketed his pride and asked him to come and see him.

As Master Nathaniel paced up and down his pipe-room (as his private den was called) waiting for the doctor, the full horror of what had happened swept over him. Ranulph had committed the unmentionable crime – he had eaten fairy fruit. If it ever became known – and these sort of things always did become known – the boy would be ruined socially for ever. And, in any case, his health would probably be seriously affected for years to come. Up and down like a see-saw went the two aspects of the case in his anxious mind . . . a Chanticleer had eaten fairy fruit; little Ranulph was in danger.

Then the page announced Endymion Leer.

He was a little rotund man of about sixty, with a snub nose, a freckled face, and with one eye blue and the other brown.

As Master Nathaniel met his shrewd, slightly contemptuous

glance he had an uncomfortable feeling which he had often before experienced in his presence, namely that the little man could read his thoughts. So he did not beat about the bush, but told him straight away why he had called him in.

Endymion Leer gave a low whistle. Then he shot at Master Nathaniel a look that was almost menacing and said sharply, 'Who gave him the stuff?'

Master Nathaniel told him it was a lad who had once been in his service called Willy Wisp.

'Willy Wisp?' cried the doctor hoarsely. 'Willy Wisp?'

'Yes, Willy Wisp . . . confound him for a double-dyed villain,' said Master Nathaniel fiercely. And then added in some surprise, 'Do you know him?'

'Know him? Yes, I know him. Who doesn't know Willy Wisp?' said the doctor. 'You see not being a merchant or a Senator,' he added with a sneer, 'I can mix with whom I choose. Willy Wisp with his pranks was the plague of the town while he was in it, and his Worship the Mayor wasn't altogether blessed by the townsfolk for keeping such a rascally servant.'

'Well, anyway, when I next meet him I'll thrash him within an inch of his life,' cried Master Nathaniel violently; and Endymion Leer looked at him with a queer little smile.

'And now you'd better take me to see your son and heir,' he said, after a pause.

'Do you . . . do you think you'll be able to cure him?' Master Nathaniel asked hoarsely, as he led the way to the parlour.

'I never answer that kind of question before I've seen the patient, and not always then,' answered Endymion Leer.

Ranulph was lying on a couch in the parlour, and Dame Marigold was sitting embroidering, her face pale and a little defiant. She was still feeling every inch a Vigil and full of resentment against the two Chanticleers, father and son, for having involved her in this horrible business.

Poor Master Nathaniel stood by, faint with apprehension, while Endymion Leer examined Ranulph's tongue, felt his pulse and, at the same time, asked him minute questions as to his symptoms.

Finally he turned to Master Nathaniel and said, 'I want to be left alone with him. He will talk to me more easily without you and your dame. Doctors should always see their patients alone.'

But Ranulph gave a piercing shriek of terror. 'No, no, no!' he cried. 'Father! Father! Don't leave me with him.'

And then he fainted.

Master Nathaniel began to lose his head, and to buzz and bang again like a cockchafer. But Endymion Leer remained perfectly calm. And the man who remains calm inevitably takes command of a situation. Master Nathaniel found himself gently but firmly pushed out of his own parlour, and the door locked in his face. Dame Marigold had followed him, and there was nothing for them to do but to await the doctor's good pleasure in the pipe-room.

'By the Sun, Moon and Stars, I'm going back!' cried Master Nathaniel wildly. 'I don't trust that fellow, I'm not going to leave Ranulph alone with him, I'm going back.'

'Oh, nonsense, Nat!' said Dame Marigold wearily. 'Do *please* be calm. One really *must* allow a doctor to have his way.'

For about a quarter of an hour Master Nathaniel paced the room with ill-concealed impatience.

The parlour was opposite the pipe-room, with only a narrow passage between them, and as Master Nathaniel had opened the door of the pipe-room, he soon was able to hear a murmur of voices proceeding from the parlour. This was comforting, for it showed that Ranulph must have come to.

Then, suddenly, his whole body seemed to stiffen, the pupils of his eyes dilated, he went ashy white, and in a low terrified voice he cried, 'Marigold, do you hear?'

In the parlour somebody was singing. It was a pretty, plaintive air, and if one listened carefully one could distinguish the words.

*'And can the physician make sick men well.*
*And can the magician a fortune divine*
*Without lily, germander, and sops in wine?*
*With sweet-brier*

*And bon-fire*
*And straw-berry wire*
*And columbine.'*

'Good gracious, Nat!' cried Dame Marigold, with a mocking look of despair. 'What on *earth* is the matter now?'

'Marigold! Marigold!' he cried hoarsely, seizing her wrists, 'don't you *hear?*'

'I hear a vulgar old song, if that's what you mean. I've known it all my life. It is very kind and domesticated of Endymion Leer to turn nursemaid and rock the cradle like this!'

*But what Master Nathaniel had heard was the Note.*

For a few seconds he stood motionless, the sweat breaking out on his forehead. Then blind with rage, he dashed across the corridor. But he had forgotten the parlour was locked, so he dashed out by the front door and came bursting in by the window that opened on to the garden.

The two occupants of the parlour were evidently so absorbed in each other that they had noticed neither Master Nathaniel's violent assault on the door nor yet his entry by the window.

Ranulph was lying on the couch with a look on his face of extraordinary peace and serenity, and there was Endymion Leer, crouching over him and softly crooning the tune to which he had before been singing words.

Master Nathaniel, roaring like a bull, flung himself on the doctor, and, dragging him to his feet, began to shake him as a terrier does a rat, at the same time belabouring him with every insulting epithet he could remember, including, of course, 'Son of a Fairy'.

As for Ranulph, he began to whimper, and complain that his father had spoiled everything, for the doctor had been making him well.

The din caused terrified servants to come battering at the door, and Dame Marigold came hurrying in by the garden window, and, pink with shame, she began to drag at Master Nathaniel's coat, almost hysterically imploring him to come to his senses.

But it was only to exhaustion that he finally yielded, and relaxed his hold on his victim, who was purple in the face and gasping for breath – so severe had been the shaking.

Dame Marigold cast a look of unutterable disgust at her panting, triumphant husband, and overwhelmed the little doctor with apologies and offers of restoratives. He sank down on a chair, unable for a few seconds to get his breath, while Master Nathaniel stood glaring at him, and poor Ranulph lay whimpering on the couch with a white scared face. Then the victim of Master Nathaniel's fury got to his feet, gave himself a little shake, took out his handkerchief and mopped his forehead, and with a little chuckle and in a voice in which there was no trace of resentment, remarked, 'Well, a good shaking is a fine thing for settling the humours. Your Worship has turned doctor! Thank you . . . thank you kindly for your physic.'

But Master Nathaniel said in a stern voice, 'What were you doing to my son?'

'What was I doing to him? Why, I was giving him medicine. Songs were medicines long before herbs.'

'He was making me well,' moaned Ranulph.

'What was that song?' demanded Master Nathaniel, in the same stern voice.

'A very old song. Nurses sing it to children. You must have known it all your life. What's it called again? You know it, Dame Marigold, don't you? *Columbine* – yes, that's it. *Columbine.*'

The trees in the garden twinkled and murmured. The birds were clamorous. From the distance came the chimes of the Guildhall clock, and the parlour smelt of spring flowers and pot-pourri.

Something seemed to relax in Master Nathaniel. He passed his hand over his forehead, gave an impatient little shrug, and, laughing awkwardly, said, 'I . . . I really don't quite know what took me. I've been anxious about the boy, and I suppose it had upset me a little. I can only beg your pardon, Leer.'

'No need to apologize . . . no need at all. No doctor worth his salt takes offence with . . . sick men,' and the look he shot at Master Nathaniel was both bright and strange.

Again Master Nathaniel frowned, and very stiffly he murmured 'Thank you.'

'Well,' went on the doctor in a matter-of-fact voice, 'I should like to have a little private talk with you about this young gentleman. May I?'

'Of course, of course, Dr Leer,' cried Dame Marigold hastily, for she saw that her husband was hesitating. 'He will be delighted, I am sure. Though I think you're a very brave man to trust yourself to such a monster. Nat, take Dr Leer into the pipe-room.'

And Master Nathaniel did so.

Once there the doctor's first words made him so happy as instantly to drive away all traces of his recent fright and to make him even forget to be ashamed of his abominable behaviour.

What the doctor said was, 'Cheer up, your Worship! I don't for a moment believe that boy of yours has eaten – what one mustn't mention.'

'What? What?' cried Master Nathaniel joyfully. 'By the Golden Apples of the West! It's been a storm in a tea-cup then? The little rascal, what a fright he gave us!'

Of course, he had known all the time that it could not be true! Facts could never be as stubborn as that, and as cruel.

And this incorrigible optimist about facts was the same man who walked in daily terror of the unknown. But perhaps the one state of mind was the outcome of the other.

Then, as he remembered the poignancy of the scene between himself and Ranulph last night and, as well, the convincingness of Ranulph's story, his heart once more grew heavy.

'But . . . but,' he faltered, 'what was the good of this cock and bull story, then? What purpose did it serve? There's no doubt the boy's ill both in mind and body, and why, in the name of the Milky Way, should he go to the trouble of inventing a story about Willy Wisp's giving him a taste of that *damned* stuff?' and he looked at Endymion Leer appealingly, as much as to say, 'Here are the facts. I give them to you. Be merciful and give them a less ugly shape.'

This Endymion Leer proceeded to do.

'How do we know it was . . . "that damned stuff"?' he asked. 'We have only Willy Wisp's word for it, and from what I know of that gentleman, his word is about as reliable as . . . as the wind in a frolic. All Lud knows of his practical jokes . . . he'd say anything to give one a fright. No, no, believe me, he was just playing off one of his pranks on Master Ranulph. I've had some experience in the real thing – I've an extensive practice, you know, down at the wharf – and your son's symptoms aren't the same. No, no, your son is no more likely to have eaten fairy fruit – than you are.'

Master Nathaniel smiled, and stretched his arms in an ecstasy of relief. 'Thank you, Leer, thank you,' he said huskily. 'The whole thing was appalling that really I believe it almost turned my head. And you are a very kind fellow not to bear me a grudge for my monstrous mishandling of you in the parlour just now.'

For the moment Master Nathaniel felt as if he really loved the queer, sharp-tongued, little upstart.

'And now,' he went on gleefully, 'to show me that it is *really* forgotten and forgiven, we must pledge each other in some wild-thyme gin . . . my cellar is rather noted for it, you know,' and from a corner cupboard he brought out two glasses and a decanter of the fragrant green cordial, left over from the supper party of the previous night.

For a few minutes they sat sipping in silent contentment.

Then Endymion Leer, as if speaking to himself, said dreamily, 'Yes, this is perhaps the solution. Why should we look for any other cure when we have the wild-thyme distilled by our ancestors? *Wild* time? No, time isn't wild . . . time-gin, sloe-gin. It is very soothing.'

Master Nathaniel grunted. He understood perfectly what Endymion Leer meant, but he did not choose to show that he did. Any remark verging on the poetical or philosophical always embarrassed him. Fortunately, such remarks were rare in Lud-in-the-Mist.

So he put down his glass and said briskly, 'Now then, Leer, let's get to business. You've removed an enormous load from my mind, but, all the same, the boy's not himself. What's the matter with him?'

Endymion Leer gave a little odd smile. And then he said, slowly and deliberately, 'Master Nathaniel, what is the matter with *you?*'

Master Nathaniel started violently.

'The matter with me?' he said coldly. 'I have not asked you in to consult you about my own health. We will, if you please, keep to that of my son.'

But he rather spoiled the dignified effect his words might have had by gobbling like a turkey cock, and muttering under his breath, 'Damn the fellow and his impudence!' Endymion Leer chuckled.

'Well, I may have been mistaken,' he said, 'but I have sometimes had the impression that our Worship the Mayor was well, a whimsical fellow, given to queer fancies. Do you know my name for your house? I call it the Mayor's Nest. The Mayor's Nest!'

And he flung back his head and laughed heartily at his own joke, while Master Nathaniel glared at him, speechless with rage.

'Now, your Worship,' he went on in a more serious voice. 'If I have been indiscreet you must forgive me . . . as I forgave you in the parlour. You see, a doctor is obliged to keep his eyes open . . . it is not from what his patients tell him that he prescribes for them, but from what he notices himself. To a doctor everything is a symptom . . . the way a man lights his pipe even. For instance, I once had the honour of having your Worship as my partner at a game of cards. You've forgotten probably – it was years ago at the Pyepowders. We lost that game. Why? Because each time that you held the most valuable card in the pack – the Lyre of Bones – you discarded it as if it had burnt your fingers. Things like that set a doctor wondering, Master Nathaniel. You are a man who is frightened about something.'

Master Nathaniel slowly turned crimson. Now that the doctor mentioned it, he remembered quite well that at one time he objected to holding the Lyre of Bones. Its name caused him to connect it with the Note. As we have seen, he was apt to regard innocent things as taboo. But to think that somebody should have noticed It!

'This is a necessary preface to what I have got to say with regard to your son,' went on Endymion Leer. 'You see, I want to make it clear that, though one has never come within a mile of fairy fruit, one can have all the symptoms of being an habitual consumer of it. Wait! Wait! Hear me out!'

For Master Nathaniel, with a smothered exclamation, had sprung from his chair.

'I am not saying that *you* have all these symptoms . . . far from it. But you know that there are spurious imitations of many diseases of the body – conditions that imitate exactly all the symptoms of the disease, and the doctors themselves are often taken in by them. You wish me to confine my remarks to your son . . . well, I consider that he is suffering from a spurious surfeit of fairy fruit.'

Though still angry, Master Nathaniel was feeling wonderfully relieved. This explanation of his own condition that robbed it of all mystery and, somehow, made it rational, seemed almost as good as a cure. So he let the doctor go on with his disquisition without any further interruption except the purely rhetorical one of an occasional protesting grunt.

'Now, I have studied somewhat closely the effects of fairy fruit,' the doctor was saying. 'These effects we regard as a malady. But, in reality, they are more like a melody – a tune that one can't get out of one's head,' and he shot a very sly little look at Master Nathaniel, out of his bright bird-like eyes.

'Yes,' he went on in a thoughtful voice, 'its effects, I think, can best be described as a changing of the inner rhythm by which we live. Have you ever noticed a little child of three or four walking hand in hand with its father through the streets? It is almost as if the two were walking in time to perfectly different tunes. Indeed, though they hold each other's hand, they might be walking on different planets . . . each seeing and hearing entirely different things. And while the father marches on steadily towards some predetermined goal, the child pulls against his hand, laughs without cause, makes little bird-like swoops at invisible objects. Now, anyone who has tasted fairy fruit (your Worship will excuse my calling a spade a spade in this way, but in my profession one can't be mealy-mouthed) – anyone, then, who has tasted fairy fruit walks through life beside other people to a different tune from theirs . . . just like the little child beside its father. But one can be *born* to a different tune . . . and that, I believe, is the case with Master Ranulph. Now, if he is ever to become a useful citizen, though he need not lose his own tune, he must learn to walk in time to other people's. He will not learn to do that here – at present. Master Nathaniel, *you are not good for your son.*'

Master Nathaniel moved uneasily in his chair, and in a stifled voice he said, 'What then do you recommend?'

'I should recommend his being taught another tune,' said the doctor briskly. 'A different one from any he has heard before . . . but one to which other people walk as well as he. You must have captains and mates, Master Nathaniel, with little houses down at the seaport town. Is there no honest fellow among them with a sensible wife with whom the lad could lodge for a month or two? Or stay,' he went on, without giving Master Nathaniel time to answer, 'life on a farm would do as well – better, perhaps. Sowing and reaping, quiet days, smells and noises that are like old tunes, healing nights . . . slow-time gin! By the Harvest of Souls, Master Nathaniel, I'd rather any day, be a farmer than a merchant . . . waving corn is better than the sea, and waggons are better than ships, and freighted with sweeter and more wholesome merchandise than all your silks and spices; for in their cargo are peace and a quiet mind. Yes. Master Ranulph must spend some months on a farm, and I know the very place for him.'

Master Nathaniel was more moved than he cared to show by the doctor's words. They were like the cry of the cock, without its melancholy. But he tried to make his voice dry and matter of fact, as he asked where this marvellous farm might be.

'Oh, it's to the west,' the doctor answered vaguely. 'It belongs to an old acquaintance of mine – the widow Gibberty. She's a fine, fresh, bustling woman and knows everything a woman ought to know, and her granddaughter, Hazel, is a nice, sensible, hard-working girl. I'm sure . . .'

'Gibberty, did you say?' interrupted Master Nathaniel. He seemed to have heard the name before.

'Yes. You may remember having heard her name in the law courts – it isn't a common one. She had a case many years ago. I think it was a thieving labourer her late husband had thrashed and dismissed who sued her for damages.'

'And where exactly is this farm?'

'Well, it's about sixty miles away from Lud, just out of a village called Swan-on-the-Dapple.'

'Swan-on-the-Dapple? Then it's quite close to the Elfin Marches!' cried Master Nathaniel indignantly.

'About ten miles away,' replied Endymion Leer imperturbably. 'But what of that? Ten miles on a busy self-supporting farm is as great a distance as a hundred would be at Lud. Still, under the circumstances, I can understand your fighting shy of the west. I must think of some other plan.'

'I should think so indeed!' growled Master Nathaniel.

'However,' continued the doctor, 'you have really nothing to fear from that quarter. He would, in reality, be much further moved from temptation there than here. The smugglers, whoever they are, run great risks to get the fruit into Lud, and they're not going to waste it on rustics and farmhands.'

'All the same,' said Master Nathaniel doggedly, 'I'm not going to have him going so damnably near to . . . a certain place.'

'The place that does not exist in the eye of the law, eh?' said Endymion Leer with a smile.

Then he leaned forward in his chair, and gazed steadily at Master Nathaniel. This time, his eyes were kind as well as piercing. 'Master Nathaniel, I'd like to reason with you a little,' he said. 'Reason I know, is only a drug, and, as such, its effects are never permanent. But, like the juice of the poppy, it often gives a temporary relief.'

He sat silent for a few seconds, as if choosing in advance the words he meant to use. Then he began, 'We have the misfortune of living in a country that marches with the unknown; and that is apt to make the fancy sick. Though we laugh at old songs and old yarns, nevertheless, they are the *yarn* with which we weave our picture of the world.'

He paused for a second to chuckle over his own pun, and then went on, 'But, for once, let us look things straight in the face, and call them by their proper names. Fairyland, for instance . . . no one has been there within the memory of man. For generations it has been a forbidden land. In consequence, curiosity, ignorance, and unbridled fancy have put their heads together and concocted a country of golden trees hanging with pearls and rubies, the inhabitants of which are immortal and terrible through unearthly gifts – and so on. But – and in this I am in no way subscribing to a certain antiquary of ill odour – there is not a single homely thing that, looked at from a certain angle, does not become fairy. Think of the Dapple, or the Dawl, when they roll the sunset towards the east. Think of an autumn wood, or a hawthorn in May. *A hawthorn in May – there's* a miracle for you! Who would ever have dreamed that that gnarled stumpy old tree had the power to do *that?* Well, all these things are familiar sights, but what should we think if never having seen them we read a description of them, or saw them for the first time? A golden river! Flaming trees! Trees that suddenly break into flower! For all we know, it may be Dorimare that is Fairyland to the people across the Debatable Hills.'

Master Nathaniel was drinking in every word as if it was nectar. A sense of safety was tingling in his veins like a generous wine . . . mounting to his head, even, a little bit, so unused was he to that particular intoxicant.

Endymion Leer eyed him, with a little smile. 'And now,' he said, 'perhaps your Worship will let me talk a little of your own case. The malady you suffer from should, I think, be called "life-sickness". You are, so to speak, a bad sailor, and the motion of life makes you brain-sick. There, beneath you, all round you, there surges and swells, and ebbs and flows, that great, ungovernable, ruthless element that we call life. And its motion gets into your blood, turns your head dizzy. Get your sea legs, Master Nathaniel!

By which I do not mean you must cease feeling the motion . . . go on feeling it, but learn to like it; or if not to like it, at any rate to bear it with firm legs and a steady head.'

There were tears in Master Nathaniel's eyes and he smiled a little sheepishly. At that moment his feet were certainly on *terra firma*; and so convinced are we that each mood while it lasts will be the permanent temper of our soul that for the moment he felt that he would never feel 'life-sickness' again.

'Thank you, Leer, thank you,' he murmured. 'I'd do a good deal for you, in return for what you've just said.'

'Very well, then,' said the doctor briskly, 'give me the pleasure of curing your son. It's the greatest pleasure I have in life, curing people. Let me arrange for him to go to this farm.'

Master Nathaniel, in his present mood, was incapable of gainsaying him. So it was arranged that Ranulph should shortly leave for Swan-on-the-Dapple.

It was with a curious solemnity that, just before he took his leave, Endymion Leer said, 'Master Nathaniel, there is one thing I want you to bear in mind – *I have never in my life made a mistake in a prescription.*'

As Endymion Leer trotted away from the Chanticleers he chuckled to himself and softly rubbed his hands. 'I can't help being a physician and giving balm,' he muttered. 'But it was monstrous good policy as well. He never would have allowed the boy to go, otherwise.'

Then he started, and stood stock-still, listening. From far away there came a ghostly sound. It might have been the cry of a very distant cock, or else it might have been the sound of faint, mocking laughter.

# 5

## RANULPH GOES TO THE WIDOW GIBBERTY'S FARM

But Endymion Leer was right. Reason is only a drug, and its effects cannot be permanent. Master Nathaniel was soon suffering from life-sickness as much as ever.

For one thing, there was no denying that in the voice of Endymion Leer singing to Ranulph, he had once again heard the Note; and the fact tormented him, reason with himself as he might.

But it was not sufficient to make him distrust Endymion Leer – one might hear the Note, he was convinced, in the voices of the most innocent; just as the mocking cry of the cuckoo can rise from the nest of the lark or hedgesparrow. But he was certainly not going to let him take Ranulph away to that western farm.

And yet the boy was longing, nay, craving to go, for Endymion Leer, when he had been left alone with him in the parlour that morning, had fired his imagination with its delights.

When Master Nathaniel questioned him as to what other things Endymion Leer had talked about, he said that he had asked him a great many questions about the stranger in green he had seen dancing, and had made him repeat to him several times what exactly he had said to him.

'Then,' said Ranulph, 'he said he would sing me well and happy. And I was just beginning to feel so wonderful, when you came bursting in, father.'

'I'm sorry, my boy,' said Master Nathaniel. 'But why did you first of all scream so and beg not to be left alone with him?'

Ranulph wriggled and hung his head. 'I suppose it was like the cheese,' he said sheepishly. 'But, father, I want to go to that farm. *Please* let me go.'

For several weeks Master Nathaniel steadily refused his consent. He kept the boy with him as much as his business and his official duties would permit, trying to find for him occupations and amusements that would teach him a 'different tune'. For Endymion Leer's words, in spite of their having had so little effect on his spiritual condition, had genuinely and permanently impressed him. However, he could not but see that Ranulph was daily wilting and that his talk was steadily becoming more fantastic; and he began to fear that his own objection to letting him go to the farm sprang merely from a selfish desire to keep him with him.

Hempie, oddly enough, was in favour of his going. The old woman's attitude to the whole affair was a curious one. Nothing would make her believe that it was *not* fairy fruit that Willy Wisp had given him. She said she had suspected it from the first, but to have mentioned it would have done no good to anyone.

'If it wasn't *that* what was it then?' she would ask scornfully. 'For what is Willy Wisp himself? He left his place – and his wages not paid, too – during the twelve nights of Yuletide. And when dog or servant leaves, sudden like, at *that* time, we all know what to think.'

'And what are we to think, Hempie?' enquired Master Nathaniel.

At first the old woman would only shake her head and look mysterious. But finally she told him that it was believed in the country districts that, should there be a fairy among the servants, he was bound to return to his own land on one of the twelve nights after the winter solstice; and should there be among the dogs one that belonged to Duke Aubrey's pack, during these nights he would howl and howl, till he was let out of his kennel, and then vanish into the darkness and never be seen again.

Master Nathaniel grunted with impatience.

'Well, it was you dragged the words from my lips, and though you *are* the Mayor and the Lord High Seneschal, you can't come lording it over my thoughts . . . I've a right to them!' cried Hempie, indignantly.

'My good Hempie, if you really believe the boy has eaten . . . a certain thing, all I can say is you seem very cheerful about it,' growled Master Nathaniel.

'And what good would it do my pulling a long face and looking like one of the old statues in the fields of Grammary I should like to know?' flashed back Hempie. And then she added, with a meaning nod, 'Besides, whatever happens, no harm can ever come to a Chanticleer. While Lud stands the Chanticleers will thrive. So come rough, come smooth, you won't find me worrying. But if I was you, Master Nat, I'd give the boy his way. There's nothing like his own way for a sick person – be he child or grown man. His own way to a sick man is what grass is to a sick dog.'

Hempie's opinion influenced Master Nathaniel more than he would like to admit; but it was a talk he had with Mumchance, the captain of the Lud Yeomanry, that finally induced him to let Ranulph have his way.

The Yeomanry combined the duties of a garrison with those of a police corps, and Master Nathaniel had charged their captain to try and find the whereabouts of Willy Wisp.

It turned out that the rogue was quite familiar to the Yeomanry, and Mumchance confirmed what Endymion Leer had said about his having turned the town upside down with his pranks during the few months he had been in Master Nathaniel's service. But since his disappearance at Yule-tide, nothing had been seen or heard of him in Lud-in-the-Mist, and Mumchance could find no traces of him.

Master Nathaniel fumed and grumbled a little at the inefficiency of the Yeomanry; but, at the bottom of his heart he was relieved. He had a lurking fear that Hempie was right and Endymion Leer was wrong, and that it had really been fairy fruit after all that Ranulph had eaten. But it is best to let sleeping facts lie. And he feared that if confronted with Willy Wisp the facts might wake up and begin to bite. But what was this that Mumchance was telling him?

It would seem that during the past months there had been a marked increase in the consumption of fairy fruit – in the low quarters of the town, of course.

'It's got to be stopped, Mumchance, d'ye hear?' cried Master Nathaniel hotly. 'And what's more, the smugglers must be caught and clapped into gaol, every mother's son of them. This has gone on too long.'

'Yes, your Worship,' said Mumchance stolidly, 'it went on in the time of my predecessor, if your Worship will pardon the expression' (Mumchance was very fond of long words, but he had a feeling that it was presumption to use them before his betters), 'and in the days of *his* predecessor . . . and way back. And it's no good trying to be smarter than our forebears. I sometimes think we might as well try and catch the Dapple and clap it into prison as them smugglers. But these are sad times, your Worship, sad times – the 'prentices wanting to be masters, and every little tradesman wanting to be a Senator, and every dirty little urchin thinking he can give impudence to his betters! You see, your Worship, I sees and hears a good deal in my way of business, if you'll pardon the expression . . . but the things one's eyes and ears tells one, they ain't in words, so to speak, and it's not easy to tell other folks what they say . . . no more than the geese can tell you how they know it's going to rain,' and he laughed apologetically. 'But I shouldn't be surprised – no, I shouldn't – *if there wasn't something brewing.*'

'By the Sun, Moon and Stars, Mumchance, don't speak in riddles!' cried Master Nathaniel irritably. 'What d'ye mean?'

Mumchance shifted uneasily from one foot to the other: 'Well, your Worship,' he began, 'it's this way. Folks are beginning to take a wonderful interest in Duke Aubrey again. Why, all the girls are wearing bits of tawdry jewellery with his picture, and bits of imitation ivy and squills stuck in their bonnets, and there ain't a poor street in this town where all the cockatoos that the sailors bring don't squawk at you from their cages that the Duke will come to his own again . . . or some such rubbish, and . . .'

'My good Mumchance!' broke in Master Nathaniel, impatiently, 'Duke Aubrey was a rascally sovereign who died more than two hundred years ago. You don't believe he's going to come to life again do you?'

'I don't say that he will, your Worship,' answered Mumchance evasively. 'But all I knows is that when Lud begins talking about him, it generally bodes trouble. I remember as how old Tripsand, he who was Captain of the Yeomanry when I was a little lad, used always to say that there was a deal of that sort of talk before the great drought.'

'Fiddlesticks!' cried Master Nathaniel.

Mumchance's theories about Duke Aubrey he immediately dismissed from his mind. But he was very much disturbed by what he had said about fairy fruit, and began to think that Endymion Leer had been right in maintaining that Ranulph would be further from temptation at Swan-on-the-Dapple than in Lud.

He had another interview with Leer, and the long and the short of it was that it was decided that as soon as Dame Marigold and Hempie could get Ranulph ready he should set out for the widow Gibberty's farm. Endymion Leer said that he wanted to look for herbs in the neighbourhood, and would be very willing to escort him there.

Master Nathaniel, of course, would much have preferred to have gone with him himself; but it was against the law for the Mayor to leave Lud, except on circuit.

In his stead, he decided to send Luke Hempen, old Hempie's grand-nephew. He was a lad of about twenty, who worked in the garden and had always been the faithful slave of Ranulph.

On a beautiful sunny morning, about a week later, Enydmion Leer came riding up to the Chanticleers' to fetch Ranulph, who was impatiently awaiting him, booted and spurred, and looking more like his old self than he had done for months.

Before Ranulph mounted, Master Nathaniel, blinking away a tear or two, kissed him on the forehead and whispered, 'The black rooks will fly away, my son, and you'll come back as brown as a berry, and as merry as a grig. And if you want me, just send a word by Luke, and I'll be with you as fast as horses can gallop – law or no law'. And from her latticed window at the top of the house appeared the head and shoulders of old Hempie in her nightcap, shaking her fist, and crying, 'Now then, young Luke, if you don't take care of my boy – you'll *catch it!*'

Many a curious glance was cast at the little cavalcade as they trotted down the cobbled streets. Miss Lettice and Miss Rosie Prim, the two buxom daughters of the leading watchmaker who were returning from their marketing considered that Ranulph looked sweetly pretty on horseback. 'Though,' added Miss Rosie, 'they do say he's a bit . . . *queer*, and it *is* a pity, I must say, that he's got the Mayor's ginger hair.'

'Well, Rosie,' retorted Miss Lettice, 'at least he doesn't cover it up with a black wig, like a certain apprentice I know!'

And Rosie laughed, and tossed her head.

A great many women, as they watched them pass, called down blessings on the head of Endymion Leer; adding that it was a pity that *he* was not Mayor and High Seneschal. And several rough looking men scowled ominously at Ranulph. But Mother Tibbs, the half-crazy washerwoman, who, in spite of her forty summers danced more lightly than any maiden, and was, in consequence, in great request as a partner at those tavern dances that played so great a part in the life of the masses in Lud-in-the-Mist – crazy, disreputable, Mother Tibbs, with her strangely noble innocent face, tossed him a nosegay and cried in her sing-song penetrating voice, 'Cockadoodle doo! Cockadoodle doo! The little master's bound for the land where the eggs are all gold!'

But no one ever paid any attention to what Mother Tibbs might say.

Nothing worth mentioning occurred during their journey to Swan; except the endless pleasant things of the country in summer. There were beech spinneys, wading up steep banks through their own dead leaves; fields all blurred with meadow-sweet and sorrel; brown old women screaming at their goats; acacias in full flower, and willows blown by the wind into white blossom.

From time to time, terrestrial comets – the blue flash of a

kingfisher, the red whisk of a fox – would furrow and thrill the surface of the earth with beauty.

And in the distance, here and there, standing motionless and in complete silence by the flowing Dapple, were red-roofed villages – the least vain of all fair things, for they never looked at their own reflexion in the water, but gazed unblinkingly at the horizon.

And there were ruined castles covered with ivy – the badge of the old order, clinging to its own; and into the ivy doves dived, seeming to leave in their wake a trail of amethyst, just as a clump of bottle-green leaves is shot with purple by the knowledge that it hides violets. And the round towers of the castles looked as if they were so firmly encrusted in the sky that, to get to their other side, one would have to hew out a passage through the celestial marble.

And the sun would set, and then our riders could watch the actual process of colour fading from the world. Was that tree still *really* green, or was it only that they were remembering how a few seconds ago it had been green?

And the nymph whom all travellers pursue and none has ever yet caught – the white high-road, glimmered and beckoned to them through the dusk.

All these things, however, were familiar sights to every Ludite. But on the third day (for Ranulph's sake they were taking the journey in easy stages) things began to look different – especially the trees; for instead of acacias, beeches, and willows – familiar living things forever murmuring their secret to themselves – there were pines and liege-oaks and olives. Inanimate works of art they seemed at first and Ranulph exclaimed, 'Oh, look at the funny trees! They are like the old statues of dead people in the Fields of Grammary!'

But, as well, they were like an old written tragedy. For if human, or superhuman, experience, and the tragic clash of personality can be expressed by plastic shapes, then one might half believe that these tortured trees had been bent by the wind into the spiritual shape of some old drama.

Pines and olives, however, cannot grow far away from the sea.

And surely the sea lay to the east of Lud-in-the-Mist, and with each mile they were getting further away from it?

It was the sea beyond the Hills of the Elfin Marches – the invisible sea of Fairyland – that caused these pines and olives to flourish.

It was late in the afternoon when they reached the village of Swan-on-the-Dapple – a score of houses straggling round a triangle of unreclaimed common, on which grew olives and stunted fruit-trees, and which was used as the village rubbish heap. In the distance were the low, pine-covered undulations of the Debatable Hills – a fine unchanging background for the changing colours of the seasons. Indeed, they lent a dignity and significance to everything that grew, lay, or was enacted, against them; so that the little children in their blue smocks who were playing among the rubbish on the dingy common as our cavalcade rode past, seemed to be performing against the background of Destiny some tremendous action, similar to the one expressed by the shapes of the pines and olives.

When they had left the village, they took a cart-track that branched off from the high-road to the right. It led into a valley, the gently sloping sides of which were covered with vine-yards and corn-fields. Sometimes their path led through a little wood of liege-oaks with trunks, where the bark had been stripped, showing as red as blood, and everywhere there were short, wiry, aromatic shrubs, beset by myriads of bees.

Every minute the hills seemed to be drawing nearer, and the pines with which they were covered began to stand out from the carpet of heath in a sort of coagulated relief, so that they looked like a thick green scum of watercress on a stagnant purple pond.

At last they reached the farm – a fine old manor-house, standing among a cluster of red-roofed barns, and supported, heraldically, on either side by two magnificent plane-trees, with dappled trunks of tremendous girth.

They were greeted by the barking of five or six dogs, and this brought the widow hurrying out accompanied by a pretty girl of about seventeen whom she introduced as her granddaughter Hazel.

Though she must have been at least sixty by then, the widow Gibberty was still a strikingly handsome woman – tall, imposing-looking, and with hair that must once have had as many shades of red and brown as a bed of wallflowers smouldering in the sun.

Then a couple of men came up and led away the horses, and the travellers were taken up to their rooms.

As befitted the son of the High Seneschal, the one given to Ranulph was evidently the best. It was large and beautifully proportioned, and in spite of its homely chintzes and the plain furniture of a farmhouse, in spite even of the dried rushes laid on the floor instead of a carpet, it bore unmistakable traces of the ancient magnificence when the house had belonged to nobles instead of farmers.

For instance, the ceiling was a fine specimen of the flat enamelled ceilings that belonged to the Duke Aubrey period in domestic architecture. There was just such a ceiling in Dame Marigold's bedroom in Lud. She had stared up at it when in travail with Ranulph – just as all the mothers of the Chanticleers had done in the same circumstances – and its colours and pattern had become inextricably confused with her pain and delirium.

Endymion Leer was put next to Ranulph, and Luke was given a large pleasant room in the attic.

Ranulph was not in the least tired by his long ride, he said. His cheeks were flushed, his eyes bright, and when the widow had left him alone with Luke, he gave two or three little skips of glee, and cried, 'I do *love* this place, Luke'.

At six o'clock a loud bell was run outside the house, presumably to summon the labourers to supper; and, as the widow had told them it would be in the kitchen, Ranulph and Luke, both feeling very hungry, went hurrying down.

It was an enormous kitchen, running the whole length of the house; in the olden days it had been the banqueting hall. It was solidly stone-vaulted, and the great chimney place was also of stone, and decorated in high-relief with the skulls and flowers and arabesques of leaves ubiquitous in the art of Dorimare. It was flanked by giant fire-dogs of copper. The floor was tiled with a mosaic of brown and red and grey-blue flag-stones.

Down the centre of the room ran a long narrow table laid with pewter plates and mugs, for the labourers and maid servants who came flocking in, their faces shining from recent soap and scrubbing, and stood about in groups at the lower end of the room, grinning and bashful from the presence of company. According to the good old yeoman custom they had their meals with their masters.

It was a most delicious supper – a great ham with the aromatic flavour of wood-smoke, eaten with pickled cowslips; brawn; a red-deer pie, and, in honour of the distinguished guests, a fat roast swan. The wine was from the widow's own grapes and was flavoured with honey and blackberries.

Most of the talking was done by the widow and Endymion Leer. He was asking her if many trout had been caught that summer in the Dapple, and what were their markings. And she told him that a salmon had recently been landed weighing ten pounds.

Ranulph, who had been munching away in silence, suddenly looked up at them, with that little smile of his that people always found a trifle disconcerting.

'That isn't *real* talk,' he said. 'That isn't the way you really talk to each other. That's only pretence talk.'

The widow looked very surprised and very much annoyed. But Endymion Leer laughed heartily and asked him what he meant by '*real* talk'; Ranulph, however, would not be drawn.

But Luke Hempen, in a dim inarticulate way, understood what he meant. The conversation between the widow and the doctor had *not* rung true; it was almost as if their words had a double meaning known only to themselves.

A few minutes later, a wizened old man with very bright eyes came into the room and sat down at the lower end of the table. And then Ranulph really did give everyone a fright, for he stopped eating, and for a few seconds stared at him in silence. Then he gave a piercing scream.

All eyes turned towards him in amazement. But he sat as if petrified, his eyes round and staring, pointing at the old man.

'Come, come, young fellow!' cried Endymion Leer, sharply, 'what's the meaning of this?'

'What ails you, little master?' cried the widow.

But he continued pointing in silence at the old man, who was leering and smirking and ogling, in evident delight at being the centre of attention.

'He's scared by Portunus, the weaver,' tittered the maids.

And the words 'Portunus,' 'old Portunus the weaver' were bandied from mouth to mouth down the two sides of the table.

'Yes, Portunus, the weaver,' cried the widow, in a loud voice, a hint of menace in her eye. 'And who, I should like to know, does not love Portunus, the weaver?'

The maids hung their heads, the men sniggered deprecatingly.

'Well?' challenged the widow,

Silence.

'And who,' she continued indignantly, 'is the handiest most obliging old fellow to be found within twenty miles?'

She paused glared down the table, and then repeated her question.

As if compelled by her eye, the company murmured 'Portunus'.

'And if the cheeses won't curdle, or the butter won't come, or the wine in the vats won't get a good head, who comes to the rescue?'

'Portunus,' murmured the company.

'And who is always ready to lend a helping hand to the maids – to break or bolt hemp, to dress flax, or to spin? And when their work is over to play them tunes on his fiddle?'

'Portunus,' murmured the company.

Suddenly Hazel raised her eyes from her plate and they were sparkling with defiance and anger.

'And who,' she cried shrilly, 'sits by the fire when he thinks no one is watching him roasting little live frogs and eating them? Portunus.'

With each word her voice rose higher, like a soaring bird. But at the last word it was as if the bird when it had reached the ceiling suddenly fell down dead. And Luke saw her flinch under the cold indignant stare of the widow.

And he had noticed something else as well.

It was the custom in Dorimare, in the houses of the yeomanry and the peasantry, to hang a bunch of dried fennel over the door of every room; for fennel was supposed to have the power of keeping away the Fairies. And when Ranulph had given his eerie scream, Luke had, as instinctively as in similar circumstances a mediaeval papist would have made the sign of the Cross, glanced towards the door to catch a reassuring glimpse of the familiar herb.

But there was no fennel hanging over the door of the widow Gibberty.

The men grinned, the maids tittered at Hazel's outburst; and then there was an awkward silence.

In the meantime, Ranulph seemed to have recovered from his fright and was going on stolidly with his supper, while the widow was saying to him reassuringly, 'Mark my words, little master, you'll get to love Portunus as much as we all do. Trust Portunus for knowing where the trout rise and where all the birds' nests are to be found . . . eh, Portunus?'

And Portunus chuckled with delight and his bright eyes twinkled.

'Why,' the widow continued, 'I have known him these twenty years. He's the weaver in these parts, and goes the round from farm to farm, and the room with the loom is always called "Portunus' parlour". And there isn't a wedding or a merrymaking within twenty miles where he doesn't play the fiddle.'

Luke, whose perceptions owing to the fright he had just had were unusually alert, noticed that Endymion Leer was very silent, and that his face as he watched Ranulph was puzzled and a little anxious.

When supper was over the maids and labourers vanished, and so did Portunus; but the three guests sat on, listening to the pleasant whirr of the widow's and Hazel's spinning-wheels, saying but little, for the long day in the open air had made all three of them sleepy.

At eight o'clock a little scrabbling noise was heard at the door. 'That's the children,' said Hazel, and she went and opened it, upon which three or four little boys came bashfully in from the dusk.

'Good evening, my lads,' said the widow, genially. 'Come for your bread and cheese . . . eh?'

The children grinned and hung their heads, abashed by the sight of three strangers.

'The little lads of the village, Master Chanticleer, take it in turn to watch our cattle all night,' said the widow to Ranulph. 'We keep them some miles away along the valley where there is good pasturage, and the herdsman likes to come back to his own home at night.'

'And these little boys are going to be out *all night*?' asked Ranulph in an awed voice.

'That they are! And a fine time they'll have of it too. They build themselves little huts out of branches and light fires in them. Oh, they enjoy themselves.'

The children grinned from ear to ear; and when Hazel had provided each of them with some bread and cheese they scuttled off into the gathering dusk.

'I'd like to go some night, too,' said Ranulph.

The widow was beginning to expostulate against the idea of young Master Chanticleer's spending the night out of doors with cows and village children, when Endymion Leer said, decidedly, 'That's all nonsense! I don't want my patient coddled . . . eh! Ranulph? I see no reason why he shouldn't go some night if it amuses him. But wait till the nights are warmer.'

He paused just a second, and added, 'towards *Midsummer*, let us say.'

They sat on a little longer; saying but little, yawning a great deal. And then the widow suggested that they should all go off to bed.

There were home-made tallow candles provided for everyone, except Ranulph, whose social importance was emphasised by a wax one from Lud.

Endymion Leer lit it for him, and then held it at arm's length and contemplated its flame, his head on one side, his eyes twinkling.

'Thrice blessed little herb!' he began in a whimsical voice. 'Herb o' *grease*, with thy waxen stem and blossom of flame! Thou are more potent against spells and terrors and the invisible menace than fennel or dittany or rue. Hail! antidote to the deadly nightshade! Blossoming in the darkness, thy virtues are heartsease and quiet sleep. Sick people bless thee, and women in travail, and people with haunted minds, and all children.'

'Don't be a buffoon, Leer,' said the widow roughly; in quite a different voice from the one of bluff courtesy in which she had hitherto addressed him. To an acute observer it would have suggested that they were in reality more intimate than they cared to show.

For the first time in his life Luke Hempen had difficulty in getting off to sleep.

His grand-aunt had dinned into him for the past week, with many a menacing shake of her old fist, that should anything happen to Master Ranulph she would hold him, Luke, responsible, and even before leaving Lud, the honest, but by no means heroic, lad, had been in somewhat of a panic; and the various odd little incidents that had taken place that evening were not of a nature to reassure him.

Finally, he could stand it no longer. So up he got, lit his candle, and crept down the attic stairs and along the corridor to Ranulph's room.

Ranulph, too, was wide awake. He had not put out his candle, and was lying staring up at the fantastic ceiling.

'What do you want, Luke?' he cried peevishly. 'Why won't anyone ever leave me alone?'

'I was just wondering if you were all right, sir,' said Luke apologetically.

'Of course I am. Why shouldn't I be?' and Ranulph gave an impatient little plunge in his bed.

'Well, I was just wondering, you know.'

Luke paused; and then said imploringly, 'Please, Master Ranulph, be a good little chap and tell me what took you at supper time when that doitered old weaver came in. You gave me quite a turn, screaming like that.'

'Ah, Luke! Wouldn't you like to know!' teased Ranulph.

Finally he admitted that when he had been a small child he had frequently seen Portunus in his dreams, 'And that's rather frightening, you know, Luke.'

Luke, much relieved, admitted that he supposed it was. He himself was not given to dreaming; nor did he take seriously the dreams of others.

Ranulph noticed his relief; and rather an impish expression stole into his eyes.

'But there's something else, Luke,' he said. 'Old Portunus, you know, is a dead man.'

This time Luke was really alarmed. Was his charge going off his head?

'Get along with you, Master Ranulph!' he cried, in a voice that he tried to make jocose.

'All right, Luke, you needn't believe it unless you like,' said Ranulph. 'Good-night, I'm off to sleep.'

And he blew out his candle and turned his back on Luke, who, thus dismissed, must needs return to his own bed, where he soon fell fast asleep.

# 6

## THE WIND IN THE CRABAPPLE BLOSSOMS

About a week later, Mistress Hempen received the following letter from Luke:

DEAR AUNTIE, – I trust this finds you well as it leaves me. I'm remembering what you said, and trying to look after the little master, but this is a queer place and no mistake, and I'd liefer we were both safe back in Lud. Not that I've any complaint to make as to victuals and lodging, and I'm sure they treat Master Ranulph as if he was a king – wax candles and linen sheets and everything that he gets at home. And I must say I've not seen him looking so well, nor so happy for many a long day. But the widow woman she's a rum customer and no mistake, and wonderful fond of fishing, for a female. She and the doctor are out all night sometimes together after trout, but never a trout do we see on the table. And sometimes she looks so queerly at Master Ranulph that it fairly makes my flesh creep. And there's no love lost between her and her granddaughter, her step-granddaughter I *should* say, her who's called Miss Hazel, and they say as what by the old farmer's will the farm belongs to her and not to the widow. And she's a stuck-up young miss, very high and keeping herself *to* herself. But I'm glad she's in the house all the same, for she's well liked by all the folk on the farm and I'd take my oath that though she's high she's straight. And there's a daft old man that they call Portunus and it's more like having a tame magpie in the house than a human man, for he can't talk a word of sense, it's all scraps of rhyme, and he's always up to mischief. He's a weaver and as cracked as Mother Tibbs, though he do play the fiddle beautiful. And it's my belief the widow walks in fear of her life for that old bird, though why she should beats me to know. For the old fellow's harmless enough, though a bit spiteful at times. He sometimes pinches the maids till their arms are as many colours as a mackerel's back. And he seems sweet on Miss Hazel though she can't abear him, though when I ask her about him she snaps my head off and tells me to mind my own business. And I'm afraid the folk on the farm must think me a bit high myself through me minding what you told me and keeping myself *to* myself. Because it's my belief if I'd been a bit more friendly at the beginning (such as it's my nature to be) I'd have found out a thing or two. And that cracked old weaver seems quite smitten by an old stone statue in the orchard. He's always cuting capers in front of it, and pulling faces at it, like a clown at the fair. But the widow's scared of him, as sure as my name's Luke Hempen. And Master Ranulph does talk so queer about him – things as I wouldn't demean myself to write to an old lady. And I'd be very glad, auntie, if you'd ask his Worship to send for us back, because I don't like this place, and that's a fact, and not so much as a sprig of fennel do they put above their doors.

– And I am,

Your dutiful grandnephew, LUKE HEMPEN

Hempie read it through with many a frown and shake of her head, and with an occasional snort of contempt; as, for instance, where Luke intimated that the widow's linen sheets were as fine as the Chanticleers'.

Then she sat for a few minutes in deep thought.

'No, no,' she finally said to herself, 'my boy's well and happy and that's more than he was in Lud, these last few months. What must be must be, and it's never any use worrying Master Nat.'

So she did not show Master Nathaniel Luke Hempen's letter.

As for Master Nathaniel, he was enchanted by the accounts he received from Endymion Leer of the improvement both in Ranulph's health and state of mind. Ranulph himself too wrote little letters saying how happy he was and how anxious to stay on at the farm. It was evident that, to use the words of Endymion Leer, he was learning to live life to a different tune.

And then Endymion Leer returned to Lud and confirmed what he had said in his letters by his accounts of how well and happy Ranulph was in the life of a farm.

The summer was simmering comfortably by, in its usual sleepy way, in the streets and gardens of Lud-in-the-Mist. The wives of Senators and burgesses were busy in still-room and kitchen making cordials and jams; in the evening the streets were lively with chattering voices and the sounds of music, and 'prentices danced with their masters' daughters in the public square, or outside taverns, till the grey twilight began to turn black. The Senators yawned through each other's speeches, and made their own as short as possible that they might hurry off to whip the Dapple for trout or play at bowls on the Guildhall's beautiful velvety green. And when one of their ships brought in a particularly choice cargo of rare wine or exotic sweetmeats they invited their friends to supper, and washed down the dainties with the good old jokes.

Mumchance looked glum, and would sometimes frighten his wife by gloomy forebodings; but he had learned that it was no use trying to arouse the Mayor and the Senate.

Master Nathaniel was missing Ranulph very much; but as he continued to get highly satisfactory reports of his health he felt that it would be selfish not to let him stay on, at any rate till the summer was over.

Then, the trees, after their long silence, began to talk again, in yellow and red. And the days began to shrink under one's very eyes. And Master Nathaniel's pleached alley was growing yellower and yellower, and on the days when a thick white mist came rolling up from the Dapple it would be the only object in his garden that was not blurred and dimmed, and would look like a pair of gigantic golden compasses with which a demiurge is measuring chaos.

It was then that things began to happen; moreover, they began at the least likely place in the whole of Lud-in-the-Mist – Miss Primrose Crabapple's Academy for young ladies.

Miss Primrose Crabapple had for some twenty years 'finished' the daughters of the leading citizens; teaching them to sing, to dance, to play the spinet and the harp, to preserve and candy fruit, to wash gauzes and lace, to bone chickens without cutting the back, to model groups of still life in every imaginable plastic material, edible and non-edible – wax, butter, sugar – and to embroider in at least a hundred different stitches – preparing them, in fact, to be one day useful and accomplished wives.

When Dame Marigold Chanticleer and her contemporaries had first been pupils at the Academy, Miss Primrose had been only a young assistant governess, very sentimental and affected, and full of nonsensical ideas. But nonsensical ideas and great practical gifts are sometimes found side by side, and sentimentality is a quality that rarely has the slightest influence on action.

Anyhow, the ridiculous gushing assistant managed bit by bit to get the whole direction of the establishment into her own hands, while the old dame to whom the school belonged became as plastic to her will as were butter, sugar or wax to her clever fingers; and when the old lady died she left her the school.

It was an old rambling red-brick house with a large pleasant garden, and stood a little back from the highroad, about half a mile beyond the west gate of Lud-in-the-Mist.

The Academy represented to the ladies of Lud all that they knew of romance. They remembered the jokes they had laughed at within its walls, the secrets they had exchanged walking up and down its pleached alleys, far more vividly than anything that had afterwards happened to them.

Do not for a moment imagine that they were sentimental about it. The ladies of Lud were never sentimental. It was as an old comic song that they remembered their school-days. Perhaps it is always with a touch of wistfulness that we remember old comic songs. It was at any rate as near as the ladies of Lud could get to the poetry of the past. And whenever Dame Marigold Chanticleer and Dame Dreamsweet Vigil and the rest of the old pupils of the Academy foregathered to eat syllabub and marzipan and exchange new stitches for their samplers, they would be sure sooner or later to start bandying memories about these funny old days and the ridiculous doings of Miss Primrose Crabapple.

'Oh, *do* you remember,' Dame Marigold would cry, 'how she wanted to start what she called a "Mother's Day", when we were all to dress up in white and green, and pretend to be lilies standing on our mothers graves?'

'Oh, yes!' Dame Dreamsweet would gurgle, 'And mother was so angry when she found out about it. "How dare the ghoulish creature bury me alive like this?" she used to say.'

And then they would laugh till the tears ran down their cheeks.

Each generation had its own jokes and its own secrets; but they were always on the same pattern; just as when one of the china cups got broken, it was replaced by another exactly like it, with the same painted border of squills and ivy.

There were squills and ivy all over the Academy, embroidered on the curtains in each bedroom, and on all the cushions and screens, painted in a frieze around the wall of the parlour, and even stamped on the pats of butter. For one of Miss Primrose Crabapple's follies was a romantic passion for Duke Aubrey – a passion similar to that cherished by high-church spinsters of the last century for the memory of Charles I. Over her bed hung a little reproduction in water-colours of his portrait in the Guildhall. And on the anniversary of his fall, which was kept in Dorimare as a holiday, she always appeared in deep mourning.

She knew perfectly well that she was an object of ridicule to her pupils and their mothers. But her manner to them was not a whit less gushing in consequence; for she was much too practical to allow her feelings to interfere with her bread and butter.

However, on the occasions when her temper got the better of her prudence she would show them clearly her contempt for their pedigree, sneering at them as commercial upstarts and interlopers.

She seemed to forget that she herself was only the daughter of a Lud grocer, and at times to imagine that the Crabapples had belonged to the vanished aristocracy.

She was grotesque, too, in appearance, with a round moon face, tiny eyes, and an enormous mouth that was generally stretched into an ingratiating smile. She always wore a green turban and a gown cut in the style of the days of Duke Aubrey. Sitting in her garden among her pretty little pupils she was like a brightly-painted Aunt Sally, placed there by a gardener with a taste for the baroque to frighten away the birds from his cherries and greengages.

Though it was flowers that her pupils resembled more than fruit – sweetpeas, perhaps, when fragrant, gay, and demure, in muslin frocks cut to a pattern, but in various colours, and in little poke-bonnets with white frills, they took their walk, two and two, through the streets of Lud-in-the-Mist.

At any rate it was something sweet and fresh that they suggested, and in the town they were always known as 'the Crabapple Blossoms'.

Recently they had been in a state of gleeful ecstasy. They had reason to believe that Miss Primrose was being courted, and by no less a person than Endymion Leer.

He was the school physician, and hence to them all a familiar figure. But, until quite lately, Miss Primrose had been a frequent victim of his relentless tongue, and many a time a little patient had been forced to stuff the sheet into her mouth to stifle her laughter, so quaint and pungent were the snubs he administered to their unfortunate school marm.

But nearly every evening this summer his familiar cane and bottle-green hat had been seen in the hall. And his visits, they had learned from the servants, were not professional; unless it be part of a doctor's duties to drop in of an evening to play a game of cribbage with his patients, and sample their cakes and cowslip wine.

Moreover, never before had Miss Primrose appeared so frequently in new gowns.

'Perhaps she's preparing her bridal chest!' tittered Prunella Chanticleer. And the very idea sent them all into convulsions of mirth.

'But do you *really* think he'll marry her? How *could* he!' said Penstemmon Fliperarde. 'She's such an old fright, and such an old goose, too. And they say *he's* so clever.'

'Why, then they'll be the goose and the sage!' laughed Prunella.

'I expect he wants her savings,' said Viola Vigil, with a wise little nod.

'Or perhaps he wants to add her to his collection of antiques,' tittered Ambrosine Pyepowders.

'Or to stick her up like an old sign over his dispensary!' suggested Prunella Chanticleer.

'But it's hard on Duke Aubrey,' laughed Moonlove Honeysuckle, 'to be cut out like this by a snuffy old doctor.'

'Yes,' said Viola Vigil. 'My father says it's a great pity she doesn't take rooms in the Duke Aubrey Arms, because,' and Viola giggled and blushed a little, 'it would be as near as *she'd* ever get to his arms, or to anybody else's!'

But the laughter that greeted this last sally was fast a trifle shame-faced; for the Crabapple Blossoms found it a little too daring.

At the beginning of autumn, Miss Primrose suddenly sent all the servants back to their homes in distant villages; and, to the indignation of the Crabapple Blossoms, their places were filled (only temporarily, Miss Primrose maintained) by the crazy washer-woman, Mother Tibbs, and a handsome, painted, deaf-mute, with bold black eyes. Mother Tibbs made but an indifferent housemaid, for she spent most of her time at the garden gate, waving her handkerchief to the passers-by. And if, when at her work, she heard the sound of a fiddle or flute, however distant, she would instantly stop whatever she was doing and start dancing, brandishing wildly in the air broom, or warming-pan, or whatever domestic implement she may have been holding in her hands at the time.

As for the deaf-mute – she was quite a good cook, but

was, perhaps, scarcely suited to employment in a young ladies' academy, as she was known in the town as 'Bawdy Bess'.

One morning Miss Primrose announced that she had found them a new dancing master (the last one had been suddenly dismissed, no one knew for what reason), and that when they had finished their seams they were to come up to the loft for a lesson.

So up they tripped to the cool, dark, pleasant loft, which smelt of apples, and had bunches of drying grapes suspended from its rafters. Long ago the Academy had been a farm-house, and on the loft's oak panelled walls were carved the interlaced initials of many rustic lovers, dead hundreds of years ago. To these Prunella Chanticleer and Moonlove Honeysuckle had recently added a monogram formed of the letters P. C. and E. L.

Their new dancing-master was a tall, red-haired youth, with a white pointed face and very bright eyes. Miss Primrose, who always implied that it was at great personal inconvenience and from purely philanthropic motives that their teachers gave them their lessons, introduced him as 'Professor Wisp, who had *very* kindly consented to teach them dancing,' and the young man made his new pupils a low bow, and turning to Miss Primrose, he said, 'I've got you a fiddler, ma'am. Oh, a rare fiddler! It's your needlework that has brought him. He's a weaver by trade, and he dearly loves pictures in silk. And he can give you some pretty patterns to work from – can't you Portunus?' and he clapped his hands twice.

Whereupon, 'like a bat dropped from the rafters,' as Prunella, with an inexplicable shudder, whispered to Moonlove, a queer wizened old man with eyes as bright as Professor Wisp's, all mopping and mowing, with a fiddle and bow under his arm, sprang suddenly out of the shadows.

'Young ladies!' cried Professor Wisp, gleefully, 'this is Master Portunus, fiddler to his Majesty the Emperor of the Moon, jester-in-chief to the Lord of Ghosts and Shadows . . . though his jests are apt to be silent ones. And he has come a long long way young ladies, to set your feet a dancing. *Ho, ho, hoh*!'

And the professor sprang up at least three feet in the air, and landed on the tips of his toes, as light as a ball of thistledown, while Master Portunus stood rubbing his hands, and chuckling with senile glee.

'What a *vulgar* young man! Just like a cheap Jack on market-day,' whispered Viola Vigil to Prunella Chanticleer.

But Prunella, who had been looking at him intently, whispered back, 'I'm sure at one time he was one of our grooms. I only saw him once, but I'm sure it's he. What *can* Miss Primrose be thinking of to engage such low people as teachers?'

Prunella had, of course, not been told any details as to Ranulph's illness.

Even Miss Primrose seemed somewhat disconcerted. She stood there, mouthing and blinking, evidently at a loss what to say. Then she turned to the old man, and, in her best company manner, said she was delighted to meet another needle-work enthusiast; and, turning to Professor Wisp, added in her most cooing treacly voice, 'I must embroider a pair of slippers for the dear doctor's birthday, and I want the design to be very ori-i-ginal, so perhaps this gentleman would kindly lend me his sampler.'

At this the professor made another wild pirouette, and, clapping his hands with glee, cried, 'Yes, yes, Portunus is your man. Portunus will set your stitches dancing to his tunes, *ho, ho, hoh*!'

And he and Portunus dug each other in the ribs and laughed till the tears ran down their cheeks.

At last, pulling himself together, the Professor bade Portunus tune up his fiddle, and requested that the young ladies should form up into two lines for the first dance.

'We'll begin with *Columbine*,' he said.

'But that's nothing but a country dance for farm servants,' pouted Moonlove Honeysuckle.

And Prunella Chanticleer boldly went up to Miss Primrose, and said, 'Please, mayn't we go on with the jigs and quadrilles we've always learned? I don't think mother would like me learning new things. And *Columbine's* so vulgar.'

'Vulgar! New!' cried Professor Wisp, shrilly. 'Why, my pretty

Miss, *Columbine* was danced in the moonlight when Lud-in-the-Mist was nothing but a beech wood between two rivers. It is the dance that the Silent People dance along the Milky Way. It's the dance of laughter and tears.'

'Professor Wisp is going to teach you very old and aristocratic dances, my dear,' said Miss Primrose reprovingly. 'Dances such as were danced at the court of Duke Aubrey – were they not, Professor Wisp?'

But the queer old fiddler had begun to tune up, and Professor Wisp, evidently thinking that they had, already, wasted enough time, ordered his pupils to stand up and be in readiness to begin.

Very sulkily it was that the Crabapple Blossoms obeyed, for they were all feeling as cross as two sticks at having such a vulgar buffoon for their master, and at being forced to learn silly old-fashioned dances that would be of no use to them when they were grown-up.

But, surely, there was magic in the bow of that old fiddler! And, surely, no other tune in the world was so lonely, so light-footed, so beckoning! Do what one would one must needs up and follow it.

Without quite knowing how it came about, they were soon all tripping and bobbing and gliding and tossing, with their minds on fire, while Miss Primrose wagged her head in time to the measure, and Professor Wisp, shouting directions the while, wound himself in and out among them, as if they were so many beads, and he the string on which they were threaded.

Suddenly the music stopped, and flushed, laughing, and fanning themselves with their pocket handkerchiefs, the Crabapple Blossoms flung themselves down on the floor, against a pile of bulging sacks in one of the corners, indifferent for probably the first time in their lives to possible damage to their frocks.

But Miss Primrose cried out sharply, 'Not there, dears! Not there!'

In some surprise they were about to move, when Professor Wisp whispered something in her ear, and, with a little meaning nod to him, she said, 'Very well, dears, stay where you are. It was only that I thought the floor would be dirty for you.'

'Well, it wasn't such bad fun after all,' said Moonlove Honeysuckle.

'No,' admitted Prunella Chanticleer reluctantly. 'That old man *can* play!'

'I wonder what's in these sacks; it feels too soft for apples,' said Ambrosine Pyepowders, prodding in idle curiosity the one against which she was leaning.

'There's rather a queer smell coming from them,' said Moonlove.

'Horrid!' said Prunella, wrinkling up her little nose.

And then, with a giggle, she whispered, 'We've had the goose and the sage, so perhaps these are the onions!'

At that moment Portunus began to tune his fiddle again, and Professor Wisp called out to them to form up again in two rows.

'This time, my little misses,' he said, 'it's to be a sad solemn dance, so Miss Primrose must foot it with you – "a very aristocratic dance, such as was danced at the court of Duke Aubrey"!' and he gave them a roguish wink.

So admirable had been his imitation of Miss Primrose's voice that, for all he was such a vulgar buffoon, the Crabapple Blossoms could not help giggling.

'But I'll ask you to listen to the tune before you begin to dance it,' he went on. 'Now then, Portunus!'

'Why! It's just *Columbine* over again . . .' began Prunella scornfully.

But the words froze on her lips, and she stood spellbound and frightened.

It was *Columbine*, but with a difference. For, since they had last heard it, the tune might have died, and wandered in strange places, to come back to earth, an angry ghost.

'Now, then, *dance*!' cried Professor Wisp, in harsh, peremptory tones.

And it was in sheer self-defence that they obeyed – as if by dancing they somehow or other escaped from that tune, which seemed to be themselves.

*'Within and out, in and out, round as a ball,*
*With hither and thither, as straight as a line,*
*With lily, germander, and sops in wine.*
*With sweet-brier*
*And bon-fire*
*And strawberry-wire*
*And columbine,'*

sang Professor Wisp. And in and out, in and out of a labyrinth of dreams wound the Crabapple Blossoms.

But now the tune had changed its key. It was getting gay once more – gay, but strange, and very terrifying.

*'Any lass for a Duke, a Duke who wears green*
*In lands where the sun and the moon do not shine,*
*With lily, germander, and sops in wine.*
*With sweet-briar*
*And bon-fire*
*And strawberry-wire*
*And columbine.'*

sang Professor Wisp, and in and out he wound between his pupils – or, rather, not *wound*, but dived, darted, flashed, while every moment his singing grew shriller, his laughter more wild.

And then – whence and how they could not say – a new person had joined the dance.

He was dressed in green and he wore a black mask. And the curious thing was that, in spite of all the crossings and recrossings and runs down the middle, and the endless shuffling in the positions of the dancers, demanded by the intricate figures of this dance, the newcomer was never beside you – it was always with somebody else that he was dancing. *You* never felt the touch of his hand. This was the experience of each individual Crabapple Blossom.

But Moonlove Honeysuckle caught a glimpse of his back; and on it there was a hump.

# 7

## MASTER AMBROSE HONEYSUCKLE CHASES A WILD GOOSE AND HAS A VISION

Master Ambrose Honeysuckle had finished his midday meal, and was smoking his churchwarden on his daisy-powdered lawn, under the branches of a great, cool, yellowing lime; and beside him sat his stout comfortable wife, Dame Jessamine, placidly fanning herself to sleep, with her pink-tongued mushroom-coloured pug snoring and choking on her lap.

Master Ambrose was ruminating on the consignment he was daily expecting of flower-in-amber – a golden eastern wine, for the import of which his house had the monopoly in Dorimare.

But he was suddenly roused from his pleasant reverie by the sound of loud excited voices proceeding from the house, and turning heavily in his chair, he saw his daughter, Moonlove, wild-eyed and dishevelled, rushing towards him across the lawn, followed by a crowd of servants with scared faces and all chattering at once.

'My dear child, what's this? What's this?' he cried testily.

But her only answer was to look at him in agonized terror, and then to moan, 'The horror of midday!'

Dame Jessamine sat up with a start and rubbing her eyes exclaimed, 'Dear me, I believe I was napping. But . . . Moonlove! Ambrose! What's happening?'

But before Master Ambrose could answer, Moonlove gave three blood-curdling screams, and shrieked out, 'Horror! Horror! The tune that never stops! *Break* the fiddle! *Break* the fiddle! Oh, Father, quietly, on tiptoe behind him, cut the strings. Cut the strings and let me out, I want the dark.'

For an instant, she stood quite still, head thrown back, eyes alert and frightened, like a beast at bay. Then, swift as a hare, she tore across the lawn, with glances over her shoulder as if something were pursuing her, and, rushing through the garden gate, vanished from their astonished view.

The servants, who till now had kept at a respectful distance, came crowding up, their talk a jumble of such exclamations and statements as 'Poor young lady!', 'It's a sunstroke, as sure as my name's Fishbones!', 'Oh, my! it quite gave me the palpitations to hear her shriek!'

And the pug yapped with such energy that he nearly burst his mushroom sides, and Dame Jessamine began to have hysterics.

For a few seconds Master Ambrose stood bewildered, then, setting his jaw, he pounded across the lawn, with as much speed as was left him by nearly fifty years of very soft living, out at the garden gate, down the lane, and into the High Street.

Here he joined the tail of a running crowd that, in obedience to the law that compels man to give chase to a fugitive, was trying hard to catch up with Moonlove.

The blood was throbbing violently in Master Ambrose's temples, and his brains seemed congested. All that he was conscious of, on the surface of his mind, was a sense of great irritation against Master Nathaniel Chanticleer for not having had the cobbles on the High Street recently renewed – they were so damnably slippery.

But, underneath this surface irritation, a nameless anxiety was buzzing like a hornet.

On he pounded at the tail end of the hunt, blowing, puffing, panting, slipping on the cobbles, stumbling across the old bridge that spanned the Dapple. Vaguely, as in delirium, he knew that windows were flung open, heads stuck out, shrill voices enquiring what was the matter, and that from mouth to mouth were bandied the words, 'It's little Miss Honeysuckle running away from her papa'.

But when they reached the town walls and the west gate, they had to call a sudden halt, for a funeral procession, that of a neighbouring farmer, to judge from the appearance of the mourners, was winding its way into the town, bound for the Fields of

Grammary, and the pursuers had perforce to stand in respectful silence while it passed, and allow their quarry to disappear down a bend of the high road.

Master Ambrose was too impatient and too much out of breath consciously to register impressions of what was going on round him. But in the automatic unquestioning way in which at such moments the senses do their work, he saw through the windows of the hearse that a red liquid was trickling from the coffin.

This enforced delay broke the spell of blind purpose that had hitherto united the pursuers into one. They now ceased to be a pack, and broke up again into separate individuals, each with his own business to attend to.

'The little lass is too nimble-heeled for us,' they said, grinning ruefully.

'Yes, she's a wild goose, that's what she is, and I fear has led us a wild goose chase,' said Master Ambrose with a short embarrassed laugh.

He was beginning to be acutely conscious of the unseemliness of the situation – he, an ex-Mayor, a Senator and judge, and, what was more, head of the ancient and honourable family of Honeysuckle, to be pounding through the streets of Lud-in-the-Mist at the tail end of a crowd of 'prentices and artisans, in pursuit of his naughty, crazy, wild goose of a little daughter!

'Pity it isn't Nat instead of me!' he thought to himself. 'I believe *he'd* rather enjoy it.'

Just then, a farmer came along in his gig, and seeing the hot breathless company standing puffing and mopping their brows, he asked them if they were seeking a little lass, for, if so, he had passed her quarter of an hour ago beyond the turnpike, running like a hare, and he'd called out to her to stop, but she would not heed him.

By this time Master Ambrose was once more in complete possession of his wits and his breath.

He noticed one of his own clerks among the late pursuers, and bade him run back to his stables and order three of his grooms to ride off instantly in pursuit of his daughter.

Then he himself, his face very stern, started off for the Academy.

It was just as well that he did not hear the remarks of his late companions as they made their way back to town; for he would have found them neither sympathetic nor respectful. The Senators were certainly not loved by the rabble. However, not having heard Moonlove's eldritch shrieks nor her wild remarks, they supposed that her father had been bullying her for some mild offence, and that, in consequence, she had taken to her heels.

'And if all these fat pigs of Senators,' they said, 'were set running like that a little oftener, why, then, they'd make better bacon!'

Master Ambrose had to work the knocker of the Academy door very hard before it was finally opened by Miss Primrose herself.

She looked flustered, and, as it seemed to Master Ambrose, a little dissipated, her face was so pasty and her eyelids so very red.

'Now, Miss Crabapple!' he cried in a voice of thunder, 'What, by the Harvest of Souls, have you been doing to my daughter, Moonlove? And if she's been ill, why have we not been told, I should like to know? I've come here for an explanation, and I mean to get it.'

Miss Primrose, mopping and mowing, and garrulously inarticulate, took the fuming gentleman into the parlour. But he could get nothing out of her further than disjointed murmurs about the need for cooling draughts, and the child's being rather headstrong, and a possible touch of the sun. It was clear that she was scared out of her wits, and, moreover, that there was something she wished to conceal.

Master Ambrose, from his experience on the Bench, soon realized that this was a type of witness upon whom it was useless to waste his time; so he said sternly. 'You are evidently unable to talk sense yourself, but perhaps some of your pupils possess that useful accomplishment. But I warn you if . . . if anything happens to my daughter it is you that will be held responsible. And now, send . . . let me see . . . send me down Prunella Chanticleer, she's always been a sensible girl with a head on her shoulders. She'll be able to tell me what exactly is the matter with Moonlove – which is more than *you* seem able to do.'

Miss Primrose, now almost gibbering with terror, stammered out something about 'study hours', and 'regularity being so desirable', and 'dear Prunella's having been a little out of sorts herself recently'.

But Master Ambrose repeated in a voice of thunder, 'Send me Prunella Chanticleer, at *once*.'

And standing there, stern and square, he was a rather formidable figure.

So Miss Primrose could only gibber and blink her acquiescence and promise him that 'dear Prunella' should instantly be sent to him.

When she had left him. Master Ambrose paced impatiently up and down, frowning heavily, and occasionally shaking his head.

Then he stood stock-still, in deep thought. Absently, he picked up from the work-table a canvas shoe, in process of being embroidered with wools of various brilliant shades.

At first, he stared at it with unseeing eyes.

Then, the surface of his mind began to take stock of the object. Its half finished design consisted of what looked like wild strawberries, only the berries were purple instead of red.

It was certainly very well done. There was no doubt but that Miss Primrose was a most accomplished needle-woman.

'But what's the good of needlework? It doesn't teach one common sense,' he muttered impatiently.

'And how like a woman!' he added with a contemptuous little snort. 'Aren't *red* strawberries good enough for her? Trying to improve on nature with her stupid fancies and her purple strawberries!'

But he was in no mood for wasting his time and attention on a half embroidered slipper, and tossing it impatiently away he was about to march out of the room and call loudly for Prunella Chanticleer, when the door opened and in she came.

Had a stranger wanted to see an upper class maiden of Lud-in-the-Mist, he would have found a typical specimen in Prunella Chanticleer.

She was fair, and plump, and dimpled; and, as in the case of her mother, the ruthless common sense of her ancestors of the revolution had been trivialized, though not softened, into an equally ruthless sense of humour.

Such *had* been Prunella Chanticleer.

But, as she now walked into the room, Master Ambrose exclaimed to himself, 'Toasted cheese! How plain the girl has grown!'

But that was a mere matter of taste; some people might have thought her much prettier than she had ever been before. She was certainly less plump than she used to be, and paler. But it was the change in the expression of her eyes that was most noticeable.

Hitherto, they had been as busy and restless (and, in justice to the charms of Prunella let it be added, as golden brown) as a couple of bees in summer – darting incessantly from one small object to another, and distilling from each what it held of least essential, so that in time they would have fashioned from a thousand trivialities that inferior honey that is apt to be labelled 'feminine wisdom'.

But, now, these eyes were idle.

Or, rather, her memory seemed to be providing them with a vision so absorbing that nothing else could arrest their gaze.

In spite of himself, Master Ambrose felt a little uneasy in her presence. However, he tried to greet her in the tone of patronizing banter that he always used when addressing his daughter or her friends. But his voice had an unnatural sound as he cried, 'Well, Prunella, and what have you all been doing to my Moonlove, eh? She came running home after dinner, and if it hadn't been broad daylight, I should have said that she had seen a ghost. And then off she dashed, up hill and down dale, like a paper chaser without any paper. What have you all been doing to her, eh?'

'I don't think we've been doing anything to her, Cousin Ambrose,' Prunella answered in a low, curiously toneless voice.

Ever since the scene with Moonlove that afternoon, Master

Ambrose had had an odd feeling that facts were losing their solidity; and he had entered this house with the express purpose of bullying and hectoring that solidity back to them. Instead of which they were rapidly vanishing, becoming attenuated to a sort of nebulous atmosphere.

But Master Ambrose had stronger nerves and a more decided mind than Master Nathaniel. Two facts remained solid, namely that his daughter had run away, and that for this Miss Crabapple's establishment was responsible. These he grasped firmly as if they had been dumb-bells that, by their weight, kept him from floating up to the ceiling.

'Now, Prunella,' he said sternly, 'there's something very queer about all this, and I believe you can explain it. Well? I'm waiting.'

Prunella gave a little enigmatical smile.

'What did she say when you saw her?' she asked.

'Say? Why, she was evidently scared out of her wits, and didn't know *what* she was saying. She babbled away about the sun being too hot – though it seems to me very ordinary autumn weather that we're having. And then she went on about cutting somebody's fiddle strings . . . oh, I don't know what!'

Prunella gave a low cry of horror.

'*Cut the fiddle strings!*' she repeated incredulously. And then she added with a triumphant laugh, 'she *can't* do that!'

'Now, young lady,' he cried roughly, 'no more of this rubbish! Do you or do you *not* know what has taken Moonlove?'

For a second or two she gazed at him in silence, and then she said slowly, 'Nobody ever knows what happens to other people. But, supposing . . . supposing she has eaten fairy fruit?' and she gave a little mocking smile.

Silent with horror, Master Ambrose stared at her.

Then he burst out furiously, 'You foul-mouthed little hussy! Do you *dare* to insinuate . . .'

But Prunella's eyes were fixed on the window that opened on to the garden, and instinctively he looked in that direction too.

For a second he supposed that the portrait of Duke Aubrey that hung in the Senate Room of the Guildhall had been moved to the wall of Miss Primrose's parlour. Framed in the window, against the leafy background of the garden stood, quite motionless, a young man in antique dress. The face, the auburn ringlets, the suit of green, the rustic background – everything, down to the hunting horn entwined with flowers that he held in one hand, and the human skull that he held in the other, were identical with those depicted in the famous portrait.

'By the White Ladies of the Fields!' muttered Master Ambrose, rubbing his eyes.

But when he looked again the figure had vanished.

For a few seconds he stood gaping and bewildered, and Prunella seized the opportunity of slipping unnoticed from the room.

Then he came to his senses, on a wave of berserk rage. They had been playing tricks, foul, vulgar, tricks, on him, on Ambrose Honeysuckle, Senator and ex-Mayor. But they should pay for it, by the Sun, Moon and Stars, they should pay for it! And he shook his fist at the ivy and squill bedecked walls.

But, in the meantime, it was he himself who was paying for it. An appalling accusation had been made against his only child; and, perhaps, the accusation was true.

Well, things must be faced. He was now quite calm, and, with his stern set face, a much more formidable person than the raging spluttering creature of a few seconds ago. He was determined to get to the bottom of this affair, and either to vindicate his daughter from the foul insinuation made by Prunella Chanticleer, or else, if the horrible thing were true (and a voice inside him that would not be silenced kept saying that it *was* true) to face the situation squarely, and, for the good of the town, find out who was responsible for what had happened and bring them to the punishment they merited.

There was probably no one in all Lud-in-the-Mist who would suffer in the same degree from such a scandal in his family as Master Ambrose Honeysuckle. And there was something fine in the way he thus unflinchingly faced the possibility. Not for a moment did he think of hushing the matter up to shield his daughter's reputation.

No, justice should run its course even if the whole town had to know that Ambrose Honeysuckle's only child – and she a girl, which seemed, somehow, to make it more horrible – had eaten fairy fruit.

As to his vision of Duke Aubrey, *that* he dismissed as an hallucination due to his excited condition and perhaps, as well, to the hysterical atmosphere that seemed to lie like a thick fog over the Academy.

Before he left Miss Primrose's parlour his eye fell on the half embroidered slipper he had impatiently tossed away on the entrance of Prunella Chanticleer.

He smiled grimly; perhaps, after all it had not been due to mere foolish feminine fancy that the strawberries were purple instead of red. She may have had real models for her embroidery.

He put the slipper in his pocket. It might prove of value in the law courts.

But Master Ambrose was mistaken in supposing that the berries embroidered on the slipper were fairy fruit.

## 8

## ENDYMION LEER LOOKS FRIGHTENED, AND A BREACH IS MADE IN AN OLD FRIENDSHIP

Master Ambrose fully expected on reaching home to find that one of the grooms he had despatched after Moonlove had returned with her in safe custody.

This, however, was not the case, and he was confronted with another frightful contingency. Moonlove had last been seen running, at a speed so great and so unflagging as to hint at some sustaining force that was more than human, *due West*. What if she were making for the Debatable Hills? Once across those hills she would never again be seen in Dorimare.

He must go to Mumchance at once, and give the alarm. Search parties must immediately be sent to ransack the country from one end to the other.

On his way out he was stopped by Dame Jessamine in the fretful complaining condition that he always found so irritating.

'Where *have* you been, Ambrose?' she cried querulously. 'First Moonlove screaming like a mad cockatoo! And then you rushing off, just after your dinner too, and leaving me like that in the lurch when I was so upset that I was on the verge of swooning! Where did you *go* to Ambrose?' and her voice grew shrill. 'I do wish you would go to Miss Primrose and tell her she must *not* let Moonlove be such a tom-boy and play practical jokes on her parents . . . rushing home in the middle of the day like that and talking such silly nonsense. She really is a very naughty girl to give us such a fright. I feel half inclined to go straight off to the Academy and give her a good scolding.'

'Stop chattering, Jessamine, and let me go,' cried Master Ambrose. 'Moonlove is *not* at the Academy.'

And he found a sort of savage satisfaction in calling back over his shoulder as he hurried from the room, 'I very much fear you will never see your daughter again, Jessamine.'

About half an hour later, he returned home even more depressed than when he had set out, owing to what he had learned from Mumchance as to the recent alarming spread in the town of the consumption of fairy fruit. He found Endymion Leer sitting in the parlour with his wife.

Her husband's parting words had brought on an attack of violent hysterics and the alarmed servants, fearing a seizure, had, on their own responsibility, summoned the only doctor of Lud in whom they had any faith, Endymion Leer. And, judging from Dame Jessamine's serene and smiling face, he had succeeded in removing completely the terrible impression produced by her husband's parting words, and in restoring to what she was pleased to call her mind its normal condition, namely that of a kettle that contains just enough water to simmer comfortably over a low fire.

She greeted Master Ambrose with a smile that for her was quite eager.

'Oh, Ambrose!' she cried, 'I have been having such a pleasant talk with Dr Leer. He says girls of her age often get silly and excited, though I'm sure *I* never did, and that she's sure to be brought home before night. But I do think we'd better take her away from Miss Primrose's. For one thing she has really learned quite enough now – I know no one who can make prettier groups in butter. So I think we had better give a ball for her before the winter, so if you will excuse me, Dr Leer, I have just a few things to see to . . .' and off she bustled to overhaul Moonlove's bridal chest, which, according to the custom of Dorimarite mothers, she had been storing, ever since her daughter's birth, with lace and velvets and brocade.

Not without reason, Dame Jessamine was considered the stupidest woman in Lud-in-the-Mist. And, in addition, the Ludite's lack of imagination and inability to feel serious emotions, amounted in her to a sort of affective idiocy.

So Master Ambrose found himself alone with Endymion Leer; and, though he had never liked the man, he was very glad to have the chance of consulting him. For, socially, however great his shortcomings might be, Master Ambrose knew him to be undeniably the best doctor in the country, and a very clever fellow into the bargain.

'Leer,' he said solemnly, when Dame Jessamine had let the room, 'there are very queer things happening at that Academy . . . *very* queer things.'

'Indeed?' said Endymion Leer, in a tone of surprise. 'What sort of things?'

Master Ambrose gave a short laugh: 'Not the sort of things, if my suspicions are correct, that one cares to talk about – even between men. But I can tell you, Leer, though I'm not what one could call a fanciful man, I believe if I'd stayed much longer in that house I should have gone off my head, the whole place stinks with . . . well, with pernicious nonsense, and I actually found myself, I, Ambrose Honeysuckle, *seeing* things – ridiculous things.'

Endymion Leer looked interested.

'What sort of things, Master Ambrose?' he asked.

'Oh, it's not worth repeating – except in so far as it shows that the fancies of silly overwrought women can sometimes be infectious. I actually imagined that I saw the Senate room portrait of Duke Aubrey reflected on the window. And if *I* take to fancying things – well, there must be something very fishy in the offing.'

Endymion Leer's expression was inscrutable.

'Optical delusions *have* been known before, Master Ambrose,' he said calmly. 'Even the eyes of Senators may sometimes play them tricks. Optical delusions, legal fictions – and so the world wags on.'

Master Ambrose grunted. He loathed the fellow's offensive way of putting things.

But he was sore at heart and terribly anxious, and he felt the need of having his fears either confirmed or dispelled, so, ignoring the sneer, he said with a weary sigh: 'However, that's a mere trifle. I have grave reasons for fearing that my daughter has . . . has . . . well, not to put too fine a point on things, I'm afraid that my daughter *has eaten fairy fruit.*'

Endymion Leer flung up his hands in horror, and then he laughed incredulously.

'Impossible, my dear sir, impossible! Your good lady told me you were sadly anxious about her, but let me assure you such an idea is mere morbidness on your part. The thing's impossible.'

'Is it?' said Master Ambrose grimly; and producing the slipper from his pocket he held it out, saying, 'What do you say to that? I found it in Miss Crabapple's parlour. I'm not much of a botanist, but I've never seen purple strawberries in Dorimare . . . Toasted cheese! What's taken the man?'

For Endymion Leer had turned livid, and was staring at the design on the shoe with eyes as full of horror as if it had been some hideous goblin.

Master Ambrose interpreted this as corroboration of his own theory.

He gave a sort of groan: 'Not so impossible after all, eh?' he said gloomily. 'Yes, *that* I very much fear is the sort of stuff my poor little girl has been given to eat.'

Then his eyes flashed, and clenching his fist he cried, 'But it's not her I blame. Before I'm many days older I'll smoke out that nest of wasps! I'll hand that simpering old woman from her own doorpost. By the Golden Apples of the West I'll . . .'

Endymion Leer had by this time, at any rate externally, recovered his equanimity.

'Are you referring to Miss Primrose Crabapple?' he asked in his usual voice.

'Yes, *Miss Primrose Crabapple*!' boomed Master Ambrose, 'nonsensical, foul-minded, obscene old . . .'

'Yes, yes,' interrupted Endymion Leer with good-humoured impatience, 'I daresay she's all of that and a great deal more, but, all the same, I don't believe her capable of having given your daughter what you think she has. I admit, when you first showed me that slipper I was frightened. Unlike you, I am a bit of a botanist, and I certainly have never seen a berry like that in Dorimare. But after all that does not prove that it grows . . . across the hills. There's many a curious fruit to be found in the

Cinnamon Isles, or in the oases of the Amber desert . . . why, your own ships, Master Ambrose, sometimes bring such fruit. The ladies of Lud have no lack of exotic fruit and flowers to copy in their embroidery, No, no, you're a bit unhinged this evening, Master Ambrose, else you would not allow so much as the shadow of foul suspicions like these to cross your mind.'

Master Ambrose groaned.

And then he said a little stiffly, 'I am not given, Dr Leer, to harbouring foul suspicions without cause. But a great deal of mischief is sometimes done by not facing facts. How is one to explain my daughter's running away, due west, like one possessed? Besides, Prunella Chanticleer as much as told me she had . . . eaten a certain thing . . . and . . . and . . . I'm old enough to remember the great drought, so I know the smell, so to speak, of evil, and there is something very strange going on in that Academy.'

'Prunella *Chanticleer*, did you say?' queried Endymion Leer with an emphasis on the last word, and with a rather odd expression in his eyes.

Master Ambrose looked surprised.

'Yes,' he said. 'Prunella Chanticleer, her school fellow and intimate friend.'

Endymion Leer gave a short laugh.

'The Chanticleers are . . . rather curious people,' he said drily, 'Are you aware that Ranulph Chanticleer has done the very thing you suspect your daughter of having done?'

Master Ambrose gaped at him.

Ranulph had certainly always been an odd and rather disagreeable boy, and there had been that horrid little incident at the Moongrass cheese supper-party . . . but that he actually should have eaten fairy fruit!

'Do you mean? Do you mean . . . ?' he gasped.

Endyniom Leer nodded his head significantly: 'One of the worst cases I have ever known.'

'And Nathaniel knows?'

Again Endymion Leer nodded.

A wave of righteous indignation swept over Master Ambrose. The Honeysuckles were every bit as ancient and as honourable a family as the Chanticleers, and yet here was he, ready to tarnish his escutcheon for ever, ready if need be to make the town-crier trumpet his disgrace from the market-place, to sacrifice money, position, family pride, everything, for the good of the community. While the only thought of Nathaniel, and he the Mayor, was to keep his skeleton safely hidden in the cupboard.

'Master Ambrose,' continued Endymion Leer, in a grave impressive voice, 'if what you fear about your daughter be true, then it is Master Nathaniel who is to blame. No, no, hear me out,' as Master Ambrose raised a protesting hand. 'I happen to know that some months ago Mumchance warned him of the alarming increase there has been recently in Lud in the consumption of . . . a certain commodity. And I know that this is true from my practice in the less genteel parts of the town. Take it from me, Master Ambrose, you Senators make a great mistake in ignoring what takes place in those low haunts. Nasty things have a way of not always staying at the bottom, you know – stir the pond and they rise to the top. Anyway, Master Nathaniel was warned, yet he took no steps.'

He paused for a few seconds, and then, fixing his eyes searchingly on Master Ambrose, he said, 'Did it never strike you that Master Nathaniel Chanticleer was a rather . . . curious man?'

'Never,' said Master Ambrose coldly. 'What are you insinuating, Leer?'

Endymion Leer gave a little shrug: 'Well, it is you who have set the example in insinuations. Master Nathaniel is a haunted man, and a bad conscience makes a very good ghost. If a man has once tasted fairy fruit he is never the same again. I have sometimes wondered if perhaps, long ago, when he was a young man . . .'

'Hold your tongue, Leer!' cried Master Ambrose angrily. 'Chanticleer is a very old friend of mine, and, what's more, he's my second cousin. There's nothing wrong about Nathaniel.'

But was this true? A few hours ago he would have laughed to

scorn any suggestion to the contrary. But since then, his own daughter . . . ugh!

Yes, Nathaniel had certainly always been a very queer fellow – touchy, irascible, whimsical.

A swarm of little memories, not noticed at the time, buzzed in Master Ambrose's head . . . irrational actions, equivocal remarks. And, in particular, one evening, years and years ago, when they had been boys . . . Nat's face at the eerie sound produced by an old lute. The look in his eyes had been like that in Moonlove's to-day.

No, no. It would never do to start suspecting everyone – above all his oldest friend.

So he let the subject of Master Nathaniel drop and questioned Endymion Leer as to the effects on the system of fairy fruit, and whether there was really no hope of finding an antidote.

Then Endymion Leer started applying his famous balm – a balm that varied with each patient that required it.

In most cases, certainly, there was no cure. But when the eater was a Honeysuckle, and hence, born with a healthy mind in a healthy body there was every reason to hope that no poison could be powerful enough to undermine such a constitution.

'Yes, but suppose she is already across the border?' said Master Ambrose. Endymion Leer gave a little shrug.

'In that case, of course, there is nothing more one can do,' he replied.

Master Ambrose gave a deep sigh and leant back wearily in his chair, and for a few minutes they sat in silence.

Drearily and hopelessly Master Ambrose's mind wandered over the events of the day and finally settled, as is the way with a tired mind, on the least important – the red juice he had noticed oozing out of the coffin, when they had been checked at the west gate by the funeral procession.

'Do the dead bleed, Leer?' he said suddenly.

Endymion Leer sprang from his chair as if he had been shot. First he turned white, then he turned crimson.

'What the . . . what the . . .' he stuttered, 'what do you mean by that question, Master Ambrose?'

He was evidently in the grip of some violent emotion.

'Busty Bridget!' exclaimed Master Ambrose, testily, 'what, by the Harvest of Souls, has taken you now, Leer? It may have been a silly question, but it was quite a harmless one. We were stopped by a funeral this afternoon at the west gate, and I thought I saw a red liquid oozing from the coffin. But, by the White Ladies of the Fields, I've seen so many queer things to-day that I've ceased to trust my own eyes.'

These words completely restored Endymion Leer's good humour. He flung back his head and laughed till the tears rolled down his cheeks.

'Why, Master Ambrose,' he gurgled, 'it was such a grisly question that it quite gave me a turn. Owing to the deplorable ignorance of this country I'm used to my patients asking me rather queer things . . . but that beats anything I've yet heard. 'Do the dead bleed?' Do pigs fly? Ha, ha, ha, ha!'

Then, seeing that Master Ambrose was beginning to look stiff and offended, he controlled his mirth, and added, 'Well, well, a man as sorely tried as you have been to-day, Master Ambrose, is to be excused if he has hallucinations . . . it is wonderful what queer things we imagine we see when we are unhinged by strong emotion. And now I must be going. Birth and death, Master Ambrose, they wait for no man – not even for Senators. So I must be off and help the little Ludites into the world, and the old ones out of it. And in the meantime don't give up hope. At any moment one of Mumchance's good Yeomen may come galloping up with the little lady at his saddle-bow. And then – even if she should have eaten what you fear she has – I shall be much surprised if a Honeysuckle isn't able with time and care to throw off all effects of that foul fodder and grow up into as sensible a woman – as her mother.'

And, with these characteristic words of comfort, Endymion Leer bustled off on his business.

Master Ambrose spent a most painful evening, his ears, on the one hand, alert for every sound of a horse's hoof, for every knock at the front door, in case they might herald news of Moonlove; and, at the same time, doing their best not to hear Dame Jessamine's ceaseless prattle.

'Ambrose, I wish you'd remind the clerks to wipe their shoes before they come in. Have you forgotten you promised me we should have a separate door for the warehouse? I've got it on paper.

'How nice it is to know that there's nothing serious the matter with Moonlove, isn't it? But I don't know what I should have done this afternoon if that kind Doctor Leer hadn't explained it all to me. How *could* you run away a second time, Ambrose, and leave me in that state without even fetching my hartshorn? I do think men are so heartless.

'What a naughty girl Moonlove is to run away like this! I wonder when they'll find her and bring her back. But it will be nice having her at home this winter, won't it? What a pity Ranulph Chanticleer isn't older, he'd do so nicely for her, wouldn't he? But I suppose Florian Baldbreeches will be just as rich, and he's nearer her age.

'Do you think Marigold and Dreamsweet and the rest of them will be shocked by Moonlove's rushing off in this wild way? However, as Dr Leer said, in his quaint way, girls *will* be girls.

'Oh, Ambrose, do you remember my deer-coloured tuftaffity, embroidered with forget-me-nots and stars? I had it in my bridal chest. Well, I think I shall have it made up for Moonlove. There's nothing like the old silks, or the old dyes either – there were no galls or gum-syrups used in *them*. You remember my deer-coloured tuftaffity, don't you?'

But Master Ambrose could stand it no longer. He sprang to his feet, and cried roughly, 'I'll give you a handful of Yeses and Noes, Jessamine, and it'll keep you amused for the rest of the evening sorting them out, and sticking them on to your questions. I'm going out.'

He would go across to Nat's . . . Nat might not be a very

efficient Mayor, but he was his oldest friend, and he felt he needed his sympathy.

'If . . . if any news comes about Moonlove, I'll be over at the Chanticleers. Let me know at once,' he called over his shoulder, as he hurried from the room.

Yes, he was longing for a talk with Nat. Not that he had any belief in Nat's judgment; but he himself could provide all that was needed.

And, apart from everything else, it would be comforting to talk to a man who was in the same boat as himself – if, that is to say, the gossip retailed by Endymion Leer were true. But whether it were true or not Leer was a vulgar fellow, and had had no right to divulge a professional secret.

So huge did the events of the day loom in his own mind, that he felt sure of finding their shadow lying over the Chanticleers; and he was prepared to be magnanimous and assure the conscience-stricken Master Nathaniel that though, as Mayor, he may have been a little remiss and slack, nevertheless, he could not, in fairness, be held responsible for the terrible thing that had happened.

But he had forgotten the gulf that lay between the Magistrates and the rest of the town. Though probably the only topics of conversation that evening in every kitchen, in every tavern, in every tradesman's parlour, were the good run for his money little Miss Honeysuckle had given her revered father that afternoon, and the search parties of Yeomen that were scouring the country for her – not to mention the terrible suspicions as to the cause of her flight he had confided to Mumchance; nevertheless not a word of it all had reached the ears of the other Magistrates.

So, when the front-door of the Chanticleers was opened for him, he was greeted by sounds of uproarious laughter proceeding from the parlour.

The Polydore Vigils were spending the evening there, and the whole party was engaged in trying to catch a moth – flicking at it with their pocket-handkerchiefs, stumbling over the furniture, emulating each other to further efforts in the ancient terms of stag-hunting.

'Come and join the fun, Ambrose,' shouted Master Nathaniel, crimson with exertion and laughter.

But Master Ambrose began to see red.

'You . . . you . . . heartless, gibbering idiots!' he roared.

The moth-hunters paused in amazement.

'Suffering Cats! What's taken you, Ambrose?' cried Master Nathaniel. 'Stag-hunting, they say, was a royal sport. Even the Honeysuckles might stoop to it!'

'Don't the Honeysuckles consider a moth a stag, Ambrose?' laughed Master Polydore Vigil.

But that evening the old joke seemed to have lost its savour.

'Nathaniel,' said Master Ambrose solemnly, 'the curse of our country has fallen on you and me . . . and you are hunting moths!'

Now, *curse* happened to be one of the words that had always frightened Master Nathaniel. So much did he dislike it that he even avoided the words that remotely resembled it in sound, and had made Dame Marigold dismiss a scullery-maid, merely because her name happened to be Kirstie.

Hence, Master Ambrose's words sent him into a frenzy of nervous irritation.

'Take that back, Ambrose! Take that back!' he roared. 'Speak for yourself. The . . . the . . . the cur . . . nothing of that sort is on *me*!'

'That is not true, Nathaniel,' said Master Ambrose sternly. 'I have only too good reason to fear that Moonlove is stricken by the same sickness as Ranulph, and . . .'

'You lie!' shouted Master Nathaniel.

'And in both cases,' continued Master Ambrose, relentlessly, 'the cause of the sickness was . . . fairy fruit.'

Dame Dreamsweet Vigil gave a smothered scream, Dame Marigold blushed crimson, and Master Polydore exclaimed, in a deeply shocked voice, 'By the Milky Way, Ambrose, you are going a little too far – even if there were not ladies present.'

'No, Polydore. There come times when even ladies must face facts. You see before you two dishonoured men – Nathaniel and myself. One of our statutes says that in the country of Dorimare each member of a family shall be the master of his own possessions, and that nothing shall be held in common but disgrace. And before you are many days older, Polydore, your family, too, may be sharing that possession. Each one of us is threatened in what is nearest to us, and our chief citizen – hunts moths!'

'No, no, Nathaniel,' he went on in a louder and angrier voice, 'you needn't glare and growl! I consider that you, as Mayor of this town, are responsible for what has happened to-day, and . . .'

'By the Sun, Moon and Stars!' bellowed Master Nathaniel, 'I haven't the slightest idea what you mean by "what has happened to-day," but whatever it is, I know very well I'm not responsible. Were *you* responsible last year when old Mother Pyepowder's yapping little bitch chewed up old Matt's pet garters embroidered by his first sweetheart, and when . . .'

'You poor, snivelling, feeble-minded buffoon! You criminal nincompoop! Yes, *criminal*, I say,' and at each word Master Ambrose's voice grew louder. 'Who was it that knew of the spread of this evil thing and took no steps to stop it? Whose own son has eaten it? By the Harvest of Souls you may have eaten it yourself for all I know . . .'

'Silence, you foul-mouthed, pompous, brainless, wind-bag! You . . . you . . . foul gibbering Son of a Fairy!' sputtered Master Nathaniel.

And so they went at it, hammer and tongs, doing the best to destroy in a few minutes the fabric built up by years of fellowship and mutual trust.

And the end of it was that Master Nathaniel pointed to the door, and in a voice trembling with fury, told Master Ambrose to leave his house, and never to enter it again.

# 9

## PANIC AND THE SILENT PEOPLE

The following morning Captain Mumchance rode off to search Miss Primrose Crabapple's Academy for fairy fruit. And in his pocket was a warrant for the arrest of that lady should his search prove successful.

But when he reached the Academy he found that the birds had flown. The old rambling house was empty and silent. No light feet tripped down its corridors, no light laughter wakened its echoes. Some fierce wind had scattered the Crabapple Blossoms. Miss Primrose, too, had disappeared.

A nameless dread seized Captain Mumchance as he searched through the empty silent rooms.

He found the bedrooms in disorder – drawers half opened, delicately tinted clothing heaped on the floor – indicating that the flitting had been a hurried one.

Beneath each bed, too, he found a little pair of shoes, very down at heel, with almost worn-out soles, looking as if the feet that had worn them must have been very busy.

He continued his search down to the kitchen premises, where he found Mother Tibbs sitting smiling to herself, and crooning.

'Now, you cracked harlot,' he cried roughly, 'what have you been up to, I'd like to know? I've had my eye on you, my beauty, for a very long time. If *I* can't make you speak, perhaps the judges will. What's happened to the young ladies? Just you tell me *that*!'

But Mother Tibbs was more crazy than usual that day, and her only answer was to trip up and down the kitchen floor, singing snatches of old songs about birds set free, and celestial flowers, and the white fruits that grow on the Milky Way.

Mumchance was holding one of the little shoes, and catching

sight of it, she snatched it from him, and tenderly stroked it, as if it had been a wounded dove.

'Dancing, dancing, dancing!' she muttered, 'dancing day and night! It's stony dancing on dreams.'

And with an angry snort Mumchance realized, not for the first time in his life, that it was waste of time trying to get any sense out of Mother Tibbs.

So he started again to search the house, this time for fairy fruit.

However, not a pip, not a scrap of peel could he find that looked suspicious. But, finally, in the loft he discovered empty sacks with great stains of juice on them, and it could have been no ordinary juice, for some of the stains were colours he had never seen before.

The terrible news of the Crabapple Blossoms' disappeareance spread like wild-fire through Lud-in-the-Mist. Business was at a standstill. Half the Senators, and some of the richer tradesmen, had daughters in the Academy, and poor Mumchance was besieged by frantic parents who seemed to think that he was keeping their daughters concealed somewhere on his person. They were all, too, calling down vengeance on the head of Miss Primrose Crabapple, and demanding that she should be found and handed over to justice.

It was Endymion Leer who got the credit for finding her. He brought her, sobbing and screaming, to the guard-room of the Yeomanry. He said he had discovered her wandering about, half frantic, on the wharf, evidently hoping to take refuge in some outward bound vessel.

She denied all knowledge of what had happened to her pupils, and said she had woken up that morning to find the birds flown.

She also denied, with passionate protestations, having given them fairy fruit. In this, Endymion Leer supported her. The smugglers, he said, were men of infinite resource and cunning, and what more likely than that they should have inserted the evil stuff into a consignment of innocent figs and grapes?

'And school-girls being one quarter boy and three quarters bird,' he added with his dry chuckle, 'they cannot help being orchard thieves . . . and if there isn't an orchard to rob, why, they'll rob the loft where the apples are kept. And if the apples turn out not to be apples – why, then, no one is to blame!' Nevertheless, Miss Primrose was locked up in the room in the Guildhall reserved for prisoners of the better class, pending her trial on a charge of receiving contraband goods in the form of woven silk – the only charge, owing to the wilful blindness of the law, on which she could be tried.

In the meantime a couple of the Yeomen, who had been scouring the country for Moonlove Honeysuckle, returned with the news that they had chased her as far as the Debatable Hills, and had last seen her scrambling like a goat up their sides. And no Dorimarite could be expected to follow her further.

A couple of days later the Yeomen sent to search for the other Crabapple Blossoms returned with similar news. All along the West Road they had heard rumours of a band of melancholy maidens flitting past to the sound of sad wild ditties. And, finally, they had come upon a goatherd who had seen them disappearing, like Moonlove, among the folds of the terrible hills.

So there was nothing further to be done. The Crabapple Blossoms had by now surely perished in the Elfin Marches, or else vanished for ever into Fairyland.

These were sad days in Lud-in-the-Mist – all the big houses with their shutters down, the dancing halls and other places of amusement closed, sad, frightened faces in the streets – and, as if in sympathy with human things, the days shortening, the trees yellowing, and beginning to shed their leaves.

Endymion Leer was much in request – especially in the houses that had hitherto been closed to him. Now, he was in and out of them all day long, exhorting, comforting, advising. And wherever he went he managed to leave the impression that somehow or other Master Nathaniel Chanticleer was to blame for the whole business.

There was no doubt of it, Master Nathaniel, these days, was the most unpopular man in Lud-in-the-Mist.

In the Senate he got nothing but sour looks from his colleagues;

threats and insults were muttered behind him as he walked down the High Street; and one day, pausing at a street corner where a puppet-show was being exhibited, he found that he himself was the villain of the piece. For when the time-honoured climax was reached and the hero was belabouring the villain's wooden head with his cudgel, the falsetto voice of the concealed showman punctuated the blows with such comments as: 'There, Nat Cock o' the Roost, is a black eye to you for small loaves . . . and there's another for sour wine . . . and there's a bloody nose to you for being too fond of *papples* and *ares*'.

Here the showman changed his voice and said, 'Please, sir, what are *papples* and *ares*?', 'Ask Nat Cock o' the Roost,' came the falsetto, 'and he'll tell you they're apples and pears that come from across the hills!'

Most significant of all, for the first time since Master Nathaniel had been head of the family, Ebeneezor Prim did not come himself to wind the clocks. Ebeneezor was a paragon of dignity and respectability, and it was a joke in Lud society that you could not really be sure of your social status till he came to wind your clocks himself, instead of sending one of his apprentices.

However, the apprentice he sent to Master Nathaniel was almost as respectable looking as he was himself. He wore a neat black wig, and his expression was sanctimonious in the extreme, with the corners of his mouth turned down, like one of his master's clocks that had stopped at 7:25.

Certainly a very respectable young man, and one who was evidently fully aware of the unsavoury rumours that were circulating concerning the house of Chanticleer; for he looked with such horror at the silly moon-face with its absurd revolving moustachios of Master Nathaniel's grandfather's clock, and opened its mahogany body so gingerly, and, when he had adjusted its pendulum, wiped his fingers on his pocket handkerchief with such an expression of disgust, that the innocent timepiece might have been the wicked Mayor's familiar – a grotesque hobgoblin tabby cat, purring, and licking her whiskers after an obscene orgy of garbage.

But Master Nathaniel was indifferent to these manifestations of unpopularity. Let mental suffering be intense enough and it becomes a sort of carminative.

When the news first reached him of the flight of the Crabapple Blossoms he very nearly went off his head. Facts suddenly seemed to be becoming real.

For the first time in his life his secret shadowy fears began to solidify – to find a real focus; and the focus was Ranulph.

His first instinct was to fling municipal obligations to the winds and ride post-haste to the farm. But what would that serve after all? It would be merely playing into the hands of his enemies, and by his flight giving the public reason to think that the things that were said about him were true.

It would be madness, too, to bring Ranulph back to Lud. Surely there was no place in Dorimare more fraught with danger for the boy these days than was the fairy fruit-stained town of Lud. He felt like a rat in a trap.

He continued to receive cheerful letters from Ranulph himself and good accounts of him from Luke Hempen, and gradually his panic turned into a sort of lethargic nightmare of fatalism, which seemed to free him from the necessity of taking action. It was as if the future were a treacly adhesive fluid that had been spilt all over the present, so that everything he touched made his fingers too sticky to be of the slightest use.

He found no comfort in his own home. Dame Marigold, who had always cared for Prunella much more than for Ranulph, was in a condition of nervous prostration.

Each time the realization swept over her that Prunella had eaten fairy fruit and was either lost in the Elfin Marches or in Fairyland itself, she would be seized by nausea and violent attacks of vomiting.

Indeed, the only moments of relief he knew were in pacing up and down his own pleached alley, or wandering in the Fields of Grammary. For the Fields of Grammary gave him a foretaste of death – the state that will turn one into a sort of object of art (that is to say it one is remembered by posterity) with all one's deeds and passions simplified, frozen into beauty; an absolutely silent thing that people gaze at, and that cannot in its turn gaze back at them.

And the pleached alley brought him the peace of *still* life – life that neither moves nor suffers, but only grows in silence and slowly matures its secret.

The Silent People! How dearly he would have liked to be one of them!

But sometimes, as he wandered in the late afternoon about the streets of the town, human beings themselves seemed to have found the secret of still life. For at that hour all living things seem to cease from functioning. The tradesmen would stand at the doors of their shops staring with vacant eyes down the street – as detached from business as the flowers in the gardens, which looked as if they too were resting after their day's work and peeping idly out from between their green shutters.

And lads who were taking their sweethearts for a row on the Dapple would look at them with unseeing eyes, while the maidens gazed into the distance and trailed their hands absently in the water.

Even the smithy, with its group of loungers at its open door, watching the swing and fall of the smith's hammer and the lurid red light illuminating his face, might have been no more than a tent at a fair where holiday makers were watching a lion-tamer or the feats of a professional strong man; for at that desultory hour the play of muscles, the bending of resisting things to a human will, the taming of fire, a creature more beautiful and dangerous than any lion, seemed merely an entertaining spectacle that served no useful purpose.

The very noises of the street – the rattle of wheels, a lad whistling, a pedlar crying his wares – seemed to come from *far* away, to be as disembodied and remote from the activities of man as is the song of the birds.

And if there was still some bustle in the High Street it was as soothing as that of a farmyard. And the whole street – houses, cobbles, and all – might almost have been fashioned out of growing things cut by man into patterns, as is a formal garden. So that Master Nathaniel would wander, at that hour, between its rows of shops and houses, as if between the thick green walls of a double hedge of castellated box, or down the golden tunnel of his own pleached alley.

If life in Lud-in-the-Mist could always be like that there would be no need to die.

## 10
## HEMPIE'S SONG

There were days, however, when even the silent things did not sooth Master Nathaniel; when the condition described by Ranulph as the imprisoning of all one's being into a space as narrow as a tooth, whence it irradiates waves of agony, became so overwhelming, that he was unconscious of the external world.

One late afternoon, a prey to this mood, he was mooning about the Fields of Grammary.

In the epitaphs on the tombstone one could read the history of Dorimarite sensibility from the quiet poignancy of those dating from the days of the Dukes – *Eglantine mourns for Endymion, who was Alive and now is Dead;* or *During her Life Ambrose often dreamed that Forget-Me-Not was Dead. This Time he woke up and found that it was True* – followed by the peaceful records of industry and prosperity of the early days of the Republic, down to the cheap cynicism of recent times – for instance, *Here lies Hyacinth Quirkscuttle, weaver, who stretched his life as he was wont to do the list of his cloth far beyond its natural limits, and, to the great regret of his family, died at the age of xcix.*

But, that afternoon, even his favourite epitaph, the one about the old baker, Ebeneezor Spike, who had provided the citizens of Lud-in-the-Mist with fresh sweet loaves for sixty years, was powerless to comfort Master Nathaniel.

Indeed, so strangled was he in the coils of his melancholy that the curious fact of the door of his family chapel being ajar caused in him nothing but a momentary, muffled surprise.

The chapel of the Chanticleers was one of the loveliest monuments of Lud. It was built of rose-coloured marble, with delicately fluted pillars, and worked in low relief with the flowers and leaves and panic stricken fugitives, so common in the old art of Dorimare. Indeed, it looked like an exquisite little pleasure-house; and tradition said that this it had originally been – one of Duke Aubrey's, in fact. And it certainly was in accordance with his legend to make a graveyard the scene of his revels.

No one ever entered it except Master Nathaniel and his household to fill it with flowers on the anniversaries of his parents' death. Nevertheless, the door was certainly ajar.

The only comment he made to himself was to suppose that the pious Hempie had been up that day to commemorate some anniversary, remembered only by herself, in the lives of her dead master and mistress, and had forgotten to lock it again.

Drearily he wandered to the western wall and gazed down upon Lud-in-the-Mist, and so drugged was he with despair that at first he was incapable of reacting in the slightest degree to what his eyes were seeing.

Then, fast as sometimes the flowing of the Dapple was reflected in the trunks of the beeches that grew on its banks, so that an element that looked as if it were half water, half light, seemed rippling down them in ceaseless zones – so did the objects he saw beneath him begin to be reflected in fancies, rippling down the hard, unyielding fabric of his woe; the red-roofed houses scattered about the side of the hill looked as if they were crowding helter-skelter to the harbour, eager to turn ships themselves and sail away – a flock of clumsy ducks on a lake of swans; the houses beyond the harbour seemed to be preening themselves preparatory to having their portrait taken. The chimneys were casting becoming velvet shadows on the high-pitched slanting roofs. The belfries seemed to be standing on tiptoe behind the houses – like tall serving lads, who, unbeknown to their masters, have succeeded in squeezing themselves into the family group.

Or, perhaps, the houses were more like a flock of barn-door fowls, of different shapes and sizes, crowding up at the hen wife's 'Chick! chick! chick!' to be fed at sunset.

Anyhow, however innocent they might look, they were the repositories of whatever dark secrets Lud might contain. Houses counted among the Silent People. Walls have ears, but no tongues. Houses, trees, the dead – they tell no tales.

His eye travelled beyond the town to the country that lay beyond, and rested on the fields of poppies and golden stubble, the smoke of distant hamlets, the great blue ribbon of the Dawl, the narrow one of the Dapple – one coming from the north, one from the west, but, for some miles beyond Lud-in-the-Mist, seeming to flow in parallel lines, so that their convergence at the harbour struck one as a geometrical miracle.

Once more he began to feel the balm of silent things, and seemed to catch a glimpse of that still, quiet landscape the future, after he had himself died.

And yet . . . there was that old superstition of the thraldom in Fairyland, the labour in the fields of gillyflowers.

No, no. Old Ebeneezer Spike was not a thrall in Fairyland.

He left the Fields of Grammary in a gentler mood of melancholy than the frost-bound despair in which he had gone there.

When he got home he found Dame Marigold sitting dejectedly in the parlour, her hands lying limply on her lap, and she had had the fire already lighted although evening had not yet set in.

She was very white, and there were violet shadows under her eyes.

Master Nathaniel stood silently at the door for a few seconds watching her.

There came into his head the lines of an old song of Dorimare: –

*I'll weave her a wreath of the flowers of grief*
*That her beauty may show the brighter.*

And suddenly he saw her with the glamour on her that used to madden him in the days of his courtship, the glamour of something that is delicate, and shadowy, and far-away – the glamour that lets loose the lust of the body of a man for the soul of a woman.

'Marigold,' he said in a low voice.

Her lips curled in a little contemptuous smile: 'Well, Nat, have you been out baying the moon, and chasing your own shadow?'

'Marigold!' and he came and leaned over the back of her chair.

She started violently. Then she cried in a voice, half petulant, half apologetic, 'I'm sorry! But, you know, I can't bear having the back of my neck touched! Oh, Nat, what a sentimental old thing you are!'

And then it all began over again – the vain repinings, the veiled reproaches; while the desire to make him wince struggled for the ascendency with the habit of mercy, engendered by years of a mild, slightly contemptuous tenderness.

Her attitude to the calamity was one of physical disgust, mingled with petulance, a sense of ill-usage, and, incredible though it may seem, a sense of its ridiculous aspect.

Occasionally she would stop shuddering, to make some such remark as: 'Oh, dear! I can't help wishing that old Primrose herself had gone off with them, and that I could have seen her prancing to the fiddle and screeching like an old love-sick tabby cat.'

Finally Master Nathaniel could stand it no longer. He sprang to his feet, exclaiming violently, 'Marigold, you *madden* me! You're . . . you're not a woman. I believe what *you* need is some of that fruit yourself. I've a good mind to get some, and force it down your throat!'

But it was an outrageous thing to have said. And no sooner were the words out of his mouth than he would have given a hundred pounds to have them unsaid.

What had taken his tongue! It was as if an old trusty watch-dog had suddenly gone mad and bitten him.

But he could stay no longer in the parlour, and face her cold, disgusted stare. So, sheepishly mumbling an apology, he left the room.

Where should he go? Not to the pipe-room. He could not face the prospect of his own company. So he went upstairs and knocked at Hempie's door.

However much in childhood a man may have loved his nurse, it is seldom that, after he has grown up, he does not feel ill at ease and rather bored when he is with her. A relationship that has become artificial, and connected, on one side, with a sense of duty rather than with spontaneous affection, is always an uncomfortable one.

And, for the nurse, it is particularly bitter when it is the magnanimous enemy – the wife – who has to keep her 'boy' up to his duty.

For years Dame Marigold had had to say at intervals, 'Nat, *have* you been up to see Hempie lately?' or 'Nat, Hempie has lost one of her brothers. *Do* go and tell her you're sorry'.

So, when Master Nathaniel found himself in the gay little room, he felt awkward and tongue-tied, and was too depressed to have recourse to the somewhat laboured facetiousness with which he was in the habit of greeting the old woman.

She was engaged in darning his stockings, and she indignantly showed him a particularly big hole, shaking her head, and exclaiming, 'There never was a man so hard on his stockings as you, Master Nat! I'd very much like to find out before I die what you do to them; and Master Ranulph is every bit as bad.'

'Well, Hempie, as I always say, you've no right to blame me if my stockings go into holes, seeing that it's you who knitted them,' retorted Master Nathaniel automatically.

For years Hempie's scolding about the condition in which she found his stockings had elicited this reply. But, after these days of nightmare, there was something reassuring in discovering that there were still people in the world sane enough, and with quiet enough minds, to be put out by the holes in a pair of worsted stockings.

Hempie had, indeed, taken the news of the Crabapple Blossoms very calmly. It was true she had never cared very much for Prunella, maintaining always that 'she was just her mother over again'. All the same, Prunella remained Master Nathaniel's daughter and Ranulph's sister, and hence had a certain borrowed preciousness in the eyes of Hempie. Nevertheless she had refused to indulge in lamentations, and had preserved on the subject a rather grim silence.

His eye roved restlessly over the familiar room. It was certainly a pleasant one – fantastic and exquisitely neat. 'Neat as a Fairy's parlour' – the old Dorimarite expression came unbidden to his mind.

There was a bowl of autumn roses on the table, faintly scenting the air with the hospitable, poetic perfume that is like a welcome to a little house with green shutters and gay chintzes and lavender-scented sheets. But the host who welcomes you is dead, the house itself no longer stands except in your memory – it is the cry of the cock turned into perfume. Are there bowls of roses in the Fairies' parlours?

'I say, Hempie, these are new, aren't they?' he said, pointing to a case of shells on the chimney-piece – very strange shells, as thin as butterfly's wings and as brightly coloured. And, as well, there were porcelain pots, which looked as if they had been made out of the petals of poppies and orchids, nor could their strange shapes ever have been turned on a potter's wheel in Dorimare.

Then he gave a low whistle, and, pointing to a horse-shoe of pure gold, nailed on to the wall, he added, 'And that, too! I'll swear I've never seen it before. Has your ship come in, Hempie?'

The old woman looked up placidly from her darning: 'Oh! these came when my poor brother died and the old home was broken up. I'm glad to have them, as I never remember a time when they weren't in the old kitchen at home. I often think it's strange how bits of chiney and brittle stuff like that lives on, long after solid flesh and bone has turned to dust. And it's a queer thing, Master Nat, as one gets old, how one lives among the dumb. Bits of chiney . . . and the Silent People,' and she wiped a couple of tears from her eyes.

Then she added, 'Where these old bits of things came from I never rightly knew. I suppose the horse-shoe's valuable, but even in bad harvests my poor father would never turn it into money. He used to say it had been above our door in his father's time, and in his grandfather's time, and it had best stay there. I shouldn't wonder if he thought it had been dropped by Duke Aubrey's horse. And as for the shells and pots . . . when we were children, we used always to whisper that they came *from beyond the hills*.'

Master Nathaniel gave a start, and stared at her in amazement. '*From beyond the hills?*' he repeated, in a low, horrified voice.

'Aye, and why not?' cried Hempie, undaunted. 'I was country-bred, Master Nat, and I learned not to mind the smell of a fox or of a civet cat . . . or of a Fairy. They're mischievous creatures, I daresay, and best left alone. But though we can't always pick and choose our neighbours, neighbourliness is a virtue all the same. For my part, I'd never have chosen the Fairies for my neighbours – but they were chosen for me. And we must just make the best of them.'

'By the Sun, Moon and Stars, Hempie!' cried Master Nathaniel in a horrified voice, 'you don't know what you're talking about, you . . .'

'Now, Master Nat, don't you try on your hoighty-toighty-his-Worship-the-Mayor-of-Lud-in-the-Mist-knock-you-down-and-be-thankful-for-small-mercies ways with *me*!' cried Hempie, shaking her fist at him. 'I know very *well* what I'm talking about. Long, long ago I made up my mind about certain things. But a good nurse must keep her mind to herself – if it's not the same as that of her master and mistress. So I never let on to you when you were a little boy, nor to Master Ranulph neither, what I thought about these things. But I've never held with fennel and such like. If folks know they're not wanted, it just makes them all the more anxious to come – be they Fairies or Dorimarites. It's just because we're all so scared of our neighbours that we get bamboozled by them. And I've always held that a healthy stomach could digest anything . . . even fairy fruit. Look at my boy now, at Ranulph – young Luke writes he's never looked so bonny. No, fairy fruit nor nothing else can poison a clean stomach.'

'I see,' said Master Nathaniel drily. He was fighting against the sense of comfort that, in spite of himself, her words were giving him. 'And are you quite happy, too, about Prunella?'

'Well, and even if I'm not,' retorted Hempie, 'where's the good of crying, and retching, and belching, all day long, like your lady downstairs? Life has its sad side, and we must take the rough with the smooth. Why, maids have died on their marriage eve, or, what's worse bringing their first baby into the world, and the world's wagged on all the same. Life's sad enough, in all conscience, but there's nothing to be frightened about in it or to turn one's stomach. I was country-bred, and as my old granny used to say, "There's no clock like the sun and no calendar like the stars." And why? Because it gets one used to the look of Time. There's no bogey from over the hills that scares one like Time. But when one's been used an one's life to seeing him naked, as it were, instead of shut up in a clock, like he is in Lud, one learns that he is as quiet and peaceful as an old ox dragging the plough. And to watch Time teaches one to sing. They say the fruit from over the hills makes one sing. I've never tasted so much as a sherd of it, but for all that I can sing.'

Suddenly, all the pent-up misery and fear of the last thirty years seemed to be loosening in Master Nathaniel's heart – he was sobbing, and Hempie, with triumphant tenderness, was stroking his hands and murmuring soothing words, as she had done when he was a little boy.

When his sobs had spent themselves, he sat down on a stool at her feet, and, leaning his head against her knees, said, 'Sing to me, Hempie.'

'Sing to you, my dear? And what shall I sing to you? My voice isn't what it once was . . . well, there's that old song – *Columbine*, I think they call it – that they always seem to be singing in the streets these days – that's got a pretty tune.'

And in a voice, cracked and sweet, like an old spinet, she began to sing:

*'When Aubrey did live there lived on poor,*
*The lord and the beggar on roots did dine*
*With lily, germander, and sops in wine.*
*With sweet-brier*
*And bon-fire*
*And strawberry-wire*
*And columbine.'*

As she sang, Master Nathaniel again heard the Note. But, strange to say, this time it held no menace. It was as quiet as trees and pictures and the past, as soothing as the drip of water, as peaceful as the lowing of cows returning to the byre at sunset.

# 11

## A STRONGER ANTIDOTE THAN REASON

Master Nathaniel sat on at his old nurse's feet for some minutes after she had stopped singing. Both his limbs and his mind seemed to be bathed in a cool, refreshing pool.

So Endymion Leer and Hempie had reached by very different paths the same conclusion – that, after all, there was nothing to be frightened about; that, neither in sky, sea, nor earth was there to be found a cavern dark and sinister enough to serve as a lair for IT – his secret fear.

Yes, but there were facts as well as shadows. Against facts Hempie had given him no charm. Supposing that what had happened to Prunella should happen to Ranulph? That he should vanish for ever across the Debatable Hills.

But it had not happened yet – nor should it happen as long as Ranulph's father had wits and muscles.

He might be a poor, useless creature when menaced by the figments of his own fancy. But, by the Golden Apples of the West, he would no longer sit there shaking at shadows, while, perhaps, realities were mustering their battalions against Ranulph.

It was for him to see that Dorimare became a country that his son could live in in security.

It was as if he had suddenly seen something white and straight – a road or a river – cutting through a sombre, moonlit landscape. And the straight, white thing was his own will to action.

He sprang to his feet and took two or three paces up and down the room.

'But I tell you, Hempie,' he cried, as if continuing a conversation, 'they're all against me. How can I work by myself! They're all against me, I say.'

'Get along with you, Master Nat!' jeered Hempie tenderly. 'You were always one to think folks were against you. When you were a little boy it was always, "You're not cross with me, Hempie, are you?" and peering up at me with your little anxious eyes – and there was me with no more idea of being cross with you than of jumping over the moon!'

'But, I tell you, they are all against me,' he cried impatiently. 'They blame me for what has happened, and Ambrose was so insulting that I had to tell him never to put his foot into my house again.'

'Well, it isn't the first time you and Master Ambrose have quarrelled – and it won't be the first time you make it up again. It was, "Hempie, Brosie won't play fair!" or "Hempie, it's my turn for a ride on the donkey, and Nat won't let me!" And then, in a few minutes, it was all over and forgotten. So you must just step across the Master Ambrose's, and walk in as if nothing had happened, and, you'll see, he'll be as pleased as Punch to see you.'

As he listened, he realized that it would be very pleasant to put his pride in his pocket and rush off to Ambrose and say that he was willing to admit anything that Ambrose chose – that he was a hopelessly inefficient Mayor, that his slothfulness during these past months had been criminal – even, if Ambrose insisted, that he was an eater of, and smuggler of, and receiver of, fairy fruit, all rolled into one – if only Ambrose would make friends again.

Pride and resentment are not indigenous in the human heart; and perhaps it is due to the gardener's innate love of the exotic that we take such pains to make them thrive.

But Master Nathaniel was a self-indulgent man, and ever ready to sacrifice both dignity and expediency to the pleasure of yielding to a sentimental velleity.

'By the Golden Apples of the West, Hempie,' he cried joyfully, 'you're right! I'll dash across to Ambrose's before I'm a minute older,' and he made eagerly for the door.

On the threshold he suddenly remembered how he had found the door of his chapel ajar, and he paused to ask Hempie if she had been up there recently, and had forgotten to lock it.

But she had not been there since early spring.

'That's odd!' said Master Nathaniel.

And then he dismissed the matter from his mind, in the exhilarating prospect of 'making up' with Ambrose.

It is curious what tricks a quarrel, or even a short absence, can play with our mental picture of even our most intimate friends. A few minutes later, as Master Ambrose looked at his old playmate standing at the door, grinning a little sheepishly, he felt as if he had just awakened from a nightmare. This was not 'the most criminally negligent Mayor with whom the town of Lud-in-the-Mist had ever been cursed'; still less was it the sinister figure evoked by Endymion Leer. It was just queer old Nat, whom he had known all his life.

Just as on a map of the country round Lud, in the zig-zagging lines he could almost see the fish and rushes of the streams they represented, could almost count the milestones on the straight lines that stood for roads; so, with regard to the face of his old friend – every pucker and wrinkle was so familiar that he felt he could have told you every one of the jokes and little worries of which they were the impress.

Master Nathaniel, still grinning a little sheepishly, stuck out his hand. Master Ambrose frowned, blew his nose, tried to look severe, and then grasped the hand. And they stood there fully two minutes, wringing each other's hand, and laughing and blinking to keep away the tears.

And then Master Ambrose said, 'Come into the pipe-room, Nat, and try a glass of my new flower-in-amber. You old rascal, I believe it was that that brought you!'

A little later, when Master Ambrose was conducting Master Nathaniel back to his house, his arm linked in his, they happened to pass Endymion Leer.

For a few seconds he stood staring after them as they glimmered down the lane beneath the faint moonlight. And he did not look overjoyed.

*

That night was filled to the brim for Master Nathaniel with sweet, dreamless sleep. As soon as he laid his head on the pillow he seemed to dive into some pleasant unknown element – fresher than air, more caressing than water; an element in which he had not bathed since he had first heard the Note, thirty years ago. And he woke up the next morning light-hearted and eager; so fine a medicine was the will to action.

He had been confirmed in it by his talk the previous evening with Master Ambrose. He had found his old friend by no means crushed by his grief. In fact, his attitude to the loss of Moonlove rather shocked Master Nathaniel, for he had remarked grimly that to have vanished for ever over the hills was perhaps, considering the vice to which she had succumbed, the best thing that could have happened to her. There had always been something rather brutal about Ambrose's common sense.

But he was as anxious as Master Nathaniel himself that drastic measures should immediately be taken for stopping the illicit trade and arresting the smugglers. They had decided what these measures ought to be, and the following days were spent in getting them approved and passed by the Senate.

Though the name of Master Nathaniel stank in the nostrils of his colleagues, their respect for the constitution was too deep seated to permit their opposing the Mayor of Lud-in-the-Mist and High Seneschal of Dorimare; besides, Master Ambrose Honeysuckle was a man of considerable weight in their councils, and they were not uninfluenced by the fact that he was the seconder of all the Mayor's proposals.

So a couple of Yeomen were placed at each of the gates of Lud, with orders to examine not only the baggage of everyone entering the town, but, as well, to rummage through every waggon of hay, every sack of flour, every frail of fruit or vegetables. As well, the West road was patrolled from Lud to the confines of the Elfin Marches, where a consignment of Yeomanry were sent to camp out, with orders day and night to watch the hills. And the clerk to the Senate was ordered to compile a *dossier* of every inhabitant of Lud.

The energy displayed by Master Nathaniel in getting these measures past did a good deal towards restoring his reputation among the townsfolk. Nevertheless that social barometer, Ebeneezor Prim, continued to send his new apprentice, instead of coming himself, to wind his clocks. And the grandfather's clock, it would seem, was protesting against the slight. For according to the servants, it would suddenly move its hands rapidly up and down its dial, which made it look like a face, alternating between a smirk and an expression of woe. And one morning Pimple, the little indigo page, ran screaming with terror into the kitchen, for, he vowed, from the orifice at the bottom of the dial, there had come shooting out a green tongue like a lizard's tail.

As none of Master Nathaniel's measures brought to light a single smuggler or a single consignment of fairy fruit, the Senate were beginning to congratulate themselves on having at last destroyed the evil that for centuries had menaced their country, when Mumchance discovered in one day three people clearly under the influence of the mysterious drug and with their mouth and hands stained with strangely coloured juices.

One of them was a pigmy pedlar from the North, and as he scarcely knew a word of Dorimarite no information could be extracted from him as to how he had procured the fruit. Another was a little street urchin who had found some sherds in a dustbin, but was in too dazed a state to remember exactly where. The third was the deaf-mute known as Bawdy Bess. And, of course, no information could be got from a deaf-mute.

Clearly, then, there was some leakage in the admirable system of the Senate.

As a result, libellous lampoons against the inefficient Mayor were found nailed to the doors of the Guildhall, and Master Nathaniel received several anonymous letters of a vaguely threatening nature, bidding him cease to meddle with matters that did not concern him, lest they should prove to concern him but too much.

But so well had the antidote of action been agreeing with his constitution that he merely flung them into the fire with a grim laugh and a vow to redouble his efforts.

## 12

## DAME MARIGOLD HEARS THE TAP OF A WOODPECKER

Miss Primrose Crabapple's trial was still dragging on, clogged by all the foolish complications arising from the legal fiction that had permitted her arrest. If you remember, in the eye of the law fairy fruit was regarded as woven silk, and many days were wasted in a learned discussion of the various characteristics of gold tissues, stick tuftaffities, figured satins, wrought grograines, silk mohair and ferret ribbons.

Urged partly by curiosity and, perhaps, also by a subconscious hope that in the comic light of Miss Primrose's personality recent events might lose something of their sinister horror, one morning Dame Marigold set out to visit her old schoolmistress in her captivity.

It was the first time she had left the house since the tragedy, and, as she walked down the High Street she held her head high and smiled a little scornful smile – just to show the vulgar herd that even the worst disgrace could not break the spirit of a Vigil.

Now, Dame Marigold had very acute senses. Many a time had she astonished Master Nathaniel by her quickness in detecting the faintest whiff of any of the odours she disliked – shag, for instance, or onions.

She was equally quick in psychological matters, and would detect the existence of a quarrel or a love affair long before they were known to anyone except the parties concerned. And as she made her way that morning to the Guildhall she became conscious in everything that was going on round her of what one can only call a change of key.

She could have sworn that the baker's boy with the tray of loaves on his head was not whistling, that the maid-servant, leaning out of a window to tend her mistress's pot-flowers, was not humming the same tune that they would have been some months ago.

This, perhaps, was natural enough. Tunes, like fruit, have their seasons, and are, besides, ever forming new species. But even the voices of the hawkers chanting *Yellow Sand!* or *Knives and Scissors!* sounded disconcertingly different.

Instinctively, Dame Marigold's delicate nostrils expanded, and the corners of her mouth turned down in an expression of disgust, as if she had caught a whiff or a disagreeable smell.

On reaching the Guildhall, she carried matters with a high hand: No, no there was no need whatever to disturb his Worship. He had given her permission to visit the prisoner, so would the guardian take her up immediately to her room.

Dame Marigold was one of those women who, though they walk blindfold through the fields and woods, if you place them between four walls have eyes as sharp as a naturalist's for the objects that surround them. So, in spite of her depression, her eyes were very busy as she followed the guardian up the splendid spiral staircase, and along the panelled corridors, hung, here and there, with beautiful bits of tapestry. She made a mental note to tell Master Nathaniel that the caretaker had not swept the staircase, and that some of the panelling was worm-eaten and should be attended to. And she would pause to finger a corner of the tapestry and wonder if she could find some silk just that powder-blue, or just that old rose, for her own embroidery.

'Why, I do declare, this panel is beginning to go too!' she murmured, pausing to tap on the wall.

Then she cried in a voice of surprise, 'I do believe it's hollow here!'

The guardian smiled indulgently: 'You are just like the doctor, ma'am – Dr Leer. We used to call him the Woodpecker, when he was studying the Guildhall for his book, for he was for ever hopping about and tapping on the walls. It was almost as if he were looking for something, we used to say. And I'd never be surprised myself to come on a sliding panel. They do say as what those old Dukes were a wild crew, and it might have suited their book very well to have a secret way out of their place!' and he gave a knowing wink.

'Yes, yes, it certainly might,' said Dame Marigold, thoughtfully.

They had now come to a door padlocked and bolted. 'This is where we have put the prisoner, ma'am,' said the guardian unlocking it. And then he ushered her into the presence of her old schoolmistress.

Miss Primrose was sitting bolt upright in a straight backed old fashioned chair, against a background of fine old tapestries, faded to the softest loveliest pastel tints – as incongruous with her grotesque ugliness as had been the fresh prettiness of the Crab-apple Blossoms.

Dame Marigold stood staring at her for a few seconds in silent indignation. Then she sank slowly on to a chair, and said sternly, 'Well, Miss Primrose? I wonder how you dare sit there so calmly after the *appalling* thing you have brought about.'

But Miss Primrose was in one of her most exalted moods – 'On her high hobby-horse,' as the Crabapple Blossoms used to call it. So she merely glittered at Dame Marigold contemptuously out of her little eyes, and, with a lordly wave of her hand, as if to sweep away from her all mundane trivialities, she exclaimed pityingly, 'My poor blind Marigold! Perhaps of all the pupils who have passed through my hands you are the one who are the least worthy of your noble birthright.'

Dame Marigold bit her lip, raised her eyebrows, and said in a low voice of intense irritation, 'What *do* you mean, Miss Primrose?'

Miss Primrose cast her eyes up to the ceiling, and, in her most treacly voice she answered, 'The great privilege of having been born a wooooman!'

Her pupils always maintained that 'woman,' as pronounced by Miss Primrose, was the most indecent word in the language.

Dame Marigold's eyes flashed: 'I may not be a woman, but, at any rate, I am a mother – which is more than you are!' she retorted.

Then, in a voice that at each word grew more indignant, she said, 'And, Miss Primrose, do you consider that you yourself have been "worthy of your noble birthright" in betraying the trust that has been placed in you? Are vice and horror and disgrace and breaking the hearts of parents "true womanliness" I should like to know? You are worse than a murderer – ten times worse. And there you sit, gloating over what you have done, as if you were a martyr or a public benefactor – as complacent and smug and misunderstood as a princess from the moon forced to herd goats! I do really believe . . .'

But Miss Primrose's shrillness screamed down her low-toned indignation: 'Shake me! Stick pins in me! Fling me into the Dapple!' she shrieked. 'I will bear it all with a smile, and wear my shame like a flower given by *him*!'

Dame Marigold groaned in exasperation: 'Who, on earth, do you mean by *"him"*, Miss Primrose?'

Then her irrepressible sense of humour broke out in a dimple, and she added, 'Duke Aubrey or Endymion Leer?'

For, of course, Prunella had told her all the jokes about the goose and the sage.

At this question Miss Primrose gave an unmistakable start; 'Duke Aubrey, of course!' she answered, but the look in her eyes was sly, suspicious, and distinctly scared.

None of this was lost upon Dame Marigold. She looked her slowly up and down with a little mocking smile; and Miss Primrose began to writhe and to gibber.

'Hum!' said Dame Marigold, meditatively.

She had never liked the smell of Endymion Leer's personality.

The recent crisis had certainly done him no harm. It had doubled his practice, and trebled his influence.

Besides, it cannot have been Miss Primrose's beauty and charms that had caused him to pay her recently such marked attentions.

At any rate, it could do no harm to draw a bow at a venture.

'I am beginning to understand, Miss Primrose,' she said slowly. 'Two . . . *outsiders*, have put their heads together to see if they could find a plan for humiliating the stupid, stuck-up, *"so-called* old families of Lud!" Oh! don't protest, Miss Primrose. You have never taken any pains to hide your contempt for us. And I have always realized that yours was not a forgiving nature. Nor do I blame you. We have laughed at you unmercifully for years – and you have resented it. All the same I think your revenge has been an unnecessarily violent one; though, I suppose, to "a true wooo-man", nothing is too mean, too spiteful, too base, if it serves the interests of "*him*"!'

But Miss Primrose had gone as green as grass, and was gibbering with terror: 'Marigold! Marigold!' she cried, wringing her hands, '*How* can you think such things? The dear, devoted Doctor! The best and kindest man in Lud-in-the-Mist! Nobody was angrier with me over what he called my "criminal carelessness" in allowing that *horrible* stuff to be smuggled into my loft, I assure you he is quite rabid on the subject of . . . er . . . *fruit*. Why, when he was a young man at the time of the great drought he was working day and night trying to stop it, he . . .'

But not for nothing was Dame Marigold descended from generations of judges. Quick as lightning, she turned on her: 'The great drought? But that must be forty years ago . . . long before Endymion Leer came to Dorimare.'

'Yes, yes, dear . . . of course . . . quite so . . . I was thinking of what another doctor had told me . . . since all this trouble my poor head gets quite muddled,' gibbered Miss Primrose. And she was shaking from head to foot.

Dame Marigold rose from her chair, and stood looking down on her in silence for a few seconds, under half-closed lids, with a rather cruel little smile.

Then she said, 'Good-bye, Miss Primrose. You have provided me with most interesting food for thought.'

And then she left her, sitting there with frightened face against the faded tapestry.

That same day, Master Nathaniel received a letter from Luke Hempen that both perplexed and alarmed him.

It was as follows: –

Your Worship, – I'd be glad if you'd take Master Ranulph away from this farm, because the widow's up to mischief, I'm sure of that, and some of the folks about here say as what in years gone by she murdered her husband, and she and somebody else, though I don't know who seem to have a grudge against Master Ranulph, and, if I might take the liberty, I'll just tell your Worship what I heard.

It was this way – one night, I don't know how it was, but I couldn't get to sleep, and thinking that a bite, may be, of something would send me off, towards midnight I got up from my bed to go and look in the kitchen for a bit of bread. And half-way down the stairs I heard the sound of low voices, and someone said, 'I fear the Chanticleers,' so I stood still where I was, and I listened. And I peeped down and the kitchen fire was nearly out, but there was enough left for me to see the widow, and a man wrapped up in a cloak, sitting opposite to her with his back to the stairs, so I couldn't see his face. Their talk was low and at first I could only hear words here and there, but they kept making mention of the Chanticleers, and the man said something that sounded like keeping the Chanticleers and Master Ambrose Honeysuckle apart, because Master Ambrose had had a vision of Duke Aubrey. And if I hadn't known the widow and how she was a deep one and as fly as you make them, I'd have thought they were two poor daft old gossips, whose talk had turned wild and nasty with old age. And then the man laid his hand on her knee, and his voice was low, but this time it was so clear that I could hear it all, and I think I can remember every word of it, so I'll write it down for your Worship: '*I fear counter orders. You know the Chief and his ways – at any moment he might betray his agents. Willy Wisp gave young Chanticleer fruit without my knowledge. And I told you how he and that doitered old weaver of yours have been putting their heads together, and that's what has frightened me most.*'

And then his voice became too low for me to hear, till he

said, '*Those who go by the Milky Way often leave footprints. So let him go by the other.*'

And then he got up to go, and I crept back to my room. But not a wink of sleep did I get that night for thinking over what I had heard. For though it seemed gibberish, it gave me the shivers, and that's a fact. And mad folks are often as dangerous as bad ones, so I hope your Worship will excuse me writing like this, and that you'll favour me with an answer by return, and take Master Ranulph away, for I don't like the look in the widow's eye when she looks at him, that I don't.

And hoping this finds your Worship well as it leaves me,

– I am, Your Worship's humble obedient servant,

LUKE HEMPEN.

How Master Nathaniel longed to jump on to his horse and ride post-haste to the farm! But that was impossible. Instead, he immediately despatched a groom with orders to ride night and day and deliver a letter to Luke Hempen, which bade him instantly take Ranulph to the farm near Moongrass (a village that lay some fifteen miles north of Swan-on-the-Dapple) from which for years he had got his cheeses.

Then he sat down and tried to find some meaning in the mysterious conversation Luke had overheard.

Ambrose seeing a vision! An unknown Chief! Footprints on the Milky Way!

Reality was beginning to become very shadowy and menacing.

He must find out something about this widow. Had she not once appeared in the law-courts? He decided he must look up the case without a moment's delay.

He had inherited from his father a fine legal library; and the book-shelves in his pipe-room were packed with volumes bound in vellum and old calf of edicts, codes, and trials, Some of them belonged to the days before printing had been introduced into Dorimare, and were written in the crabbed hand of old town-clerks.

It made the past very real, and threw a friendly, humorous light upon the dead, to come upon, when turning those yellow parchment pages, some personal touch of the old scribe's, such as a sententious or facetious insertion of his own – for instance, *The Law bides her Time, but my Dinner doesn't!* or the caricature in the margin of some forgotten judge. It was just as if one of the grotesque plaster heads on the old houses were to give you, suddenly, a sly wink.

But it was the criminal trials that, in the past, had given Master Nathaniel the keenest pleasure. The dry style of the Law was such a magnificent medium for narrative. And the little details of everyday life, the humble objects of daily use, became so startlingly vivid, when, like scarlet geraniums breaking through a thick autumn mist, they blazed out from that grey style . . . so vivid, and, often, fraught with such tragic consequences.

Great was his astonishment when he discovered from the index that it was among the criminal trials that he must look for the widow Gibberty's. What was more, it was a trial for murder.

Surely Endymion Leer had told him, when he was urging him to send Ranulph to the farm, that it had been quite a trivial case, concerning an arrear of wages, or something, due to a discharged servant?

As a matter of fact the plaintiff, a labourer of the name of Diggory Carp, *had* been discharged from the service of the late Farmer Gibberty. But the accusation he brought against the widow was that she had poisoned her husband with the sap of osiers.

However, when he had finished the trial, Master Nathaniel found himself in complete sympathy with the judge's pronouncement that the widow was innocent, and with his severe reprimand to the plaintiff, for having brought such a serious charge against a worthy woman on such slender grounds.

But he could not get Luke's letter out of his head, and he felt that he would not have a moment's peace till the groom returned with news from the farm.

As he sat that evening by the parlour fire, wondering for the hundredth time who the mysterious cloaked stranger could have been whose back had been seen by Luke, Dame Marigold suddenly broke the silence by saying, 'What do you know about Endymion Leer, Nat?'

'What do I know of Endymion Leer?' he repeated absently. 'Why, that he's a very good leech, with very poor taste in cravats, and, if possible, worse taste in jokes. And that, for some unknown reason, he has a spite against me . . .'

He broke off in the middle of his sentence, and muttered beneath his breath, 'By the Sun, Moon and Stars! Supposing it should be . . .'

Luke's stranger had said he feared the Chanticleers.

A strange fellow, Leer! The Note had once sounded in his voice. Where did he come from? Who was he? Nobody knew in Lud-in-the-Mist.

And, then, there were his antiquarian tastes. They were generally regarded as a harmless, unprofitable hobby. And yet . . . the past was dim and evil, a heap of rotting leaves. The past was silent and belonged to the Silent People . . . But Dame Marigold was asking him another question, a question that had no apparent connection with her previous one: 'What was the year of the great drought?'

Master Nathaniel answered that it was exactly forty years ago, and added quizzically, 'Why this sudden interest in history, Marigold?'

Again she answered by asking him a question, 'And when did Endymion Leer first arrive in Dorimare?'

Master Nathaniel began to be interested. 'Let me see,' he said thoughtfully, 'It was certainly long before we married. Yes, I remember, we called him in to a consultation when my mother had pleurisy, and that was shortly after his arrival, for he still could only speak broken Dorimarite . . . it must be thirty years ago.'

'I see,' said Dame Marigold drily. 'But I happen to know that he was already in Dorimare at the time of the drought.'

And she proceeded to repeat to him her conversation that morning with Miss Primrose.

'And,' she added, 'I've got another idea,' and she told him about the panel in the Guildhall that sounded hollow and what the guardian had said about the woodpecker ways of Endymion Leer. 'And if, partly for revenge for our coldness to him, and partly from a love of power,' she went on. 'It is he who has been behind this terrible affair, a secret passage would be very useful in smuggling, and would explain how all your precautions have been useless. And who would be more likely to know about a secret passage in the Guildhall than Endymion Leer!'

'By the Sun, Moon and Stars!' exclaimed Master Nathaniel excitedly, 'I shouldn't be surprised if you were right, Marigold. You've got a head on your shoulders with something in it more useful than porridge!'

And Dame Marigold gave a little complacent smile.

Then he sprang from his chair, 'I'm off to tell Ambrose!' he cried eagerly.

But would he be able to convince the slow and obstinate mind of Master Ambrose? Mere suspicions are hard to communicate. They are rather like the wines that will not travel, and have to be drunk on the spot.

At any rate, he could but try.

'Have you ever had a vision of Duke Aubrey, Ambrose?' he cried, bursting into his friend's pipe-room.

Master Ambrose frowned with annoyance. 'What are you driving at, Nat?' he said, huffily.

'Answer my question. I'm not chaffing you, I'm in deadly earnest. Have you ever had a vision of Duke Aubrey?'

Master Ambrose moved uneasily in his chair. He was far from proud of that vision of his. 'Well,' he said, gruffly, 'I suppose one might call it that. It was at the Academy – the day that wretched girl of mine ran away. And I was so upset that there was some excuse for what you call visions.'

'And did you tell anyone about it?'

'Not I!' said Master Ambrose emphatically; then he caught himself up and added, 'Oh! yes I believe I did though. I mentioned it to that spiteful little quack, Endymion Leer. I'm sure I wish I hadn't. Toasted Cheese! What's the matter now, Nat?'

For Master Nathaniel was actually cutting a caper of triumph and glee.

'I was right! I was right!' he cried joyfully, so elated by his own acumen that for the moment his anxiety was forgotten.

'Read that, Ambrose,' and he eagerly thrust into his hands Luke Hempen's letter.

'Humph!' said Master Ambrose when he had finished it. 'Well, what are you so pleased about?'

'Don't you see, Ambrose!' cried Master Nathaniel impatiently. 'That mysterious fellow in the cloak must be Endymion Leer . . . nobody else knows about your vision.'

'Oh, yes, Nat, blunt though my wits may be I saw *that*. But I fail to see how the knowledge helps us in any way.'

Then Master Nathaniel told him about Dame Marigold's theories and discoveries.

Master Ambrose hummed and hawed, and talked about women's reasoning, and rash conclusions. But perhaps he was more impressed, really, than he chose to let Master Nathaniel see. At any rate he grudgingly agreed to go with him by night to the Guildhall and investigate the hollow panel. And, from Master Ambrose, this was a great concession; for it was not the sort of escapade that suited his dignity.

'Hurrah, Ambrose!' shouted Master Nathaniel. 'And I'm ready to bet a Moongrass cheese against a flask of your best flower-in-amber that we'll find that rascally quack at the bottom of it all!'

'You'd always a wonderful eye for a bargain, Nat,' said Master Ambrose with a grim chuckle. 'Do you remember, when we were youngsters, how you got my pedigree pup out of me for a stuffed pheasant, so moth-eaten that it had scarcely a feather to its name, and, let me see, what else? I think there was half a packet of mouldy sugar-candy . . .'

'And I threw in a broken musical-box whose works used to go

queer in the middle of *To War, Bold Sons of Dorimare*, and burr and buzz like a drunk cockchafer,' put in Master Nathaniel proudly. 'It was quite fair – quantity for quality.'

# 13

## WHAT MASTER NATHANIEL AND MASTER AMBROSE FOUND IN THE GUILDHALL

Master Nathaniel was much too restless and anxious to explore the Guildhall until the groom returned whom he had sent with the letter to Luke Hempen.

But he must have taken the order to ride night and day literally – in so short a time was he back again in Lud. Master Nathaniel was, of course, enchanted by his despatch, though he was unable to elicit from him any detailed answers to his eager questions about Ranulph. But it was everything to know that the boy was well and happy, and it was but natural that the fellow should be bashful and tongue-tied in the presence of his master.

But the groom had not, as a matter of fact, come within twenty miles of the widow Gibberty's farm.

In a road-side tavern he had fallen in with a red-haired youth, who had treated him to glass upon glass of an extremely intoxicating wine; and, in consequence, he had spent the night and a considerable portion of the following morning sound asleep on the floor of the tavern.

When he awoke, he was horrified to discover how much time he had wasted. But his mind was set at rest on the innkeeper's giving him a letter from the red-haired youth, to say that he deeply regretted having been the indirect cause of delaying a messenger sent on pressing business by the High Seneschal (in his cup the groom had boasted of the importance of his errand), and had, in consequence, ventured to possess himself of the letter, which he guaranteed to deliver at the address on the wrapper as soon, or sooner, as the messenger could have done himself.

The groom was greatly relieved. He had not been long in Master Nathaniel's service. It was *after* Yuletide he had entered it.

*

So it was with a heart relieved from all fears for Ranulph and free to throb like a schoolboy's with the lust of adventure that Master Nathaniel met Master Ambrose on the night of the full moon at the splendid carved doors of the Guildhall.

'I say, Ambrose,' he whispered, 'I feel as if we were lads again, and off to rob an orchard!'

Master Ambrose snorted. He was determined, at all costs, to do his duty, but it annoyed him that his duty should be regarded in the light of a boyish escapade.

The great doors creaked back on their hinges. Shutting them as quietly as they could, they tip-toed up the spiral staircase and along the corridor described by Dame Marigold: whenever a board creaked under their heavy steps, one inwardly cursing the other for daring to be so stout and unwieldy.

All round them was darkness, except for the little trickles of light cast before them by their two lanthorns.

A house with old furniture has no need of ghosts to be haunted. As we have seen, Master Nathaniel was very sensitive to the silent things – stars, houses, trees; and often in his pipe-room, after the candles had been lit, he would sit staring at the bookshelves, the chairs, his father's portrait – even at his red umbrella standing up in the corner, with as great a sense of awe as if he had been a star-gazer.

But that night, the brooding invisible presences of the carved panels, the storied tapestries, affected even the hard-headed Master Ambrose. It was as if that silent population was drawing him, by an irresistible magnetism, into the zone of its influence.

If only they would speak, or begin to move about – those silent rooted things! It was like walking through a wood by moonlight.

Then Master Nathaniel stood still.

'This, I think, must roughly be the spot where Marigold found the hollow panel,' he whispered, and began tapping cautiously along the wainscotting.

A few minutes later, he said in an excited whisper, 'Ambrose!

Ambrose! I've got it. Hark! You can hear, can't you? It's as hollow as a drum.'

'Suffering Cats! I believe you're right,' whispered back Master Ambrose, beginning, in spite of himself, to be a little infected with Nat's absurd excitement.

And then, yielding to pressure, the panel slid back, and by the light of their lanthorns they could see a twisting staircase.

For a few seconds they gazed at each other in silent triumph. Then Master Nathaniel chuckled, and said, 'Well, here goes – down with our buckets into the well! And may we draw up something better than an old shoe or a rotten walnut!' and straightway he began to descend the stairs, Master Ambrose valiantly following him.

The stairs went twisting down, down – into the very bowels of the earth, it seemed. But at last they found themselves in what looked like a long tunnel.

'Tally ho! Tally ho!' whispered Master Nathaniel, laughing for sheer joy of adventure, 'take it at a gallop, Brosie; it may lead to an open glade . . . and the deer at bay!'

And digging him in the ribs, he added, 'Better sport than moth hunting, eh?' which showed the completeness of their reconciliation.

Nevertheless, it was very slowly, and feeling each step, that they groped their way along the tunnel.

After what seemed a very long time Master Nathaniel halted, and whispered over his shoulder, 'Here we are. There's a door . . . Oh, thunder and confusion on it for ever! *It's locked.*'

And, beside himself with irritation at this unlooked-for obstacle, he began to batter and kick at the door, like one demented.

He paused a minute for breath, and from the inside could be heard a shrill female voice demanding the pass-word.

'Pass-word?' bellowed back Master Nathaniel, 'by the Sun, Moon and Stars and the Golden Apples of the West, what . . .'

But before he could finish his sentence, the door was opened from the other side, and they marched into a low, square room, which was lit by one lamp swinging by a chain from the ceiling – for which there seemed but little need for a light more brilliant than that of any lamp, and yet as soft as moonlight, seemed to issue from the marvellous tapestries that hung on the walls.

They were dumb with amazement. This was as different from all the other tapestry they had ever seen as is an apple-tree in full blossom against a turquoise sky in May to the same tree in November, when only a few red leaves still cling to its branches, and the sky is leaden. Oh, those blues, and pinks, and brilliant greens! In what miraculous dyes had the silks been dipped?

As to the subjects, they were those familiar to every Dorimarite – hunting scenes, fugitives chased by the moon, shepherds and shepherdesses tending their azure sheep. But, depicted in these brilliant hues, they were like the ashes of the past, suddenly, under one's very eyes, breaking into flame. Heigh-presto! The men and women of a vanished age, noisy, gaudy, dominant, are flooding the streets, and driving the living before them like dead leaves.

And what was all this lying in heaps on the floor? Pearls and sapphires, and monstrous rubies? Or windfalls of fruit, marvellous fruit, fallen from the trees depicted on the tapestry?

Then, as their eyes grew accustomed to all the brilliance, the two friends began to get their bearings; there could be no doubt as to the nature of that fruit lying on the floor – it was fairy fruit, or their names were not respectively Chanticleer and Honeysuckle.

And, to their amazement, the guardian of this strange treasure was none other than their old acquaintance Mother Tibbs.

Her clear, child-like eyes that shone like lamps out of her seared weather-beaten face, were gazing at them in a sort of mild surprise.

'If it isn't Master Hyacinth and Master Josiah!' she exclaimed, adding, with her gay, young laugh, 'to think of *their* knowing the pass-word!'

Then she peered anxiously into their faces: 'Are your stockings wearing well yonder? The last pair I washed for you didn't take the soap as they should. Marching down the Milky Way, and tripping it beyond the moon, is hard on stockings.'

Clearly, she took them for their own fathers.

Meanwhile, Master Ambrose was drawing in his breath, with a noise as if he were eating soup, and creasing his double chins – sure signs, to anyone who had seen him on the Bench, that he was getting ready to hector.

But Master Nathaniel gave him a warning nudge, and said cordially to their hostess, 'Why, our stockings, and boots too, are doing very nicely, thank you. So you didn't expect us to know the pass-word, eh? Well, well, perhaps we know more than you think,' then, under his breath to Master Ambrose, 'By my Great-aunt's Rump, Ambrose, what *was* the pass-word?'

Then turning again to Mother Tibbs, who was slightly swaying from her hips, as if in time to some jig, which she alone could hear, he said, 'You've got some fine tapestry. I don't believe I've ever seen finer!'

She smiled, and then coming close up to him, said in a low voice, 'Does your Worship know what makes it so fine? No? Why, *it's the fairy fruit!*' and she nodded her head mysteriously, several times.

Master Ambrose gave a sort of low growl of rage, but again Master Nathaniel shot him a warning look, and said in a voice of polite interest, 'Indeed! Indeed! And where, may I ask, does the . . . er . . . *fruit* come from?'

She laughed merrily, 'Why the gentlemen bring it! All the pretty gentlemen, dressed in green, with their knots of ribands, crowding down in the sunrise from their ships with the scarlet sails to suck the golden apricocks, when all in Lud are fast asleep! And then the cock says *Cockadoodledoo!* Cockadoodledooooo!' and her voice trailed off, far-away and lonely, suggesting, somehow, the first glimmer of dawn on ghostly hayricks.

'And I'll tell you something, Master Nat Cock o' the Roost,' she went on, smiling mysteriously, and coming close up to him, *'you'll soon be dead!'*

Then she stepped back, smiling and nodding encouragingly, as if to say, '*There's* a pretty present I've given you! Take care of it.'

'And as for Mother Tibbs,' she went on triumphantly, 'she'll soon be a fine lady, like the wives of the Senators, dancing all night under the moon! The gentlemen have promised.'

Master Ambrose gave a snort of impatience, but Master Nathaniel said with a good-humoured laugh, 'So that's how you think the wives of the Senators spend their time, eh? I'm afraid they've other things to do. And as to yourself, aren't you getting too old for dancing?'

A slight shadow passed across her clear eyes. Then she tossed her head with the noble gesture of a wild creature, and cried, 'No! No! As long as my heart dances my feet will too. And nobody will grow old when the Duke comes back.'

But Master Ambrose could contain himself no longer. He knew only too well Nat's love of listening to long rambling talk – especially when there happened to be some serious business on hand.

'Come, come!' he cried in a stern voice, 'in spite of being crack-brained, my good woman, you may soon find yourself dancing to another tune. Unless you tell us in double quick time who exactly these *gentlemen* are, and who it was that put you on guard here, and who brings that filthy fruit, and who takes it away, we will . . . why, we will cut the fiddle strings that you dance to!'

This threat was a subconscious echo of the last words he had heard spoken by Moonlove. Its effect was instantaneous.

'Cut the fiddle strings! Cut the fiddle strings!' she wailed; adding coaxingly, 'No, no, pretty master, you would never do that! Would he now?' and she turned appealingly to Master Nathaniel. 'It would be like taking away the poor man's strawberries. The Senator has peaches and roasted swans and peacocks' hearts, and a fine coach to drive in, and a feather bed to lie late in of a morning. And the poor man has black bread and baked haws, and work . . . but in the summer he has strawberries and tunes to dance to. No, no, you would never cut the fiddle strings!'

Master Nathaniel felt a lump in his throat. But Master Ambrose was inexorable: 'Yes, of course I would!' he blustered; 'I'd cut the strings of every fiddle in Lud. And I will, too, unless you tell us what we want to know. Come, Mother Tibbs, speak out – I'm a man of my word.'

She gazed at him beseechingly, and then a look of innocent cunning crept into her candid eyes and she placed a finger on her lips, then nodded her head several times and said in a mysterious whisper, 'If you'll promise not to cut the fiddle strings I'll show you the prettiest sight in the world – the sturdy dead lads in the Fields of Grammary hoisting their own coffins on their shoulders, and tripping it over the daisies. Come!' and she darted to the side of the wall, drew aside the tapestry and revealed to them another secret door. She pressed some spring, it flew open disclosing another dark tunnel.

'Follow me, pretty masters,' she cried.

'There's nothing to be done,' whispered Master Nathaniel, 'but to humour her. She may have something of real value to show us.'

Master Ambrose muttered something about a couple of lunatics and not having left his fireside to waste the night in indulging their fantasies; but all the same he followed Master Nathaniel, and the second secret door shut behind them with a sharp click.

'Phew!' puffed Master Nathaniel; 'Phew!' puffed Master Ambrose, as they pounded laboriously along the passage behind their light-footed guide.

Then they began to ascend a flight of stairs, which seemed interminable, and finally fell forward with a lurch on to their knees, and again there was a click of something shutting behind them.

They groaned and cursed and rubbed their knees and demanded angrily to what unholy place she had been pleased to lead them.

But she clapped her hands gleefully, 'Don't you know, pretty masters? Why, you're where the dead cocks roost! You've come back to your own snug cottage, Master Josiah Chanticleer. Take your lanthorn and look round you.'

This Master Nathaniel proceeded to do, and slowly it dawned on him where they were.

'By the Golden Apples of the West, Ambrose!' he exclaimed, 'if we're not in my own chapel!'

And, sure enough, the rays of the lanthorns revealed the shelves lined with porphyry coffins, the richly wrought marble ceiling, and the mosaic floor of the home of the dead Chanticleers.

'Toasted Cheese!' muttered Master Ambrose in amazement.

'It must have two doors, though I never knew it,' said Master Nathaniel. 'A secret door opening on to that hidden flight of steps. There are evidently people who know more about my chapel than I do myself,' and suddenly he remembered how the other day he had found its door ajar.

Mother Tibbs laughed gleefully at their surprise, and then, placing one finger on her lips, she beckoned them to follow her; and they tiptoed after her out into the moonlit Fields of Grammary, where she signed to them to hide themselves from view behind the big trunk of a sycamore.

The dew, like lunar daisies, lay thickly on the grassy graves. The marble statues of the departed seemed to flicker into smiles under the rays of the full moon; and, not far from the sycamore, two men were digging up a newly-made grave. One of them was a brawny fellow with the gold rings in his ears worn by sailors, the other was – Endymion Leer.

Master Nathaniel shot a look of triumph at Master Ambrose, and whispered, 'A cask of flower-in-amber, Brosie!'

For some time the two men dug on in silence, and then they pulled out three large coffins and laid them on the grass.

'We'd better have a peep, Sebastian,' said Endymion Leer, 'to see that the goods have been delivered all right. We're dealing with tricky customers.'

The young man, addressed as Sebastian, grinned, and taking a clasp knife from his belt, began to prise open one of the coffins.

As he inserted the blade into the lid, our two friends behind the sycamore could not help shuddering; nor was their horror lessened by the demeanour of Mother Tibbs, for she half closed her eyes, and drew the air in sharply through her nostrils, as if in expectation of some delicious perfume.

But when the lid was finally opened and the contents of the

coffin exposed to view, they proved not to be cere cloths and hideousness, but – closely packed fairy fruit.

'Toasted Cheese!' muttered Master Ambrose; 'Busty Bridget!' muttered Master Nathaniel.

'Yes, that's the goods all right,' said Endymion Leer, 'and we'll take the other two on trust. Shut it up again, and help to hoist it on to my shoulder, and do you follow with the other two – we'll take them right away to the tapestry-room. We're having a council there at midnight, and it's getting on for that now.'

Choosing a moment when the backs of the two smugglers were turned, Mother Tibbs darted out from behind the sycamore, and shot back into the chapel, evidently afraid of not being found at her post. And she was shortly followed by Endymion Leer and his companion.

At first, the sensations of Master Nathaniel and Master Ambrose were too complicated to be expressed in words, and they merely stared at each other, with round eyes. Then a slow smile broke over Master Nathaniel's face, 'No Moongrass cheese for you this time, Brosie,' he said. 'Who was right, you or me?'

'By the Milky Way, it was you, Nat!' cried Master Ambrose, for once, in a voice of real excitement. 'The rascal! The unmitigated rogue! So it's him, is it, we parents have to thank for what has happened! But he'll hang for it, he'll hang for it – though we have to change the whole constitution of Dorimare! The *blackguard*!'

'Into the town probably as a hearse,' Master Nathaniel was saying thoughtfully, 'then buried here, then down through my chapel to the secret room in the Guildhall, whence, I suppose, they distribute it by degrees. It's quite clear now how the stuff gets into Lud. All that remains to clear up is how it gets past our Yeomen on the border . . . but what's taken you, Ambrose?'

For Master Ambrose was simply shaking with laughter; and he did not laugh easily.

'Do the dead bleed?' he was repeating between his guffaws; 'why, Nat, it's the best joke I've heard these twenty years!'

And when he had sufficiently recovered he told Master Nathaniel about the red juice oozing out of the coffin, which he had taken for blood, and how he had frightened Endymion Leer out of his wits by asking him about it.

'When, of course, it was a bogus funeral, and what I had seen was the juice of that damned fruit!' and again he was seized with paroxysms of laughter.

But Master Nathaniel merely gave an absent smile; there was something vaguely reminiscent in that idea of the dead bleeding – something he had recently read or heard; but, for the moment, he could not remember where.

In the meantime, Master Ambrose had recovered his gravity. 'Come, come,' he cried briskly, 'we've not a moment to lose. We must be off at once to Mumchance, rouse him and a couple of his men, and be back in a twinkling to that tapestry-room, to take them red-handed.'

'You're right, Ambrose! You're right!' cried Master Nathaniel. And off they went at a sharp jog trot, out at the gate, down the hill, and into the sleeping town.

They had no difficulty in rousing Mumchance and in firing him with their own enthusiasm. As they told him in a few hurried words what they had discovered, his respect for the Senate went up in leaps and bounds – though he could scarcely credit his ears when he learned of the part played in the evening's transactions by Endymion Leer.

'To think of that! To think of that!' he kept repeating, 'and me who's always been so friendly with the Doctor, too!'

As a matter of fact, Endymion Leer had for some months been the recipient of Mumchance's complaints with regard to the slackness and inefficiency of the Senate; and, in his turn, had succeeded in infecting the good Captain's mind with sinister suspicions against Master Nathaniel. And there was a twinge of conscience for disloyalty to his master, the Mayor, behind the respectful heartiness of his tones as he cried, 'Very good, your Worship. It's Green and Juniper what are on duty tonight. I'll go and fetch them from the guard-room, and we should be able to settle the rascals nicely.'

As the clocks in Lud-in-the-Mist were striking midnight the five of them were stepping cautiously along the corridors of the Guildhall. They had no difficulty in finding the hollow panel, and having pressed the spring, they made their way along the secret passage.

'Ambrose!' whispered Master Nathaniel flurriedly, 'what was it exactly that I said that turned out to be the pass-word? What with the excitement and all I've clean forgotten it.'

Master Ambrose shook his head. 'I haven't the slightest idea,' he whispered back. 'To tell you the truth, I couldn't make out what she meant about your having used a pass-word. All *I* can remember your saying was "Toasted Cheese!" or "Busty Bridget!" – or something equally elegant.'

Now they had got to the door, locked from the inside as before.

'Look here, Mumchance,' said Master Nathaniel, ruefully, 'we can't remember the pass-word, and they won't open without it.'

Mumchance smiled indulgently, 'Your Worship need not worry about the pass-word,' he said. 'I expect we'll be able to find another that will do as well . . . eh, Green and Juniper? But perhaps first – just to be in order – your Worship would knock and command them to open.'

Master Nathaniel felt absurdly disappointed. For one thing, it shocked his sense of dramatic economy that they should have to resort to violence when the same result could have been obtained by a minimum expenditure of energy. Besides, he had so looked forward to showing off his new little trick!

So it was with a rueful sigh that he gave a loud rat-a-tat-tat on the door, calling out, 'Open in the name of the Law!'

These words, of course, produced no response, and Mumchance, with the help of the other four, proceeded to put into effect his own pass-word, which was to shove with all their might against the door, two of the hinges of which he had noticed looked rusty.

It began to creak, and then to crack, and finally they burst into . . . an empty room. No strange fruit lay heaped on the floor; nothing hung on the walls but a few pieces of faded moth-eaten tapestry. It looked like a room that had not been entered for centuries.

When they had recovered from their first surprise, Master Nathaniel cried fiercely, 'They must have got wind that we were after them, and given us the slip, taking their loads of filthy fruits with them, I'll . . .'

'There's no fruit been here, your Worship,' said Mumchance in a voice that he was trying hard to keep respectful; 'it always leaves stains, and there ain't any stains here.'

And he couldn't resist adding, with a wink to Juniper and Green, 'I daresay it's your Worship's having forgotten the pass-word that's done it!' And Juniper and Green grinned from ear to ear.

Master Nathaniel was too chagrined to heed this insolence; but Master Ambrose – ever the champion of dignity in distress – gave Mumchance such a look that he hung his head and humbly hoped that his Worship would forgive his little joke.

# 14

## DEAD IN THE EYE OF THE LAW

The following morning Master Nathaniel woke late, and got up on the wrong side of his bed, which, in view of the humiliation and disappointment of the previous night, was, perhaps, pardonable.

His temper was not improved by Dame Marigold's coming in while he was dressing to complain of his having smoked green shag elsewhere than in the pipe-room: 'And you *know* how it always upsets me, Nat. I'm feeling quite squeamish this morning, the whole house reeks of it . . . Nat! you know you *are* an old blackguard!' and she dimpled and shook her finger at him, as an emolient to the slight shrewishness of her tone.

'Well, you're wrong for once,' snapped Master Nathaniel; 'I haven't smoked shag even in the pipe-room for at least a week – so *there*! Upon my word, Marigold, your nose is a nuisance – you should keep it in a bag, like a horse!'

But though Master Nathaniel might be in a bad temper he was far from being daunted by what had happened the night before.

He shut himself into the pipe-room and wrote busily for about a quarter of an hour; then he paced up and down committing what he had written to memory. Then he set out for the daily meeting of the Senate. And so absorbed was he with the speech he had been preparing that he was impervious, in the Senators' tiring-room, to the peculiar glances cast at him by his colleagues.

Once the Senators had donned their robes of office and taken their places in the magnificent room reserved for their councils, their whole personality was wont suddenly to alter, and they would cease to be genial, easy-going merchants who had known each other all their lives and become grave, formal – even hierophantic, in manner; while abandoning the careless colloquial diction of every day, they would adopt the language of their forefathers, forged in more strenuous and poetic days than the present.

In consequence the stern look in Master Nathaniel's eye that morning, when he rose to address his colleagues, the stern tone in which he said 'Senators of Dorimare!' might have heralded nothing more serious than a suggestion that they should, that year, have geese instead of turkeys at their public dinner.

But his opening words showed that this was to be no usual speech.

'Senators of Dorimare!' he began, 'I am going to ask you this morning to awake. We have been asleep for many centuries, and the Law has sung us lullabies. But many of us here have received the accolade of a very heavy affliction. Has that wakened us? I fear not. The time has come when it behoves us to look facts in the face – even if these facts bear a strange likeness to dreams and fancies.

'My friends, the ancient foes of our country are abroad. Tradition says that the Fairies' (he brought out boldly the horrid word) 'fear iron; and we, the descendants of the merchant-heroes, must still have left in us some veins of that metal. The time has come to prove it. We stand to lose everything that makes life pleasant and secure – laughter, sound sleep, the merriment of fire-sides, the peacefulness of gardens. And if we cannot bequeath the certainty of these things to our children, what will boot them their inheritance? It is for us, then, as fathers as well as citizens, once and for all to uproot this menace, the roots of which are in the past, the branches of which cast their shadow on the future.

'I and another of your colleagues have discovered at last who it was that brought this recent grief and shame upon so many of us. It will be hard, I fear, to prove his guilt, for he is subtle, stealthy, and mocking, and, like his invisible allies, his chief weapon is delusion. I ask you all, then, to parry that weapon with faith and loyalty, which will make you take the word of old and trusty friends as the only touchstone of truth. And, after that – I have sometimes thought that less blame attaches to deluding others than to deluding oneself. Away, then, with flimsy legal fictions! Let us call things by their names – not grograine or tuftaffity, but *fairy fruit*. And if it be proved that any man has brought such merchandise into Dorimare, let him hang by the neck till he be dead.'

Then Master Nathaniel sat down.

But where was the storm of applause he had expected would greet his words? Where were the tears, the eager questions, the tokens of deeply stirred feelings?

Except for Master Ambrose's defiant 'Bravos!' his speech was received in profound silence. The faces all round him were grim and frigid, with compressed lips and frowning brows – except the portrait of Duke Aubrey – he, as usual, was faintly smiling.

Then Master Polydore Vigil rose to his feet, and broke the grim silence.

'Senators of Dorimare!' he began, 'the eloquent words we have just listened to from his Worship the Mayor, can, strangely enough, serve as a prelude – a golden prelude – to my poor, leaden words. I, too, came here this morning resolved to call your attention to legal fictions – which sometimes, it may be, have their uses. But perhaps before I say my say, his Worship will allow the clerk to read us the oldest legal fiction in our Code. It is to be found in the first volume of the Acts of the twenty-fifth year of the Republic, Statute 5, chapter 9.'

Master Polydore Vigil sat down, and a slow grim smile circulated round the hall, and then seemed to vanish and subside in the mocking eyes of Duke Aubrey's portrait.

Master Nathaniel exchanged puzzled glances with Master Ambrose; but there was nothing for it but to order the clerk to comply with the wishes of Master Polydore.

So, in a small, high, expressionless voice, which might have been the voice of the Law herself, the clerk read as follows:—

*'Further, we ordain that nothing but death alone shall have power to dismiss the Mayor of Lud-in-the-Mist and High Seneschal of Dorimare before the five years of his term of office shall fully have expired. But, the dead, being dumb, feeble, treacherous and given to vanities, if any Mayor*

*at a time of menace to the safety of the Dorimarites be held by his colleagues to be any of these things, then let him be accounted dead in the eye of the Law, and let another be elected in his stead.'*

# 15

## 'HO, HO, HOH!'

The clerk shut the great tome, bowed low, and withdrew to his place; and an ominous silence reigned in the hall.

Master Nathaniel sat watching the scene with an eye so cold and aloof that the Eye of the Law itself could surely not have been colder. What power had delusion or legal fictions against the mysterious impetus propelling him along the straight white road that led he knew not whither?

But Master Ambrose sprang up and demanded fiercely that the honourable Senator would oblige them by an explanation of his offensive insinuations.

Nothing loth, Master Polydore again rose to his feet, and, pointing a menacing finger at Master Nathaniel, he said: 'His Worship the Mayor has told us of a man stealthy, mocking, and subtle, who has brought this recent grief and shame upon us. That man is none other than his Worship the Mayor himself.'

Master Ambrose again sprung to his feet, and began angrily to protest, but Master Nathaniel, *ex cathedra*, sternly ordered him to be silent and to sit down.

Master Polydore continued: 'He has been dumb, when it was the time to speak, feeble, when it was the time to act, treacherous, as the desolate homes of his friends can testify, and *given to vanities*. Aye, *given to vanities*, for what,' and he smiled ironically, 'but vanity in a man is too great a love for grogaines and tuftaffities and other costly silks? Therefore, I move that in the eye of the Law he be accounted dead.'

A low murmur of approval surged over the hall.

'Will he deny that he is over fond of *silk*?'

Master Nathaniel bowed, in token that he did deny it.

Master Polydore asked if he would then be willing to have his house searched; again Master Nathaniel bowed.

There and then?

And Master Nathaniel bowed again.

So the Senate rose and twenty of the Senators, without removing their robes, filed out of the Guildhall and marched two and two towards Master Nathaniel's house.

On the way who should tag himself on to the procession but Endymion Leer. At this, Master Ambrose completely lost his temper. He would like to know why this double-dyed villain, this shameless Son of a Fairy, was putting his rancid nose into the private concerns of the Senate! But Master Nathaniel cried impatiently, 'Oh, let him come, Ambrose, if he wants to. The more the merrier!'

You can picture the consternation of Dame Marigold when, a few minutes later, her brother – with a crowd of Senators pressing up behind him – bade her, with a face of grave compassion, to bring him all the keys of the house.

They proceeded to make a thorough search, ransacking every cupboard, chest, and bureau. But nowhere did they find so much as an incriminating pip, so much as a stain of dubious colour.

'Well,' began Master Polydore, in a voice of mingled relief and disappointment, 'it seems that our search has been a . . .'

'*Fruitless* one, eh?' prompted Endymion Leer, rubbing his hands, and darting his bright eyes over the assembled faces. 'Well, perhaps it has. Perhaps it has.'

They were standing in the hall, quite close to the grandfather's clock, which was ticking away, as innocent and foolish-looking as a newly-born lamb.

Endymion Leer walked up to it and gazed at it quizzically, with his head on one side. Then he tapped its mahogany case – making Dame Marigold think of what the guardian at the Guildhall had said of his likeness to a woodpecker.

Then he stood back a few paces and wagged his finger at it in comic admonition ('Vulgar buffoon!' said Master Ambrose quite audibly), and then the wag turned to Master Polydore and said,

'Just before we go, to make quite sure, what about having a peep inside this clock?'

Master Polydore had secretly sympathised with Master Ambrose's ejaculation, and thought that the Doctor, by jesting at such a time, was showing a deplorable lack of good breeding.

All the same, the Law does not shrink from reducing thoroughness to absurdity, so he asked Master Nathaniel if he would kindly produce the key of the clock.

He did so, and the case was opened; Dame Marigold made a grimace and held her pomander to her nose, and to the general amazement that foolish, innocent-looking grandfather's clock stood revealed as a veritable cornucopia of exotic, strangely coloured, sinister-looking fruits.

Vine-like tendrils, studded with bright, menacing berries were twined round the pendulum and the chains of the two leaden weights; and at the bottom of the case stood a gourd of an unknown colour, which had been scooped hollow and filled with what looked like crimson grapes, tawny figs, raspberries of an emerald green, and fruits even stranger than these, and of colour and shape not found in any of the species of Dorimare.

A murmur of horror and surprise arose from the assembled company. And, was it from the clock, or down the chimney, or from the ivy peeping in at the window? – from somewhere quite close came the mocking sound of 'Ho, ho, *hoh*!'

Of course, before many hours were over the whole of Lud-in-the-Mist was laughing at the anti-climax to the Mayor's high falutin' speech that morning in the Senate. And in the evening he was burned in effigy by the mob, and among those who danced round the bonfire were Bawdy Bess and Mother Tibbs. Though it is doubtful whether Mother Tibbs really understood what was happening. It was an excuse for dancing, and that was enough for *her*.

It was reported, too, that the Yeomanry and their Captain, though not actually taking part in these demonstrations, stood looking on with indulgent smiles.

Among the respectable tradesmen in the far from unsympathetic crowd of spectators was Ebeneezor Prim the clockmaker. He had, however, not allowed his two daughters to be there; and they were sitting dully at home, keeping the supper hot for their father and the black-wigged apprentice.

But Ebeneezor came back without him, and Rosie and Lettice were too much in awe of their father to ask any questions. The evening dragged wearily on – Ebeneezor sat reading *The Good Mayor's Walk Through Lud-in-the-Mist* (a didactic and unspeakably dreary poem, dating from the early days of the Republic), and from time to time he would glance severely over the top of his spectacles at his daughters, who were whispering over their tatting, and looking frequently towards the door.

But when they finally went upstairs to bed the apprentice had not yet come in, and in the privacy of their bedroom the girls admitted to each other that it was the dullest evening they had spent since his arrival, early in spring. For it was wonderful what high spirits were concealed behind that young man's prim exterior.

Why, it was sufficient to enliven even an evening spent in the society of papa to watch the comical grimaces he pulled behind that gentleman's respectable back! And it was delicious when the shrill 'Ho, ho, *hoh*!' would suddenly escape him, and he would instantly snap down on the top of it his most sanctimonious expression. And then, he seemed to possess an inexhaustible store of riddles and funny songs, and there was really no end to the invention and variety of his practical jokes.

The Misses Prim, since their earliest childhood, had craved for a monkey or a cockatoo, such as sailor brothers or cousins brought to their friends; their father, however, had always sternly refused to have any such creature in his house. But the new apprentice had been ten times more amusing than any monkey or cockatoo that had ever come from the Cinnamon Isles.

The next morning, as he did not come for his usual early roll and glass of home-made cordial, the two girls peeped into his room, and found that his bed has not been slept in; and lying neglected on the floor was the neat black wig. Nor did he ever come back to claim it. And when they timidly asked their father what had happened to him, he sternly forbade them ever again to mention his name, adding, with a mysterious shake of the head, 'For some time I have had my suspicions that he was not what he appeared.'

And then he sighed regretfully, and murmured, 'But never before have I had an apprentice with such wonderfully skilful fingers.'

As for Master Nathaniel – while he was being burned in effigy in the market-place, he was sitting comfortably in his pipe-room, deep in an in-folio.

He had suddenly remembered that it was something in the widow Gibberty's trial that was connected in his mind with Master Ambrose's joke about the dead bleeding. And he was re-reading that trial – this time with absorption.

As he read, the colours of his mental landscape were gradually modified, as the colours of a real landscape are modified according to the position of the sun. But if a white road cuts through the landscape it still gleams white – even when the moon has taken the place of the sun. And a straight road still gleamed white across the landscape of Master Nathaniel's mind.

# 16

## THE WIDOW GIBBERTY'S TRIAL

The following day, with all the masquerading that the Law delights in, Master Nathaniel was pronounced in the Senate to be dead. His robes of office were taken off him, and they were donned by Master Polydore Vigil, the new Mayor. As for Master Nathaniel – he was wrapped in a shroud, laid on a bier and carried to his home by four of the Senators, the populace lining the streets and greeting the mock obsequies with catcalls and shouts of triumph.

But the ceremony over, when Master Ambrose, boiling with indignation at the outrage, came to visit his friend, he found a very cheerful corpse who greeted him with a smack on the back and a cry of, 'Never say die, Brosie! I've something here that should interest you,' and he thrust into his hand an open in-folio.

'What's this?' asked the bewildered Master Ambrose.

There was a certain solemnity in Master Nathaniel's voice as he replied, 'It's the Law, Ambrose – the homœopathic antidote that our forefathers discovered to delusion. Sit down this very minute and read that trial through.'

As Master Ambrose knew well, it was useless trying to talk to Nat about one thing when his mind was filled with another. Besides, his curiosity was aroused, for he had come to realize that Nat's butterfly whims were sometimes the disguise of shrewd and useful intuitions. So, through force of long habit, growling out a protest about this being no time for tomfoolery and rubbish, he settled down to read the volume at the place where Master Nathaniel had opened it, namely, at the account of the trial of the widow Gibberty for the murder of her husband.

The plaintiff, as we have seen, was a labourer, Diggory Carp by name, who had been in the employ of the late farmer. He said he had been suddenly dismissed by the defendant just after harvest, when it was not easy to find another job.

No reason was given for his dismissal, so Diggory went to the farmer himself, who, he said, had always been a kind and just master, to beg that he might be kept on. The farmer practically admitted that there was no reason for his dismissal except that the mistress had taken a dislike to him. 'Women are kittle cattle, Diggory,' he had said, with an apologetic laugh, 'and it's best humouring them. Though it's hard on the folks they get their knife into. So I fear it will be best for every one concerned that you should leave my service, Diggory.'

But he gave him a handful of florins over and above his wages, and told him he might take a sack of lentils from the granary – if he were careful that the mistress did not get wind of it.

Now, Diggory had a shrewd suspicion as to why the defendant wanted to get rid of him. Though she was little more than a girl – she was the farmer's second wife and more like his daughter's elder sister than her stepdame – she had the reputation of being as staid and sensible as a woman of forty. But Diggory knew better. He had discovered that she had a lover. One evening he had come on her in the orchard, lying in the arms of a young foreigner, called Christopher Pugwalker, a herbalist, who had first appeared in the neighbourhood just before the great drought.

'And from that time on,' said Diggory, 'she had got her knife into me, and everything I did was wrong. And I believe she hadn't a moment's peace till she'd got rid of me. Though, if she'd only known, I was no blab, and not one for blaming young blood and a wife half the age of her husband.'

So he and his wife and his children were turned out on the world.

The first night they camped out in a field, and when they had lighted a fire Diggory opened the sack that, with the farmer's permission, he had taken from the granary, in order that his wife might make them some lentil soup for supper. But lo and behold! instead of lentils the sack contained fruit – fruit that Diggory Carp, as a west countryman, born and bred near the Elfin Marches, recognised at the first glance to be of a kind that he would not dream of touching himself or of allowing his wife and children to touch . . . the sack, in fact, contained fairy fruit. So they buried it in the field, for, as Diggory said, 'Though the stuff be poison to men, they do say as how it's a mighty fine manure for the crops.'

For a week or so they tramped the country, living from hand to mouth. Sometimes Diggory would earn a little by doing odd jobs for the farmers, or by playing the fiddle at village weddings, for Diggory, it would seem, was a noted fiddler.

But with the coming of winter they began to feel the pinch of poverty, and his wife bethought her of the trade of basket-making she had learned in her youth; and, as they were camping at the time at the place where grew the best osiers for the purpose, she determined to see if her fingers had retained their old cunning. As the sap of these particular osiers was a deadly poison, she would not allow the children to help her to gather them.

So she set to and made wicker urns in which the farmers' wives could keep their grain in winter, and baskets of fancy shapes for lads to give to their sweethearts to hold their ribbands and fal-lals. The children peddled them about the countryside, and thus they managed to keep the pot boiling.

The following summer, shortly before harvest, Diggory's eldest girl went to try and sell some baskets in the village of Swan. There she met the defendant, whom she asked to look at her wares, relying on not being recognised as a daughter of Diggory's, through having been in service at another farm when her father was working at the Gibbertys'.

The defendant seemed pleased with the baskets, bought two or three, and got into talk with the girl about the basket-making industry, in the course of which, she learned that the best osiers for the purpose were very poisonous. Finally she asked the girl to bring her a bundle of the osiers in question, as making baskets, she said, would make a pleasant variety, of an evening, from the eternal spinning; and in the course of a few days the girl brought her, as requested, a bundle of the osiers, and was well paid for them.

Not long afterwards came the news that the farmer Gibberty had died suddenly in the night, and with it was wafted the rumour of foul play. There was an old custom in that part of the country that whenever there was a death in the house all the inmates should march in procession past the corpse. It was really a sort of primitive inquest, for it was believed that in the case of foul play the corpse would bleed at the nose as the murderer passed it. This custom, said Diggory, was universally observed in that part of the country, even in cases as free from all suspicion as those of women dying in child-bed. And in all the taverns and farmhouses of the neighbourhood it was being whispered that the corpse of the farmer Gibberty, on the defendant's walking past it, had bled copiously, and when Christopher Pugwalker's turn had come to pass it, it had bled a second time.

And, knowing what he did, Diggory Carp came to feel that it was his duty to lodge an accusation against the widow.

His two reasons, then, for thinking her guilty were that the corpse had bled when she passed it, and that she had bought from his daughter osiers the sap of which was poisonous. The motive for the crime he found in her having a young lover, whom she wished should stand in her dead husband's shoes. It was useless for the defendant to deny that Pugwalker was her lover – the fact had for months been the scandal of the neighbourhood, and she had finally lost all sense of shame and had actually had him to lodge in the farm for several months before her husband's death. This was proved beyond a shadow of a doubt by the witnesses summoned by Diggory.

As for the bleeding of the corpse: vulgar superstitions did not fall within the cognizance of the Law, and the widow ignored it in her defence. However, with regard to that other vulgar superstition to which the plaintiff had alluded, fairy fruit, she admitted, in passing, that very much against her wishes her late husband had sometimes used it as manure – though she had never discovered how he procured it.

As to the osiers – she allowed that she had bought a bundle from the plaintiff's daughter; but that it was for no sinister purpose she was able conclusively to prove. For she summoned various witnesses – among others the midwife from the village, who was always called in in cases of sickness – who had been present during the last hours of the farmer, and who all of them swore that his death had been a painless one. And various physicians, who were summoned as expert witnesses, all maintained that the victim of the poisonous sap of osiers always died in agony.

Then she turned the tables on the plaintiff. She proved that Diggory's dismissal had been neither sudden nor unjust; for, owing to his thieving propensities, he had often been threatened with it by her late husband, and several of the farm-servants testified to the truth of her words.

As to the handful of florins and the sack of lentils, all she could say was that it was not like the farmer to load a dishonest servant with presents. But nothing had been said about two sacks of corn, a pig, and a valuable hen and her brood, which had disappeared simultaneously with the departure of the plaintiff. Her husband, she said, had been very angry about it, and had wanted to have Diggory pursued and clapped into gaol; but she had persuaded him to be merciful.

The long and the short of it was that the widow left the court without a stain on her character, and that a ten years' sentence for theft was passed on Diggory.

As for Christopher Pugwalker, he had disappeared before the trial, and the widow denied all knowledge of his whereabouts.

## 17

## THE WORLD-IN-LAW

'Well,' said Master Ambrose, as he laid down the volume, 'the woman was clearly as innocent as you are. And I should very much like to know what bearing the case has upon the present crisis.'

Master Nathaniel drew up his chair close to his friend's and said in a low voice, as if he feared an invisible listener, 'Ambrose, do you remember how you startled Leer with your question as to whether the dead could bleed?'

'I'm not likely to forget it,' said Master Ambrose, with an angry laugh. 'That was all explained the night before last in the Fields of Grammary.'

'Yes, but supposing he had been thinking of something else – not of fairy fruit. What if Endymion Leer and Christopher Pugwalker were one and the same?'

'Well, I don't see the slightest reason for thinking so. But even if they were – what good would it do us?'

'Because I have an instinct that hidden in that old case is a good honest hempen rope, too strong for all the gossamer threads of Fairie.'

'You mean that we can get the rascal hanged? By the Harvest of Souls, you're an optimist, Nat. If ever a fellow died quietly in his bed from natural causes, it was that fellow Gibberty. But, for all that, there's no reason to lie down under the outrageous practical joke that was played off on you yesterday. By my Great-aunt's Rump, I thought Polydore and the rest of them had more sense than to be taken in by such tomfoolery. But the truth of it is that that villain Leer can make them believe what he chooses.'

'Exactly!' cried Master Nathaniel eagerly. 'The original meaning of Fairie is supposed to be delusion. They can juggle with appearances – we have seen them at it in that tapestry room. How are we to make any stand against an enemy with such powers behind him?'

'You don't mean that you are going to lie down under it, Nat?' cried Master Ambrose indignantly.

'Not ultimately – but for a time I must be like the mole and work in secret. And now I want you to listen to me, Ambrose, and not scold me for what you call wandering from the point and being prosy. Will you listen to me?'

'Well, yes, if you've got anything sensible to say,' said Master Ambrose grudgingly.

'Here goes then! What do you suppose the Law was invented for, Ambrose?'

'What was the Law invented for? What *are* you driving at, Nat? I suppose it was invented to prevent rapine, and robbery, and murder, and all that sort of thing.'

'But you remember what my father said about the Law being man's substitute for fairy fruit? Fairy things are all of them supposed to be shadowy cheats – delusion. But man can't live without delusion, so he creates for himself another form of delusion – the world-in-law, subject to no other law but the will of man, where man juggles with facts to his heart's content, and says, 'If I choose I shall make a man old enough to be my father my son, and if I choose I shall turn fruit into silk and black into white, for this is the world I have made myself, and here I am master'. And he creates a monster to inhabit it – the man-in-law, who is like a mechanical toy and always behaves exactly as he is expected to behave, and is no more like you and me than are the fairies.'

For the life of him, Master Ambrose could not suppress a grunt of impatience. But he was a man of his word, so he refrained from further interruption.

'Beyond the borders of the world-in-law,' continued Master Nathaniel, 'that is to say, the world as we choose for our own convenience that it should appear, there is delusion – or reality. And the people who live there are as safe from our clutches as if they lived on another planet. No, Ambrose, you needn't purse up your lips like that . . . everything I've been saying is to be found more or less in my father's writings, and nobody ever thought *him* fantastic – probably because they never took the trouble to read his books. I must confess I never did myself till just the other day.'

As he spoke he glanced up at the portrait of the late Master Josiah, taken in the very arm-chair he, Nathaniel, was at that very moment sitting in, and following his son's every movement with a sly, legal smile. No, there had certainly been nothing fantastic about Master Josiah.

And yet . . . there was something not altogether human about these bright bird-like eyes and that very pointed chin. Had Master Josiah also heard the Note . . . and fled from it to the world-in-law?

Then he went on: 'But what I'm going to say now is my own idea. Supposing that everything that happens on the one planet, the planet that we call Delusion, reacts on the other planet; that is to say, the world as we choose to see it, the world-in-law? No, no, Ambrose! You promised to hear me out!' (For it was clear that Master Ambrose was getting restive.) 'Supposing, then, that one planet reacts on the other, but that these reactions are translated, as it were, into the terms of the other? To take an example, supposing that what on one planet is a spiritual sin should turn on the other into a felony? That what in the world of delusion are hands stained with fairy fruit should, in the world-in-law, turn into hands stained with human blood? In short, that Endymion Leer should turn into Christopher Pugwalker?'

Master Ambrose's impatience had changed to real alarm. He greatly feared that Nathaniel's brain had been unhinged by his recent misfortunes. Master Nathaniel burst out laughing: 'I believe you think I've gone off my head, Brosie – but I've not, I promise you. In plain language, unless we can find that this fellow Leer has been guilty of something in the eye of the Law he'll go on triumphing over us and laughing at us in his sleeve and ruining our country for our children till, finally, all the Senate, except you and me, follows his funeral procession, with weeping and wailing, to the Fields of Grammary. It's our one hope of getting even with him, Brosie. Otherwise, we might as soon hope to catch a dream and put it in a cage.'

'Well, according to your ideas of the Law, Nat, it shouldn't be difficult,' said Master Ambrose drily. 'You seem to consider that in what you call the world-in-law one does what one likes with facts – launch a new legal fiction, then, according to which, for your own particular convenience, Endymion Leer is for the future Christopher Pugwalker.'

Master Nathaniel laughed: 'I'm in hopes we can prove it without a legal fiction,' he said. 'The widow Gibberty's trial took place thirty-six years ago, four years after the great drought, when, as Marigold has discovered, Leer was in Dorimare, though he has always given us to understand that he did not arrive till considerably later . . . and the reason would be obvious if he left as Pugwalker, and returned as Leer. Also, we know that he is intimate with the widow Gibberty. Pugwalker was a herbalist; so is Leer. And then there is the fright you gave him with your question, "Do the dead bleed?" Nothing will make me believe that that question immediately suggested to him the mock funeral and the coffin with fairy fruit . . . he might think of that on second thoughts, not right away. No, no, I hope to be able to convince you, and before very long, that I am right in this matter, as I was in the other – it's our one hope, Ambrose.'

'Well, Nat,' said Master Ambrose, 'though you talk more nonsense in half an hour than most people do in a lifetime, I've been coming to the conclusion that you're not such a fool as you look – and, after all, in Hempie's old story it was the village idiot who put salt on the dragon's tail.'

Master Nathaniel laughed, quite pleased by this equivocal compliment – it was so rarely that Ambrose paid one a compliment at all.

'Well,' continued Master Ambrose, 'and how are you going to set about launching your legal fiction, eh?'

'Oh, I'll try and get in touch with some of the witnesses in the trial – Diggory Carp himself may turn out to be still alive. At any rate, it will give me something to do, and Lud's no place for me just now.'

Master Ambrose groaned: 'Has it really come to this, Nat, that you have to leave Lud, and that we can do nothing against this . . . this . . . this sort of cobweb of lies and buffoonery and . . . well, *delusion*, if you like? I can tell you, I haven't spared Polydore and the rest of them the rough side of my tongue – but it's as if that fellow Leer had cast a spell on them.'

'But we'll *break* the spell, by the Golden Apples of the West, we'll break it, Ambrose!' cried Master Nathaniel buoyantly; 'we'll dredge the shadows with the net of the Law, and Leer shall end on the gallows, or my name's not Chanticleer!'

'Well,' said Master Ambrose, 'seeing you've got this bee in your bonnet about Leer you might like a little souvenir of him; it's the embroidered slipper I took from that gibbering criminal old woman's parlour, and now that her affair is settled there's no more use for it.' (The variety of 'silk' found in this Academy had finally been decided to be part 'barratine tuftaffity' and part 'figured mohair,' and Miss Primrose had been heavily fined and set at liberty.) 'I told you how the sight of it made him jump, and though the reason is obvious enough – he thought it was fairy fruit – it seems to take so little to set your brain romancing there's no knowing what you mayn't discover from it! I'll have it sent over to you tonight.'

'You're very kind, Ambrose. I'm sure it will be most valuable,' said Master Nathaniel ironically.

During Miss Primrose's trial the slipper had from time to time been handed round among the judges, without its helping them in the slightest in the delicate distinctions they were drawing between tuftaffity and mohair. In Master Nathaniel it had aroused a vague sense of boredom and embarrassment, for it suggested a long series of birthday presents from Prunella that had put him to the inconvenience of pumping up adequate expressions of gratitude and admiration. He had little hope of being able to extricate any useful information from that slipper – still, Ambrose must have his joke.

They sat in silence for a few minutes, and then Master Nathaniel rose to his feet and said, 'This may be a long business, Ambrose, and we may not have an opportunity for another talk. Shall we pledge each other in wild thyme gin?'

'I'm not the man to refuse your wild thyme gin, Nat. And you don't often give one a chance of tasting it, you old miser,' said Master Ambrose, trying to mask his emotion with facetiousness. When he had been given a glass filled with the perfumed grass-green syrup, he raised it, and smiling at Master Nathaniel, began, 'Well, Nat . . .'

'Stop a minute, Ambrose!' interrupted Master Nathaniel. 'I've got a sudden silly whim that we should take an oath I must have read when I was a youngster in some old book . . . the words have suddenly come back to me. They go like this: *We* (and then we say our own names), *Nathaniel Chanticleer and Ambrose Honeysuckle, swear by the Living and the Dead, by the Past and the Future, by Memories and Hopes, that if a Vision comes begging at our door we will take it in and warm it at our hearth, and that we will not be wiser than the foolish nor more cunning than the simple, and that we will remember that he who rides the Wind needs must go where his Steed carries him.* Say it after me, Ambrose.'

'By the White Ladies of the Fields, never in my life have I heard such fustian!' grumbled Master Ambrose.

But Nat seemed to have set his heart on this absurd ceremony, and Master Ambrose felt that the least he could do was to humour him, for who could say what the future held in store and when they might meet again. So, in a protesting and excessively matter-of-fact voice, he repeated after him the words of the oath.

When, and in what book had Master Nathaniel found it? For it was the vow taken by the candidates for initiation into the first degree of the ancient Mysteries of Dorimare.

Do not forget that, in the eye of the Law, Master Nathaniel was a dead man.

# 18

## MISTRESS IVY PEPPERCORN

The tasks assigned to the clerks in Master Nathaniel's counting-house did not always concern cargoes and tonnage. For instance, once for two whole days they had not opened a ledger, but had been kept busy, under their employer's superintendence, in cutting out and pinning together fantastic paper costumes to be worn at Ranulph's birthday party. And they were quite accustomed to his shutting himself into his private office, with strict injunctions that he was not to be disturbed, while he wrote, say, a comic valentine to old Dame Polly Pyepowders, popping his head frequently round the door to demand their help in finding a rhyme. So they were not surprised that morning when told to close their books and to devote their talents to discovering, by whatever means they chose, whether there were any relations living in Lud of a west country farmer called Gibberty who had died nearly forty years ago.

Great was Master Nathaniel's satisfaction when one of them returned from his quest with the information that the late farmer's widowed daughter, Mistress Ivy Peppercorn, had recently bought a small grocer's shop in Mothgreen, a village that lay a couple of miles beyond the north gate.

There was no time to be lost, so Master Nathaniel ordered his horse, put on the suit of fustian he wore for fishing, pulled his hat well down over his eyes, and set off for Mothgreen.

Once there, he had no difficulty in finding Mistress Ivy's little shop, and she herself was sitting behind the counter.

She was a comely, apple-cheeked woman of middle age, who looked as if she would be more in her element among cows and meadows than in a stony little shop, redolent of the various necessities and luxuries of a village community.

She seemed of a cheerful, chatty disposition, and Master Nathaniel punctuated his various purchases with quips and cranks and friendly questions.

By the time she had weighed him out two ounces of snuff and done them up into a neat little paper poke she had told him that her maiden name had been Gibberty, and that her husband had been a ship's captain, and she had lived till his death in the sea-port town. By the time she had provided him with a quarter of lollipops, he knew that she much preferred a country life to trade. And by the time a woollen muffler had been admired, purchased and done up in a parcel, she had informed him that she would have liked to have settled in the neighbourhood of her old home, but – *there were reasons*.

What these reasons were took time, tact and patience to discover. But never had Master Nathaniel's wistful inquisitiveness, masquerading as warm-hearted sympathy, stood him in better stead. And she finally admitted that she had a stepmother whom she detested, and whom, moreover, she had good reason to distrust.

At this point Master Nathaniel considered he might begin to show his hand. He gave her a meaning glance; and asked her if she would like to see justice done and rascals getting their deserts, adding, 'There's no more foolish proverb than the one which says that dead men tell no tales. To help dead men to find their tongues is one of the chief uses of the Law.'

Mistress Ivy looked a little scared. 'Who may you be, sir, please?' she asked timidly.

'I'm the nephew of a farmer who once employed a labourer called Diggory Carp,' he answered promptly.

A smile of enlightenment broke over her face.

'Well, who would have thought it!' she murmured. 'And what may your uncle's name have been? I used to know all the farmers and their families round our part.'

There was a twinkle in Master Nathaniel's candid hazel eyes: 'I doubt I've been too sharp and cut myself!' he laughed. 'You see, I've worked for the magistrates, and that gets one into the habit of setting traps for folk . . . the Law's a wily lady. I've no uncle in the West, and I never knew Diggory Carp. But I've always taken an interest in crime and enjoyed reading the old trials. So when you said your name had been Gibberty my mind at once flew back to a certain trial that had always puzzled me, and I thought, perhaps, the name Diggory Carp might unlock your tongue. I've always felt there was more behind that trial than met the eye.'

'Did you indeed?' said Mistress Ivy evasively. 'You seem mighty interested in other folks' affairs,' and she looked at him rather suspiciously.

This put Master Nathaniel on his mettle. 'Now, hark'ee, Mistress Ivy, I'm sure your father took a pleasure in looking at a fine crop, even if it was in another man's field, and that your husband liked good seamanship . . .'

And here he had to break off his dissertation and listen, which he did very patiently, to a series of reminiscences about the tastes and habits of her late husband.

'Well, as I was saying,' he went on, when she paused for a moment to sigh, and smile, and wipe her eyes with the corner of her apron, 'what the sight of a field filled to the brim with golden wheat was to your father, and that of a ship skilfully piloted into harbour was to your husband, the sight of Justice crouching and springing on her prey is to me. I'm a bachelor, and I've managed to put by a comfortable little nest-egg, and there's nothing I'd like to spend it on better than in preventing Justice being baulked of her lawful prey, not to mention helping to avenge a fine fellow like your father. We old bachelors, you know, have our hobbies . . . they're quieter about the house than a crowd of brats, but they're sometimes quite as expensive,' and he chuckled and rubbed his hands.

He was thoroughly enjoying himself, and seemed actually to have become the shrewd, honest, somewhat bloodthirsty old fellow he had created. His eyes shone with the light of fanaticism when he spoke of Justice, the tiger; and he could picture the snug little house he lived in in Lud – it had a little garden gay with flowers, and a tiny lawn, and espalier fruit trees, to the care of which he dedicated his leisure hours. And he had a dog, and a canary, and an old housekeeper. Probably, when he got home tonight, he would sit down to a supper of sausages and mashed, followed by toasted cheese. And then, when he had finished his supper, he would get out his collection of patibulary treasures, and over a bowl of negus finger lovingly the various bits of gallows rope, the blood-stained glove of a murdered strumpet, the piece of amber worn as a charm by a notorious brigand chief, and gloat over the stealthy steps of his pet tiger, the Law. Yes, his obscure little life was as gay with hobbies as his garden was with flowers. How comfortable were other men's shoes!

'Well, if what you mean,' said Mistress Ivy, 'is that you'd like to help to punish wicked people, why, I wouldn't mind lending a hand myself. All the same,' and again she looked at him suspiciously, 'what makes you think my father didn't come by a natural death?'

'My nose, good lady, my nose!' and, as he spoke, he laid a knowing finger alongside the said organ. 'I smelt blood. Didn't it say in the trial that the corpse bled?'

She bridled, and cried scornfully, 'And you, to be town-bred too, and an educated man from the looks of you, to go believing that vulgar talk! You know what country people are, setting everything that happens to the tunes of old songs. It was two drops of blood when the story was told in the tavern at Swan, and by the time it had reached Moongrass it was a gallon. I walked past the corpse with the others, and I can't say I noticed any blood – but then, my eyes were all swelled with crying. All the same, it's what made Pugwalker leave the country.'

'Indeed?' cried Master Nathaniel, and his voice was very eager.

'Yes. My stepmother was never the kind to be saucy with – though I had no cause to love her, I must say she looked like a queen, but he was a foreigner and a little bit of a chap, and the boys in the village and all round gave him no peace, jumping out at him from behind hedges and chasing him down the street, shouting, "Who made the corpse of Farmer Gibberty bleed?" and such like. And he just couldn't stand it, and supped off one night, and I never thought to see him again. But I've seen him in the streets of Lud, and not long ago too – though he didn't see me.'

Master Nathaniel's heart was thumping with excitement. 'What is he like?' he asked breathlessly.

'Oh! very like what he was as a young man. They say there's nothing keeps you young like a good conscience!' and she laughed drily. 'Not that he was ever much to look at – squat and tubby and freckled, and such saucy prying eyes!'

Master Nathaniel could contain himself no longer, and in a voice hoarse with excitement he cried, 'Was it . . . do you mean the Lud doctor, Endymion Leer?'

Mistress Ivy pursed up her mouth and nodded meaningfully.

'Yes, that's what he calls himself now . . . and many folks set such store by him as a doctor, that, to hear them talk, one would think a baby wasn't properly born unless he'd brought it into the world, nor a man properly dead unless he'd closed his eyes.'

'Yes, yes. But are you *sure* he is the same as Christopher Pugwalker? Could you swear to him in court?' cried Master Nathaniel eagerly.

Mistress Ivy looked puzzled. 'What good would it do to swear at him?' she asked doubtfully. 'I must say I never held with foul language in a woman's mouth, nor did my poor Peppercorn – for all that he was a sailor.'

'No, no!' cried Master Nathaniel impatiently, and proceeded to explain to her the meaning of the expression.

She dimpled a little at her own blunder, and then said guardedly, 'And what would bring me into the law courts, I should like to know? The past is over and done with, and what is done can't be undone.'

Master Nathaniel fixed her with a searching gaze, and, forgetting his assumed character, spoke as himself.

'Mistress Peppercorn,' he said solemnly, 'have you no pity for the dead, the dumb, helpless dead? You loved your father, I am sure. When a word from you might help to avenge him, are you going to leave that word unsaid? Who can say that the dead are not grateful for the loving thoughts of the living, and that they do not rest more quietly in their graves when they have been avenged? Have you no time or pity left for your dead father?'

During this speech Mistress Ivy's face had begun working, and at the last words she burst into sobs. 'Don't think that, sir,' she gasped; 'don't think that! I remember well how my poor father used to sit looking at her of an evening, not a word passing his lips, but his eyes saying as clearly as if it had been his tongue, "No, Clem" (for my stepmother's name was Clementine), "I don't trust you no further than I see you, but, for all that, you can turn me round your little finger, because I'm a silly, besotted old fool, and we both know it." Oh! I've always said that my poor father had both his eyes wide open, in spite of him being the slave of her pretty face. It was not that he didn't see, or couldn't see – what he lacked was the heart to speak out.'

'Poor fellow! And now, Mistress Ivy, I think you should tell me all you know and what it is that makes you think that, in spite of the medical evidence to the contrary, your father was murdered,' and he planted his elbows on the counter and looked her squarely in the face.

But Mistress Ivy trimmed. 'I didn't say that poor father was poisoned with osiers. He died quiet and peaceful, father did.'

'All the same, you think there was foul play. I am not entirely disinterested in this matter, now that I know Dr Leer is connected with it. I happen to bear him a grudge.'

First Mistress Ivy shut the door on to the street, and then leant over the counter, so that her face was close to his, and said in a low voice: 'Why, yes, I always did think there had been foul play, and I'll tell you for why. Just before my father died we'd been making jam. And one of poor father's funny little ways was to like the scum of jam or jelly, and we used to keep some of every boiling in a saucer for him. Well, my own little brother Robin, and *her* little girl – a little tot of three – were buzzing round the fruit and sugar like a pair of little wasps, whining for this, sticking their fingers into that, and thinking they were helping with the jam-making. And suddenly my stepmother turned round and caught little Polly with her mouth all black with mulberry juice. And, oh, the taking she was in! She caught her and shook her, and ordered her to spit out anything she might have in her mouth; and then, when she found it was mulberries, she cooled down all of a sudden and told Polly she must be a good girl and never put anything in her mouth without asking first.

'Now, the jam was boiled in great copper cauldrons, and I noticed a little pipkin simmering on the hearth, and I asked my stepmother what it was. And she answered carelessly, "Oh, it's some mulberry jelly, sweetened with honey instead of sugar, for my old grandfather at home." And at the time I didn't give the matter another thought. But the evening before my father died . . . and I've never mentioned this to a soul except my poor Peppercorn . . . after supper he went and sat out in the porch to smoke his pipe, leaving her and him to their own doings in the kitchen; for she'd been brazen-faced enough, and my father weak enough, actually to have the fellow living there in the house. And my father was a queer man in that way – too proud to sit where he wasn't wanted, even in his own kitchen. And I'd come out, too, but I was hid from him by the corner of the house, for I had been waiting for the sun to go down to pick flowers, to take to a sick neighbour the next day. But I could hear him talking to his spaniel, Ginger, who was like his shadow and followed him wherever he went. I remember his words as clearly as if it had been yesterday: "Poor old Ginger!" he said, "I thought it would be me who would dig your grave. But it seems not, Ginger, it seems not. Poor old lady, by this time to-morrow I'll be as dumb as you are . . . and you'll miss our talks, poor Ginger." And then Ginger gave a howl that made my blood curdle, and I came running round the corner of the house and asked father if he was ailing, and if I could fetch him anything. And he laughed, but it was as different as chalk from cheese from the way he laughed as a rule. For poor father was a frank-hearted, open-handed man, and not one to hoard up bitterness any more than he would hoard up money; but that laugh – the last I heard him give – was as bitter as gall. And he said, "Well, Ivy, my girl, would you like to fetch me some peonies and marigolds and shepherd's thyme from a hill where the Silent

People have danced, and make me a salad from them?" And seeing me looking surprised, he laughed again, and said, "No, no. I doubt there are no flowers growing this side of the hills that could help your poor father. Come, give me a kiss – you've always been a good girl." Now, these are flowers that old wives use in love potions, as I knew from my granny, who was very wise about herbs and charms, but father had always laughed at her for it, and I supposed he was fretting over my stepmother and Pugwalker, and wondering if he could win her heart back to him.

'But that night he died, and it was then that I started wondering about that jelly in the pipkin, for him, liking scum as he did, and always having a saucer of it set aside for him, it wouldn't have been difficult to have boiled up some poison for him without any danger of other folks touching it. And Pugwalker knew all about herbs and such like, and could have told her what to use. For it was as plain as print that poor father knew he was going to die, and peonies make a good purge; and I've wondered since if it was as a purge that he wanted these flowers. And that's all I know, and perhaps it isn't much, but it's been enough to keep me awake many a night of my life wondering what I should have done if I'd been older. For I was only a little maid of ten at the time, with no one I could talk to, and as frightened of my stepmother as a bird of a snake. If I'd been one of the witnesses, I dare say it would have come out in court, but I was too young for that.'

'Perhaps we could get hold of Diggory Carp?'

'Diggory Carp?' she repeated in surprise. 'But surely you heard what happened to him? Ah, that was a sad story! You see, after he was sent to gaol, there came three or four terrible lean years, one after the other. And food was so dear, no one, of course, had any money over for buying fancy goods like baskets . . . and the long and the short of it was that when Diggory came out of gaol he found that his wife and children had died of starvation. And it seemed to turn his wits, and he came up to our farm, raging against my stepmother, and vowing that some day he'd get his own back on her. And that night he hanged himself from one of the trees in our orchard, and he was found there dead the next morning.'

'A sad story,' said Master Nathaniel. 'Well, we must leave him out of our calculations. All you've told me is very interesting – very interesting indeed. But there's still a great deal to be unravelled before we get to the rope I'm looking for. One thing I don't understand is Diggory Carp's story about the osiers. Was it a pure fabrication of his?'

'Poor Diggory! He wasn't, of course, the sort of man whose word one would be very ready to take, for he did deserve his ten years – he was a born thief. But I don't think he would have had the wits to invent all that. I expect the story he told was true enough about his daughter selling her the osiers, but that it was only for basket-making that she wanted them. Guilt's a runny thing – like a smell, and one often doesn't quite know where it comes from. I think Diggory's nose was not mistaken when it smelt out guilt, but it led him to the wrong clue. My father wasn't poisoned by osiers.'

'Can you think what it was, then?'

She shook her head. 'I've told you everything I know.'

'I wish you knew something more definite,' said Master Nathaniel a little fretfully. 'The Law dearly loves something it can touch – a blood-stained knife and that sort of thing. And there's another matter that puzzles me. Your father seems, on your showing, to have been a very indulgent sort of husband, and to have kept his jealousy to himself. What *cause* was there for the murder?'

'Ah! that I think I can explain to you,' she cried. 'You see, our farm was very conveniently situated for . . . well, for smuggling a certain thing that we don't mention. It stands in a sort of hollow between the marches and the west road, and smugglers like a friendly, quiet place where they can run their goods. And my poor father, though he may have sat like a dumb animal in pain when his young wife was gallivanting with her lover, all the same, if he had found out what was being stored in his granary, Pugwalker would have been kicked out of the house, and she could have whistled for him till she was black in the face. My father was easy-going enough in some ways, but there were places in him as hard as nails, and no woman, be she never so much of a fool (and, fair play to my stepmother, she was no fool), can live with a man without finding out where these places are.'

'Oh, ho! So what Diggory Carp said about the contents of that sack was true, was it?' And Master Nathaniel inwardly thanked his stars that no harm had come to Ranulph during his stay in such a dangerous place.

'Oh, it was true, and no mistake; and, child though I was at the time, I cried through half one night with rage when they told me what the hussy had said in court about my father using the stuff as manure and her begging him not to! Begging him not to, indeed! I could have told them a very different story. And it was Pugwalker that was at the back of that business, and got the granary key from her, so that they could run their goods there. And shortly before my father died he got wind of it – I know that from something I overheard. The room I shared with my little brother Robin opened into theirs, and we always kept the door ajar, because Robin was a timid child, and fancied he couldn't go to sleep unless he heard my father snoring. Well, about a week before my father died I heard him talking to her in a voice I'd never known him use to her before. He said he'd warned her twice already that year, and that this was the last time. Up to that time he'd held his head high, he said, because his hands were clean and all his doings straight and fair, and now he warned her for the last time that unless this business was put a stop to once and for all, he'd have Pugwalker tarred and feathered, and make the neighbourhood too hot for him to stay in it. And, I remember, I heard him hawking and spitting, as if he'd rid himself of something foul. And he said that the Gibbertys had always been respected, and that the farm, ever since they had owned it, had helped to make the people of Dorimare straight-limbed and clean-blooded, for it had sent fresh meat and milk to market, and good grain to the miller, and sweet grapes to the vintner, and that he would rather sell the farm than that poison and filth should be sent out of his granary, to turn honest lads into idiots gibbering at the moon. And then she started coaxing him, but she spoke too low for me to catch the words. But she must have been making him some promise, for he said gruffly, "Well, see that it's done, then, for I'm a man of my word".

'And in not much more than a week after that he was dead – poor father. And I count it a miracle that I ever grew up and am sitting here now telling you all this. And a still greater one that little Robin grew up to be a man, for he inherited the farm. But it was her own little girl that died, and Robin grew up and married, and though he died in his prime it was through a quinsy in his throat, and he always got on with our stepmother, and wouldn't hear a word against her. And she has brought up his little girl, for her mother died when she was born. But I've never seen the lass, for there was never any love lost between me and my stepmother, and I never went back to the old house after I married.'

She paused, and in her eyes was that wistful, tranced look that always comes when one has been gazing at things that happened to one long ago.

'I see, I see,' said Master Nathaniel meditatively. 'And Pug-walker? Did you ever see him again till you recognized him in the streets of Lud the other day?'

She shook her head. 'No, he disappeared, as I told you, just before the trial. Though I don't doubt that *she* knew his where-abouts and heard from him – met him even; for she was always going out by herself after nightfall. Well, well, I've told you everything I know – though perhaps I'd have better held my tongue, for little good comes of digging up the past.'

Master Nathaniel said nothing; he was evidently pondering her story.

'Well,' he said finally, 'everything you have told me has been very interesting – very interesting indeed. But whether it will lead to anything definite is another matter. All the evidence is purely circumstantial. However, I'm very grateful to you for having spoken to me as freely as you've done. And if I find out anything further I'll let you know. I shall be leaving Lud shortly, but I shall keep in touch with you. And, under the circumstances, perhaps it would be prudent to agree on some word or token by which you would recognize a messenger as really coming from me, for the fellow you knew as Pugwalker has not grown less cunning with advancing years – he's full of guile, and let him once get wind of what we're after, he'd be up to all sorts of tricks to make our plans miscarry. What shall the token be?'

Then his eyes began to twinkle; 'I've got it!' he cried. 'Just to give you a little lesson in swearing, which you say you dislike so much, we'll make it a good round oath. You'll know a messenger comes from me if he greets you with the words, *By the Sun, Moon and Stars and the Golden Apples of the West!*'

And he rubbed his hands in delight, and shouted with laughter. Master Nathaniel was a born tease.

'For shame, you saucy fellow!' dimpled Mistress Ivy. 'You're as bad as my poor Peppercorn. He used always . . .'

But even Master Nathaniel had had his fill of reminiscences. So he cut her short with a hearty good-bye, and renewed thanks for all she had told him.

But he turned back from the door to hold up his finger and say with mock solemnity, 'Remember, it's to be *By the Sun, Moon and Stars and the Golden Apples of the West!*'

# 19

## THE BERRIES OF MERCIFUL DEATH

Late into that night Master Nathaniel paced the floor of his pipe-room, trying to pierce through the intervening medium of the dry words of the Law and the vivider though less reliable one of Mistress Ivy's memory, and reach that old rustic tragedy, as it had been before the vultures of Time had left nothing of it but dry bones.

He felt convinced that Mistress Ivy's reconstruction was correct – as far as it went. The farmer had been poisoned, though not by osiers. But by what? And what had been the part played by Pugwalker, *alias* Endymion Leer? It was, of course, gratifying to his vanity that his instinctive identification of the two had proved correct. But how tantalizing it would be if this dead man's tale was to remain but a vague whisper, too low to be heard by the ear of the Law!

On his table was the slipper that Master Ambrose had facetiously suggested might be of use to him. He picked it up, and stared at it absently. Ambrose had said the sight of it had made Endymion Leer jump out of his skin, and that the reason was obvious. And yet those purple strawberries did not look like fairy fruit. Master Nathaniel had recently become but too familiar with the aspect of that fruit not to recognize it instantly, whatever its variety. Though he had never seen berries exactly like these, he was certain that they did not grow in Fairyland.

He walked across to his bookcase and took out a big volume bound in vellum. It was a very ancient illustrated herbal of the plants of Dorimare.

At first he turned its pages somewhat listlessly, as if he did not really expect to find anything of interest. Then suddenly he came on an illustration, underneath which was written THE BERRIES OF MERCIFUL DEATH. He gave a low whistle, and fetching the slipper laid it beside the picture. The painted berries and the embroidered ones were identical.

On the opposite page the berries were described in a style that a literary expert would have recognized as belonging to the Duke Aubrey period. The passage ran thus:—

THE BERRIES OF MERCIFUL DEATH

*These berries are wine-coloured, and crawl along the ground, and have the leaves of wild strawberries. They ripen during the first quarter of the harvest moon, and are only to be found in certain valleys of the West, and even there they grow but sparsely; and, for the sake of birds and children and other indiscreet lovers of fruit, it is well that such is the case, for they are a deadly and insidious poison, though very tardy in their action, often lying dormant in the blood for many days. Then the poison begins to speak in itchings of the skin, while the tongue, as though in punishment for the lies it may have told, becomes covered with black spots, so that it has the appearance of the shards of a ladybird, and this is the only warning to the victim that his end is approaching. For, if evil things ever partake of the blessed virtues, then we may say that this malign berry is mercifully cruel, in that it spares its victims belchings and retchings and fiery humours and racking colics. And, shortly before his end, he is overtaken by a pleasant drowsiness, yielding to which he falls into a peaceful sleep, which is his last. And now I will give you a receipt which, if you have no sin upon your conscience, and are at peace with the living and the dead, and have never killed a robin, nor robbed an orphan, nor destroyed the nest of a dream, it may be will prove an antidote to the poison – and may be it will not. This, then, is the receipt: Take one pint of salad oil and put it into a vial glass, but first wash it with rose-water, and marygold flower water, the flowers being gathered towards the West. Wash it till the oil comes white; then put it into the glass, and then put thereto the buds of Peonies, the flowers of Marygold and the flowers and tops of Shepherd's Thyme. The Thyme must be gathered near the side of a hill where Fairies are said to dance.*

Master Nathaniel laid down the book, and his eyes were more frightened than triumphant. There was something sinister in the silent language in which dead men told their tales – with sly malice embroidering them on old maids' canvas work, hiding them away in ancient books, written long long before they were born; and why were his ears so attuned to this dumb speech?

For him the old herbalist had been describing a murderer, subtle, sinister, mitigating dark deeds with mercy – a murderer, the touch of whose bloody hands was balm to the sick in body, and whose voice could rock haunted minds to sleep. And, as well, in the light of what he already knew, the old herbalist had told a story. A violent, cruel, reckless woman had wished to rid herself of her enemy by the first means that came to her hand – osiers, the sap of which produced an agonizing, cruel death. But her discreet though murderous lover took the osiers from her, and gave her instead the berries of merciful death.

The herbalist had proved beyond the shadow of a doubt that the villain of the story was Endymion Leer.

Yes, but how should he make the dead tell their tale loud enough to reach the ear of the Law?

In any case, he must leave Lud, and that quickly.

Why should he not visit the scene of this old drama, the widow Gibberty's farm? Perhaps he might there find witnesses who spoke a language understood by all.

The next morning he ordered a horse to be saddled, packed a few necessaries in a knapsack, and then he told Dame Marigold that, for the present, he could not stay in Lud. 'As for you,' he said, 'you had better move to Polydore's. For the moment I'm the most unpopular man in the town, and it would be just as well that they should think of you as Vigil's sister rather than as Chanticleer's wife.'

Dame Marigold's face was very pale that morning and her eyes were very bright. 'Nothing would induce me,' she said in a low voice, 'ever again to cross the threshold of Polydore's house. I shall never forgive him for the way he has treated you. No, I shall stay here – in *your* house. And,' she added, with a little scornful laugh, 'you needn't be anxious about me. I've never yet met a member of the lower classes that was a match for one of ourselves – they fall to heel as readily as a dog. I'm not a bit afraid of the mob, or anything they could do to me.'

Master Nathaniel chuckled: 'By the Sun, Moon and Stars!' he cried proudly, 'you're a chip off the old block, Marigold!'

'Well, don't stay too long away, Nat,' she said, 'or else when you come back you'll find that I've gone mad like everybody else, and am dancing as wildly as Mother Tibbs, and singing songs about Duke Aubrey!' and she smiled her charming crooked smile.

Then he went up to say good-bye to old Hempie.

'Well, Hempie,' he cried gaily. 'Lud's getting too hot for me. So I'm off with a knapsack on my back to seek my fortune, like the youngest son in your old stories. Will you wish me luck?'

There were tears in the old woman's eyes as she looked at him, and then she smiled.

'Why, Master Nat,' she cried, 'I don't believe you've felt so light-hearted since you were a boy! But these are strange times when a Chanticleer is chased out of Lud-in-the-Mist! And wouldn't I just like to give those Vigils and the rest of them a bit of my mind!' and her old eyes flashed. 'But don't you ever get down-hearted, Master Nat, and don't ever forget that there have always been Chanticleers in Lud-in-the-Mist, and that there always will be! But it beats me how you're to manage with only three pairs of stockings, and no one to mend them.'

'Well, Hempie,' he laughed, 'they say the Fairies are wonderfully neat-fingered, and, who knows, perhaps in my wanderings I may fall in with a fairy housewife who will darn my stockings for me,' and he brought out the forbidden word as lightly and easily as if it had been one in daily use.

About an hour after Master Nathaniel had ridden away Luke Hempen arrived at the house, wild-eyed, dishevelled, and with very startling news. But it was impossible to communicate it to Master Nathaniel, as he had left without telling anyone his destination.

# 20

## WATCHING THE COWS

In the interval between his two letters – the one to Hempie, and the one to Master Nathaniel – Luke decided that his vague suspicions had been groundless, for the days at the farm were buzzing by with a soothing hum like that of summer insects, and Ranulph was growing gay and sunburned.

Then towards autumn Ranulph had begun to wilt, and finally Luke overheard the strange conversation he had reported in his letter to Master Nathaniel, and once again the farm grew hateful to him, and he followed Ranulph as if he were his shadow and counted the hours for the order to come from Master Nathaniel bidding them return to Lud.

Perhaps you may remember that on his first evening at the farm Ranulph had wanted to join the children who watched the widow's cows at night, but it had evidently been nothing but a passing whim, for he did not express the wish again.

And then at the end of June – as a matter of fact it was Midsummer day – the widow had asked him if he would not like that night to join the little herdsmen. But towards evening had come a steady downfall of rain, and the plan had fallen through.

It was not alluded to again till the end of October, three or four days before Master Nathaniel left Lud-in-the-Mist. It had been a very mild autumn in the West and the nights were fresh rather than cold, and when, that evening, the little boys came knocking at the door for their bread and cheese, the widow began to jeer at Ranulph, in a hearty jovial way, for being town-bred and never having spent a night under the sky.

'Why don't you go tonight with the little herdsmen? You

wanted to when you first came here, and the Doctor said it would do you no harm.'

Now Luke was feeling particularly downcast that night; no answer had come from Master Nathaniel to his letter, though it was well over a week since he had written. He felt forlorn and abandoned, with a weight of responsibility too heavy for his shoulders, and he was certainly not going to add to that weight by allowing Ranulph to run the risk of catching a bad chill. And as well, any suggestion that came from the widow was greeted by him with suspicion.

'Master Ranulph,' he cried excitedly, 'I can't let you go. His Worship and my old auntie wouldn't like it, what with the nights getting damp and all. No, Master Ranulph, be a good little chap and go to your bed as usual.'

As he was speaking he caught Hazel's eye, and she gave him an almost imperceptible nod of approval.

But the widow cried, with a loud scornful laugh, in which Ranulph shrilly joined: 'Too damp, indeed! When we haven't had so much as a drop of rain these four weeks! Don't you let yourself be coddled, Master Ranulph. Young Hempen's nothing but an old maid in breeches. He's as bad as my Hazel, I've always said that if she doesn't die an old maid, it isn't that she wasn't born one!'

Hazel said nothing, but she fixed her eyes beseechingly on Luke.

But Ranulph, I fear, was a very spoiled little boy, and, into the bargain, he dearly loved annoying Luke; so he jumped up and down, shouting, 'Old maid Hempen! Old maid Hempen! I'm *going* – so there!'

'That's right, little master!' laughed the widow. 'You'll be a man before I am.'

And the three little herdsmen, who had been watching this scene with shy amusement, grinned from ear to ear.

'Do as you like, then,' said Luke sullenly, 'but I'm coming too. And, anyway, you must wrap up as warmly as you can.'

So they went upstairs to put on their boots and mufflers.

When they came down Hazel, with compressed lips and a little frown knitting her brows, gave them their rations of cheese and bread and honey, and then, with a furtive glance in the direction of the widow, who was standing with her back turned, talking to the little herdsmen, she slipped two sprigs of fennel into Luke's buttonhole. 'Try and get Master Ranulph to wear one of them,' she whispered.

This was not reassuring. But how is an undergardener, not yet turned eighteen, to curb the spoiled son of his master – especially when a strong-willed, elderly woman throws her weight into the other scale?

'Well, well,' said the widow, bustling up, 'it's high time you were off. You have a full three miles' walk before you.'

'Yes, yes, let's be off!' cried Ranulph excitedly; Luke felt it would be useless to protest further, so the little cavalcade dived into the moonlit night.

The world was looking very beautiful. At one end of the scale of darkness stood the pines, like rich black shadows; at the other end of the scale were the farm buildings, like white glimmering human masks. And in between these two extremes were all the various degrees of greyness – the shimmer of the Dapple that was more white than grey, and all the different trees – plane trees, liege-oaks, olives – and one could almost recognize their foliage by their lesser or greater degree of density.

On they trudged in silence, up the course of the Dapple – Luke too anxious and aggrieved to talk, Ranulph buried too deep in dreams, and the little herdsmen far too shy.

There were nothing but rough cattle paths in the valley – heavy enough going by day, and doubly so by night, and before they had yet gone half the way Ranulph's feet began to lag.

'Would you like to rest a bit and then go back?' asked Luke eagerly.

But Ranulph shook his head scornfully and mended his pace.

Nor did he allow himself to lag again till they reached their destination – a little oasis of rich pasturage, already on rising ground though still a mile or two away from the hills.

Once here – in their own kingdom, as it were – the little

herdsmen became lively and natural; laughing and chatting with Ranulph, as they set about repairing such breaches as had been made in the huts by the rough and tumble of twelve odd hours. Then there was wood to be collected, and a fire to be lit – and into these tasks Ranulph threw himself with a gay, though rather feverish, vigour.

At last they settled down to their long watch – squatting round the fire, and laughing for sheer love of adventure as good campaigners should; for were there not marching towards them some eight dark hours equipped with who could say what curious weapons from the rich arsenal of night and day?

The cattle crouched round them in soft shadowy clumps, placidly munching, and dreaming with wide-open eyes. The narrow zone of colour created by the firelight was like the planet Earth – a little freak of brightness in a universe of impenetrable shadows.

Suddenly Luke noticed that each of the three little herdsmen was, like himself, wearing a sprig of fennel.

'I say! Why are all you little chaps wearing fennel?' he blurted out.

They stared at him in amazement.

'But you be wearing a bit yourself, Master Hempen,' said Toby, the eldest.

'I know' – and he could not resist adding in an offhand tone – 'it was a present from a young lady. But do you always wear a bit in these parts?' he added.

'Always on *this* night of the year,' said the children. And as Luke looked puzzled, Toby cried in surprise, 'Don't you wear fennel in Lud on the last night of October?'

'No, we don't,' answered Luke, a little crossly, 'and why should we, I should like to know?'

'Why,' cried Toby in a shocked voice, 'because this is the night when the Silent People – the dead, you know – come back to Dorimare.'

Ranulph looked up quickly. But Luke scowled; he was sick to death of western superstitions, and into the bargain he was feeling frightened. He removed the second sprig of fennel given him by

Hazel from his button-hole, and holding it out to Ranulph, said, 'Here, Master Ranulph! Stick that in your hatband or somewhere.'

But Ranulph shook his head, 'I don't want any fennel, thank you, Luke,' he said. 'I'm not frightened.'

The children gazed at him in half-shocked admiration, and Luke sighed gloomily.

'Not frightened of . . . the Silent People?' queried Toby.

'No,' answered Ranulph curtly. And then he added, 'At least not tonight.'

'I'll wager the widow Gibberty, at any rate, isn't wearing any fennel,' said Luke, with a harsh laugh.

The children exchanged queer little glances and began to snigger. This aroused Luke's curiosity: 'Now then, out with it, youngsters! Why doesn't the widow Gibberty wear fennel?'

But their only answer was to nudge each other, and snigger behind their fingers.

This put Luke on his mettle. 'Look here, you bantams,' he cried, 'don't you forget that you've got the High Seneschal's son here, and if you know anything about the widow that's . . . well, that's a bit fishy, it's your duty to let me know. If you don't, you may find yourselves in gaol some day. So you just spit it out!' and he glared at them as fiercely as his kindly china-blue eyes would allow.

They began to look scared. 'But the widow doesn't know we've seen anything . . . and if she found out, and that we'd been blabbing, oh my! wouldn't we catch it!' cried Toby, and his eyes grew round with terror at the mere thought.

'No, you won't catch it. I'll give you my word,' said Luke. 'And if you've really anything worth telling, the Seneschal will be very grateful, and each of you may find yourselves with more money in your pockets than your three fathers put together have ever had in all their lives. And, anyhow, to begin with, if you'll tell me what you know, you can toss up for this knife, and there's not a finer one to be found in all Lud,' and he waved before their dazzled eyes his greatest treasure, a magnificent six-bladed knife, given him one Yule-tide by Master Nathaniel, with whom he had always been a favourite. At the sight of this marvel of cutlery, the little boys proved venal, and in voices scarcely above a whisper and with frequent frightened glances over their shoulders, as if the widow might be lurking in the shadows listening to them, they told their story.

One night, just before dawn, a cow called Cornflower, from the unusually blue colour of her hide, who had recently been added to the herd, suddenly grew restless and began to *moo*, the strange *moo* of blue cows that was like the cooing of doves, and then rose to her feet and trotted away into the darkness. Now Cornflower was a very valuable cow and the widow had given them special injunctions to look after her, so Toby, leaving the other two to mind the rest of the herd, dashed after her into the thinning darkness and though she had got a good start of him was able to keep in her track by the tinkling of her bell. Finally he came on her standing at the brink of the Dapple and nozzling the water. He went close up to her and found that she had got her teeth into something beneath the surface of the stream and was tearing at it in intense excitement. Just then who should drive up in a cart but the widow and Dr Endymion Leer. They appeared much annoyed at finding Toby, but they helped him to get Cornflower away from the water. Bits of straw were hanging from her mouth and it was stained with juices of a colour he had never seen before. The widow then told him to go back to his companions, and said she would herself take Cornflower back to the herd in the morning. And, to account for her sudden appearance on the scene, she said she had come with the doctor to try and catch a very rare fish that only rose to the surface an hour before sunrise. 'But you see,' went on Toby, 'my dad's a great fisherman, and often takes me out with him, but he'd never told me about this fish in the Dapple that can only be caught before sunrise, and I thought I'd just like to have a peep at it. So instead of going back to the others right away, I hid, I did, behind some trees. And they took some nets, they did, out of the cart, but it wasn't fish they drew up in them . . . no it wasn't.' He was suddenly seized with embarrassment, and he and his two little friends again began to snigger.

'Out with it!' cried Luke impatiently. '*What* was in their nets? You'll not get the knife for only half a story, you know.'

'You say, Dorian,' said Toby bashfully, nudging the second eldest boy; but Dorian, too, would only giggle and hang his head.

'I don't mind saying!' cried Peter, the youngest, valiantly. 'It was *fairy fruit* – that's what it was!'

Luke sprang to his feet. 'Busty Bridget!' he exclaimed in a horrified voice. Ranulph began to chuckle. 'Didn't you guess right away what it was, Luke?' he asked.

'Yes,' went on Peter, much elated by the effect his words had produced, 'it was wicker baskets all full of fairy fruit, I know, because Cornflower had torn off the top of one of them.'

'Yes,' interrupted Toby, beginning to think that little Peter had stolen enough of his thunder, 'she had torn off the top of one of the baskets, and I've never seen fruit like it; it was as if coloured stars had fallen from the sky into the grass, and were making all the valley bright, and Cornflower, she was eating as if she would never stop . . . more like a bee among flowers, she was, than a common cow. And the widow and the doctor, though of course they were put out, they couldn't help laughing to see her. And her milk the next morning – oh my! it tasted of roses and shepherd's thyme, but she never came back to the herd, for the widow sold her to a farmer who lived twenty miles away, and . . .'

But Luke could contain himself no longer. 'You little rascals!' he cried, 'to think of all the trouble there is in Lud just now, and the magistrates and the town guard racking their brains to find out how the stuff gets across the border, and three little bantams like you knowing all about it, and not telling a soul! Why did you keep it to yourselves like that?'

'We were frightened of the widow,' said Toby sheepishly. 'You won't tell that we've blabbed,' he added in an imploring voice.

'No, I'll see that you don't get into trouble,' said Luke. 'Here's the knife, and a coin to toss up for it with . . . Toasted Cheese! A nice place this, we've come to! Are you sure, young Toby, it was Dr Leer you saw?' Toby nodded his head emphatically. 'Aye, it was Dr Leer and no mistake – here's my hand on it.' And he stuck out a brown little paw.

'Well, I'm blessed! *Dr Leer!*' exclaimed Luke; and Ranulph gave a little mocking laugh.

Luke fell into a brown study; surprise, indignation, and pleasant visions of himself swaggering in Lud, praised and flattered by all as the man who had run the smugglers to earth, chasing each other across the surface of his brain. And, in the light of Toby's story, could it be that the stranger whose mysterious conversation with the widow he had overheard was none other than the popular, kindly doctor, Endymion Leer? It seemed almost incredible.

But on one thing he was resolved – for once he would assert himself, and Ranulph should not spend another night at the widow Gibberty's farm.

Toby won the toss and pocketed the knife with a grin of satisfaction, and by degrees the talk became as flickering and intermittent as the light of the dying fire, which they were too idle to feed with sticks; and finally it was quenched in silence, and they yielded to the curious drugged sensation that comes from being out of doors and wide-awake at night.

It was as if the earth had been translated to the sky, and they had been left behind in chaos, and were gazing up at its towns and beasts and heroes flattened out into constellations and looking like the stippled pictures in a neolithic cave. And the Milky Way was the only road visible in the universe.

Now and then a toad harped on its one silvery note, and from time to tame a little breeze would spring up and then die down.

Suddenly Ranulph broke the silence with the startling question, 'How far is it from here to Fairyland?'

The little boys nudged one another and again began to snigger behind their hands.

'For shame, Master Ranulph!' cried Luke indignantly, 'talking like that before youngsters!'

'But I want to *know*!' said Ranulph petulantly.

'Tell what your old granny used to say, Dorian,' giggled Toby.

And Dorian was finally persuaded to repeat the old saying: 'A thousand leagues by the great West Road and ten by the Milky Way.'

Ranulph sprang to his feet, and with rather a wild laugh, he cried, 'Let's have a race to Fairyland. I bet it will be me that gets there first. One, two, three – and *away*!'

And he would actually have plunged off into the darkness, had not the little boys, half shocked, half admiring, flung themselves on him and dragged him back.

'There's an imp of mischief got into you tonight, Master Ranulph,' growled Luke.

'You shouldn't joke about things like that . . . specially tonight, Master Chanticleer,' said Toby gravely.

'You're right there, young Toby,' said Luke, 'I only wish he had half your sense.'

'It was just a bit of fun, wasn't it, Master Chanticleer? You didn't *really* want us to race to . . . yonder?' asked little Peter, peering through the darkness at Ranulph with scared eyes.

'Of course it was only fun,' said Luke.

But Ranulph said nothing.

Again they lapsed into silence. And all round them, subject to blind taciturn laws, and heedless of man, myriads of things were happening, in the grass, in the trees, in the sky.

Luke yawned and stretched himself. 'It must be getting near dawn,' he said.

They had successfully doubled the dangerous cape of midnight, and he began to feel secure of safely weathering what remained of their dark voyage.

It was the hour when night-watchers begin to idealize their bed, and, with Sancho Panza, to bless the man who invented it. They shuddered, and drew their cloaks closer round their shoulders.

Then, something happened. It was not so much a modification of the darkness, as a sigh of relief, a slight relaxing of tension, so that one *felt*, rather than saw, that the night had suddenly lost a shade of its density . . . ah! yes; there! between these two shoulders of the hills she is bleeding to death.

At first the spot was merely a degree less black than the rest of the sky. Then it turned grey, then yellow, then red. And the earth was undergoing the same transformation. Here and there patches of greyness broke out in the blackness of the grass, and after a few seconds one saw that they were clumps of flowers. Then the greyness became filtered with a delicate sea-green; and next, one realized that the grey-green belonged to the foliage, against which the petals were beginning to show white – and then pink, or yellow, or blue; but a yellow like that of primroses, a blue like that of certain wild periwinkles, colours so elusive that one suspects them to be due to some passing accident of light, and that, were one to pick the flower, it would prove to be pure white.

Ah, there can be no doubt of it now! The blues and yellows are real and perdurable. Colour is steadily flowing through the veins of the earth, and we may take heart, for she will soon be restored to life again. But had we kept one eye on the sky we should have noticed that a star was quenched with every flower that reappeared on earth.

And now the valley is again red and gold with vineyards, the hills are clothed with pines, and the Dapple is rosy.

Then a cock crowed, and another answered it, and then another – a ghostly sound, which, surely, did not belong to the smiling, triumphant earth, but rather to one of those distant dying stars.

But what had taken Ranulph? He had sprang to his feet and was standing motionless, a strange light in his eyes.

And then again, from a still more distant star, it seemed, another cock crowed, and another answered it.

'The piper! The piper!' cried Ranolph in a loud triumphant voice. And, before his astonished companions could get to their feet, he was dashing up one of the bridle-paths towards the Debatable Hills.

# 21
## THE OLD GOATHERD

For a few seconds they stood petrified, and then Luke was seized with panic, and, calling to the little boys to stay where they were, dashed off in pursuit.

Up the path he pounded, from time to time shouting angrily to Ranulph to come back, but the distance between them grew ever wider.

Luke's ears began to sing and his brain to turn to fire, and he seemed to lose all sense of reality – it was not on the earth that he was running, but through the airless deserts of space.

He could not have said how long he struggled on, for he who runs hard leaves time behind as well as space. But finally his strength gave way, and he fell, breathless and exhausted, to the ground.

When he had sufficiently recovered to think of starting off again the diminishing speck that had been Ranulph had completely vanished.

Poor Luke began to swear – at both Ranulph and himself.

Just then he heard a tinkle of bells, and down the bridle-path came a herd of goats and a very ancient herdsman – to judge, at least, from his bowed walk, for his face was hidden by a hood.

When he had got up to Luke, he stood still, leaning heavily on his stick, and peered down at him from underneath the overhanging flap of his hood with a pair of very bright eyes.

'You've been running hard, young master, by the looks of ye,' he said, in a quavering voice. 'You be the second young fellow as what I've seen running this morning.'

'The second?' cried Luke eagerly. 'Was the other a little lad of about twelve years old with red hair, in a green leathern jerkin embroidered in gold?'

'Well, his hair was red and no mistake, though as to the jerkin . . .' And here he was seized with a violent attack of coughing, and it took all Luke's patience not to grab him by the shoulders and shake the words out of him.

'Though as to the jerkin – my eyes not being as sharp as they once were . . .'

'Oh! never mind about the jerkin,' cried Luke. 'Did you stop and speak to him?'

'But about that jerkin – you do cut an old man short, you do . . . it might have been green, but then again it might have been yellow. But the young gentleman what I saw was not the one as *you're* after.'

'How do you know?'

'Why, because he was the Seneschal's son – the one *I* saw,' said the old man proudly, as if the fact put him at once into a superior position to Luke.

'But it's the Seneschal's son – Master Ranulph Chanticleer, that 'I'm after, too!' cried Luke, eagerly. 'How long is it since you saw him? I *must* catch up with him.'

'You'll not do that, on your two feet,' said the goatherd calmly. 'That young gentleman, and his yellow jerkin and his red hair, must be well on the way to Moongrass by now.'

'To Moongrass?' And Luke stared at him in amazement.

'Aye, to Moongrass, where the cheeses come from. You see it was this way. I'm goatherd to the Lud Yeomanry what the Seneschal has sent to watch the border to keep out you know what. And who should come running into their camp about half an hour ago with his red jerkin and his green hair but your young gentleman. "Halt!" cries the Yeoman on guard. "Let me pass. I'm young Master Chanticleer," cries he. "And where are you bound for?" cries the Yeoman. "For Fairyland," says he. And then didn't they all laugh! And the little chap flew into quite a rage, and said he was off to Fairyland, and no one should stop him. And, of course, that just made them laugh all the more. But though they wouldn't let him go to Fairyland, the young rascal . . .' And here the old man was seized with a paroxysm of wheezy laughter which brought on another bout of coughing.

'Well, as I was saying,' he went on, when he had recovered, 'they wouldn't let him through to Fairyland, but they said they would ride back with him where he came from. "No, you won't," says he; "my dad," says he, "don't want me to go back there, never any more." And he whisks out a letter signed by the Seneschal, bidding him leave the widow Gibberty's farm, where he was staying, and go straight off to Farmer Jellygreen's at Moongrass. So one of the Yeomen saddled his horse, and the youngster got up behind him, and they set off for Moongrass by one of the cattle-paths running northeast, which comes out at about the middle of the road between Swan and Moongrass. So that's that, my young fellow.'

In his relief Luke tossed his cap into the air. 'The young rascal!' he cried joyfully; 'fancy his never having told me he'd got a letter from his Worship, and me expecting that letter for the last three days, and getting stomach-ache with worry at it's not coming! And saying he was off to a certain place, too! A nice fright he's given me. But thank'ee, gaffer, thank'ee kindly. And here's something for you to drink the health of Master Ranulph Chanticleer,' and with a heart as light as a bird's, he began to retrace his steps down the valley.

But what was that faint sound behind him? It sounded suspiciously like the *Ho, ho, hoh!* of that impudent Willy Wisp, who for a short time, had been one of his Worship's grooms.

He stopped, and looked round. No one was visible except the old goatherd in the distance, leaning on his stick. What he had heard could have been nothing but the distant tinkle of the goat bells.

When he reached the farm, he found it in a tumult. The little boys had frightened Hazel out of her wits, and confirmed her worst fears by the news that 'Master Ranulph had run away towards the hills, and that Master Hempen had run after him.'

'Granny!' cried Hazel, wringing her hands, 'a messenger must be sent off post-haste to the Seneschal!'

'Stuff and nonsense!' cried the widow, angrily. 'You mind your own business, miss! Long before any messenger could reach Lud, the lads will be back safe and sound. Towards the hills, indeed! That Luke Hempen is a regular old woman. It's just a bit of Master Ranulph's fun. He's hiding behind a tree, and will jump out on them with a "Boo!" Never in my life have I heard so much fuss about nothing.' And then, turning to the farm-servants, who were clustering round the children with scared, excited eyes, she bade them go about their business, and let her hear no more nonsense.

Her words sounded like good sense, but, for all that, they did not convince Hazel. Her deep distrust of the widow was almost as old as herself, and her instinct had told her for some time that the widow was hostile to Ranulph.

Never for a moment did Hazel forget that *she*, not the widow, was the rightful owner of the farm. Should she for once assert her position, and, in direct defiance of the widow, report what had happened to the law-man of the district and send a messenger to Master Nathaniel?

But, as everybody knows, legal rights can be but weaklings – puny little child princes, cowed by their bastard uncles, Precedent and Seniority.

No, she must wait till she was of age, or married, or . . . was there *any* change of condition that could alter her relations with the widow, and destroy the parasite growth of sullen docility which, for as long as she could remember, had rotted her volition and warped her actions?

Hazel clenched her fists and set her teeth . . . *She would assert herself! – she would!* . . . Now, at once? Why not give them, say, till noon, to come back? Yes, she would give them till noon.

But, before then, a rather shamefaced Luke arrived with his confession that Master Ranulph had made proper fools of them.

'So, Miss Hazel, if you'll give me a bite of something, and lend me a horse, I'll go after the young scamp to Moongrass. To think of his giving us the slip like that and never having told me he'd heard from his father! And there was me expecting a letter from his Worship every day, telling us to leave at once, and . . .'

Hazel raised her eyebrows. 'You were expecting a letter ordering you to leave us? How was that?'

Luke turned red, and mumbled something inaudible. Hazel stared at him for a few seconds in silence, and then she said quietly: 'I'm afraid you were wise if you asked the Seneschal to remove Master Ranulph.'

He gave her a shrewd glance. 'Yes . . . I fear this is no place for Master Ranulph. But if you'd excuse me being so bold, miss, I'd like to give you a word of warning – don't you trust that Endymion Leer further than you see him, and don't you ever let your Granny take you out *fishing*!'

'Thank you, Master Hempen, but I am quite able to look after myself,' said Hazel haughtily. And then an anxious look came into her eyes. 'I hope – oh! I hope that you'll find Master Ranulph safe and sound at Moongrass! It's all so . . . well, so very strange. That old goatherd, who do you suppose he was? One meets strange people near the Elfin Marches. You'll let me know if all is well . . . won't you?'

Luke promised. Hazel's words had damped his spirits and brought back all his anxiety, and the fifteen miles to Moongrass, in spite of a good horse, seemed interminable.

Alas! there was no Ranulph at the Jellygreens' farm; but, to Luke's bewilderment, it turned out that the farmer had been expecting him, as he had, a few days previously, received a letter from Master Nathaniel, from which it was clear that he imagined his son was already at Moongrass. So there was nothing for Luke but, with a heavy heart, to start off the next morning for Lud, where, as we have seen, he arrived a few hours after Master Nathaniel had left it.

# 22

## WHO IS PORTUNUS?

About half-way to Swan, Master Nathaniel, having tethered his horse to a tree, was reclining drowsily under the shade of another. It was midday, and the further west he rode the warmer it grew; it was rather as if he were riding backward through the months.

Suddenly he was aroused by a dry little laugh, and looking round, he saw crouching beside him, an odd-looking old man, with very bright eyes.

'By my Great-aunt's rump, and who may *you* be?' enquired Master Nathaniel testily.

The old man shut his eyes, gulped several times, and replied:

*'Who are you? Who is me?*
*Answer my riddle and come and see,'*

and then he stamped impatiently, as if that had not been what he had wished to say.

'Some cracked old rustic, I suppose,' thought Master Nathaniel, and closed his eyes; in the hopes that when the old fellow saw he was not inclined for conversation he would go away.

But the unwelcome visitor continued to crouch beside him, now and then giving him little jogs in the elbow, which was very irritating when one happened to be hot and tired and longing for forty winks.

'What are you doing?' cried Master Nathaniel irritably.

*'I milk blue ewes; I reap red flowers,*
*I weave the story of dead hours,'*

answered the old man.

'Oh, do you? Well, I wish you'd go now, this moment, and milk your red ewes . . . I want to go to sleep,' and he pulled his hat further down over his eyes and pretended to snore.

But suddenly he sprang to his feet with a yap of pain. The old man had prodded him in his belly, and was standing looking at him out of his startlingly bright eyes, with his head slightly on one side.

'Don't you try that on, old fellow!' cried Master Nathaniel angrily. 'You're a nuisance, that's what *you* are. Why can't you leave me alone?'

The old man pointed eagerly at the tree, making little inarticulate sounds; it was as if a squirrel or a bird had been charged with some message that they could not deliver.

Then he crept up to him, put his mouth to his ear, and whispered, 'What is it that's a tree, and yet not a tree, a man and yet not a man, who is dumb and yet can tell secrets, who has no arms and yet can strike?'

Then he stepped back a few paces as if he wished to observe the impression his words had produced, and stood rubbing his hands and cackling gleefully.

'I suppose I must humour him,' thought Master Nathaniel; so he said good-naturedly, 'Well, and what's the answer to your riddle, eh?'

But the old man seemed again to have lost the power of articulate speech, and could only reiterate eagerly, 'Dig . . . dig . . . dig.'

' "dig, dig, dig." . . . So that's the answer, is it? Well, I'm afraid I can't stay here the whole afternoon trying to guess your riddles. If you've got anything to tell me, cant you say it a bit plainer?'

Suddenly he remembered the old superstition that when the Silent People returned to Dorimare they could only speak in riddles and snatches of rhyme. He looked at the old man searchingly. 'Who are you?' he said.

But the answer was the same as before. 'Dig . . . dig . . . dig.'

'Try again. Perhaps after a bit the words will come more easily,' said Master Nathaniel. 'You are trying to tell me your name.'

The old man shut his eyes tight, took a long breath, and,

evidently making a tremendous effort, brought out very slowly, 'Seize – your – op-por-tun-us. Dig . . . dig. Por-tun-us is my name.'

'Well, you've got it out at last. So your name is Portunus, is it?'

But the old man stamped his foot impatiently. 'Hand! hand!' he cried.

'Is it that you want to shake hands with me, old fellow?' asked Master Nathaniel.

But the old man shook his head peevishly. 'Farm hand,' he managed to bring out. 'Dig . . . dig.'

And then he lapsed into doggerel:

*'Dig and delve, delve and dig,*
*Harness the mare to the farmer's gig.'*

Finally Master Nathaniel gave up trying to get any sense out of him and untethered his horse. But when he tried to mount, the old man seized the stirrup and looking up at him imploringly, repeated 'Dig . . . dig . . . dig.' And Master Nathaniel was obliged to shake him off with some roughness. And even after he had left him out of sight he could hear his voice in the distance, shouting, 'Dig . . . dig.'

'I wonder what the old fellow was trying to tell me,' said Master Nathaniel to himself.

On the morning of the following day he arrived at the village of Swan-on-the-Dapple.

Here the drama of autumn had only just reached its gorgeous climax, and the yellow and scarlet trees were flaming out their silent stationary action against the changeless chorus of pines, dark green against the distant hills.

'By the Golden Apples of the West!' muttered Master Nathaniel, 'I'd no idea those accursed hills were so near. I'm glad Ranulph's safe away.'

Having inquired his way to the Gibbertys' farm, he struck off the high road into the valley – and very lovely it was looking in its autumn colouring. The vintage was over, and the vines were now golden and red. Some of the narrow oblong leaves of the wild cherry had kept their bottle-green, while others, growing on the same twig, had turned to salmon-pink, and the mulberries alternated between canary-yellow and grass-green. The mountain ash had turned a fiery rose (more lovely, even, than had been its scarlet berries) and often an olive grew beside it, as if ready, lovingly, to quench its fire in its own tender grey. The birches twinkled and quivered, as if each branch were a golden divining rod trembling to secret water; and the path was strewn with olives, looking like black oblong dung. It was one of those mysterious autumn days that are intensely bright though the sun is hidden; and when one looked at these lambent trees one could almost fancy them the source of the light flooding the valley.

From time to time a tiny yellow butterfly would flit past, like a little yellow leaf shed by one of the birches; and now and then one of the bleeding, tortured looking liege-oaks would drop an acorn, with a little flop – just to remind you, as it were, that it was leading its own serene, vegetable life, oblivious of the agony ascribed to it by the fevered fancy of man.

Not a soul did Master Nathaniel pass after he had left the village, though from time to time he saw in the distance labourers following the plough through the vineyards, and their smocks provided the touch of blue that turns a picture into a story; there was blue smoke, too, to tell of human habitations; and an occasional cock strutting up and down in front of one of the red vines, like a salesman before his wares, flaunting, by way of advertisement, a crest of the same material as the vine leaves, but of a more brilliant hue; and in the distance were rushes, stuck up in sheaves to dry, and glimmering with the faint, whitish, pinky-grey of faraway fruit trees in blossom.

While, as if the eye had not enough to feed on in her own domain, the sounds, even, of the valley were pictorial – a tinkling of distant bells, conjuring up herds of goats; the ominous, melancholy roar which tells that somewhere a waggoner is goading on his oxen; and the distant bark of dogs that paints a picture of homesteads and sunny porches.

As Master Nathaniel jogged leisurely along, his thoughts turned to the farmer Gibberty, who many a time must have jogged along this path, in just such a way, and seen and heard the very same things that he was seeing and hearing now.

Yes, the farmer Gibberty had once been a real living man, like himself. And so had millions of others, whose names he had never heard. And one day he himself would be a prisoner, confined between the walls of other people's memory. And then he would cease even to be that, and become nothing but a few words cut in stone. What would these words be, he wondered.

A sudden longing seized him to hold Ranulph again in his arms. How pleasant would have been the thought that he was waiting to receive him at the farm!

But he must be nearing his journey's end, for in the distance he could discern the figure of a woman, leisurely scrubbing her washing on one of the sides of a stone trough.

'I wonder if that's the widow,' thought Master Nathaniel. And a slight shiver went down his spine.

But as he came nearer the washerwoman proved to be quite a young girl.

He decided she must be the granddaughter, Hazel; and so she was.

He drew up his horse beside her and asked if this were the widow Gibberty's farm.

'Yes, sir,' she answered shortly, with that half-frightened, half-defiant look that was so characteristic of her.

'Why, then, I've not been misdirected. But though they told me I'd find a thriving farm and a fine herd of cows, the fools forgot to mention that the farmer was a rose in petticoats,' and he winked jovially.

Now this was not Master Nathaniel's ordinary manner with young ladies, which, as a matter of fact, was remarkably free from flirtatious facetiousness. But he had invented a rôle to play at the farm, and was already beginning to identify himself with it.

As it turned out, this opening compliment was a stroke of luck. For Hazel bitterly resented that she was not recognized as the lawful owner of the farm, and Master Nathaniel's greeting of her as the farmer thawed her coldness into dimples.

'If you've come to see over the farm, I'm sure we'll be very pleased to show you everything,' she said graciously.

'Thank'ee, thank'ee kindly. I'm a cheesemonger from Lud-in-the-Mist. And there's no going to sleep quietly behind one's counter these days in trade, if one's to keep one's head above water. It's competition, missy, competition that keeps old fellows like me awake. Why, I can remember when there weren't more than six cheesemongers in the whole of Lud; and now there's as many in my street alone. So I thought I'd come myself and have a look round and see where I could get the best dairy produce. There's nothing like seeing for oneself.'

And here he launched into an elaborate and gratuitous account of all the other farms he had visited on his imaginary tour of inspection. But the one that had pleased him best, he said, had been that of a very old friend of his – and he named the farmer near Moongrass with whom, presumably, Ranulph and Luke were now staying.

Here Hazel looked up eagerly, and, in rather an unsteady voice, asked if he'd seen two lads there – a big one, and a little one who was the son of the Seneschal

'Do you mean little Master Ranulph Chanticleer and Luke Hempen? Why, of course I saw them! It was they who told me to come along here . . . and very grateful I am to them, for I have found something well worth looking at.'

A look of indescribable relief flitted over Hazel's face.

'Oh . . . oh! I'm so *glad* you saw them,' she faltered.

'Aha! My friend Luke has evidently been making good use of his time – the young dog!' thought Master Nathaniel; and he proceeded to retail a great many imaginary sayings and doings of Luke at his new abode.

Hazel was soon quite at home with the jovial, facetious old cheesemonger. She always preferred elderly men to young ones, and was soon chatting away with the abandon sometimes observable when naturally confiding people, whom circumstances have made suspicious, find someone whom they think they can trust; and Master Nathaniel, was, of course, drinking in every word and longing to be in her shoes.

'But, missy, it seems all work and no play!' he cried at last 'Do you get no frolics and junketings?'

'Sometimes we dance of an evening, when old Portunus is here,' she answered.

'Portunus?' he cried sharply. 'Who's he?'

But this question froze her back into reserve. 'An old weaver with a fiddle,' she answered stiffly.

'A bit doited?'

Her only answer was to look at him suspiciously and say, 'Do you know Portunus, sir?'

'Well, I believe I met him – about half-way between here and Lud. The old fellow seemed to have something on his mind, but couldn't get it out – I've known many a parrot that talked better than he.'

'Oh, I've often thought that, too! That he'd something on his mind, I mean,' cried Hazel on another wave of confidence. 'It's as if he were trying hard to tell one something. And he often follows me as if he wanted me to do something for him. And I sometimes think I should try and help him and not be so harsh with him – but he just gives me the creeps, and I can't help it.'

'He gives you the creeps, does he?'

'That he does!' she cried with a little shiver. 'To see him gorging himself with green fruit! It isn't like a human being the way he does it – it's like an insect or a bird. And he's like a cat, too, in the way he always follows about the folk that don't like him. Oh, he's *nasty!* And he's spiteful, too, and mischievous. But maybe that's not to be wondered at, if . . .' and she broke off abruptly.

Master Nathaniel gave her a keen look. 'If what?' he said.

'Oh, well – just silly talk of the country people,' said Hazel evasively.

'That he's – er, for instance, one of what you call the Silent People?'

'How did you know?' And Hazel looked at him suspiciously.

'Oh, I guessed. You see, I've heard a lot of that sort of talk since I've been in the west. Well, the old fellow certainly seemed to have something he wanted to tell me, but I can't say he was very explicit. He kept saying, over and over again, "Dig, dig." '

'Oh, that's his great word,' cried Hazel. 'The old women round about say that he's trying to tell one his name. You see, they think that . . . well, that he's a dead man come back and that when he was on earth he was a labourer, by name Diggory Carp.'

'Diggory Carp?' cried Master Nathaniel sharply.

Hazel looked at him in surprise. 'Did you know him, sir?' she asked.

'No, no; not exactly. But I seem to have heard the name somewhere. Though I dare say in these parts it's a common enough one. Well, and what do they say about this Diggory Carp?'

Hazel looked a little uneasy. 'They don't say much, sir – to me. I sometimes think there must have been some mystery about him. But I know that he was a merry, kind, sort of man, well liked all round, and a rare fiddler. But he came to a sad end, though I never heard what happened exactly. And they say,' and here she lowered her voice mysteriously, 'that once a man joins the Silent People he becomes mischievous and spiteful, however good-natured he may have been when he was alive. And if he'd been unfairly treated, as they say he was, it would make him all the more spiteful, I should think. I often think he's got something he wants to tell us, and I sometimes wonder if it's got anything to do with the old stone herm in our orchard . . . he's so fond of dancing round it.'

'Really? And where is this old herm? I want to see all the sights of the country, you know; get my money's worth of travel!' And Master Nathaniel donned again the character of the cheerful cheesemonger, which, in the excitement of the last few minutes, he had, unwillingly, sloughed.

As they walked to the orchard, which was some distance from the washing trough, Hazel said, nervously:

'Perhaps you haven't heard, sir, but I live here with my granny; at least, she isn't my real granny, though I call her so. And . . .

and . . . well, she seems fond of old Portunus, and perhaps it would be as well not to mention to her that you had met him.'

'Very well; I won't mention him to her . . . at present.' And he gave rather a grim little smile.

Though the orchard had been stripped of its fruit, what with the red and yellow leaves, and the marvellous ruby-red of the lateral branches of the peach trees there was colour enough in the background of the old grey herm, and, in addition, there twined around him the scarlet and gold of a vine.

'I often think he's the spirit of the farm,' said Hazel shyly, looking to see if Master Nathaniel was admiring her old stone friend. To her amazement, however, as soon as his eyes fell on it he clapped his hand against his thigh, and burst out laughing.

'By the Sun, Moon and Stars!' he cried, 'here's the answer to Portunus' riddle: "the tree yet not a tree, the man yet not a man," ' and he repeated to Hazel the one consecutive sentence that Portunus had managed to enunciate.

' "Who has no arms and yet can strike, who is dumb and yet can tell secrets," ' she repeated after him. 'Can you strike and tell secrets, old friend?' she asked whimsically, stroking the grey lichened stone. And then she blushed and laughed as if to apologize for this exhibition of childishness.

With country hospitality Hazel presumed that their uninvited guest had come to spend several days at the farm, and accordingly she had his horse taken to the stables and ordered the best room to be prepared for his use.

The widow, too, gave him a hearty welcome, when he came down to the midday meal in the big kitchen.

When they had been a few minutes at table, Hazel said, 'Oh, granny, this gentleman has just come from the farm near Moongrass, where little Master Chanticleer and young Hempen have gone. And he says they were both of them blooming, and sent us kind messages.'

'Yes,' said Master Nathaniel cheerfully, ever ready to start romancing, 'my old friend the farmer is delighted with them.

The talk in Lud was that little Chanticleer had been ill, but all I can say is, you must have done wonders for him – his face is as round and plump as a Moongrass cheese.'

'Well, I'm glad you're pleased with the young gentleman's looks, sir,' said the widow in a gratified voice. But in her eyes there was the gleam of a rather disquieting smile.

Dinner over, the widow and Hazel had to go and attend to their various occupations, and Master Nathaniel went and paced up and down in front of the house, thinking.

Over and over again his thoughts returned to the odd old man, Portunus.

Was it possible that he had really once been Diggory Carp, and that he had returned to his old haunts to try and give a message?

It was characteristic of Master Nathaniel that the metaphysical possibilities of the situation occupied him before the practical ones. If Portunus were, indeed, Diggory Carp, then these stubble-fields and vineyards, these red and golden trees, would be robbed of their peace and stability. For he realized at last that the spiritual balm he had always found in silent things was simply the assurance that the passions and agonies of man were without meaning, roots, or duration – no more part of the permanent background of the world than the curls of blue smoke that from time to time were wafted through the valley from the autumn bonfires of weeds and rubbish, and that he could see winding like blue wraiths in and out of the foliage of the trees.

Yes, their message, though he had never till now heard it distinctly, had always been that Fairyland was nothing but delusion – there was life and death, and that was all. And yet, had their message always comforted him? There had been times when he had shuddered in the company of the silent things.

'Aye, aye,' he murmured dreamily to himself, and then he sighed.

But he had yielded long enough to vain speculations – there were things to be *done*. Whether Portunus were the ghost of Diggory Carp or merely a doited old weaver, he evidently knew something that he wanted to communicate – and it was connected with the orchard herm. Of course, it might have nothing whatever to do with the murder of the farmer Gibberty, but with the memory of the embroidered slipper fresh in his mind, Master Nathaniel felt it would be rank folly to neglect a possible clue.

He went over in his mind all the old man's words. 'Dig, dig,' . . . that word had been the ever recurring burden.

Then he had a sudden flash of inspiration – why should not the word be taken in its primary meaning? Why, instead of the first syllable of Diggory Carp, should it not be merely an order to dig . . . with a spade or a shovel? In that case it was clear that the place to dig in was under the herm. And he decided that he would do so as soon as an opportunity presented itself.

# 23

## THE NORTHERN FIRE-BOX AND DEAD MEN'S TALES

That night Hazel could not get to sleep. Perhaps this was due to having noticed something that afternoon that made her vaguely uneasy. The evenings were beginning to be chilly, and, shortly before supper, she had gone up to Master Nathaniel's room to light his fire. She found the widow and one of the maidservants there before her, and, to her surprise, they had brought down from the attic an old charcoal stove that had lain there unused for years, for Dorimare was a land of open fires, and stoves were practically unknown. The widow had brought the stove to the farm on her marriage, for, on her mother's side, she had belonged to a race from the far North.

On Hazel's look of surprise, she had said casually, 'The logs are dampish to-day, and I thought this would make our guest cosier.'

Now Hazel knew that the wood was not in the least damp: how could it be, as it had not rained for days? But that this should have made her uneasy was a sign of her deep instinctive distrust of her grandfather's widow.

Perhaps the strongest instinct in Hazel was that of hospitality – that all should be well, physically and morally, with the guests under the roof that she never forgot was hers, was a need in her much more pressing than any welfare of her own.

Meanwhile, Master Nathaniel, somewhat puzzled by the outlandish apparatus that was warming his room, had got into bed. He did not immediately put out his candle; he wished to think. For being much given to reverie, when he wanted to follow the sterner path of consecutive thought, he liked to have some tangible object on which to focus his eye, a visible goal, as it were, to keep his feet from straying down the shadowy paths that he so much preferred.

Tonight it was the fine embossed ceiling on which he fixed his eye – the same ceiling at which Ranulph used to gaze when he had slept in this room. On a ground of a rich claret colour patterned with azure arabesques, knobs of a dull gold were embossed, and at the four corners clustered bunches of grapes and scarlet berries in stucco. And though time had dulled their colour and robbed the clusters of many of their berries they remained, nevertheless, pretty and realistic objects.

But, in spite of the light, the focus, and his desire for hard thinking, Master Nathaniel found his thoughts drifting down the most fantastic paths. And, besides, he was so drowsy and his limbs felt so strangely heavy. The colours on the ceiling were getting all blurred, and the old knobs were detaching themselves from their background and shining in space like suns, moons, and stars – or was it like apples – the golden apples of the West? And now the claret-coloured background was turning into a red field – a field of red flowers, from which leered Portunus, and among which wept Ranulph. But the straight road, which for the last few months had been the projection of his unknown, buried purpose, even through this confused landscape glimmered white . . . yet, it looked different from usual . . . why, of course, it was the Milky Way! And then he knew no more.

In the meantime Hazel had been growing more and more restless, and, though she scolded herself for foolishness, more and more anxious. Finally, she could stand it no more: 'I think I'll just creep up to the gentleman's door and listen if I can hear him snoring,' she said to herself. Hazel believed that it was a masculine peculiarity not to be able to sleep without snoring.

But though she kept her ear to the keyhole for a full two minutes, not a sound proceeded from Master Nathaniel's room. Then she softly opened the door. A lighted candle was guttering to its end, and her guest was lying, to all appearance, dead, whilst a suffocating atmosphere pervaded the room. Hazel felt almost sick with terror, but she flung open the casement window as wide as it would go, poured half of the water from the ewer into the stove to extinguish its fire, and the remainder over Master Nathaniel himself. To her unspeakable relief he opened his eyes, groaned, and muttered something inaudible.

'Oh, sir, you're not dead then!' almost sobbed Hazel. 'I'll just go and fetch you a cup of cordial and get you some hartshorn.'

When she returned with the two restoratives, she found Master Nathaniel sitting up in bed, and, though he looked a little fuddled, his natural colour was creeping back, and the cordial restored him to almost his normal condition.

When Hazel saw that he was really himself again, she sank down on the floor and, spent with terror, began to sob bitterly.

'Come, my child!' said Master Nathaniel kindly, 'there's nothing to cry about. I'm feeling as well as ever I did in my life . . . though, by the Harvest of Souls, I can't imagine what can have taken me. I never remember to have swooned before in all my born days.'

But Hazel would not be comforted: 'That it should have happened, here, in my house,' she sobbed. 'We who have always stood by the laws of hospitality . . . and not a *young* gentleman, either . . . oh, dearie me; oh, dearie me!'

'Why do you take blame to yourself, my child?' asked Master Nathaniel. 'Your hospitality is in no sense to blame if, owing perhaps to recent fatigues and anxieties I should suddenly have turned faint. No, it is not you that are the bad host, but I that am the bad guest to have given so much trouble.'

But Hazel's sobs only grew wilder. 'I didn't like her bringing in that fire-box – no I didn't! An evil outlandish thing that it is! That it should have happened under *my* roof! For it *is* my roof . . . and *she'll* not pass another night under it!' And she sprang to her feet, with clenched fists and blazing eyes.

Master Nathaniel was becoming interested. 'Are you alluding to your grandfather's widow?' he asked quietly.

'Yes, I am!' cried Hazel indignantly. 'Oh! she's up to strange tricks, always . . . and none of her ways are those of honest farmers – no fennel over our doors, unholy fodder in our granary . . . and in her heart, thoughts as unholy. I saw the smile with which she looked at you at dinner.'

'Are you accusing this woman of actually having made an attempt on my life?' he asked slowly.

But Hazel flinched before this point-blank question, and her only answer was to begin again to cry. For a few minutes Master Nathaniel allowed her to do so unmolested, and then he said gently, 'I think you have cried enough for tonight, my child. *You* have been kindness itself, but it is evident that I am not very welcome to your grandfather's widow, so I must not inflict myself longer upon her. But before I leave her roof there is something I want to do, and I shall need your help.'

Then he told her who he was and how he wanted to prove something against a certain enemy of his, and had come here hoping to find a missing clue.

He paused, and looked at her meditatively. 'I think I ought to tell you, my child,' he went on, 'that if I can prove what I want, your grandmother may also be involved. Did you know that she had once been tried for the murder of your grandfather?'

'Yes,' she faltered. 'I've heard that there was a trial. But I thought she was proved innocent.'

'Yes. But there is such a thing as a miscarriage of justice. I believe that your grandfather *was* murdered, and that my enemy – whose name I don't care to mention till I have more to go upon – had a hand in the matter. And I have a shrewd suspicion that the widow was his accomplice. Under these circumstances, will you still be willing to help me?'

Hazel first turned red, and then she turned white, and her lower lip began to tremble. She disliked the widow, but had to admit that she had never been unkindly treated by her, and, though not her own kith and kin, she was the nearest approach to a relative she could remember. But, on the other hand, Hazel belonged by tradition and breed to the votaries of the grim cult of the Law. Crime must not go unpunished; moreover (and here Hazel subscribed to a still more venerable code) one's own kith and kin must not go unavenged.

But the very vehemence with which she longed to be rid of the widow's control had bred a curious irrational sense of guilt with regard to her; and, into the bargain, she was terrified of her.

Supposing this clue should lead to nothing, and the widow discover what they had been imagining? How, in that case, should she dare to face her, to go on living under the same roof with her?

And yet . . . she was certain she had tried to murder their guest that night. How dared she? How dared she?

Hazel clenched her fists, and in a little gasping voice said, 'Yes, sir, I'll help you.'

'Good!' said Master Nathaniel briskly. 'I want to take old Portunus' advice – and dig under that herm in the orchard, this very night. Though, mind you, it's just as likely as not to prove nothing but the ravings of a crazy mind; or else it may concern some buried treasure, or something else that has nothing to do with your grandfather's murder. But, in the case of our finding a valuable bit of evidence, we must have witnesses. And I think we should have the law-man of the district with us; who is he?'

'It's the Swan blacksmith, Peter Pease.'

'Is there any servant you trust whom you could send for him? Someone more attached to you than to the widow?'

'I can trust them all, and they all like me best,' she answered.

'Good. Go and wake a servant and send him off at once for the blacksmith. Tell him not to bring him up to the house, but to take him straight to the orchard . . . we don't want to wake the widow before need be. And the servant can stay and help us with the job – the more witnesses the better.'

Hazel felt as if she was in a strange, rather terrible dream. But she crept up to the attic and aroused one of the unmarried labourers – who, according to the old custom, slept in their master's house – and bade him ride into Swan and bring the blacksmith back with him on important business concerning the law.

Hazel calculated that he should get to Swan and back in less than an hour, and she and Master Nathaniel crept out of the house to wait for them in the orchard, each provided with a spade.

The moon was on the wane, but still sufficiently full to give a good light. She was, indeed, an orchard thief, for no fruit being left to rob, she had robbed the leaves of all their colour.

'Poor old moon!' chuckled Master Nathaniel, who was now in the highest of spirits, 'always filching colours with which to paint her own pale face, and all in vain! But just look at your friend, at Master Herm. He *does* look knowing!'

For in the moonlight the old herm had found his element, and under her rays his stone flickered and glimmered into living silver flesh, while his archaic smile had gained a new significance.

'Excuse me, sir,' said Hazel timidly, 'but I couldn't help wondering if the gentleman you suspected was . . . Dr Leer.'

'What makes you think so?' asked Master Nathaniel sharply.

'I don't quite know,' faltered Hazel. 'I just – wondered.'

Before long they were joined by the labourer and the law-man blacksmith – a burly, jovial, red-haired rustic of about fifty.

'Good evening,' cried Master Nathaniel briskly, 'I am Nathaniel Chanticleer' (he was sure that the news of his deposition could not yet have had time to travel to Swan), 'and if my business were not very pressing and very secret I would not, you may be sure, have had you roused from your bed at this ungodly hour. I have reason to think that something of great importance may be hidden under this herm, and I wanted you to be there to see that our proceedings are all in order,' and he laughed genially. 'And here's the guarantee that I'm no masquerader,' and he removed his signet ring and held it out to the blacksmith. It was engraved with his well-known crest, the cock, and with six chevrons, in token that six of his ancestors had been High Seneschals of Dorimare.

Both the blacksmith and the labourer were at first quite overwhelmed by learning his identity, but he pressed a spade into the hand of each and begged them to begin digging without further delay.

For some time they toiled away in silence, and then one of the spades came against something hard.

It proved to be a small iron box with a key attached to it.

'Out with it! Out with it!' cried Master Nathaniel excitedly. 'I wonder if it contains a halter! By the Sun, Moon and Stars, I wonder!'

But he was sobered by a glimpse of poor Hazel's scared face.

'Forgive me, my child,' he said gently, 'my thirst for revenge made me forget both decency and manners. And, as like as not, there will be nothing in it but a handful of Duke Aubrey crowns – the nest-egg of one of your ancestors.'

They unlocked the box and found that it contained nothing but a sealed parchment package, addressed thus:

*To the First Who Finds Me.*

'I think, Miss Hazel, it should be you who opens it. Don't you agree, Master Law-man?' said Master Nathaniel. So, with trembling fingers, Hazel broke the seal, tore open the wrapper and drew out a sheet of writing.

By the light of the blacksmith's lanthorn they read as follows:

> I, Jeremiah Gibberty, farmer and law-man of the district of Swan-on-the-Dapple, having ever been a merry man who loved his joke, do herein crack my last, this side of the Debatable Hills, in the hopes that it will not lie so long in the damp earth as to prove but a lame rocket when the time comes to fire it off. And this is my last joke, and may all who hear it hold their sides, and may the tears run down their cheeks. I, Jeremiah Gibberty, was wilfully murdered by my second wife, Clementina, daughter of Ralph Baldbreeches, sailor, and of an outlandish woman from the far North. In which crime she was aided and abetted by her lover, Christopher Pugwalker, a foreigner who called himself a herbalist. And I know by sundry itchings of my skin which torment me as I write and by my spotted tongue that I have been given what the folks who know them call death-berries. And they were boiled down to look like mulberry jelly, offered me by my dear wife, and of which I ate in my innocence. And I bid him who finds this writing to search for a little lad, by name Peter Pease, the son of a tipsy tinker. For this little lad, having

an empty stomach and being greedy for pence, came to me but an hour since with a basket full of these same deathberries and asked me if I should like to buy them. And I, to test him, asked him if he thought there was a blight in my orchard that I should be so hard put to it for fruit. And he said he thought we must like them up at Gibbertys' for he had seen the gentleman who lived with us (Christopher Pugwalker) but a week since, gathering them. And if Christopher Pugwalker should leave these parts, then let the law search for a dumpy fellow, with nut-brown hair, a pug-nose freckled like a robin's egg, and one eye brown, the other blue. And in order that my last joke may be a well-built one, I have tested the berries I bought from the little lad, though it wrung my heart to do so, on one of the rabbits of a certain little maid, by name, Marjory Beach, the daughter of my carter. And I have done so because she, being seven years old and a healthy lass, runs a good chance of being still this side of the hills when someone digs up this buried jest. And if she be alive she will not have forgotten how one of her rabbits took to scratching itself, and how its tongue was spotted like a snake, and how she found it lying dead. And I humbly beg her pardon for having played such a cruel trick on a little maid, and I ask my heirs (if so be any of them be still alive) to send her a fine buck rabbit, a ham, and ten gold pieces. And, though I am law-man and could put them under arrest before I die, yet, for a time, I hold my hand. Partly because I have been a hunter all my life, and, as the hare and the deer are given their chance to escape, so shall they have theirs; and partly because I should like to be very far on my wanderings down the Milky Way before Clementina mounts Duke Aubrey's wooden horse; because I think the sound of her strangling would hurt my ears; and, last of all, because I am very weary. And here I sign my name for the last time.

JEREMIAH GIBBERTY

# 24

## BELLING THE CAT

When they had finished reading, Hazel burst into hysterical sobs, crying alternately, 'Poor grandfather!' and 'Will they hang her for it?' Master Nathaniel soothed her as best he could, and, when she had dried her eyes, she said, 'Poor Marjory Beach! She must have that ham and that buck rabbit.'

'She's still alive, then?' asked Master Nathaniel eagerly. Hazel nodded: 'She is poor, and still a maid, and lives in Swan.'

'And what about Peter Pease, the tinker's smart little lad? Is there nothing for *him*, Miss Hazel?' cried the blacksmith with a twinkle.

Hazel stared at him in bewilderment, and Master Nathaniel cried gleefully, 'Why, it's the same name, by the Harvest of Souls! Were you, then, the little chap who saw Pugwalker picking the berries?'

And Hazel said in slow amazement, '*You* were the little boy who spoke to my grandfather . . . *that night?* I never thought . . .'

'That I'd begun so humbly, eh? Yes, I was the son of a tinker, or, as they liked to be called, of a whitesmith. And now I'm a blacksmith, and as white is better than black I suppose I've come down in the world.' And he winked merrily.

'And you remember the circumstances alluded to by the late farmer?' asked Master Nathaniel eagerly.

'That I do, my lord Seneschal. As well as if they had happened yesterday. I won't easily forget the farmer's face that night when I offered him my basketful – but though the death-berries are rare enough I found them in those days commoner to pick up than ha'pence. And I won't easily forget Master Pugwalker's face, either, while he was plucking them. And little did he know there was a squirrel watching him with a good Dorimarite tongue in his head!'

'Have you ever seen him since?'

The blacksmith winked.

'Come, come!' cried Master Nathaniel impatiently. 'Have you seen him since? This is no time for beating about the bush.'

'Well, perhaps I have,' said the blacksmith slowly, 'trotting about Swan, as brisk and as pleased with himself as a fox with a goose in his mouth. And I've often wondered whether it wasn't my duty as law-man to speak out . . . but, after all, it was very long ago, and his life seemed to be of better value than his death, for he was a wonderfully clever doctor and did a powerful lot of good.'

'It – it was Dr Leer, then?' asked Hazel in a low voice; and the blacksmith winked.

'Well, I think we should be getting back to the house,' said Master Nathaniel, 'there's still some business before us.' And, lowering his voice, he added, 'Not very pleasant business, I fear.'

'I suppose your Honour means belling the cat?' said the blacksmith, adding with a rueful laugh, 'I can't imagine a nastier job. She's a cat with claws.'

As they walked up to the house, the labourer whispered to Hazel, 'Please, missy, does it mean that the mistress killed her husband? They always say so in the village, but . . .'

'Don't, Ben; don't! I can't bear talking about it,' cried Hazel with a shudder. And when they reached the house, she ran up to her own bedroom and locked herself in.

Ben was despatched to get a stout coil of rope, and Master Nathaniel and the blacksmith, whom the recent excitement had made hungry, began to forage round for something to eat.

Suddenly a voice at the door said, 'And what, may I ask, are you looting for in my larder, gentlemen?'

It was the widow. First she scrutinized Master Nathaniel – a little pale and hollow-eyed, perhaps, but alive and kicking, for all that. Then her eyes travelled to Peter Pease. At that moment, Ben entered with the rope, and Master Nathaniel nudged the law-man, who, clearing his throat, cried in the expressionless falsetto of the Law, 'Clementina Gibberty! In the name of the country of Dorimare, and to the end that the dead, the living, and those not yet born, may rest quietly in their graves, their bed, and the womb, I arrest you for the murder of your late husband, Jeremiah Gibberty.'

She turned deadly pale, and, for a few seconds, stood glaring at him in silence. Then she gave a scornful laugh. 'What new joke of yours is this, Peter Pease? I was accused of this before, as you know well, and acquitted with the judge's compliments, and as good as an apology. Law business must be very slack in Swan that you've nothing better to do than to come and frighten a poor woman in her own house with old spiteful tales that were silenced once and for all nearly forty years ago. My late husband died quietly in his bed, and I only hope you may have as peaceful an end. And you must know very little of the law, Peter Pease, if you don't know that a person can't be tried twice for the same crime.'

Then Master Nathaniel stepped forward. 'You were tried before,' he said quietly, 'for poisoning your husband with the sap of osiers. This time it will be for poisoning him with the berries of merciful death. Tonight the dead have found their tongues.'

She gave a wild shriek, which reached upstairs to Hazel's room and caused her to spring into bed and pull the blankets over her ears, as if it had been a thunderstorm.

Master Nathaniel signed to Ben who, grinning from ear to ear, as is the way of rustics when witnessing a painful and embarrassing scene, came up to his mistress with the coil of rope. But to bind her, he needed the aid of both the blacksmith and Master Nathaniel, for, like a veritable wild cat, she struggled and scratched and bit.

When her arms were tightly bound, Master Nathaniel said, 'And now I will read you the words of the dead.'

She was, for the time, worn out by her struggles, and her only answer was an insolent stare, and he produced the farmer's document and read it through to her.

'And now,' he said, eyeing her curiously, 'shall I tell you who gave me the clue without which I should never have found that letter? It was a certain old man, whom I think you know, by name Portunus.'

Her face turned as pale as death, and in a low voice of horror she cried, 'Long ago I guessed who he was, and feared that he might prove my undoing.' Then her voice grew shrill with terror and her eyes became fixed, as if seeing some hideous vision, 'The Silent People!' she screamed. 'The dumb who speak! The bound who strike! I cherished and fed old Portunus like a tame bird. But what do the dead know of kindness?'

'If old Portunus is he whom you take him to be, I fail to see that he has much cause for gratitude,' said Master Nathaniel drily. 'Well, he has taken his revenge, on you – and your accomplice.'

'My accomplice?'

'Aye, on Endymion Leer.'

'Oh, Leer!' And she laughed scornfully. 'It was a greater than Endymion Leer who ordered the death of farmer Gibberty.'

'Indeed?'

'Yes. One who cares not for good and evil, and sows his commands like grain.'

'Whom do you mean?'

Again she laughed scornfully. 'Not one whom I would name to *you*. But set your mind at rest, he cannot be summoned in a court of law.'

She gave him a searching look, and said abruptly, 'Who are you?'

'My name is Nathaniel Chanticleer.'

'I thought as much!' she cried triumphantly. 'I wasn't sure, but I thought I'd take no risks. However, you seem to bear a charmed life.'

'I suppose you are alluding to your kind thought for my comfort – patting that nice little death-box in my room to keep me warm, eh?'

'Yes, that's it,' she answered brazenly.

Then a look of indescribable malice came into her face, and, with an evil smile, she said, 'You see, you gave yourself away – without knowing it – at dinner.'

'Indeed? And how, may I ask?'

At first she did not answer, but eyed him gloatingly as a cat might eye a mouse. And then she said slowly, 'It was that pack of lies you told me about the doings of the lads at Moongrass. Your son isn't at Moongrass – nor ever has been, nor ever will be.'

'What do you mean?' he cried hoarsely.

'Mean?' she said with a shrill, triumphant laugh. 'I mean this – on the night of the thirty-first of October, when the Silent People are abroad, he heard Duke Aubrey's summons, and followed it across the hills.'

'Woman . . . what . . . what . . . speak . . . or . . .' and the veins in Master Nathaniel's temples were swelling, and a fire seemed to have been lighted in his brain.

Her laughter redoubled. 'You'll never see your son again!' she jeered. 'Young Ranulph Chanticleer has gone to the land whence none returns.'

Not for a moment did he doubt the truth of her words. Before his inward eye there flashed the picture he had seen in the pattern on the ceiling, just before losing consciousness – Ranulph weeping among the fields of gillyflowers.

A horror of impotent tenderness swept over him. While, with the surface of his mind, he supposed that this was IT springing out at him at last. And parallel with the agony, and in no way mitigating it, was a sense of relief – the relaxing of tension, when one can say, 'Well, it has come at last.'

He turned a dull eye on the widow, and said, a little thickly, 'The land from which no one returns . . . but I can go there, too.'

'Follow him across the hills?' she cried scornfully. 'No; you are not made of *that* sort of stuff.'

He beckoned to Peter Pease, and they went out together to the front of the house. The cocks were crowing, and there was a feeling of dawn in the air.

'I want my horse,' he said dully. 'And can you find Miss Hazel for me?'

But as he spoke she joined them – pale and wild-eyed.

'From my room I heard you coming out,' she said. 'Is it – is it over?'

Master Nathaniel nodded. And then, in a quiet voice emptied of all emotion, he told her what he had just learned from the widow. She went still paler than before, and her eyes filled with tears.

Then, turning to Peter Pease, he said, 'You will immediately get out a warrant for the apprehension of Endymion Leer and send it into Lud to the New Mayor, Master Polydore Vigil. And you, Miss Hazel, you'd better leave this place at once – you will have to be plaintiff in the trial. Go to your aunt, Mistress Ivy Peppercorn, who keeps the village shop at Mothgreen. And remember, you must say nothing whatever about the part I've played in this business – that is essential. I am not popular at present in Lud. And, now, would you kindly order my horse to be saddled and brought round.'

There was something so colourless, so dead, in his voice, that both Hazel and the smith stood, for a few seconds, in awed and sympathetic silence, and then Hazel went off slowly to order his horse.

'You . . . you didn't mean what you said to the widow, sir, about . . . about going . . . *yonder*?' asked Peter Pease in an awed voice.

Suddenly the fire was rekindled in Master Nathaniel's eyes, and he cried fiercely, 'Aye, yonder, and beyond yonder, if need be . . . till I find my son.'

It did not take long for his horse to be saddled and led to the door.

'Good-bye, my child,' he said to Hazel, taking her hand, and then he added, with a smile, 'You dragged me back last night from the Milky Way . . . and now I am going by the earthly one.'

She and Peter stood watching him, riding along the valley towards the Debatable Hills, till he and his horse were just a speck in the distance.

'Well, well,' said Peter Pease, 'I warrant it'll be the first time in the history of Dorimare that a man has loved his son well enough to follow him *yonder*.'

# 25

## THE LAW CROUCHES AND SPRINGS

Literally, Master Polydore Vigil received the severest shock of his life, when a few days after the events recorded in the last chapter there reached him the warrant against Endymion Leer, duly signed and sealed by the law-man of the district of Swan-on-the-Dapple.

Dame Marigold had been right in saying that her brother was now completely under the dominion of the doctor. Master Polydore was a weak, idle man, who, nevertheless, dearly loved the insignia of authority. Hence, his present position was for him an ideal one – he had all the glory due to the first citizen, who has, moreover, effected a *coup d'état*, and none of the real responsibility that such a situation entails.

And now, this terrible document had arrived – it was like an attempt to cut off his right hand. His first instinct on receiving it was to rush off and take counsel with Endymion Leer himself – surely the omniscient resourceful doctor would be able to reduce to wind and thistledown even a thing as solid as a warrant. But respect for the Law, and the belief that though everything else may turn out vanity and delusion, the Law has the terrifying solidity of Reality itself, were deep-rooted in Master Polydore. If there was a warrant out against Endymion Leer – well, then, he must bend his neck to the yoke like any other citizen and stand his trial.

Again he read through the warrant, in the hopes that on a second reading it would lose its reality – prove to be a forgery, or a hoax. Alas! Its genuineness was but too unmistakable – the Law had spoken.

Master Polydore let his hands fall to his sides in an attitude of limp dismay; then he sighed heavily; then he rose slowly to his feet – there was nothing for it but to summon Mumchance, and let the warrant instantly be put into effect. As it was possible, nay, almost certain, that the Doctor would be able to clear himself triumphantly in Court, the quicker the business was put through, the sooner Master Polydore would recover his right hand.

When Mumchance arrived, Master Polydore said, in a voice as casual as he could make it, 'Oh! yes, Mumchance, yes . . . I asked you to come, because,' and he gave a little laugh, 'a warrant has actually arrived – of course, there must be some gross misunderstanding behind it, and there will be no difficulty in getting it cleared up in Court – but, as a matter of fact, a warrant has arrived from the law-man of Swan-on-the-Dapple, against . . . well, against none other than Dr Endymion Leer!' and again he laughed.

'Yes, your Worship,' said Mumchance; and, not only did his face express no surprise, but into the bargain it looked distinctly grim.

'Absurd, isn't it?' said Master Polydore, 'and *most* inconvenient.'

Mumchance cleared his throat: 'A murderer's a murderer, your Worship,' he said. 'Me and my wife, we were spending last evening at Mothgreen – my wife's cousin keeps the tavern there, and he was celebrating his silver wedding – if your Worship will excuse me mentioning such things – and among the friends he'd asked in was the plaintiff and her aunt . . . and, well . . . there be some things that be just too big for any defendant to dodge. But I'll say no more, your Worship.'

'I should hope not, Mumchance; you have already strangely forgotten yourself,' and Master Polydore glared fiercely at the unrepentant Mumchance. All the same, he could not help feeling a little disquieted by the attitude adopted by that worthy.

Two hours later after a busy morning devoted to professional visits – and, perhaps, some unprofessional ones too – Endymion Leer sat down to his midday dinner. There was not a happier man in Lud than he – he was the most influential man in the town, deep in the counsels of the magistrates; and as for the dreaded Chanticleers – well, he had successively robbed them of their sting. Life being one and indivisible, when one has a sense that it is good its humblest manifestations are transfigured, and that morning the Doctor would have found a meal of baked haws sweet to his palate – how much more so the succulent meal that was actually awaiting him. But it was not fated that Endymion Leer should eat that dinner. There came a loud double knock at the door, and then the voice of Captain Mumchance, demanding instantly to be shown in to the Doctor. It was in vain that the housekeeper protested, saying that the Doctor had given strict orders that he was never to be disturbed at his meals, for the Captain roughly brushed her aside with an aphorism worthy of that eminent jurist, the late Master Josiah Chanticleer. 'The Law, my good lady, is no respecter of a gentleman's stomach, so I'll trouble you to stand out of the way,' and he stumped resolutely into the parlour.

'Morning, Mumchance!' cried the Doctor cheerily, 'come to share this excellent looking pigeon-pie?'

For a second or two the Captain surveyed him rather ghoulishly. It must be remembered that not only had the Captain identified himself with the Law to such a degree that he looked upon any breach of it as a personal insult, but that also he had been deeply wounded in his professional pride in that he had not immediately recognised a murderer by his smell.

Captain Mumchance was not exactly an imaginative man, but as he stood there contemplating the Doctor he could almost have believed that his features and expression had suffered a subtle and most unbecoming change since he had last seen them. It was as if he was sitting in a ghastly green light – the most disfiguring and sinister of all those effects of light with which the Law cunningly plays with appearances – the light that emanates from the word *murder*.

'No thank you,' he said gruffly, 'I don't sit down to table with the likes of you.'

The Doctor gave him a very sharp look, and then he raised his eyebrows and said drily, 'It seems to me that recently you have more than once honoured my humble board.'

The Captain snorted, and then in a stentorian and unnatural

voice, he shouted, 'Endymion Leer! I arrest you in the name of the country of Dorimare, and to the end that the dead, the living, and those not yet born may rest quietly in their graves, their beds and the womb.'

'Gammon and spinnage!' cried the Doctor, testily, 'what's your little game, Mumchance?'

'Is murder, game?' said the Captain; and at that word the Doctor blanched, and then Mumchance added, 'You're accused of the murder of the late Farmer Gibberty.'

The words acted like a spell. It was as if Endymion Leer's previous sly, ironical, bird-like personality slipped from him like a mask, revealing another soul, at once more formidable and more tragic. For a few seconds he stood white and silent, and then he cried out in a terrible voice: 'Treachery! Treachery! The Silent People have betrayed me! It is ill serving a perfidious master!'

The news of the arrest of Endymion Leer on a charge of murder flew like wildfire through Lud.

At all the street corners, little groups of tradesmen, 'prentices, sailors, were to be seen engaged in excited conversation, and from one to the other group flitted the deaf-mute harlot, Bawdy Bess, inciting them in her strange uncontrolled speech, while dogging her footsteps with her dance-like tread went old Mother Tibbs, alternately laughing in crazy glee and weeping and wringing her hands and crying out that she had not yet brought back the Doctor's last washing, and it was a sad thing that he should go for his last ride in foul linen. 'For he'll mount Duke Aubrey's wooden horse – the Gentlemen have told me so,' she added with mysterious nods.

In the meantime, Luke Hempen had reported to Mumchance what he had learned from the little herdsmen about the 'fish' caught by the widow and the Doctor. The Yeomanry stationed on the border were instantly notified and ordered to drag the Dapple near the spot where it bubbled out after its subterranean passage through the Debatable Hills. They did so, and discovered wicker frails of fairy fruit, so cunningly weighted that they were able to float under the surface of the water.

This discovery considerably altered Master Polydore's attitude to Endymion Leer.

# 26

## 'NEITHER TREES NOR MEN'

In view of the disturbance caused among the populace by the arrest of Endymion Leer, the Senate deemed it advisable that his trial, and that of the widow Gibberty, should take precedence of all other legal business; so as soon as the two important witnesses, Peter Pease and Marjory Beach, reached Lud-in-the-Mist, it was fixed for an early date.

Never, in all the annals of Dorimare, had a trial been looked forward to with such eager curiosity. It was to begin at nine o'clock in the morning, and by seven o'clock the hall of justice was already packed, while a seething crowd thronged the courtyard and overflowed into the High Street beyond.

On the front seats sat Dame Marigold, Dame Jessamine, Dame Dreamsweet, and the other wives of magistrates; the main body of the hall was occupied by tradesmen and their wives, and other quiet, well-to-do members of the community, and behind them seethed the noisy, impudent, hawking, cat-calling, riff-raff – 'prentices, sailors, pedlars, strumpets; showing clearly on what side were their sympathies by such ribald remarks as, 'My old granny's pet cockatoo is terrible fond of cherries, I think we should tell the Town Yeomanry, and have it locked up as a smuggler,' or 'Where's Mumchance! Send for Mumchance and the Mayor! Two hundred years ago an old gaffer ate a gallon of crab soup and died the same night – arrest Dr Leer and hang him for it.'

But as the clocks struck nine and Master Polydore Vigil, in his priestly-looking purple robes of office embroidered in gold with the sun and the moon and the stars, and the other ten judges clad in scarlet and ermine filed slowly in and, bowing gravely to the assembly, took their seats on the dais, silence descended on the hall; for the fear of the Law was inbred in every Dorimarite, even the most disreputable.

Nevertheless, there was a low hum of excitement when Mumchance in his green uniform, carrying an axe, and two or three others of the Town Yeomanry, marched in with the two prisoners, who took their places in the dock.

Though Endymion Leer had for long been one of the most familiar figures in Lud, all eyes were turned on him with as eager a curiosity as if he had been some savage from the Amber Desert, the first of his kind to be seen in Dorimare; and such curious tricks can the limelight of the Law play on reality that many there thought that they could see his evil sinister life writ in clear characters on his familiar features.

To the less impressionable of the spectators, however, he looked very much as usual, though perhaps a little pale and flabby about the gills. And he swept the hall with his usual impudent appraising glance, as if to say, 'Linsey-woolsey, linsey-woolsey! But one must make the best of a poor material.'

'He's going to give the judges a run for their money!'

'If he's got to die, he'll die game!' gleefully whispered various of his partisans.

As for the widow, her handsome passionate face was deadly pale and emptied of all expression; this gave her a sort of tragic sinister beauty, reminiscent of the faces of the funereal statues in the Fields of Grammary.

'Not the sort of woman I'd like to meet in a lonely lane at night,' was the general comment she aroused.

Then the Clerk of Arraigns called out 'Silence!' and in a solemn voice, Master Polydore said, 'Endymion Leer and Clementina Gibberty, hold up your hands.' They did so. Whereupon, Master Polydore read the indictment, as follows: 'Endymion Leer, and Clementina Gibberty, you are accused of having poisoned the late Jeremiah Gibberty, farmer, and law-man of the district of Swan-on-the-Dapple, thirty-six years ago, with a fruit known as the berries of merciful death.'

Then the plaintiff, a young fresh-faced girl (none other, of course, than our old friend, Hazel) knelt at the foot on the dais and was given the great seal to kiss; upon which the Clerk of Arraigns led her up into a sort of carved pulpit, whence in a voice, low, but so clear as to penetrate to the furthest corners of the hall she told, with admirable lucidity, the story of the murder of her grandfather.

Next, Mistress Ivy, flustered and timid, told the Judges, in somewhat rambling fashion, what she had already told Master Nathaniel.

Then came the testimony of Peter Pease and Marjory Beach, and, finally, the document of the late farmer was handed round among the Judges.

'Endymion Leer!' called out Master Polydore, 'the Law bids you speak, or be silent, as your conscience prompts you.'

And as Endymion Leer rose to make his defence, the silence of the hall seemed to be trebled in intensity.

'My Lords Judges!' he began. 'I take my stand, not high enough, perhaps, to be out of reach of the gibbet, but well above the heads, I fancy, of everybody here to-day. And, first of all, I would have you bear in mind that my life has been spent in the service of Dorimare.' (Here there was a disturbance at the back of the hall and shouts of 'Down with the Senators!', 'Long live the good Doctor!' But the would-be rioters were cowed by the thunder of the Law, rumbling in the 'Silence!' of the Clerk of Arraigns.)

'I have healed and preserved your bodies – I have tried to do the same for your souls. First, by writing a book – published anonymously some years ago – in which I tried to show the strange seeds that are sleeping in each of you. But the book hardly aroused the enthusiasm that it so justly deserved' (and he gave his old dry chuckle). 'In fact, not to put too fine a point on it, the copies were burned by the common hangman – and could you have found the author you would gladly have burned him too. I can tell you since writing it I have gone in fear of my life, and have hardly dared to look a red-haired man in the face – still less a blue cow!' and here some of his partisans at the back of the hall laughed uproariously.

He paused, and then went on in a graver voice, 'Why have I

taken all this trouble with you? Why have I spent my erudition and my skill on you thus? To speak truth, I hardly know myself . . . perhaps because I like playing with fire; perhaps because I am relentlessly compassionate.

'My friends, you are outcasts, though you do not know it, and you have forfeited your place on earth. For there are two races – trees and man; and for each there is a different dispensation. Trees are silent, motionless, serene. They live and die, but do not know the taste of either life or death; to them a secret has been entrusted but not revealed.

'But the other tribe – the passionate, tragic, rootless tree – man? Alas! he is a creature whose highest privileges are a curse. In his mouth is ever the bitter-sweet taste of life and death, unknown to the trees. Without respite he is dragged by the two wild horses, memory and hope; and he is tormented by a secret that he can never tell. For every man worthy of the name is an initiate; but each one into different Mysteries. And some walk among their fellows with the pitying, slightly scornful smile, of an adept among catechumens. And some are confiding and garrulous, and would so willingly communicate their own unique secret – in vain! For though they shout it in the market-place, or whisper it in music and poetry, what they say is never the same as what they know, and they are like ghosts charged with a message of tremendous import who can only trail their chains and gibber.

'Such then are the two tribes. Citizens of Lud-in-the-Mist, to which do you belong? To neither; for you are not serene, majestic, and silent, nor are you restless, passionate, and tragic.

'I could not turn you into trees; but I had hoped to turn you into men.

'I have fed and healed your bodies; and I would feign have done the same for your souls.' (He paused to mop his brow; clearly it was more of an effort for him to speak than one would have guessed. Then he went on, and his voice had in it a strange new thrill.) 'There is a land where the sun and the moon do not shine; where the birds are dreams, the stars are visions, and the immortal flowers spring from the thoughts of death. In that land grow fruit, the juices of which sometimes cause madness, and sometimes manliness; for that fruit is flavoured with life and death, and it is the proper nourishment for the souls of man. You have recently discovered that for years I have helped to smuggle that fruit into Dorimare. The farmer Gibberty would have deprived you of it – and so I prescribed for him the berries of merciful death.' (This admission of guilt caused another disturbance at the back of the hall, and there were shouts of 'Don't you believe him!', 'Never say die, Doctor!', and so on. The Yeomanry had to put out various rough looking men, and Master Ambrose, sitting up on the dais, recognised among them the sailor, Sebastian Thug, whom he and Master Nathaniel had seen in the Fields of Grammary. When silence and order had been restored Endymion Leer went on.) 'Yes, I prescribed for him the berries of merciful death. What could it matter to the world whether he reaped the corn-fields of Dorimare, or the fields of gillyflowers beyond the hills?

'And now, my Lords Judges, I will forestall your sentence. I have pleaded guilty, and you will send me for a ride on what the common folk call Duke Aubrey's wooden horse; and you will think that you are sending me there because I helped to murder the farmer Gibberry. But, my Lords Judges, you are purblind, and, even in spectacles, you can only read a big coarse script. It is not *you* that are punishing me, but others for a spiritual sin. During these days of my imprisonment I have pondered much on my own life, and I have come to see that I have sinned. But how? I have prided myself on being a good chemist, and in my crucibles I can make the most subtle sauces yield up their secret – whether it be white arsenic, rosalgar, mercury sublimate, or cantharides. But where is the crucible or the chemist that can analyse a spiritual sin?

'But I have not lived in vain. You will send me to ride on Duke Aubrey's wooden horse, and, in time, the double-faced Doctor will be forgotten; and so will you, my Lords Judges. But Lud-in-the-Mist will stand, and the country of Dorimare, and the dreaded country beyond the hills. And the trees will continue to suck life from the earth and the clouds, and the winds will howl o' nights, and men will dream dreams. And who knows? Some day, perhaps, my fickle bitter-sweet master, the lord of life and death, of laughter and tears, will come dancing at the head of his silent battalions to make wild music in Dorimare.

'This then, my Lords Judges, is my defence,' and he gave a little bow towards the dais.

While he had been speaking, the Judges had shown increasing symptoms of irritation and impatience. This was not the language of the Law.

As for the public – it was divided. One part had sat taut with attention – lips slightly parted, eyes dreamy, as if they were listening to music. But the majority – even though many of them were partisans of the Doctor – felt that they were being cheated. They had expected that their hero, whether guilty or not, would in his defence quite bamboozle the judges by his juggling with the evidence and brilliant casuistry. Instead of which his speech had been obscure, and, they dimly felt, indecent; so the girls tittered, and the young men screwed their mouths into those grimaces which are the comment of the vulgar on anything they consider both ridiculous and obscene.

'Terribly bad taste, I call it,' whispered Dame Dreamsweet to Dame Marigold (the sisters-in-law had agreed to bury the hatchet), 'you always said that little man was a low vulgar fellow.' But Dame Marigold's only answer was a little shrug, and a tiny sigh.

Then came the turn of the widow Gibberty to mount the pulpit and make her defence.

Before she began to speak, she fixed in turn the judges, plaintiff, and public, with an insolent scornful stare. Then, in her deep, almost masculine, voice, she began: 'You've asked me a question to which you know the answer well enough, else I shouldn't be standing here now. Yes, I murdered Gibberty – and a good riddance too. I was for killing him with the sap of osiers, but the fellow you call Endymion Leer, who was always a squeamish, tenderhearted, sort of chap (if there was nothing to lose by it, that's to say) got me the death-berries and made me give them to him in a jelly, instead of the osiers.' (It was a pity Master Nathaniel was not there to glory in his own acumen!) 'And it was not only because they caused a painless death that he preferred the berries. He had never before seen them at their work, and he was always a death-fancier – tasting, and smelling, and fingering death, like a farmer does samples of grain at market. Though, to give him his due, if it hadn't been for him, that girl over there who has just been standing up to denounce him and me,' (and she nodded in the direction on the pale, trembling, Hazel) 'and her father before her, would long ago have gone the way of the farmer. And this I say in the hope that the wench's conscience may keep her awake sometimes in the nights to come, remembering how she dealt with the man who had saved her life. It will be but a small prick, doubtless; but it is the last that I can give her.

'And now, good people, here's a word of advice to you, before I go my last ride, a pillion to my old friend Endymion Leer. Never you make a pet of a dead man. For the dead are dirty curs and bite the hand that has fed them,' and with an evil smile she climbed down from the pulpit; while more than one person in the audience felt faint with horror and would willingly have left the hall.

There was nothing left but for Master Polydore to pronounce the sentence; and though the accused had stolen some of his thunder, nevertheless the solemn time-honoured words did not fail to produce their wonted thrill:

'Endymion Leer and Clementina Gibberty, I find you guilty of murder, and I consign your bodies to the birds, and your souls to whence they came. And may all here present take example from your fate, correcting their conduct if it needs correction, or, if it be impeccable, keeping it so. For every tree can be a gallows, and every man has a neck to hang.'

The widow received her sentence with complete stolidity; Endymion Leer with a scornful smile. But as it was pronounced there was a stir and confusion at the back of the hall, and a grotesque frenzied figure broke loose from the detaining grip of her neighbours, and, struggling up to the dais, flung herself at the feet of Master Polydore. It was Miss Primrose Crabapple.

'Your Worship! Your Worship!' she cried, shrilly, 'Hang me instead of him! My life for his! Was it not I who gave your daughters fairy fruit, with my eyes open! And I glory in the knowledge that I was made a humble instrument of the same master whom he has served so well. Dear Master Polydore, have mercy on your country, spare your country's benefactor, and if the law must have a victim let it be me – a foolish useless woman, whose only merit was that she believed in loveliness though she had never seen it.'

Weeping and struggling, her face twisted into a grotesque tragic mask, they dragged her from the hall, amid the laughter and ironical cheers of the public.

That afternoon Mumchance came to Master Polydore to inform him that a young maid-servant from the Academy had just been to the guard-room to say that Miss Primrose Crabapple had killed herself.

Master Polydore at once hurried off to the scene of the tragedy, and there in the pleasant old garden where so many generations of Crabapple Blossoms had romped, and giggled, and exchanged their naughty little secrets, he found Miss Primrose, hanging stone-dead from one of her own apple-trees.

'Well, as the old song has it, Mumchance,' said Master Polydore – ' "*Here hangs a maid who died for love.*" '

Master Polydore was noted for his dry humour.

A gibbet had been set up in the great court of the Guildhall, and the next day, at dawn, Endymion Leer and the widow Gibberty were hanged by the neck till they died.

Rumour said that as the Doctor's face was contorted in its last grimace strange silvery peals of laughter were heard proceeding from the room where long ago Duke Aubrey's jester had killed himself.

## 27
## THE FAIR IN THE ELFIN MARCHES

About two hours after he had set out from the farm, Master Nathaniel reached a snug little hollow at the foot of the hills, chosen for their camp by the consignment of the Lud Yeomanry stationed, by his own orders, at the foot of the Debatable Hills.

'Halt!' cried the sentry. And then he dropped his musket in amazement. 'Well, I'm blessed if it ain't his Worship!' he cried. Some six or seven of his mates, who were lounging about the camp, some playing cards, some lying on their backs and staring up at the sky, came hurrying up at the sound of the challenge, and, speechless with astonishment, they stared at Master Nathaniel.

'I have come to look for my son,' he said. 'I have been told that . . . er . . . he came this way some two or three nights ago. If so, you must have seen him.'

The Yeomen shook their heads. 'No, your Worship, we've not seen no little boy. In fact, all the weeks we've been here we've not seen a living soul. And if there *are* any folks about they must be as swift as swallows and as silent-footed as cats, and as hard to see – well, as the dead themselves. No, your Worship, little Master Chanticleer has not passed this way.'

Master Nathaniel sighed wearily. 'I had a feeling that you would not have seen him,' he said; adding dreamily more to himself than to them: 'Who knows? He may have gone by the Milky Way.'

And then it struck him that this was probably the last normal encounter he would ever have with ordinary human beings, and he smiled at them wistfully.

'Well, well,' he said, 'you're having a pleasant holiday, I expect . . . nothing to do and plenty to eat and drink, eh? Here's a couple of crowns for you. Send to one of the farms for a pigskin of red wine and drink my health . . . and my son's. I'm off on what may prove a very long journey; I suppose this bridle-path will be as good a route as any?'

They stared at him in amazement.

'Please, your Worship, if you'll excuse me mentioning it, you must be making a mistake,' said the sentry, in a shocked voice. 'All the bridle-paths about here lead to nowhere but the Elfin Marches . . . and beyond.'

'It is for beyond that I am bound,' answered Master Nathaniel curtly. And digging his spurs into his horse's flanks, he dashed past the horrified Yeomen, and up one of the bridle-paths, as if he would take the Debatable Hills by storm.

For a few seconds they stood staring at one another, with scared, astonished eyes. Then the sentry gave a low whistle.

'He must be powerful fond of that little chap,' he said.

'If the little chap really slipped past without our seeing him, that will be the third Chanticleer to cross the hills. First there was the little missy at the Academy, then the young chap, then the Mayor.'

'Aye, but *they* didn't do it on an empty stomach – leastways, we know the Crabapple Blossoms didn't, and if the talk in Lud be true, the little chap had had a taste too of what he oughtn't,' said another. 'But it's another story to go when you're in your right mind. Dr Leer can't have been in the right when he said all them Magistrates were played out, for it's the bravest thing has ever been done in Dorimare.'

Master Nathaniel, for how long he could not have said, went riding up and up the bridle-path that wound in and out among the foothills, which gradually grew higher and higher. Not a living creature did he meet with – not a goat, not so much as a bird. He began to feel curiously drowsy, as if he were riding in a dream.

Suddenly his consciousness seemed to have gone out of gear, to have missed one of the notches in time or space, for he found himself riding along a high-road, in the midst of a crowd of peasants in holiday attire. Nor did this surprise him – his passive uncritical mood was impervious to surprise.

And yet . . . what were these people with whom he had mingled? An ordinary troop of holiday-making peasants? At first sight, so they seemed. There were pretty girls, with sunny hair escaping from under red and blue handkerchiefs, and rustic dandies cross-gartered with gay ribands, and old women with quiet, nobly-lined faces – a village community bound for some fair or merry-making.

But why were their eyes so fixed and strange, and why did they walk in *absolute silence*?

And then the invisible cicerone of dreams, who is one's other self, whispered in his ear, *These are they whom men call dead.*

And, like everything said by that cicerone, these words seemed to throw a flood of light on the situation, to make it immediately normal, even prosaic.

Then the road took a sudden turn, and before them stretched a sort of heath, dotted with the white booths of a fair.

'That is the market of souls,' whispered the invisible cicerone.

'Of course, of course,' muttered Master Nathaniel, as if all his life he had known of its existence. And, indeed, he had forgotten all about Ranulph, and thought that to visit this fair had been the one object of his journey.

They crossed the heath, and then they paid their gate-money to a silent old man. And though Master Nathaniel paid with a coin of a metal and design he had never seen before, it was with no sense of a link missing in the chain of cause and effect that he produced it from his pocket.

Outwardly, there was nothing different in this fair from those in Dorimare. Pewterers, shoemakers, silversmiths were displaying their wares; there were cows and sheep and pigs, and refreshment booths and raree-shows. But instead of the cheerful, variegated din that is part of the fun of the every-day fair, over this one there reigned complete silence; for the beasts were as silent as the people. Dead silence, and blazing sun.

Master Nathaniel started off to investigate the booths. In one of them they were flinging darts at a pasteboard target, on which were painted various of the heavenly bodies, with the moon in the centre. Anyone whose dart stuck in the moon was allowed to choose a prize from a heap of glittering miscellaneous objects – golden feathers, shells painted with curious designs, brilliantly-coloured pots, fans, silver sheep-bells.

'They're like Hempie's new ornaments,' thought Master Nathaniel.

In another booth there was a merry-go-round of silver horses and gilded chariots – both sadly tarnished. It was a primitive affair that moved not by machinery, but by the ceaseless trudging round of a live pony – a patient, dingy little beast – tied to it with a rope. And the motion generated a thin, cracked music – tunes that had been popular in Lud-in-the-Mist when Master Nathaniel had been a little boy.

There was *Oh, you Little Charmer with your pretty Puce Bow*, there was *Old Daddy Popinjay fell down upon his Rump*, there was *Why did she cock her Pretty Blue Eye at the Lad with the Silver Buckles?*

But, except for one solitary little boy, the tarnished horses and chariots whirled round without riders; and the pert tunes sounded so thin and wan as to accentuate rather than destroy the silence and atmosphere of melancholy.

In a hopeless, resigned sort of way, the little boy was sobbing. It was as if he felt that he was doomed by some inexorable fate to whirl round for ever and ever with the tarnished horses and chariots, the dingy, patient pony, and the old cracked tunes.

'It is not long,' said the invisible cicerone, 'since that little boy was stolen from the mortals. He still can weep.'

Master Nathaniel felt a sudden tightening in his throat. Poor little boy! Poor little lonely boy! What was it he reminded him of? Something painful, and very near his heart.

Round and round trudged the pony, round and round went the hidden musical-box, grinding out its thin, blurred tunes.

*Why did she cock her pretty blue eye*
*At the lad with the silver buckles,*
*When the penniless lad who was handsome and spry*
*Got nought but a rap on his knuckles?*

These vulgar songs, though faded, were not really old. Nevertheless, to Master Nathaniel, they were the oldest songs in existence – sung by the Morning Stars when all the world was young. For they were freighted with his childhood, and brought the memory, or, rather, the tang, the scent, of the solemn innocent world of children, a world *sans* archness, *sans* humour, *sans* vulgarity, where they had sounded as pure and silvery as a shepherd's pipe. Where the little charmer with her puce bow, and the scheming hussy who had cocked her blue eye had been own sisters to the pretty fantastic ladies of the nursery rhymes, like them walking always to the accompaniment of tinkling bells and living on frangipane and sillabubs of peaches and cream; and whose gestures were stylised and actions preposterous – nonsense actions that needed no explanation. While mothers-in-law, shrewish wives, falling in love – they were just pretty words like brightly-coloured beads, strung together without meaning.

As Master Nathaniel listened, he knew that other people would have heard other tunes – whatever tunes through the milkman's whistle, or the cracked fiddle of a street musician, or the voices of young sparks returning from the tavern at midnight, the Morning Stars may have happened to sing in their own particular infancy.

*Oh, you little charmer with your pretty puce bow,*
*I'll tell mamma if you carry on so!*

Round and round whirled the tarnished horses and chariots with their one pathetic little rider; round and round trudged the pony – the little dusty, prosaic pony.

Master Nathaniel rubbed his eyes and looked round; he felt as if after a dive he were slowly rising to the surface of the water. The fair seemed to be coming alive – the silence had changed into a low murmur. And now it was swelling into the mingled din of chattering voices, lowing cows, grunting pigs, blasts from tin trumpets, hoarse voices of cheapjacks praising their wares – all the noises, in short, that one connects with an ordinary fair.

He sauntered away from the merry-go-round and mingled with

the crowd. All the stall-keepers were doing a brisk trade, but, above all, the market gardeners – *their* stalls were simply thronged.

But, lo and behold! the fruit that they were selling was of the kind he had seen in the mysterious room of the Guildhall, and concealed inside the case of his grandfather's clock – it was fairy fruit; but the knowledge brought no sense of moral condemnation.

Suddenly he realized that his throat was parched with thirst and that nothing would slake it but one of these translucent globes.

The wizened old woman who was selling them cried out to him coaxingly, 'Three for a penny, sir! Or, for you, I'll make it four for a penny . . . for the sake of your hazel eyes, lovey! You'll find them as grateful as dew to the flowers – four for a penny, pretty master. Don't say no!'

But he had the curious feeling that one sometimes has in dreams, namely, that he himself was inventing what was happening to him, and could make it end as he chose.

'Yes,' he said to himself, 'I am telling myself one of Hempie's old stories, about a youngest son who has been warned against eating anything offered him by strangers, so, of course, I shall not touch it.'

So with a curt 'No, thank'ee, nothing doing today,' he contemptuously turned his back on the old woman and her fruit.

But whose was that shrill voice? Probably that of some cheapjack whose patter or whose wares, to judge from the closely-packed throng hiding him from view, had some particularly attractive quality. The voice sounded vaguely familiar, and, his curiosity aroused, Master Nathaniel joined the crowd of spectators.

He could discern nothing but the top of a red head, but the patter was audible: 'Now's your chance, gentlemen! Beauty doesn't keep, but rots like apples. Appleshies! Four points if you hit her on the breast, six if you hit her on the mouth, and he who first gets twenty points wins the maid. Don't fight shy of the appleshies! Apples and beauty do not keep – there's a worm in both. Step up, step up, gentlemen!'

Yes, he had heard that voice before. He began to shoulder his way through the crowd. It proved curiously yielding, and he had no difficulty in reaching the centre of attraction, a wooden platform on which gesticulated, grimaced and pirouetted . . . who but his rascally groom Willy Wisp, dressed as a harlequin. But Willy Wisp was not the strangest part of the spectacle. Out of the platform grew an apple tree, and tied to it was his own daughter, Prunella, while grouped around her in various attitudes of woe were the other Crabapple Blossoms.

Suddenly Master Nathaniel felt convinced that this was not merely a story he was inventing himself, but, as well, it was a dream – a grotesque, illogical, synthesis of scraps of reality, to which he could add what elements he chose.

'What's happening?' he asked his neighbour.

But he knew the answer – Willy Wisp was selling the girls to the highest bidder, to labour in the fields of gillyflowers.

'But you have no right to do this!' he cried out in a loud angry voice, 'no right whatever. This is not Fairyland – it is only the Elfin Marches. They cannot be sold until they have crossed over into Fairyland – I say they *cannot be sold*.'

All round him he heard awed whispers, 'It is Chanticleer – Chanticleer the dreamer, who has never tasted fruit.'

Then he found himself giving a learned dissertation on the law of property, as observed in the Elfin Marches. The crowd listened to him in respectful silence. Even Willy Wisp was listening, and the Crabapple Blossoms gazed at him with inexpressible gratitude.

With what seemed to him a superbly eloquent peroration he brought his discourse to an end. Prunella stretched out her arms to him, crying, 'Father, you have saved us! You and the Law.'

'You and the Law! You and the Law!' echoed the other Crabapple Blossoms.

'Chanticleer and the Law! Chanticleer and the Law!' shouted the crowd.

The fair had vanished. He was in a strange town, and was one of a great crowd of people all hurrying in the same direction.

'They are looking for the bleeding corpse,' whispered the

invisible cicerone, and the words filled Master Nathaniel with an unspeakable horror.

Then the crowd vanished, leaving him alone in a street as silent as the grave. He pressed forward, for he knew that he was looking for something; but what it was he had forgotten. At every street corner he came on a dead man, guarded by a stone beggar with a face like the herm in the Gibberty's orchard. He was almost choked by the horror of it. The terror became articulate: 'Supposing one of the corpses should turn out to be that little lonely boy on the merry-go-round!'

This possibility filled him with an indescribable anguish.

Suddenly he remembered about Ranulph. Ranulph had gone to the country from which there is no return.

*But he was going to follow him there and fetch him back.* Nothing would stop him – he would push, if necessary, through fold after fold of dreams until he reached their heart.

He bent down and touched one of the corpses. It was warm, and it moved. As he touched it he realized that he had incurred the danger of contamination from some mysterious disease.

'But it isn't real, it isn't real,' he muttered. 'I'm inventing it all myself. And so, whatever happens, I shan't mind, *because it isn't real.*'

It was growing dark. He knew that he was being followed by one of the stone beggars, who had turned into a four-footed animal called Portunus. In one sense the animal was a protection, in another a menace, and he knew that in summoning him he must be very careful to use the correct ritual formulary.

He had reached a square, on one side of which was a huge building with a domed roof. Light streamed from it through a great window of stained glass, on which was depicted a blue warrior fighting with a red dragon . . . no, it was not a stained glass window but merely the reflection on the white walls of the building from a house in complete darkness in the opposite side of the square, inhabited by creatures made of red lacquer. He knew that they were expecting him to call, because they believed that he was courting one of them.

'What else could bring him here save all this lovely spawn?' said a voice at his elbow.

He looked round – suddenly the streets were pullulating with strange semi-human *fauna*: tiny green men, the wax figures of his parents from Hemrae's chimney-piece, grimacing greybeards with lovely children gamboling round them dressed in beetles' shards.

Now they were dancing, some slow old-fashioned dance . . . in and out, in and out. Why, they were only figures on a piece of tapestry flapping in the wind!

Once more he felt his horse beneath him. But what were these little pattering footsteps behind him? He turned uneasily in his saddle, to discover that it was nothing but a gust of wind rustling a little eddy of dead leaves.

The town and its strange *fauna* had vanished, and once more he was riding up the bridle-path; but now it was night.

# 28

## 'BY THE SUN, MOON AND STARS AND THE GOLDEN APPLES OF THE WEST'

Though it was a relief to have returned to the fresh air of reality, Master Nathaniel was frightened. He realized that he was alone at dead of night in the Elfin Marches. And the moon kept playing tricks on him, turning trees and boulders into goblins and wild beasts; cracking her jokes, true humorist that she was, with a solemn impassive face. But, how was this? She was a waxing moon, and almost full, while the night before – or what he supposed was the night before – she had been a half moon on the wane.

Had he left time behind him in Dorimare?

Then suddenly, like some winged monster rushing from its lair, there sprang up a mighty wind. The pines creaked and rustled and bent beneath its onslaught, the grasses whistled, the clouds flocked together and covered the face of the moon.

Several times he was nearly lifted from his saddle. He drew his cloak closely round him, and longed, with an unspeakable longing, for his warm bed in Lud; and it flashed into his mind that what he had so often imagined in that bed, to enhance his sense of well-being, was now actually occurring – he was tired, he was cold, and the wind was finding the fissures in his doublet.

Suddenly, as if some hero had slain the monster, the wind died down, the moon sailed clear of the clouds, and the pines straightened themselves and once more stood at attention, silent and motionless. In spite of this, his horse grew strangely restive, rearing and jibbing, as if something was standing before it in the path that frightened it; and in vain Master Nathaniel tried to quiet and sooth it.

Then it shuddered all over and fell heavily to the ground.

Fortunately, Master Nathaniel was thrown clear, and was not

hurt, beyond the inevitable bruises entailed by the fall of a man of his weight. He struggled to his feet and hurried to his horse. It was stone dead.

For some time he sat beside it . . . his last link with Lud and familiar things; as yet too depressed in mind and aching in body to continue his journey on foot.

But what were these sudden strains of piercingly sweet music, and from what strange instrument did they proceed? They were too impersonal for a fiddle, too passionate for a flute, and much too sweet for any pipes or timbrels. It must be a human – or superhuman – voice, for now he was beginning to distinguish words.

*'There are windfalls of dreams, there's a wolf in the stars,*
*And Life is a nymph who will never be thine,*
*With lily, germander, and sops in wine.*
*With sweet-brier*
*And bon-fire*
*And strawberry-wine*
*And columbine.'*

The voice stopped, and Master Nathaniel buried his face in his hands and sobbed as if his heart would break.

In this magically sweet music once more he had heard the Note. It held, this time, no menace as to things to come; but it aroused in his breast an agonizing tumult of remorse for having allowed something to escape that he would never, never recapture. It was as if he had left his beloved with harsh words, and had returned to find her dead.

Through his agony he was conscious of a hand laid on his shoulder: 'Why, Chanticleer! Old John o' Dreams! What ails you? Has the cock's crow become too bittersweet for Chanticleer?' said a voice, half tender and half mocking, in his ear.

He turned round, and by the light of the moon saw standing behind him – Duke Aubrey.

The Duke smiled. 'Well, Chanticleer,' he said, 'so we meet at last! Your family has been dodging me down the centuries, but some day you were bound to fall into my snares. And, though you did not know it, you have been working for some time past as one of my secret agents. How I laughed when you and Ambrose Honeysuckle pledged each other in words taken from my Mysteries! And little did you think, when you stood cursing and swearing at the door of my tapestry-room, that you had pronounced the most potent charm in Faerie,' and he threw back his head and broke into peal upon peal of silvery laughter.

Suddenly his laughter stopped, and his eyes, as he looked at Master Nathaniel, became wonderfully compassionate.

'Poor Chanticleer! Poor John o' Dreams!' he said gently. 'I have often wished my honey were not so bitter to the taste. Believe me, Chanticleer, I fain would find an antidote to the bitter herb of life, but none grows this side of the hills – or the other.'

'And yet . . . I have never tasted fairy fruit,' said Master Nathaniel in a low broken voice.

'There are many trees in my orchard, and many and various are the fruit they bear – music and dreams and grief and, sometimes, joy. All your life, Chanticleer, you have eaten fairy fruit, and some day, it may be, you will hear the Note again – but that I cannot promise. And now I will grant you a vision – they are sometimes sweet to the taste.'

He paused. And then he said, 'Do you know why it was that your horse fell down dead? It was because you had reached the brink of Fairyland. The winds of Faerie slew him. Come with me, Chanticleer.'

He took Master Nathaniel's hand and dragged him to his feet, and they scrambled a few yards further up the bridle-path and stepped on to a broad plateau. Beneath them lay what, in the uncertain moonlight, looked like a stretch of desolate uplands.

Then Duke Aubrey raised his arms high above his head and cried out in a loud voice, 'By the Sun, Moon and Stars and the Golden Apples of the West!'

At these words the uplands became bathed in a gentle light and proved to be fair and fertile – the perpetual seat of Spring; for there were vivid green patches of young corn, and pillars of pink and white smoke, which were fruit trees in blossom, and pillars of blue blossom, which was the smoke of distant hamlets, and a vast meadow of cornflowers and daisies, which was the great inland sea of Faerie. And everything – ships, spires, houses – was small and bright and delicate, yet real. It was not unlike Dorimare, or, rather, the transfigured Dorimare he had once seen from the Fields of Grammary. And as he gazed he knew that in that land no winds ever howled at night, and that everything within its borders had the serenity and stability of trees, the unchanging peace of pictures.

Then, suddenly, it all vanished. Duke Aubrey had vanished too, and he was standing alone on the edge of a black abyss, while wafted on the wind came the echo of light, mocking laughter.

Was Fairyland, then, a delusion? Had Ranulph vanished into nothingness?

For a second or two he hesitated, and then – he leaped down into the abyss.

# 29

## A MESSAGE COMES TO HAZEL AND THE FIRST SWALLOW TO DAME MARIGOLD

The information given by Luke Hempen had enabled the authorities in Lud finally to put a stop to the import of fairy fruit. As we have seen, the Dapple had been dragged near its source, and wicker frails had been brought up, so cunningly weighted that they could float beneath the surface of the water, and closely packed with what was unmistakably fairy fruit. After that no further cases of fruit-eating came to Mumchance's notice. But, for all that, his anxieties were by no means at an end, for the execution of Endymion Leer came near to causing a popular rising. An angry mob, armed with cudgels and led by Bawdy Bess, stormed the court of the Guildhall, cut down the body – which had been left hanging on the gibbet as an example to evildoers – and bore it off in triumph; and the longest funeral procession that had been seen for years was shortly following it to the Fields of Grammary.

The cautious Mumchance considered it would be imprudent to interfere with the obsequies.

'After all, your Worship,' he said to Master Polydore, 'the Law has had his blood, and if it will mean a little peace and quiet she can do without his corpse.'

The next day many of the 'prentices and artisans went on strike, and several captains of merchant vessels reported that their crews showed signs of getting out of hand.

Master Polydore was terrified out of his wits, and Mumchance was inclined to take a very gloomy view of the situation: 'If the town chooses to rise the Yeomanry can do nothing against them,' he said dejectedly. 'We ain't organized (if your Worship win pardon the expression) for trouble – no, we ain't.'

Then, as if by a miracle, everything quieted down. The strikers, as meek as lambs, returned to their work, the sailors ceased to be turbulent, and Mumchance declared that it was years since the Yeomanry had had so little to do.

'There's nothing like taking strong measures *at once*,' Master Polydore remarked complacently to Master Ambrose (whom he had taken as his mentor in the place of Endymion Leer). 'Once let them feel that there is a strong man at the helm, and you can do anything with them. And, of course, they never felt that with poor old Nat.'

Master Ambrose's only answer was a grunt – and a rather sardonic smile. For Master Ambrose happened to be one of the few people who knew what had really happened.

The sudden calm was due neither to a miracle, nor to the strong hand of Master Polydore. It had been brought about by two humble agents – Mistress Ivy Peppercorn and Hazel Gibberty.

One evening they had been sitting in the little parlour behind the grocer's shop over the first fire of the season.

As plaintiff and principal witness in the unpopular trial, their situation was not without danger. In fact, Mumchance had advised them to move into Lud till the storm had blown over. But, to Hazel, Lud was the place where the widow was buried, and, full as she was of western superstitions, she felt that she could not bear to sleep enclosed by the same town walls as the angry corpse. Nor would she return to the farm. Her aunt had told her of Master Nathaniel's half joking plan to communicate with her, and Hazel insisted that even though he had gone beyond the Debatable Hills it was their clear duty to remain within reach of a message.

That evening Mistress Ivy was waxing a little plaintive over her obstinacy. 'I sometimes think, Hazel, your wits have been turned, living so long with that bad, bold woman . . . and I don't wonder, I'm sure, poor child; and if my poor Peppercorn hadn't come along, I don't know what would have happened to *me*. But there's no sense, I tell you, in waiting on here – with the hams and bacon at home not cured yet, nor the fish salted for winter, nor your fruit pickled or preserved. You're a farmer on your own now, and you *shouldn't* forget it. And I wish to goodness you'd get all this silly nonsense out of your head. A message from the Mayor, indeed! Though I can't get over its being him that came to see me, and me never knowing, but giving him sauce, as though he'd been nothing but a shipmate of my poor Peppercorn's! No, no, poor gentleman, we'll never hear from *him*! Leastways, not *this* side of the Debatable Hills.'

Hazel said nothing. But her obstinate little chin looked even more obstinate than usual.

Then suddenly she looked up with startled eyes.

'Hark, auntie!' she cried. 'Didn't you hear someone knocking?'

'What a girl you are for fancying things! It's only the wind,' said Mistress Ivy querulously.

'Why, auntie, there it is again! No, no, I'm sure it's someone knocking. I'll just go and see,' and she took a candle from the table; but her hand was trembling.

The knocking was audible now to Mistress Ivy as well.

'You just stay where you are, my girl!' she cried shrilly. 'It'll be one of these rough chaps from the town, and I won't have you opening the door – no, I won't.'

But Hazel paid no attention, and, though her face was white and her eyes very scared, she marched boldly into the shop and called, 'Who's there?' through the door.

'By the Sun, Moon and Stars and the Golden Apples of the West!' came the answer.

'Auntie! Auntie!' she cried shrilly. 'It's from the Mayor. He has sent a messenger, and you must come.'

This brought Mistress Ivy hurrying to her side. Though she was not an heroic character, she came of good sturdy stock, and she was not going to leave her dead brother's child to face the dangers of the unseen alone, but her teeth were chattering with terror. Evidently the messenger was growing impatient, for he began beating a tattoo on the door and singing in a shrill sweet voice:

*'Maids in your smocks*
*Look well to your locks*
*And beware of the fox*
*When the bellman knocks.'*

Hazel (not without some fumbling, for her hands were still trembling) drew the bolts, lifted the latch, and flung the door wide open. A sudden gust of wind extinguished her candle, so they could not see the face of the messenger.

He began to speak in a shrill, expressionless voice, like that of a child repeating a lesson: 'I have given the password, so you know from whom I come. I am to bid you go at once to Lud-in-the-Mist, and find a sailor, by name Sebastian Thug – he will probably be drinking at the tavern of the Unicorn – also a deaf-mute, commonly known as Bawdy Bess, whom you will probably find in the same place. You will have need of no other introduction than the words, *By the Sun, Moon and Stars and the Golden Apples of the West*. You are to tell them that there is to be no more rioting, and that they are to keep the people quiet, for the Duke will send his deputy. And next you will go to Master Ambrose Honeysuckle and bid him remember the oath with which he and Master Nathaniel pledged each other over wild-thyme gin, swearing to ride the wind with a loose rein, and to be hospitable to visions. And tell him that Lud-in-the-Mist must throw wide its gates to receive its destiny. Can you remember this?'

'Yes,' said Hazel in a low puzzled voice.

'And now just a trifle to the messenger for his pains!' and his voice became gay and challenging. 'I am an orchard thief and the citizen of a green world. Buss me, green maid!' and before Hazel had time to protest he gave her a smacking kiss on the lips and then plunged into the night, leaving the echoes of his 'Ho, ho, *hoh*!' like a silvery trail in his wake.

'Well, I never did!' exclaimed Mistress Ivy in amazement, adding with a fat chuckle, 'It would seem that it isn't only *this* side of the hills that saucy young fellows are to be found. But I don't quite know what to make of it, my girl. How are we to know he really comes from the Mayor?'

'Well, auntie, we can't know, of course, for certain – though, for my part, I don't think he was a Dorimarite. But he gave the password, so I think we must deliver the messages – there's nothing in them, after all, that could do any harm.'

'That's true,' said Mistress Ivy. 'Though I'm sure I don't want to go trudging into Lud at this time of night on a fool's errand. But, after all, a promise is a promise – and doubly so when it's been given to somebody as good as dead.'

So they put on their pattens and cloaks, lighted a lanthorn, and started off to walk into Lud, as briskly as Mistress Ivy's age and weight would allow, so as to get there before the gates were shut. Master Ambrose, as a Senator, would give them a pass to let them through on the way back.

The Unicorn was a low little tavern down by the wharf, of a not very savoury reputation. And as they peeped in at the foul noisy little den, Hazel had considerable difficulty in persuading Mistress Ivy to enter.

'And to think of the words we have to use too!' the poor woman whispered disconsolately; 'they're not at the best of times the sort of words I like to hear on a woman's lips, but in a place like this you can't be too careful of your speech . . . it's never safe to swear at folks in liquor.'

But the effect produced by the words was the exact opposite of what she had feared. On first crossing the threshold they had been greeted by hostile glances and coarse jests, which, on one of the revellers recognizing them as two of the protagonists in the trial, threatened to turn into something more serious. Whereupon, to the terror of Mistress Ivy, Hazel had made a trumpet of her hands and shouted with all the force of her strong young lungs, 'Sebastian Thug and Mistress Bess! By the Sun, Moon and Stars and the Golden Apples of the West!'

The words must indeed have contained a charm, for they instantly calmed the angry company. A tall young sailor, with very light eyes and a very sunburned face, sprang to his feet, and so did a bold-eyed, painted woman, and they hurried to Hazel's side. The young man said in a respectful voice, 'You must excuse our rough and ready ways when we first saw you, missie; we didn't know you were one of us.' And then he grinned, showing some very white teeth, and said, 'You see, pretty fresh things don't often come our way, and sea-dogs are like other dogs and bark at what they're not used to.'

Bawdy Bess's eyes had been fixed on his lips, and his last words caused her to scowl and toss her head; but from Hazel they brought forth a little, not unfriendly, smile. Evidently, like her aunt, she was not averse to seafaring men. And, after all, sailors are apt to have a charm of their own. When on dry land, like ghosts when they walk, there is a tang about them of an alien element. And Sebastian Thug was a thorough sailor.

Then in a low voice Hazel gave the message, which Thug repeated on his fingers for the benefit of Bawdy Bess. He insisted on conducting them to Master Ambrose's, and said he would wait outside for them and see them home.

Master Ambrose made them repeat the words several times, and questioned them closely about the messenger.

Then he took two or three paces up and down the room, muttering to himself, 'Delusion! Delusion!'

Then he turned suddenly to Hazel and said sharply, 'What reason have you to believe, young woman, that this fellow really came from Master Nathaniel?'

'None, sir,' answered Hazel. 'But there was nothing for us to do but to act as if he did.'

'I see, I see. You, too, ride the wind – that's the expression, isn't it? Well, well, we are living in strange times.'

And then he sank into a brown study, evidently forgetful of their presence; so they thought it best quietly to steal away.

From that evening the rabble of Lud-in-the-Mist ceased to give any trouble.

When the Yeomen stationed on the border were recalled to Lud and spread the news that they had seen Master Nathaniel riding alone towards the Elfin Marches, Dame Marigold was condoled with as a widow, and went into complete retirement, refusing even to see her oldest friends, although they had all come to regret their unjust suspicions of Master Nathaniel, and were, in consequence, filled with contrition, and eager to prove it in services to his wife.

Occasionally she made an exception for Master Ambrose; but her real support and stay was old Hempie. Nothing could shake the old woman's conviction that all was well with the Chanticleers. And the real anchor is not hope but faith – even if it be only somebody else's faith. So the gay snug little room at the top of the house, where Master Nathaniel had played when he was a little boy, became Dame Marigold's only haven, and there she would spend the most of her day.

Though Hempie never forgot that she was only a Vigil, nevertheless, in her own way, she was growing fond of her. Indeed, she had almost forgiven her for having spilled her cup of chocolate over her sheets, when, after her betrothal, she had come on a visit to Master Nathaniel's parents – almost, but not quite, for to Hempie the Chanticleers' linen was sacrosanct.

One night, at the beginning of December, when the first snow was lying on the ground, Dame Marigold, who had almost lost the power of sleep, was tossing wakefully in her bed. Her bedroom ran the whole length of the house, so one of its windows looked out on the lane, and suddenly she heard what sounded like low knocking on the front door. She sat up and listened – there it was again. Yes, someone was knocking at the door.

She sprang from bed, flung on a cloak and hurried downstairs, her heart beating violently.

With trembling fingers she drew the bolts and flung wide the door. A small, slight figure was cowering outside.

'Prunella!' she gasped. And with a sort of sob Prunella flung herself into her mother's arms.

For some minutes they stood crying and hugging each other, too profoundly moved for questions or explanations.

But they were roused by a scolding voice from the stairs: 'Dame Marigold, I'm ashamed of you, that I am, not having more sense at your age than to keep her standing there when she must be half frozen, poor child! Come up to your room this minute, Miss Prunella, and no nonsense! I'll have your fire lighted and a warming-pan put in your bed.'

It was Hempie, candle in hand, frowning severely from under

the frills of an enormous nightcap. Prunella rushed at her, half laughing, half crying, and flung her arms round her neck.

For a few seconds Hempie allowed herself to be hugged, and then, scolding hard all the time, she chivvied her up to her room. And, when Prunella was finally settled in her warm bed, with an inexorable expression she strode in carrying a cup of some steaming infusion.

It was black currant tea, for the brewing of which Hempie was famous. And it had always been one of her grievances against Dame Marigold and Prunella that they detested the stuff, and refused to drink it, even when they had a bad cold. For it had always been loved by all true Chanticleers, from old Master Josiah downwards.

'Now, miss, you just drink that down, every drop of it,' she said severely.

Prunella was too exhausted that night to tell them her adventures. But the next morning she gave a confused account of wanderings at the bottom of the sea, and how they had lost their way in a terrible marine jungle, out of which they had been guided by Master Nathaniel. It was evident that she had no very clear recollection of what had happened to her since her flight from Lud; or, rather, since 'Professor Wisp' had given his first dancing lesson.

The other Crabapple Blossoms returned to their respective homes the same night as Prunella; and each gave a different account of their adventures. Moonlove Honeysuckle said they had danced wildly down the waste places of the sky, and then had been imprisoned in a castle in the moon; Viola Vigil said they had been chased by angry trees into the Dapple, where they had got entangled in the weeds, and could not extricate themselves – and so on. But on one point all the accounts agreed namely, that it had been Master Nathaniel Chanticleer who had delivered them.

# 30

## MASTER AMBROSE KEEPS HIS VOW

At first the Crabapple Blossoms felt as if they had awakened from an evil dream, but they soon found that it was a dream that had profoundly influenced their souls. Though they showed no further desire to ran away and roam the hills, they were moody, silent, prone to attacks of violent weeping, and haunted by some nameless fear – strange melancholy denizens, in fact, of the comfortable, placid homes of their parents.

One would not have imagined that a daughter in this condition would have met with much sympathy from Master Ambrose Honeysuckle. Nevertheless, his tenderness and patience with Moonlove proved boundless. Night after night he sat by her holding her hand till she fell asleep, and by day he soothed her ravings, and in her quieter moments they would have long intimate talks together, such as they had never had before she ran away. And the result of these talks was that his still but fundamentally honest mind was beginning to creak on its hinges. And he would actually listen without protest when Moonlove expressed her conviction that although fairy fruit had robbed her of her peace of mind, nevertheless nothing but fairy fruit could restore it to her, and that at Miss Primrose Crabapple's she had either been given the wrong kind or not enough.

The reign of winter was now established, and Lud-in-the-Mist seemed at last to have settled down into its old peaceful rut.

Master Nathaniel had turned into 'poor old Nat,' and was to most people no more than a lovable ghost of the past. Indeed, Master Polydore was thinking of suggesting to Dame Marigold that two empty coffins should be placed in the Chanticleers' chapel bearing respectively the names of Nathaniel and Ranulph.

As for the Senate, it was very busy preparing for its annual banquet, which was celebrated every December in the Guildhall, to commemorate the expulsion of the Dukes; and it was kept fully occupied by such important questions as how many turkeys should be ordered and from what poulterers; which Senator was to have the privilege of providing the wine, and which the marizpan and ginger; and whether they would be justified in expending on goose liver and peacocks' hearts the sum left them in the will of a late linen-draper, to be devoted to the general welfare of the inhabitants of Lud-in-the-Mist.

But one morning a polished conceit of Master Polydore's concerning 'that sweet and pungent root commonly known as ginger, a kindly snake who stings us that we may the better enjoy the fragrant juice of the grape' was rudely interrupted by the sudden entry of Mumchance, his eyes almost starting out of his head with terror, with the appalling tidings that an army of Fairies had crossed the Debatable Hills, and that crowds of terrified peasants were pouring into Lud.

The news produced something like pandemonium in the Senate. Everyone began talking at once, and a dozen different schemes of defence were mooted, each one more senseless than the last.

Then Master Ambrose Honeysuckle rose to his feet. He was the man that carried most weight among his colleagues and all eyes were turned to him expectantly.

In a calm, matter-of-fact voice, he began thus: 'Senators of Dorimare! Before the entry of the Captain of the Yeomanry we were discussing what dessert we should have at our annual feast. It seems unnecessary to start a fresh subject of discussion before the previous one has been settled to our satisfaction. So, with your permission, I will return to the sweet and pungent (I think these were his Worship's well-chosen epithets) subject of dessert; for there is one item I should like to add to those that have already been suggested.'

He paused, and then he said in a loud challenging voice, 'Senators of Dorimare! I propose that for the first time since the foundation of our annual feast, we should partake at it of . . . *fairy fruit!*'

His colleagues stared at him in open-mouthed amazement. Was this some ill-timed jest? But Ambrose was not given to jesting . . . especially on serious occasions.

Then, with a certain rough poetry breaking through the artificial diction of the Senate, he began to speak of the events of the year that was nearly over, and the lessons to be learned from them. And the chief lessons, he said, were those of humility and faith.

He ended thus: 'One of our proverbs says, *Remember that the Dapple flows into the Dawl.* I have sometimes wondered, recently, whether we have ever really understood the true meaning of that proverb. Our ancestors built our town of Lud-in-the-Mist between these two rivers, and both have brought us their tribute. The tribute of the Dawl has been gold, and we have gladly accepted it. But the tribute of the Dapple we have ever spurned. The Dapple – our placid old friend, in whose waters we learned as lads the gentle art of angling – has silently, through the centuries, been bringing fairy fruit into Dorimare . . . a fact that, to my mind, at least, proves that fairy fruit is as wholesome and necessary for man as the various other gifts brought for our welfare by our silent friends – the Dawl's gift of gold, the earth's gift of corn, the hills' gift of shelter and pasturage, and the trees' gift of grapes and apples and shade.

'And if all the gifts of Life are good, perhaps, too, are all the shapes she chooses to take, and which we cannot alter. The shape she has taken now for Dorimare is that of an invasion by our ancient foes. Why should we not make a virtue of necessity and throw our gates wide to them as friends?'

His colleagues, at first, expressed themselves as horrified. But perhaps they, too, though unknown to themselves, had been altered by recent events.

At any rate, this was one of the crises when the strongest man inevitably finds himself at the helm. And there could be no doubt that the strongest man in the Senate was Master Ambrose Honeysuckle.

When the Senate rose, he addressed the terrified populace from the market-place, with the result that before nightfall he had quieted the panic-stricken crowds and had persuaded the citizens, with the exception of such models of old-fashioned respectability as Ebeneezor Prim, to accept with calm passivity whatever the future might hold in store.

His two most ardent supporters were Sebastian Thug and the disreputable Bawdy Bess.

Only a few months ago what would he have said if someone had told him the day would come when he, Ambrose Honeysuckle, would turn demagogue, and, assisted by a rough sailor and a woman of the town, would be exhorting the citizens of Lud-in-the-Mist to throw wide their gates and welcome in the Fairies?

So, instead of repairing its walls and testing its cannon and laying in provisions against a siege, Lud-in-the-Mist hoisted its flags and festooned its windows with wreaths of Duke Aubrey's ivy, and flung the west gate wide open; and a throng of silent, expectant people lined the streets and waited.

First of all came the sounds of wild sweet music, then the tramp of a myriad feet, and then, like hosts of leaves blown on the wind, the invading army came pouring into the town.

As he watched, Master Ambrose remembered the transfigured tapestry in the Guildhall, and the sense they had had of noisy, gaudy, dominant dreams flooding the streets and scattering reality in their wake.

Behind the battalions of mail-clad dead marched three gigantic old men, with long white beards reaching below their girdles. Their long stiff robes were embroidered in gold and jewels with strange emblems, and behind them were led sumpter mules laden with coffers of wrought gold. And the rumour passed through the waiting crowd that these were none other than the balsam-eating priests of the sun and moon.

And bringing up the rear on a great white charger was – Master Nathaniel Chanticleer, with Ranulph riding by his side.

The accounts of what took place immediately after the entry of the fairy army read more like legends than history.

It would seem that the trees broke into leaf and the masts of all the ships in the bay into blossom; that day and night the cocks crowed without ceasing; that violets and anemones sprang up through the snow in the streets, and that mothers embraced their dead sons, and maids their sweethearts drowned at sea.

But one thing seems certain, and that is that the gold-wrought coffers contained the ancient offering of fairy fruit to Dorimare. And the coffers were of such miraculous capacity that there was enough and to spare, not only for the dessert of the Senate, but for that of every household in Lud-in-the-Mist.

## 31
## THE INITIATE

You may, perhaps, have been wondering why a man so full of human failings, and set in so unheroic a mould as Master Nathaniel Chanticleer should have been cast for so great a role. Yet the highest spiritual destinies are not always reserved for the strongest men, nor for the most virtuous ones.

But though he had been chosen as Duke Aubrey's deputy and initiated into the Ancient Mysteries, he had not ceased to be in many ways the same Master Nathaniel as of old – whimsical, child-like, and, often, unreasonable. Nor, I fear, did he cease to be the prey of melancholy. I doubt whether initiation ever brings happiness. It may be that the final secret revealed is a very bitter one . . . or it may be that the final secret had not yet been revealed to Master Nathaniel.

And, strange to say, far from being set up by his new honours, he felt oddly ashamed of them – it was almost as if he was for the first time running the gauntlet of his friends' eyes after having been afflicted by some physical disfigurement.

When things had returned again to their usual rut, Master Ambrose came to spend a quiet evening with Master Nathaniel.

They sat for some time in silence puffing at their pipes, and then Master Ambrose said, 'Tell me what your theory is about Endymion Leer, Nat. He was a double-dyed villain, all right, I suppose?'

Master Nathaniel did not answer at once, and then he said thoughtfully, 'I suppose so. I read the report of his defence, however, and his words seemed to me to ring true. But I think there was some evil lurking in his soul, and everything he touched was contaminated by it, even fairy fruit – even Duke Aubrey.'

'And that spiritual sin he accused himself of . . . what do you suppose it was?'

'I think,' said Master Nathaniel slowly, 'he may have mishandled the sacred objects of the Mysteries.'

'What are these sacred objects, Nat?'

Master Nathaniel moved uneasily in his chair, and said, with an embarrassed little laugh, 'Life and death, I suppose.' He hated being asked about these sorts of things.

Master Ambrose sat for a few moments pondering, and then he said, 'It was curious how in all his attacks on you he defeated his own ends.'

'Yes,' cried Master Nathaniel, with much more animation than he had hitherto shown, 'that was really very curious. Everything he did produced exactly the opposite effect he had intended it should. He feared the Chanticleers, and wanted to be rid of them, so he gets Ranulph off to Fairyland, whence nobody had ever before returned. And he manages to get me so discredited that I have to leave Lud, and he thinks me safely out of the way. But, in reality, he was only bringing about his own downfall. I have to leave Lud, and so I go to the farm, and there I find old Gibberty's incriminating document. While the fact of Ranulph's having gone off yonder sends me after him, and that is why, I suppose, I come back as Duke Aubrey's deputy,' and again he gave an embarrassed laugh; and then added dreamily, 'It is useless to try and circumvent the Duke.'

'"He who rides the wind needs must go where his steed carries him,"' quoted Master Ambrose.

Master Nathaniel smiled, and for some minutes they puffed at their pipes in silence.

Then Master Nathaniel gave a reminiscent chuckle: 'These were queer months that we lived through, Ambrose!' he cried. 'All of us, that's to say those of us who had parts to play, seemed to be living each others' dreams or dreaming each others' lives, whichever way you choose to put it, and the most incongruous things began to rhyme – apples and bleeding corpses and trees and ghosts. Yes, all our dreams got entangled. Leer makes a speech about men and trees, and I find the solution of the situation under a herm, which is half a man and half a tree, and you see the juice of fairy fruit and think it is the dead bleeding – and so on. Yes, my adventures went on getting more and more like a dream till . . . the climax,' and he paused abruptly.

A long silence followed, broken at last by Master Ambrose. 'Well, Nat,' he said, 'I think I've had a lesson in humility. I used to have as good an opinion of myself as most men, I think, but now I've learned I'm a very ordinary sort of fellow, made of very inferior clay to you and my Moonlove – all the things that you know at first hand I can only take on faith.'

'Suppose, Ambrose, that what we know at first hand is only this – that there is nothing to know?' said Master Nathaniel a little sadly. Then he sank into a brown study, and Master Ambrose, thinking he wanted to be alone, stole quietly from the room.

Master Nathaniel sat gazing moodily into the fire; and his pipe went out without his noticing it. Then the door opened softly, and someone stole in and stood behind his chair. It was Dame Marigold. All she said was, 'Funny old Nat!' but her voice had a husky tenderness. And then she knelt down beside him and took him into her soft warm arms. And a new hope was borne in upon Master Nathaniel that some day he would hear the Note again, and all would be clear.

# 32

## CONCLUSION

I should like to conclude with a few words as to the fate of the various people who have appeared in these pages.

Hazel Gibberty married Sebastian Thug – and an excellent husband he made her. He gave up the sea and settled on his wife's farm. Mistress Ivy Peppercorn came and lived with them and every summer they had a visit from Master Nathaniel and Ranulph. Bawdy Bess left Lud at the time of Sebastian's marriage – out of pique, said the malicious.

Luke Hempen entered the Lud Yeomanry, where he did so well that when Mumchance retired he was elected Captain in his place.

Hempie lived to a ripe old age – long enough to tell her stories to Ranulph's children; nor had she any scruples about telling *them* her views on 'neighbourliness'. And when she died, as a tribute to her long and loving service, she was buried in the family chapel of the Chanticleers.

Mother Tibbs, after taking a conspicuous part in the wild revels which followed on the arrival of the fairy army, vanished for ever from Dorimare. Nor did anyone ever again see Portunus. But, from time to time, at weddings and junketings, a wild red-haired youth would arrive uninvited, and having turned everything topsy-turvy with his pranks, would rush from the house, shouting 'Ho! Ho! *Hoh*!'

By degrees the Crabapple Blossoms recovered their spirits. But they certainly did not grow up into the sort of young ladies their mothers had imagined they would when they first sent them to Miss Primrose Crabapple's Academy. They were never stinted of fairy fruit, for the Dapple continued to bring its tribute to Dorimare, adding thereby considerably to the wealth of the country. For, thanks to the sound practical sense of Master Ambrose, a new industry was started – that of candying fairy fruit, and exporting it to all the countries with which they trafficked, in pretty fancy boxes, the painted lids of which showed that art was creeping back to Dorimare.

As for Ranulph, when he grew up he wrote the loveliest songs that had been heard since the days of Duke Aubrey – songs that crossed the sea and were sung by lonely fishermen in the far North, and by indigo mothers crooning to their babies by the doors of their huts in the Cinnamon Isles.

Dame Marigold continued to smile, and to nibble marzipan with her cronies. But she used sometimes sadly to wonder whether Master Nathaniel had ever really come back to her from beyond the Debatable Hills; sometimes, but not always.

And Master Nathaniel himself? Whether he ever heard the Note again I cannot say. But in time he went, either to reap the fields of gillyflowers, or to moulder in the Fields of Grammary. And below his coffin in the family chapel a brass tablet was put up with this epitaph:

HERE LIES
NATHANIEL CHANTICLEER
PRESIDENT OF THE GUILD OF MERCHANTS
THREE TIMES MAYOR OF LUD-IN-THE-MIST
TO WHOM WAS GRANTED NO SMALL SHARE OF
THE PEACE AND PROSPERITY
HE HELPED TO BESTOW ON
HIS TOWN AND COUNTRY

An epitaph not unlike those he used to con so wistfully in his visits to the Fields of Grammary.

And this is but another proof that the Written Word is a Fairy, as mocking and elusive as Willy Wisp, speaking lying words to us in a feigned voice. So let all readers of books take warning! And with this final exhortation this book shall close.

If you have enjoyed

LUD-IN-THE-MIST

here are some other classic novels to be discovered

## FLOWERS FOR ALGERNON
## Daniel Keyes

'A masterpiece of poignant brilliance . . . heartbreaking'
*Guardian*

## THE MAN IN THE HIGH CASTLE
## Philip K Dick

'Helped shape an entire field of modern fiction: alternate history. It's the definition of genre-defining'
*Guardian*

# I WANT WHAT I WANT

## Geoff Brown

A modern classic: one of the first novels to explore gender identity.

# ABOUT GOLLANCZ

Gollancz is the oldest SF publishing imprint in the world. Since being founded in 1927 Gollancz has continued to publish a focused selection of bestselling and award-winning authors. The front-list includes **Ben Aaronovitch**, **Joe Abercrombie**, **Charlaine Harris**, **Joanne Harris**, **Joe Hill**, **Alastair Reynolds**, **Patrick Rothfuss**, **Nalini Singh** and **Brandon Sanderson**.

As one of the largest Science Fiction and Fantasy imprints in the UK it is no surprise we have one of the most extensive backlists in the world. Find high-quality SF on Gateway written by such authors as **Philip K. Dick**, **Ursula Le Guin**, **Connie Willis**, **Sir Arthur C. Clarke**, **Pat Cadigan**, **Michael Moorcock** and **George R.R. Martin**.

We also have a strand of publishing in translation, which includes French, Polish and Russian authors. Gollancz is home to more award-winning authors than any other imprint, with names including **Aliette de Bodard**, **M. John Harrison**, **Paul McAuley**, **Sarah Pinborough**, **Pierre Pevel**, **Justina Robson** and many more.

**The SF Gateway**

*More than 3,000 classic, rare and previously out-of-print SF novels at your fingertips.*

**www.sfgateway.com**

**The Gollancz Blog**

*Bringing you news from our worlds to yours. Stories, interviews, articles and exclusive extracts just for you!*

**www.gollancz.co.uk**

**GOLLANCZ**
**LONDON**

# BRINGING NEWS FROM OUR WORLDS TO YOURS . . .

Want your news daily?

The Gollancz blog has instant updates on the hottest SF and Fantasy books.

Prefer your updates monthly?

Sign up for our in-depth newsletter.

**www.gollancz.co.uk**

Follow us @gollancz

Find us facebook.com/GollanczPublishing

Classic SF as you've never read it before.

Visit the SF Gateway to find out more!

**www.sfgateway.com**